ADMISSION OF LOVE

"Are the cabinets as nice as they were in the catalog?" Devon's voice was low.

Chloe shivered from the feel of his husky voice so near to her ear. Turning her head she looked over at him. "Nicer."

Their eyes met and held.

Devon began to clear up the stray packing materials, shoving them into a heavy-duty garbage bag from a box in the corner. Wordlessly, Chloe began to help him and they worked with only the sounds of construction echoing throughout the house.

"What possessed you to wear those jeans, Chloe?" He meant to sound disgusted but instead his voice came out low and husky.

Chloe stood up and whirled to face him. Self-consciously she looked down at herself. *They are mighty snug.* What's wrong with . . . my jeans?"

They were just inches apart. Nervously, her heart hammered against her chest. She licked her full lips with the tip of her fleshy tongue. His eyes darted down to watch the innocent but sexy move.

He broke.

With a hungry growl, he pulled Chloe to him, dropping the plastic garbage bag to the floor. He lowered his handsome head to taste of the sweet nectar of her lips.

Initially their kisses were short, breathing in the air between them after touching their lips together briefly. Devon used his tongue to lick the tender contours of her mouth and they both shivered with desire. She was as sweet-tasting and fulfilling as the juiciest, sweetest fruit. He felt like he could kiss her for an eternity.

BOOK YOUR PLACE ON OUR WEBSITE AND MAKE THE ARABESQUE ROMANCE CONNECTION!

We've created a customized website just for our very special Arabesque readers, where you can get the inside scoop on everything that's going on with Arabesque romance novels.

When you come online, you'll have the exciting opportunity to:

- View covers of upcoming books

- Learn about our future publishing schedule (listed by publication month and author)

- Find out when your favorite authors will be visiting a city near you

- Search for and order backlist books

- Check out author bios and background information

- Send e-mail to your favorite authors

- Join us in weekly chats with authors, readers and other guests

- Get writing guidelines

- AND MUCH MORE!

Visit our website at
http://www.arabesquebooks.com

ADMISSION OF LOVE

Niobia Bryant

ARABESQUE
★BET.
BOOKS

BET Publications, LLC
www.bet.com
www.arabesquebooks.com

ARABESQUE BOOKS are published by

BET Publications, LLC
c/o BET BOOKS
One BET Plaza
1900 W Place NE
Washington, D.C. 20018-1211

First Printing: August, 2000

10 9 8 7 6 5 4 3 2 1
Printed in the United States of America

*This is dedicated to the most phenomenal woman—
my mother, Letha Bryant*

*Thank you, Mama, for those first readings of this novel,
the photocopying, and the belief in my dreams.
I love you!*

Prologue

Paris, France

Being a supermodel isn't easy.

That's what Chloe was thinking as she stepped out of the
back of the black stretch Lincoln limousine amidst the bright
and frequent flashes of the cameras. Yells of "Chloe" rose
from the multitude of fans who crowded the streets in front
of the fashion house. Always gracious, she waved at the people who adored her, stopping to sign a few autographs before
dashing into the modern structure for the first of three runway
shows she had to complete that day.

Chloe Bolton, resplendent in her Nubian beauty, was one
of the top supermodels in the world. Her rise to fame, fortune
and glamour began eighteen years ago and she hadn't looked
back since. At thirty-three she was still sought after by the
biggest names in the fashion industry.

As Chloe entered the noisy backstage chaos, the dressing
area was filled to capacity with models in various states of
undress, hair stylists, makeup artists, photographers and the
designer with his many assistants, all working together
amongst the confusion to pull off another successful runway
show.

She weaved through the mass of people, following a slender-
hipped male assistant of Jeffrey Wilson's. He led her over to the
area where the hair stylists were stationed. As she dropped her

Fendi black leather tote carelessly onto the floor next to the chair, Chloe said a silent thanks that the stylist was black, which was rare to see in this business. As a matter of fact, it was rare to see many African-American faces in the industry at all, whether they were models, designers, photographers or anything.

Luckily she breezed through hair and makeup, although when Chloe had reached in her tote and pulled out the gold-lettered, monogrammed cache of Ashanti Cosmetics, the woman had shown reluctance before finally accepting it with a tight smile.

Ashanti Cosmetics was an African-American-owned cosmetic company based in a small town in Upstate New York. In the five years since Chloe became their spokeswoman, her personal appearances and advertisements in print, radio and television had helped the once small company become a real contender in the retail cosmetic business. It was a well-known fact that she used only Ashanti products, which was part of her contract.

She rushed over to where the six outfits she would wear were stationed on a rack with a long white card on the front. The card showed a Polaroid of each outfit with the corresponding order in which she would wear the fashions. She was first, tenth, twentieth, twenty-fifth, thirtieth and then last in the large rotation.

There was no room for modesty as Chloe stripped by a makeshift curtain to the red lace thong bikini she wore, using her arm to cover her pendulous breasts. With assistance she was soon draped in a pale pink silk and lycra blend slip dress with matching stiletto mules.

"Yes, yes Chloe! The face of an angel . . . the body of a temptress."

Chloe turned into the open arms of Jeffrey Wilson, allowing him to kiss her forehead in his elaborate fashion. His dark skin gleamed with excitement in his shocking red silk suit. She was proud and excited for him. There were many struggling African-American designers with talent, and it was uplifting to see one of them gain respect in the racist industry. But so many other talented designers were still waiting for their turn to shine.

"Oh Jeffie, when I walk the runway in your designs I am going to work it. Believe that!" She spoke of the sassy runway walk she was known for across the world.

He snapped his fingers, the diamonds on his pinky finger sparkling under the glare of the lights above them. "You better work, girl. You will of course escort me at the end of the show?"

Chloe blushed with pleasure. "Of course."

He reached behind her to take the matching full-length ostrich feather wrap off the hanger. Chloe turned and leaned backward to allow him to slide the material up her well-toned arms to settle the elaborate collar up around her face.

His eyes observed her, from her perfectly upswept hair to the elaborately made up beauty of her heartshaped face. Her hazel, cat-shaped eyes were luminous above her high, prominent cheekbones, long, wide-bridged nose and deliciously full, pouty lips. Her tall, slender frame with full, heavy breasts, thin waist and deeply curved hips were any man's fantasy. There were no imperfections to be found. He nodded his head in approval and pointed with a flare to the curtained entrance to the runway.

"You go girl, and work it!"

"Chloe!!!"

The shrill cry of her mother's voice startled the seven-year-old little girl. She sat precariously on the edge of the porcelain bathroom sink gazing at her own reflection in the mirror. This was something she did frequently as soon as she was old enough to discover how to use her slender legs and arms to climb onto the sink by way of the commode sitting next to it.

She could only look with wide, bright hazel eyes over her thin shoulder as the bathroom door opened with a creak and her mother's robust figure filled the doorway. The fear in her heart turned to happiness as she watched her mother's plump shoulders shake with laughter and her kind eyes, so like her own, fill with humorous tears.

"Ooh, child. You, little Miss Chloe Renee Bolton, are a mess. Lawd, will you look at my baby." *Adell placed her hand on her ample hip as she fought hard to pretend she was mad.* "How many times have I told you to stop playing dress-up in my things?"

Her mother's words were scolding, but the smile on her lips was tender and loving, softening the effect. Adell laughed again at the sight of her already beautiful daughter's face, done up in her makeup, and her thin body drowned in her good silk dress and jewelry.

"Ain't I beautiful, Mama?" *As long as she could remember, she'd been told she was beautiful, but she loved to hear her mother say it.*

"Yes, baby, you are . . . inside and out." *Adell chuckled.* "And you know it, because as soon as there are more than two people in a room you're modeling for them."

"Yup, and everybody says how good I am at it too," *she said proudly as she turned and kissed her reflection, leaving a garish print of red lipstick on the mirror.* "I'm gonna be famous like Beverly Johnson and Naomi Sims."

Adell reached for a washcloth from the bar behind the door and began to clean the makeup from her daughter's face. "You know what I always say, Chloe. Set a goal, reach for it, and your dreams will be recognized. And you know what?"

"Yes, ma'am?"

"I will be proud of my baby no matter what you decide to do in life. Just promise me that you'll be happy."

* * *

Ever since she began to model at the tender age of fifteen, Chloe had loved the makeup, clothes, pictures, traveling and seeing herself in magazines and on television. She had found the runway exhilarating and had conquered it with a unique flare all her own. She had dreamed of being a model all her life.

At thirty-three, the rush of the runway was quickly fading. The glamour of modeling had lost its shine for her. What she had once loved, she now found to be a tiring chore.

Chloe took her spot on the runway, posing dramatically in the silver strapless swimsuit she wore. It was the last of her three runway shows and she was glad the day of work was almost over, a new feeling for her lately. With a deep breath she walked the runway with style she owned, her hips in counter motion to her arms. It was a must to be perfectly in sync with the upbeat music blaring around her. She called this her sista walk. Flashbulbs went off and the audience applauded both her and the designer swimwear.

Chloe paused for a second longer at the end of the runway. She searched within herself for that familiar feel of the rush . . . seeking the thrill. It was not there and had not been there for a long time.

New York, New York

One week after her runway shows in Paris, Chloe strode up Madison Avenue, very aware of the impressive sight she made with her tall, graceful figure casually dressed in tight faded Versace blue jeans, matching black leather belt with silver logo buckle and a white cropped T-shirt beneath a quilted DKNY down jacket and DKNY boots. She could only wish for more time to stop in the many boutiques that lined one of the well-known avenues in New York, but she had an appointment.

Chloe pushed the double glass door open and entered the

modern glass structure housing the Woods Modeling Agency. She took time to speak to the hopeful young models who sat in the waiting area, clutching their portfolios and probably praying this would be the day they were discovered.

Chloe greeted the friendly receptionist before breezing into the plush office, with a final wave back to the girls in the foyer.

"Hi Liv," she greeted the older woman sitting behind the glass and steel office desk.

Olivia Woods was the brash and very outspoken owner of the agency, which had started out of her small home office with just five models, including a young and already beautiful Chloe. Their careers in the fashion industry had started and grown together.

Chloe walked straight to the small refrigerator in the corner of the office and grabbed a bottle of mineral water. Liv eyed her top grossing protégé. Even with no makeup and her hair in a messy ponytail, Chloe was incredibly beautiful. Olivia's keen eyes had spotted the potential in Chloe eighteen years ago when she discovered the graceful teenager working at a concession stand at Madison Square Garden. To think, if her teenaged son had not talked her into going to the Knicks basketball game that night at the Garden, she would never have discovered Chloe.

Within two years of her discovery, Chloe's name was on the lips of the hottest fashion designers clamoring to have her wear their creations. With magazines now too numerous to count, she was one of the best-known supermodels, period. Her popularity and wealth had increased over the years with her annual swimsuit calendars, fitness videos and three books on beauty and fashion. Even in the beginning when she had gained star status, she had loyally remained with Olivia's then small, African-American-owned agency, and for that Liv would always love her.

"Jeffrey, Calvin and Donna were all pleased with you in Paris last week . . . as always of course." Olivia's voice was hoarse and raspy from her chronic use of cigarettes for the past forty years. She dropped the silver Cross pen in her hand onto the desk.

Chloe slumped into the black leather swivel chair in front of Olivia's cluttered desk. "Jeffrey's collection was very elegant and feminine. I saw some of the reviews for the show and they were all raves. His sales last year should have exceeded eight hundred thousand, Liv. If he were white it would've."

Olivia shared Chloe's outspoken belief on racism in the fashion industry. The truth was just the truth. Racism touched nearly every aspect of the industry.

She ran her hand through her shoulder-length dreadlocks, inhaling deeply of the cigarette in her hand. "His collection was one of the best I've seen this season, especially that red wool jersey—"

"I'm thinking about retiring." Chloe's voice was soft but firm as she interrupted the other woman whom she adored.

Olivia started to laugh but soon saw the serious expression on Chloe's face and knew this might be for real. Her own expression became incredulous. "Why, Chloe? We have to turn down all the offers that are coming in for you. You took this biz by storm almost twenty years ago and you haven't let up so far. Why now?"

Chloe didn't need to think the question over. She had done enough of that already recently. "Modeling isn't fun anymore. Maybe that's because I'm older or because I've done all there is to do. I'm tired of competing with younger, ambitious women who want to be where I am . . . on top. The racism in this industry is only slowly getting better. I mean, why is it that there can only be one black supermodel at one time?" Chloe sighed. "I just don't want to do it anymore. Isn't that enough, Liv?"

"You could take a hiatus—"

"No."

"We'll cut back on your runway shows—"

"No."

Olivia leaned her thin frame back into her leather ergonomic chair. Her eyes narrowed to peer at Chloe through the silver blue haze of the smoke. "You're booked through June and your contract with me doesn't run out until the end of next year. Your contract with Ashanti Cosmetics is still good for one year also."

She had laid all the details on the table, now completely businesslike. Chloe nodded in understanding, having thought out the particulars. "I'll of course honor all prior commitments, but I ask as a personal favor that I not be booked for any more after June."

Now it was Liv's turn to nod. "You're asking me to release you from your contract early?"

Chloe looked the older woman in her eyes. "Yes."

Olivia sighed, torn between her friendship with this woman and her loyalty to her business. "Chloe—"

"I'm not trying to be a pain in the ass. I'm just doing what is best for me." Chloe stood and went to walk over to the wall of Liv's office where her very first *Vogue* cover hung. "I also would like for you to see if Ashanti will also release me from the last year of my contract with them."

She turned away from the glamorous image of herself at eighteen. "I need out."

Olivia nodded slowly, her woolen dreadlocks lightly swaying against her light-complected cheeks. "Well that gives me until June to change your mind."

Chloe smiled. "I don't think so, Liv. I'm done."

One

Three months later

Chloe hopped out of the back of the yellow taxi, the bustle and blaring of New York her backdrop. She pulled her leather coat tighter around her body to block the brisk February winds that were blowing. The sun was shining brightly but offered no reprieve from the cold. The weather report called for snow flurries that afternoon, something Chloe was dreading because she didn't react well to winter. She motioned for the doorman, Mr. Harrison, to retrieve her luggage from the trunk of the taxi.

"Good morning, Ms. Bolton."

"Hello, Mr. Harrison."

She pulled a fifty-dollar bill from her Coach billfold and walked over to the window to hand it to the portly taxi driver. "Keep the change."

"Thank you, Ms. Bolton!" He honked his horn briefly twice before pulling off into the static New York City traffic.

Chloe paused, the chilling air whipping around her, as she listened to the sounds of the city. She listened to the blare of car horns, the screech of car tires, the bellowing of angry New Yorkers, the shrill sound of sirens from ambulances and police vehicles, and the clattering drill of street repair.

New York. Busy, fast-paced, congested and tiring.

No longer my kind of town, Chloe thought. She hefted her

tote onto her shoulder before she entered the exclusive Central Park West building where she owned a luxury apartment.

The thirty-floor granite structure spoke of wealth and affluence. Each floor held just two spacious apartments. Her neighbors in the building were some of the wealthiest people living on the East Coast. Sometimes Chloe actually forgot that, financially, she ranked amongst them.

She took the two thirty-inch Samsonite suitcases from the doorman and politely refused his offer to assist her to her floor. Using the handles, Chloe pulled the luggage behind her onto the elevator for the short ride to the fifth floor. When she stepped off the elevator, she glanced down the Persian-carpeted hall to her neighbor's elaborately carved door. In the eight years that she owned the apartment, she'd seen the elderly Jewish couple a total of five times, and even then that was in passing in the elevator or in the foyer downstairs. She shook her head in wonder, reaching into her tote bag to retrieve her keys.

It was more than a month since she had been in her apartment. First there was the two-week photo shoot, for what would now be her last swimsuit calendar, off the coast of Spain on the beautiful Balearic Islands. After that she left for a two-week book signing tour in Europe for her just-released fourth beauty aid book, appropriately entitled *Chloe's Beauty Secrets*.

She wanted and needed time for a normal home life. Hell, she felt like a stranger in her own home. It seemed she was always on the go, always on an airplane jetting somewhere, always living out of suitcases in expensive hotels and eating restaurant food. She couldn't remember the last time she had a home-cooked meal.

Tomorrow they began shooting commercials for Ashanti's new line of moisturizing lipsticks. This meant she had one day to recuperate from her month-long travels before hitting the airport again, headed for yet another destination.

It was all too hectic.

Whenever she thought of her upcoming retirement, Chloe actually felt like a ton of weight was being lifted from her shoulders. It was like she had been running a nonstop marathon for eighteen years and now the finish line was finally in sight. It was the pure and sweet feeling of relief.

Both Liv and the board of directors for Ashanti Cosmetics had graciously agreed to release her from her contracts early. She shuddered to think of what she would have done if they had exercised the right to force her to work.

She left the suitcases in a pile by the door of the marbled foyer. The elaborately decorated and spacious apartment was a far cry from the small two-bedroom flat she had lived in with her mother before her career began. But Chloe had long since left behind the innocence and wide-eyed wonder she once had for wealth and all its trappings. She was unimpressed by her elegantly furnished home, which only hinted at the wealth she had smartly accumulated over the years.

The apartment consisted of three bedrooms, each with its own full bathroom plus another off of the den, a sunken living room with a spectacular view of New York, a full, professionally equipped kitchen and a balcony that ran the length of one side of the dining room.

When Chloe first bought the place, for a small fortune, she had hired a professional interior decorator who catered to the wealthy elite. Due to her busy schedule, Chloe had left the entire job and almost all the decisions up to the woman and her staff's discretion. The only instructions she gave were to keep it simple. Thus the ivory and gold decor throughout the entire apartment were not her doing.

Overall the apartment looked fashionable and elegant, just not what Chloe would have chosen for herself. If she had decorated her home she definitely would have toned down the crystal chandeliers and some of the more elaborate Elizabethan decor. Definitely more color would have livened up the place. Visions of warm colors like blues and maroons with lots of flowers and plants.

Well it didn't really matter now. She hardly was home anyway. But when she finally was retired she had plans for a lot of changes to be made and not just in the decor of her apartment. June just couldn't come soon enough.

After a long nap, Chloe quickly unpacked in her bedroom, adding the clothes she had taken with her and the new outfits she bought to her already bulging wardrobe. Currently every closet in her home was filled with clothes, coats, shoes and hats. She knew she needed to sort through the hundreds of outfits and accessories and donate what she didn't wear anymore to charity. Three walk-in closets and a hall closet filled with clothes was extreme to her.

Brrrnnnggg.

She glanced over to the ringing cordless telephone on the bedside table and decided to let her answering machine pick it up. She'd just gotten home and had barely had time for a good nap before the phone had begun to ring off the hook.

"Hey, Chloe here. Leave a message."

Beep.

"Chloe . . . Chloe . . . I know you're home so pick up. I'm downstairs and for the thousandth time I'm about to strangle your doorman—"

Chloe dropped the clothes she was putting on hangers and flung herself on the bed to snatch up the phone. "Hey girl. Come on up."

Her lifelong best friend Anika sucked her teeth, and Chloe could envision the full-sized beauty rolling her expressive eyes heavenward. "I would if Harrison would *let* me. I mean *why* do I have to go through this every time I try to venture into the living area of the rich and famous to see *my* best friend in the world. You know if I was—"

"Hold on, Anika." Chloe laughed as she rolled off the bed and crossed the floor to the intercom system in the hall just outside her bedroom.

She pushed the button labeled talk. "Mr. Harrison, please admit Ms. Foxx upstairs. I'm sure you know who she is," she said playfully.

"Yes Ms. Bolton. I am *very* aware of Ms. Foxx. She is hard to . . . forget."

"Then what's the problem, Mr. Harrison?"

"She refuses to sign in."

Chloe sighed and pushed the button again, knowing Anika could hear her voice as well as the doorman could. "Anika, just sign in. It's the policy of the building as you know because you've been through this with Mr. Harrison before."

The phone in her hand began to buzz, signaling that it was off the hook. Anika had obviously hung up her end of the line. Chloe pushed the button on the phone to end the noise.

Pushing the button labeled listen, Chloe heard Anika grumble as she signed the guest log book and showed the doorman her identification.

"I mean this *isn't* the White House," she heard Anika snap.

"Yes, ma'am, and you have a . . . *wonderful* day," was Mr. Harrison's reply.

Shaking her head, Chloe walked back into the bedroom and put the phone on the base before walking back out to go and open the door for her friend.

Chloe and Anika had known each other since they were in grade school. Anika and her rambunctious family, consisting of four older brothers, her obviously-in-love parents and her grandmother, had rented the one-family house next door to the three-family house where Chloe had lived with her mother. The two had become instant friends and had remained so for the past twenty-five years. Even when Chloe began modeling at the age of fifteen and moved away at eighteen, she had remained in close contact with her flamboyant friend.

Chloe never felt that Anika had envied her growing success, and she had made sure to share as much of it as she could with her. When she had passed the age of eighteen and was allowed by her mother to attend the celebrity-filled parties, she had always taken Anika along with her.

Chloe loved her to death and it was her friend, along with her mother, that had helped keep her grounded. There was no room for too much ego around Anika, because she would bring anybody back to reality in a hot second. The woman was just that brutal at times. But it had also been Anika who helped her through her grieving when her mother passed away with breast cancer eight years ago. Even though she had mourned just as deeply for the woman she lovingly called Mama Dell, Anika still had the inner strength to help her best friend through it all.

Chloe opened the door and was leaning against the door-jamb when Anika stepped off the elevator. She was statuesque and, in Chloe's opinion, one of the most beautiful women ever.

She wore her hair short in a wavy rod set that was jet black. It perfectly offset her round face, large expressive eyes of a soft mocha, a short upturned nose, high cheekbones and well-defined full lips that seemed to constantly pout. A flat mole, which she called her beauty mark, was just below her bottom lip. Her lashes were long and full. Chloe truly believed that Anika was far prettier than she was.

She was five feet eight inches tall and weighed about one hundred and eighty pounds, but every bit of her was firm and solid. No hints of overhanging fatty bulges or cellulite existed on her body. Her shoulders were broad but softly rounded, continuing down to long, toned arms. Even her stomach was flat and her long legs shapely. Her body was the epitome of an hourglass figure.

Anika's confidence lured men to her. Her sense of style made women envy her. Her sense of humor and sharp wit were the trademark that made everyone want to be around her. She was truly one of kind.

Today she wore a charcoal gray close-fitting ribbed turtle-neck with matching wool pants beneath a gray leather pea coat and matching leather high-heeled boots. The only makeup she wore on her smooth caramel complexion was clear lip gloss and mascara.

"Anika, why do you have to take Mr. Harrison through those changes every time you come to see me?" Chloe watched as Anika breezed past her to enter the apartment, leaving a cloud of raspberry scented Victoria's Secret body lotion and after bath mist behind.

She pulled off her gloves and coat. "Maybe I don't want people to know *I've* been here. I mean what if there's a murder? I might become a suspect and not know a thing about what went down in this building."

Chloe laughed. "Girl you are crazy. Where do you come up with some of the things you say?"

She winked. "I like to keep things lively. So you just got in, huh?"

Chloe nodded. "Come on back to the bedroom. I was just unpacking."

"Well hurry up because I'm starving," Anika complained as she followed her slender friend down the short hallway to the master suite.

"You want me to cook something?"

Anika flopped across the foot of the bed as Chloe stowed a now empty suitcase in the top of the closet. "Oh no. We're going to the Plaza. I heard Wesley Snipes is in this Big Apple taping a new movie and he might be staying at that luxurious hotel. This time if I spot him I'm going to make my move."

"Yeah, right," Chloe scoffed. "You'll just freeze up like you did the last time. You do remember when I introduced you to him at the premiere for *Passenger 57.*"

Chloe laughed as she sat on the bed next to her friend. "What were the words you said? I know they forever etched you into his memory."

"Aw, go to hell," Anika muttered.

"Oh yeah. I remember now." Chloe cleared her throat and faked a doe-eyed look, staring off into the distance. "Hi . . .

hi . . . my, uh, name . . . is . . . uhm . . . it's nice for you to meet me!"

Anika reached for a throw pillow on the floor as Chloe fell backward onto the bed in a fit of laughter. Playfully she swatted the gorgeous supermodel with it. "I was nervous," she said. "Besides, it *should've* been a pleasure for him to meet me just as much as it was for me to meet him."

Anika's confidence never wavered.

They fell silent as Chloe swallowed the last of her laughter with a long sigh and folded up the clothes in a jumbled pile on the bed.

"How long are you in town?"

"A day," Chloe said. "We began shooting the new commercials for Ashanti tomorrow. They have a new line of moisturizing lipsticks."

"Where ya headed this time?"

"Puerto Rico."

Anika raised a shapely brow. "Why Puerto Rico?"

Chloe stood, carrying the pile of now folded underclothes to the eight-drawer marble dresser. "They wanted Caribbean footage, and shooting there will save on production costs over traveling to Jamaica or the Bahamas. The setting's just as beautiful and doesn't one beach really resemble the next?"

"Yeah but you just missed out on a chance to frolic with a bronzed warrior with dreadlocks and a sexy accent, mon," she said, imitating the Jamaican dialect. "I mean the best part about your world-famous career, besides the money of course, is traveling to all those different places."

"Yeah and hardly spending enough time anywhere to truly enjoy it," Chloe said wryly.

"Or enough time to find a man," Anika said pointedly. "It's been three years since you dropped you know who, you know."

"Yes I do know." Chloe threw a withering look at her. "And *you* know that I'm not looking for anybody. If I wanted a man I'd have one, thank you very much. Don't hate me because I'm not in the market for heartbreak."

"Okay, okay," Anika conceded. This was an old argument she knew she would not win. She rolled off the bed to check her impeccable appearance.

"You *are* always on the go," she said, purposely changing the subject. "I get to see you a good twelve times out of the year. I don't know where you get the energy, girl."

"I don't know where I *got* the energy from either."

"Huh?" Anika turned from the mirror where she was applying one of the dozen tubes of lipstick Chloe owned. The shade was a deep mahogany.

"A few months ago I finally told Liv I was retiring. She's not accepting any more offers for me after June of this year."

Anika gasped in shock before regaining her cool composure. "Well, that's good for you, girl. You *have* been complaining a lot lately. And we both know what you promised Mama Dell."

Chloe nodded. "I know. That's the first thing that crossed my mind. I promised her I'd quit when I stopped enjoying it."

Anika turned back to the mirrored wall, skillfully applying the lipstick. "Lawd knows you've made enough money, and you will be remembered as one of the black model trailblazers in fashion. I'm proud of the dedication you've shown your work, even if I didn't see the necessity of you half naked in nothing but a thong and a smile to sell perfume."

"Ha ha ha."

"So what are you going to do now? You're only thirty-three, for goodness sakes!" Anika snorted. "Hardly the age to *truly* retire."

Chloe had pondered the same thing many times since her decision. Quite frankly she wasn't sure, although she had some ideas, like dedicating more time to charities. "I do know that I want to travel and just relax and enjoy all the places I haven't had a chance to explore because I was working. I'm also tired of New York living."

"I hear that. That's why I live in New Jersey. It's not quite as bad as New York," Anika sighed.

"It ain't much better either!"

"Funny," Anika said sarcastically as she applied blush to her high cheekbones. She jumped suddenly, startling Chloe.

"What?" Chloe asked, concerned.

"How about that land Mama Dell left you down south?"

"In Holtsville?"

"Yeah, now if that's not a 180-degree change from the Big Apple, what is?"

She had completely forgotten about the twelve acres of land she'd inherited. Her mother had loved the small town where she had been born and raised. She'd lived there until she had moved to New York at eighteen. Now the land that her mother had cherished was hers.

Her mind wandered to the stories her mother told her about growing up in Holtsville. The spacious, grass-filled land to run and play in; the animals her father raised; miles and miles of empty, uncongested land with tall trees and wildflowers; the still of the night; the fresh, home-grown foods and home remedies for whatever ailments they had; and the tightly knit community, where no one was a stranger even though the nearest neighbor was a quarter mile away. Life moved at a slower, more easygoing pace.

South Carolina. Known as "down south" to anyone who lived "up north."

Chloe could only imagine it because she couldn't remember anything about the yearly trips she and her mother made there. She had only been an arm baby and later a toddler. The trips stopped suddenly when she was just two because her grandparents had been killed by a drunk driver in a tragic automobile accident. Her mother had been an only child of two people who also had no siblings, so there weren't any more family members to travel to see in the small town.

If Holtsville was anything like her mother said, then it had to be pure paradise compared to the constant hustle and bustle of the city that *never* sleeps . . . New York.

"Well, sista friend," Anika sighed, turning to show Chloe how the lipstick perfectly suited her coloring and the outfit. "Whatever you decide to do, I'm behind you one hundred percent."

Chloe nodded, feeling even more sure of her decision.

"Okay, Chloe, let's hit the streets. Wesley awaits!"

Six Months Later

Chloe hated to admit that she was excited about the gala party being thrown in her honor. She sighed and sunk down lower into the honey- and lemon-scented bubble bath. Her chin touched the water and she closed her eyes. As the steamy water gently lapped against her body, she blocked out the noise of preparation coming from the other side of the hotel suite's bathroom door.

Woods Modeling Agency and Ashanti had collaborated on this mega-event as a final farewell to the beauty who had remained firm in her decision to retire, a decision that many questioned the reasons for. A suite of rooms at the Plaza Hotel were at her disposal to prepare for the evening. The outer rooms were filled with racks of designer original dresses on loan from some of the hottest names in fashion, all of whom wanted her to be seen in their creation for her last formal appearance. A representative from Harry Winston Jewelers, along with four burly security guards, had a selection of diamond jewelry for her to choose to wear with whatever gown she selected, also on loan. Hair and makeup stylists were primed to accentuate her natural beauty.

All were outside that door, waiting to help her celebrate her farewell to a highly successful career. They, like many others, wondered why the beauty would retire now when she was still at the height of her career. They also wondered what her plans for the future were, a question that Chloe had avidly dodged in the press.

Downstairs the ballroom was surely bustling with activity as last-minute preparations were made. This would be her last big hooray, and Chloe would admit, only to herself, that she was a little melancholy. But she was also sure that retiring was what she wanted. Her plans for the future were already in motion and she was anxious to start the new chapter in her life.

Chloe stepped out of the elevated tub, engulfing her glistening wet body in a plushly embroidered bath towel. She descended the steps leading from the platform and crossed the carpeted floor, flinging open both the double doors. The activity in the outer room halted as all eyes turned toward her. With a warm smile characteristic of her fun-loving personality, she said, "Make me beautiful."

"God beat us to it," someone yelled out and they all agreed.

Chloe blushed like a schoolgirl. "Y'all full of it."

"Chloe, you chose *my* dress. How wise of you!"

She turned to find Jeffrey appraising her with a critical eye. She smiled and struck a dramatic pose. "How do I look, Jeffie?"

He was amazed, as he was each time he saw her, that she was so beautiful and graceful. She truly would be a loss to the fashion industry. "You look gorgeous as always, Chloe."

Jeffrey had designed the dress with her in mind and it suited this mocha-skinned beauty perfectly. The cut of the slip dress was simple with slender spaghetti straps and a straight, square neckline. The fall colors were not true to the currently hot summer weather, but the rich gold, rust and mocha perfectly offset her chocolate skin and the rich auburn color of her shoulder-length tresses. She brought the sequined creation to life and he was truly honored that she chose to wear it.

As she circled once again for his approval, he decided he

would give her the dress, which could retail for six thousand dollars. No other woman could do it justice.

They posed for several publicity shots before Jeffrey moved on, eventually disappearing from Chloe's sight into the crowd with a dramatic twirl. She promised herself to keep in contact with him, because she would miss him too much to do otherwise.

It was one in the morning and Chloe was exhausted. The dancing all night with barely any reprieve, posing for pictures, and talking to all the celebrities on hand to wish her well was catching up with her. Of course there were the hordes of celebrity reporters hounding her. They all asked much of the same questions she had heard over the past six months since her imminent retirement was announced.

She begged off another dance with a well-known action adventure star and moved through the crowd toward her table of honor at the front of the room. With a smile she waved to Anika, elegant in a red halter dress, dancing with Wesley Snipes with an I-told-you-so expression on her pretty face.

Chloe didn't have to look in a mirror to know that her face was flushed and damp with perspiration. She was contemplating going to the bathroom to touch up her makeup when the tiny hairs on the back of her neck stood on end alerting her that someone was behind her. Turning in her seat, Chloe found her ex-boyfriend, Calvin Ingram, still tall and handsome, still able to arouse her, and still able to hurt her. She hated the sudden ache in her belly because it meant that even after three years he could still get to her.

Damn!

"Can I finally get you to myself?"

Chloe rolled her eyes heavenward. His voice was silky smooth and able to lull away all the defenses she put up . . . if she let him. "Hello Cal. It's . . . good to see you."

What a lie. He was the last man she wanted to see. Memories of his betrayal were still fresh in her mind and in her heart. She had loved this handsome man standing before her and the world she had shared with him crumbled the day she came home early from a photo shoot and found him in bed with another woman. Love had quickly turned to hate and then to pity, because he had no concept of fidelity.

A vision of the day flashed in front of her. Long, slender light-skinned legs wrapped around his waist. His strong, hard buttocks being grasped tightly by her hands as he wildly stroked inside the woman beneath him.

Pain shot through her and tears filled her eyes. *Damn . . . it still hurts!*

Chloe forced a tight smile onto her face. "How's Yvette?"

She received little pleasure from the uncomfortable look that showed on his face as she mentioned the name of the woman she caught him with. *Why can't he leave me alone?*

His eyes dropped as he sat down in the chair next to her. The familiar scent of his spicy cologne wafted past her nostrils and for a second she let herself get lost in the "good times" they shared.

Five years ago during an *Ebony* cover photo shoot, Chloe had spotted Calvin from across the room. The attraction was instantaneous and she couldn't keep her eyes off of him. He was, to her, the perfect male specimen: tall, bronzed, with bright eyes and an even brighter smile, straight teeth and dark chocolate skin that gleamed.

He was introduced to her as Calvin Ingram, the freelance writer who would be conducting the interview. As she shook his hand, her eyes had summed up the slender, athletic build and his towering height of six feet and five inches. She was truly interested in the man.

That interview led to a year of exclusive dating and then a nearly two-year-long courtship that ended abruptly on January the fifteenth.

Damn, three years later and I can still remember the date, she thought as she fidgeted nervously under his intense gaze.

"Chloe, you're still as beautiful as ever. I've missed you, Cat."

She winced as he reverted to his pet name for her, referring to her oddly shaped eyes. "Look Calvin. What do you want from me? We've exchanged polite pleasantries; why don't we continue on our separate paths."

He reached for her hand resting lightly on the table, but she snatched it away. "Look Cat—"

"Chloe," she stated firmly. "My name is not Cat."

"All right . . . Chloe. I haven't seen or spoken to you since that night. You'd done so well at avoiding all my advances until finally I stopped trying. You never gave me the chance to explain—"

"Explain what, Calvin?" she hissed. Her eyes glistened with anger as she stared him down, her usually beautiful mouth now a thin line. "Explain why you were banging the hell out of Yvette in the bed we shared together? Explain why I heard the man whom I thought loved me, telling another woman 'I love you' and 'You're the best piece of—' "

"Chloe." He cut her words off before she could finish. "Now is not the time nor the place."

She laughed bitterly and quelled the desire to slap his handsome and arrogant face. "You're right. Now is not the time nor the place. I don't think there will ever be that time or place. Just leave me the hell alone! Understand?"

Chloe stood abruptly from the chair, almost knocking it to the floor. She stormed away from him, not waiting for an answer to her question and thus out of earshot as he said, "I will get you back, Cat. I swear it."

Chloe hated the way that seeing Calvin disturbed her. His sudden appearance into her life should have meant nothing to her, but here she was clearly shaken.

What the hell is he doing here anyway?

She quickly crossed the room, putting space between herself and him. Olivia walked up to her dressed in a sharp black Donna Karan tuxedo styled suit and diamond jewelry. "Chloe . . . are you okay? It's time to make your speech."

A vision of Calvin's face flashed in her mind and Chloe

visibly winced. *Stay cool, Chloe,* she told herself. *Remember what Mama always said. One fool don't stop no show and life does go on.*

She took a deep breath to clear her head and gave Olivia her million-dollar smile: coy, alive, innocent yet sexy, and false. "I'm fine."

"What are you going to do with yourself?" Olivia asked, finally resigned to the fact that her jewel was lost.

Chloe thought of the tales her mother told and she was calmed instantly. She envisioned miles and miles of flowers, fresh air, peace and quiet, with only the sun and the moon as her immediate neighbors. "I'm going home."

Two

Holtsville, South Carolina (one year later)

The early morning was quiet and the sun not set to rise for another thirty minutes at six A.M. Devon Jamison stepped down off the sprawling circular porch of the house and crossed the short distance to the renovated barn that now housed the offices for Jamison Contractors Inc. He entered the one-level wooden structure and began the morning ritual of turning on all the fluorescent track lights, pouring ground beans in the coffee maker and checking the answering machine for any messages left after business hours.

Jamison Contractors was the pride and joy of Devon and his identical twin brother Deshawn. They built solid homes, and their reputation was one of excellence, even beyond South Carolina. Who knew that what they did as chores for their father growing up would become their craft?

They were skilled at their work and had brought growth to the small carpentry company their father had operated. Now their jobs ranged from building and installing woodwork and cabinets to room additions and home building. The combination of their architectural degrees from North Carolina State and the natural skill acquired from their father made them the best at what they did. He knew his parents were proud of their sons' work and smiled down on them from where they surely rested in heaven together.

Devon glanced over at the large wood-framed photograph of his parents that hung on the wall of the office. God, he missed them, something he had never said aloud but felt deeply just the same. Their deaths had affected him more than he ever let on. First he lost his father to prostate cancer and then just a few short years later his mother joined the man she loved in death as she succumbed to a stroke. It had been more than twelve years and he didn't know if he would ever be totally numb to the pain.

His father had passed on but had left behind a legacy of hard work. Like his father had, he enjoyed the physical labor. Both he and his brother were in the position financially to sit back and let their crew do all the manual work, but they both threw themselves into every aspect of building a solid, quality home for their clients.

Nothing felt better to him than the sun beating down on his bared back as he hammered, or the rough feel of the calluses on his hands. He looked down at them with pride. The hands of a man who loved rugged labor. They didn't look pretty but they were strong and skilled.

Besides, no woman had ever complained when he caressed the soft contours of their bodies. Well, no woman except Elissa. But Elissa was . . . different.

A deep scowl set on his handsome, stern face as he thought of his ex-girlfriend. He'd met her his senior year in college. The pretty, feminine traits she'd possessed had appealed to him. She was small and petite with an air about her that begged a man to take care of her. He had been more than willing to do so.

Eventually, though, her insistence on taking two or more hours to dress and her refusal to be kissed properly, because she feared her perfectly applied makeup would be altered, had become a nuisance to him. How could he love a woman who loved to look at her own reflection instead of looking at him?

Well, he couldn't. Although in the beginning of their two-year-long relationship he had honestly believed he loved the woman. But a bitter final argument over her vanity had finally split them apart.

She had been a small-town girl with big city dreams and ideals. Hardly the woman for him, a simple down-home man who needed and wanted nothing less than a down-home girl in his life. Not that he was ready to settle down and wed, but he knew that when he did lose his heart to another woman she would meet his criteria. She had to or they wouldn't last forever. The last thing he needed in his life was another prima donna. That was one mistake he would *never* make again.

He wondered briefly how Elissa was. Probably married to some well-to-do white-collar man that allowed her to be as prissy and self-indulgent as she wanted to be. Well, it didn't matter where she was as long as she was away from him. She had been his first big mistake in love and he hoped she would be the last.

Pushing all thoughts of the woman in his past aside, Devon focused his attention on the blueprints sprawled on the drafting table before him. It was their latest project: a sprawling, one-level structure for Chloe Bolton.

About nine months ago, he and Deshawn had come into the office to find a message on the answering machine from an attorney by the name of Anthony Barnett. He had said he represented Chloe Bolton and asked if someone could call him back as soon as possible at the number he gave.

They both had been more than confused by the message. Of course they knew who Chloe Bolton was. Who didn't? But the million-dollar question was: What could the supermodel need from them?

They knew she was also the grandchild of Tessa and Odis Bolton, a wonderfully loving couple who had lived in Holtsville all their lives until their untimely deaths. The twins had immediately figured that whatever it was that she wanted, it had to do with the twelve acres of land her family owned. Land that was just a half mile from Devon and his family's land.

The only way to get to the truth was to get it straight from the horse's mouth, so to speak. Or at least the horse's attorney's mouth. The day after they received the message from Mr. Barnett, an eager Deshawn had returned the call.

It seemed the beautiful supermodel wanted to build a home on the land that she inherited from her deceased mother. An award-winning architect from New York had already been contracted to design the house to the model's specifications. Her lawyer, Anthony Barnett, was now offering them the opportunity to build the house. The terms offered by him, who served as her liaison, had been very tempting and generous, so of course Deshawn had accepted the deal on his brother's and his behalf.

Two months ago, construction of the uniquely designed house began and today, as he had almost every day since that first call from her attorney, Devon wondered what the jet-setting model would possibly want in Holtsville, South Carolina. The little town would definitely be considered "roughing it."

The population of Holtsville was well under three thousand, with just five police officers and even fewer city officials. Anyone who wanted to see a movie had to drive the twenty-five minutes to nearby Walterboro, and even the movie house there never showed new movies on the day of their nationwide opening. It was sometimes weeks or more to see the new movies. No major department stores or boutiques were located in the town, and the only eating establishment was Donnie's Diner, which wasn't saying much. The only night life was a splattering of hastily opened clubs that could barely hold more than fifty people at one time. A good ride to nearby Charleston had to supply the movies, more upscale restaurants, shopping malls and other forms of entertainment for the townspeople. Holtsville, like many other small towns, was also ripe and salivating for gossip. Word of someone having an affair, or being involved in a fight, or going broke or being injured or *anything* juicy spread through the town like a brush fire. What these people could accomplish with word of mouth was amazing. Not always accurate, but amazing nonetheless.

He knew that she had not stepped foot in the small town of her mother's birth since her grandparents' death when she was a toddler. He had been a child himself and didn't remember her, just like mostly everyone didn't, but that didn't stop most of the folks from claiming her as their hometown celebrity. "Chloe Bolton's from Holtsville, you know," was their claim to fame. They had all followed her career because they knew she was the grandchild of the late Boltons, Tessa and Odis. Everyone was talking about the celebrity moving "back home," as they put it. Ever since the story leaked out about her plans for building a home there, her name stayed in the local newspapers ripe with speculation on her plans.

Like everyone, he had read the rumors about her relationships with fellow celebrities, supposed suicide attempts, drug overdoses, outrageous spending of her money and, recently, outlandish reasons for her retirement last year. Those gossip rags that his best friend and secretary, Alicia, always brought to work with her were filled with all types of tales about the beauty.

His grandmother Nana Lil, who had been close to both Tessa and Odis, found it hard to believe that anyone with their blood flowing through them could turn out as bad as the papers proclaimed. She also spoke well of her friend's level-headed and kind-natured daughter Adell, whom she was sure could never raise a drug-abusing and promiscuous child. Whenever his grandmother would tout Chloe's impeccable family ties, Devon would just think to himself, *You can lead a horse to water, but you can't make it drink!* Perhaps even with the blood of honorable people in her and being raised by a good woman, Chloe Bolton had gone to pot anyway. He did know you couldn't believe everything you read in the press, and Deshawn, a loyal fan, didn't believe any of it.

He had to admit, as he focused his attention on the blueprints before him, that although the house was grand compared to many of the small, centuries-old homes in the area, it was modest compared to what he had assumed she would want. He had been more than surprised when Barnett had arrived for their first meeting, plans in hand.

As someone with an architectural degree of his own and a critical eye, Devon was willing to admit he was impressed by the architect's unique design. The man was truly a visionary for using an Olympic-sized, glass-enclosed circular pool with a retractable glass ceiling as the centerpiece of the house. Yes, the design was artistic and still functional, but Devon had made a point to let Barnett know that both he and his brother were architects themselves.

All communication thus far had been through Barnett, who, when asked by an eager Deshawn when Ms. Bolton would arrive in town, would only say that she was out of the country traveling. It was due to the friendly attorney, they had then learned, that they had been offered the contract. It seemed he was a business associate of one of their former clients, a young African-American politician from Washington, D.C., who had wanted a vacation home built in Virginia for his family. The fact that they lived just a half mile from the site was just a bonus, he had assured them during the first week of construction when he flew into Charleston to meet with them in person to go over any last-minute details. During the couple of months after they began construction on the house, the attorney had returned several times to check on the developments.

"Morning, brother."

Devon looked up to see his mirror image walk into the office, similarly clad in well-worn baggy jeans and long sleeve henley with GAP embroidered on the front. "Good morning. Nana up yet?"

Deshawn laughed, a smile as always ready to break through on his handsome face. "Yeah, she's flipping through those three hundred channels from that satellite dish we brought her. She's in rerun heaven right about now."

Devon smiled, not as quick to laugh as his easygoing twin. It was odd because as much as they looked alike, they were different in their personalities. Nana Lil, with her ornery sense of humor, called Deshawn the "friendly one." Devon never took offense because he knew their grandmother loved them both equally and she was right. The truth was just the truth. Since before he could remember, Deshawn was always the talkative one, instantly making friends while Devon kept to himself and spoke only when he deemed it necessary. Nothing had changed over the years since their childhood. Well, except that Deshawn's charm made it hard for any woman to resist him and Devon's aloofness seemed to draw women to him in droves. They both had very active social lives.

The differences in their personalities didn't stop them from being close, as most twins were. Sometimes Devon could just shake his head in wonder when he saw that his twin had many of the same idiosyncrasies that he had, like eating with a spoon most of the time or biting his thumbnail when he was thinking something over.

The sun was just beginning to peek over the horizon, and the skies were a bluish lavender mix as day began to break. Summers in the South were one of a kind and Devon knew that by noon the temperature would sore. He made a mental note to make sure he brought the water coolers filled with ice to the site for the crew to use throughout the day. If it was anything like yesterday, then it would be another scorcher as they worked.

Deshawn walked over to look down at the blueprints. Devon steeled himself for what he knew was about to spew from his brother's mouth.

"Chloe Bolton's house, just a half mile from *my* house." He smiled heavenward, as if thanking the Great One above. "Life around here is definitely going to get real interesting when *she* gets here."

"*If* she gets here," Devon snapped. "She's probably not moving down south permanently, like I told you before.

Barnett seems to be the only one in contact with her and *he* doesn't even know when she plans on showing her face around here. She's 'out of the country,' remember? I mean, the woman didn't even care enough about the house to come check out how it's developing herself, so it might not be number one on her priority list. She's probably more concerned about getting a manicure or a facial or something else inane."

Devon sighed as he stood from his desk and began to make preparations to go to the site. "Look, you're not gonna talk me to death about her all day again? It's bad enough that it's all the whole town is concerned about and on top of that, I have to look at that damn calendar."

With a big, charming grin Deshawn walked past his brother to stand in front of where the calendar hung on the wall above his own cluttered drafting table. Opened to the current month, the calendar showed Chloe climbing up the steel stairs of an hourglass-shaped pool with clear turquoise tiles that perfectly matched the hue of the metallic two-piece string bikini she wore. Her long auburn hair was wet and straight back off her beautiful, smiling face.

She was breathtakingly beautiful, and Deshawn couldn't fathom any man in his right mind with a healthy libido not wanting the goddess as his nearest next-door neighbor. In his opinion, Devon was crazy for his paranoid suspicions of the woman's intentions on moving to Holtsville, and he was a closet eunuch for not wanting any involvement with her, beyond building the house.

"Well, even if she isn't moving here permanently, which I can't blame her for, this woman living down the road is a treat, no matter how infrequently."

Devon glanced briefly at the calendar over his shoulder as he strapped on his tool belt. "That's your opinion."

"Thanks for signing the autograph, Ms. Bolton. I'm sure the little girl will never forget this."

Chloe returned the copy of her beauty book, *Chloe's Beauty Secrets,* and the pen to the friendly flight attendant with a smile. "No problem. Tell them I appreciate the support even though I'm retired."

Her first-class flight from Montego Bay's international airport to Charleston, South Carolina, had gone smoothly but Chloe was anxious to be back on solid ground again. Excitement coursed through her as the pilot announced their imminent landing. She closed the novel she had been reading and looked out the window to the sweeping landscape beneath them.

She felt in her heart she had made the right decision. She knew her mother approved, and that was very important to Chloe. Anika had also blessed her friend's adventure, and as Chloe thought of her friend, tears filled her eyes. Although they both promised to visit and call often, Chloe was going to miss her friend. But she also knew that a friendship like theirs would weather the hundreds of miles of separation.

The plane landed smoothly with no delays, and with the pilot's approval she, along with the others in first-class, left the plane. She moved with long strides down the corridor connecting the plane to the airport terminal. With a wince, she realized her name was being yelled out. It was the voice of a child, and that's what stopped Chloe from pulling her cap farther down on her head and sprinting away.

A small child with long, slender braids, about six years old, removed her hand from an elderly woman, presumably her grandmother, and raced toward Chloe. The book she had signed earlier was under her arm.

"Thanks for da audogiraffe." She smiled, revealing missing teeth adorably.

Chloe bit back a grin as the girl mispronounced the word *autograph.* "You're welcome and thank you for buying it. It's a pretty old book from last year."

"I know dat, but my mother lost da other one she had."

Chloe smiled. "Oh, I thought the book was for you," she said playfully.

The little girl laughed. *"I'm* not old enough for makeup!"

"You're pretty enough without it anyway."

"Can I take a pidchoo with you?"

Chloe glanced around quickly, glad that the few people still left in the corridor strode by them fast, also anxious to finish their journeys. She had made every effort to be incognito, even wearing a cap and shades. Yet still this child had recognized her, and so could someone else. But how could she resist this little brown-skinned angel?

She couldn't.

"Okay." Chloe removed her cap and DKNY shades, and stooped down to little Kimani's height. She flashed her famous smile as her grandmother snapped several shots of them together.

"Thank you so much. You really made Kiki's day. Sure do 'preciate that."

Chloe smiled and wished them well before taking her leave, praying she didn't appear rude. But she didn't want to be recognized. After getting her few pieces of luggage, Chloe picked up her already reserved rental car, a red BMW convertible.

Following the directions given her by the star-struck car rental agent, Chloe was situated in her penthouse suite at the Charleston Grand Royale within thirty minutes. She called Anika at work to let her know she had arrived safely. Next she unpacked, and because she was well acclimated to hotel living, it took just minutes to empty the two suitcases and garment bag. The rest of her clothing was, of course, in her apartment in New York. There was no way she could have done the extensive traveling that she had this year with her entire wardrobe. Now all the traveling stopped here, in her new home state of South Carolina.

In fact, she had flown straight from the exclusive resort in Jamaica, and she was dying to get cleaned up. It had been a long day. After a hot bath with aromatherapeutic jasmine bath beads, Chloe dressed in a crisp white tank and cut off, stone-washed jeans. With a pair of black thong sandals on, Chloe left the penthouse suite.

As she stepped off the elevator into the elegantly furnished foyer, she was careful to look out for the hotel's overly enthusiastic manager. When she had first arrived, he and a small portion of his staff had been awaiting her arrival with the full red carpet treatment. Frankly, she wasn't in the mood for any fanfare. Really, she just wanted to see her land and her house.

Her whole purpose for leaving beautiful Jamaica early, with its white sands and black, muscled men, was to check on the development of her house. No longer could she go on Anthony's words; she *had* to see it for herself. The whole project was too important for her to be in another country while it was being constructed.

She breathed a sigh of relief as she slipped past the unsuspecting hotel manager. Within minutes she was back in the vehicle, with the top down and the radio playing the latest R&B songs. The directions she had stopped to get from a gas station cashier seemed easy enough. Most of the driving was straight down Highway 17.

As she enjoyed the late afternoon Sunday sun and the feel of the breeze as she drove, Chloe thought of the year she just spent traveling. After spending the rest of the summer at a small villa she rented in Italy, she spent the fall season cruising. It had been the best way to continue winding down after her hectic life in the New York celebrity set. Although filled with luxurious amenities, it still had been a way for Chloe to wean herself from a fast-paced life and enjoy having empty days to treat herself to the simple things she enjoyed, like reading. On many of the nights aboard the ship she had remained in her suite and just ordered pizza, or watched pay per view movies on the interactive television, or allowed her private butler to arrange a candlelit supper dinner, for one, on her veranda.

The two-week cruise to Greece had been memorable, but it was her stay at the beautiful Andromeda Hotel in Athens that had been the ultimate. Her days had been spent walking the mountains among ancient pottery remains. She had enjoyed the rich history and culture of the Acropolis and she had been amused by the sight of men astride donkeys riding through the olive groves. The last day of her three-week stay in the beautiful country, she chartered a private yacht to sightsee the Cyclades and Dodecanese islands, a sight too impressive to describe with words.

Anika had joined her for two weeks of her month-long travels in Anguilla, a tiny paradise with only one main road and a small number of hotels. It was without the downtown hustle and bustle of larger areas in the Caribbean, and ripe with quiet sophistication. Chloe and Anika had lazed the days away on the secluded crescent-shaped beaches, interspersing their time with touring the island and shopping, of course.

The rest of her time had been spent at an all-inclusive resort in Jamaica. She had spent many hours toasting the sunset from a cliffside perch. The jerk chicken, Red Stripe beer and roasted yams at the Pork Pit had been as satisfying as a meal at a four-star hotel. The resort activity of beach bashes, toga parties and reggae dancing had been unforgettable.

This year had been just what she needed, a mix of total relaxation, exploration of new places and unique experiences. She had met interesting people whom she would never forget. She had been pursued by a wide variety of men, even having to outwit several rather amorous would-be suitors. All in all she had had the best year of her life, and now the building of her dream home, on her family's land, would be the icing on the cake for her.

Chloe focused her attention back on her driving as the main highway eventually passed through a small town. She decelerated the car, pulling onto the small dirt driveway of a two-pump gas station. As she parked, a grizzly old man with silver hair and oversized overalls stepped out of the small storefront.

She stepped out of the vehicle, towering over the short man. "Good afternoon. Could you direct me to Holtsville? I think I got my directions mixed up."

Cyrus Dobbs pulled his sweat-drenched handkerchief from his back pocket and wiped his damp brow. The scorching heat was intense and Chloe felt as damp and sticky as the old man looked. She waited patiently as he tended to the moisture.

Now, his vision wasn't 20/20, but he knew a good-looking gal when he saw one. Hell, a blind man could see this one. He rocked back on his heels to look up into her face. "Great Lawd, you's a tall one," he drawled, his broken English prominent with his southern accent.

Chloe smiled and pushed her shades on top of her damp, wilting hair. "Yes, I am. Did I miss the turn for Holtsville? I haven't seen a sign or anything."

"I've been breathing for seventy-two years and I ain't seen nothin' as pretty as you since my wife Mabel." Cyrus wiped his brow again as the sweat beaded on his face. "Hot as Hades, ain't it?"

"Yes, sir, it is hot. That's why I'm trying to reach my destination." Chloe felt sweat trickle down her spine. Funny, she had been in places much hotter than this but somehow it felt worse when she wasn't surrounded by white sand beaches and dressed in a bikini.

"Where's dat?"

Chloe swatted a mosquito humming by her ear and forced a smile. "Holtsville," she said patiently.

"You got bidness in Holtsville?" Out came the cloth again.

"My mother passed away eight years ago and she left me some land and I'm having a home built there for myself."

"Didn't catch your mother's name. She grew up in Holtsville, you say?"

"Adell. My mom's name was Adell Bolton," Chloe answered, resorting to the rule of obeying her elders that her mother had preached since birth.

Cyrus wiped his brow again. "You're dat model gal building the house. Odis's grandbaby."

This was a statement, not a question.

"That land is down the road from the Jamison boys."

Chloe jumped as she realized that she may be getting somewhere with him. "Yes! Yes! Jamison Contractors are building the house . . . in Holtsville." She put emphasis on the last two words.

"I know." Cyrus smiled, revealing big white teeth which had to be false because they were just too perfect.

Maybe it was the heat, or maybe it was the fact that she had just lain around for nearly a year vacationing, but Chloe definitely felt her mind was not working at full capacity. Did this old man not know a lot of details about her, like her grandparents' name, who was building the house and where the land was located? "Is *this* Holtsville?" she asked, her husky voice incredulous.

"Yes, yes it is." He pulled a piece of wood and a sharp pocket knife from his pocket. "Them Jamison twins work hard, both of them. They sure woulda made their daddy proud. That big ol' house of yours will stand strong for plenty generations to come."

"Well I haven't seen the house yet, but I'm anxious to."

"So you're the big-time model everybody been talkin' 'bout, huh?" He had a way of asking questions that let you know he already knew the answers. He whittled as he talked, slow but steady even with his gnarled fingers.

"Yes, I am."

"Seen ya house, it's comin' along just fine." The wood was shaping into a tiny figure.

"How far to my land?" Chloe pushed off the trunk of the car where she had been leaning. There was no denying the excitement she felt.

She listened intently as he *finally* offered assistance and gave her directions to her land. Thankfully, it was just a short distance from there. Chloe moved to hop back into the car but instead turned to extend her slender sable hand to him. "Thank you Mr.—"

He wiped his hand on his overalls before he warmly clasped her own. "Cyrus Dobbs, and you're Chloe."

"Yes, Chloe Bolton. Thank you again, Mr. Dobbs."

He closed the pocket knife and opened his other hand to her. A wooden angel rested in his wrinkled palm, small and delicate. As she paused, he said, "Take it child 'fore my hand drops off."

She picked up the figure, studying it. It was barely as big as her palm, but detailed down to the sleeping face. "This is for me?"

He nodded and studied her reaction intently with wise, aged eyes.

Touched, Chloe could only smile with a husky, "Thank you, it's . . . it's beautiful."

"If you want, once you move in, I'll take you to your grandparents' grave, seeing as how you ain't got no more family in Holtsville."

Chloe felt the urge to kiss his grizzly cheek, but didn't. "I would appreciate that, Mr. Dobbs."

She climbed back into the car and started the engine, her wooden angel clutched in her palm. "I'll be seeing you."

"Yup you sure will, and welcome home, angel."

She waved and shifted into drive, steering the car back onto the main road. Chloe was glad she decided to come into town on a Sunday to see the land and the beginning structure of the house alone. Her eyes took in everything around her as she drove, and she felt an infinite connection to her mother, to the grandparents she didn't know and to the generations of Boltons who had once lived in this town.

Holtsville was everything her mother had spoken of. As she drove, she enjoyed the long stretches of uninhabited woodsy land with wildflowers and grass as tall as she. Children played noisily and freely on uncluttered spaces next to their homes. Old men sat under the shade of a willow tree playing cards on a makeshift table. Women sat on screened porches in cotton house dresses and casual wear, fanning themselves while drinking lemonade. The faint sounds of the organs and a joyful choir could be heard from the small brick church. The air was filled with the tantalizing smell of roasted ham and baked desserts.

Peace, quiet, family, love . . . Holtsville.

She waved back as many of the people she passed on the country roads greeted her, even though they didn't know her. She loved it!

A sign on her right said "Jamison Contractors straight ahead one mile on left." She was tempted to stop and introduce herself to the contractors, but she didn't because she didn't favor dropping by people's homes, especially on a Sunday, unexpectedly. Besides, she wanted to see the house alone. Tomorrow she'd call from the hotel and tell them she was in town.

She looked over as she eventually passed their house, a white, three-story affair with a large barn yards away with a sign, JAMISON CONTRACTORS INC., on the front. As she sped past she noticed a shirtless man with a well-defined, muscled body bending over washing a truck.

Just as Cyrus Dobbs had said, one half mile down from the Jamisons was her land. The car slowed under her direction as she turned left onto the grassy land. She squealed in pleasure when she first laid eyes upon the sprawling frame structure of her soon-to-be home. With her eyes closed, she could visualize the finished project. The land surrounding the cleared area, where the house stood, was green as emeralds.

Chloe reached into the car and pulled the small notepad from her Fendi tote, along with a pen. She jotted notes on the lined paper as she walked every inch of the land surrounding the house. Her plans for a colorful garden were clear in her visions, although she planned to hire a professional landscaper. She removed her sandals and relished the feel of the warm blades of grass between her scarlet-lacquered toes.

Tucking the notepad in her back pocket, Chloe climbed the

steps onto the wraparound porch. Although just the frame of the house stood now, she walked through the one-level structure. She studied the size and shape of each of the rooms, pulling out her notepad again to jot down notes on possible decorations and furnishings. Soon the lined pad was filled with ideas, and Chloe felt she could now walk around the structure blind. The house would be beautiful and she knew her mother would have loved it. She didn't stop the tears that filled her eyes as she thought of her.

As soon as she had been financially able, she had moved her mother from the small, two-bedroom apartment where they lived into a home in an upper middle class neighborhood on Staten Island. They had traveled around the world together as Chloe worked. Their relationship had been a rare mix of friendship and a solid mother-daughter relationship. Now that she was gone, Chloe truly wished she had built the home here a long time ago so that Adell could enjoy it with her.

She sighed and wiped the tears from her cheeks. Sweat traveled down the valley of her full breasts as she left the framed structure to sit on the porch. She could easily have moved anywhere in the world, but this small town her mother loved was the right choice. Freedom from New York, freedom from traveling and working, freedom from the glamorous lifestyle she left behind. For once she was moving through life at a slower pace and enjoying herself. The small amount of apprehension she felt over moving to a new place where she didn't know a soul was outweighed by her growing closeness to this land and the meaning it held for her.

Already she was reluctant to leave it, even with the sweltering heat. Instead of heading back to the comforts of the hotel in Charleston, Chloe leaned back against the porch's railing and closed her eyes. With a faint smile she envisioned days of swinging on the very same porch or planting perennials in her garden. She was at peace.

Three

Devon was washing his midnight blue Ford F-150 pickup truck on the side of the house when he saw the flash of red fly by on the road. He could only make out that it was a woman as the car rounded the bend and disappeared from sight. He didn't recognize her or the flashy vehicle.

He heard the sound of the screen door open with a long and loud squeak. "Who's that, Vonnie?"

Devon pushed back the irritation he felt at his grandmother's still addressing him with her childhood pet name for him. He continued to wash the hood with wide, circular motions and answered her the best he could. "I don't know, Nana Lil."

He smiled when she sucked her teeth, and then he heard the familiar long squeak again, just before the slam signaling that the door had closed. Devon assumed that she had gone back inside the house.

He was wrong.

"That was a fancy car, wasn't it?"

"Yup." He moved around the car, bending over to wash the side, his bare back to the house. His grandmother was nosier than a detective and he silently hoped she would let it drop, but he knew damn well she wouldn't. She was quiet for a while, only the steady "bump-bump" of her favorite maple rocking chair hitting against the solid granite porch, making noise. Devon knew that any second now she would say some—

"Ain't nothing else down that way but the house y'all build-ing on the Tessa and Odis's land for their grandbaby."

He said nothing as he sprayed water from the hose onto the truck with the nozzle. He enjoyed the feel of the cold water bouncing off the truck and onto his bare chest. It offered slight relief from the sizzling summer heat.

Lillian Jamison leaned back in her rocking chair. As she rocked, she wished that Deshawn was home, although church was a good place to be. Like her, he was talkative and curious, something the more reserved Devon called nosy. Now he was like his daddy. Devon kept everything inside and could sit for an hour straight and not say one solitary word. They were twins and the spitting image of one another, but as different as night and day. She loved them both just the same. Her boys . . . well, okay, they were grown men who owned their own business and home, but it felt good to call them her boys, so she did . . . to herself anyway.

She continued to rock in her chair, watching Devon as he waxed his truck, but keeping an eye on the road as well. Soon he finished up and came to sit on the porch, wiping the water and sweat from his chest with a towel. In the direction of the Bolton land the road eventually became a dead end, so who-ever it was in the red car would have to turn around eventually and drive back. She hadn't. Lil knew that it had to be Tessa's grandbaby, finally come home.

"Vonnie, maybe you should drive down and check things out."

Devon had to agree with his grandmother now. It had been close to a half hour since the red BMW had flown by. He pulled on his Calvin Klein white tank. "I'll drive down."

"Thank you, baby," she said, sweet as sugar now.

He pulled his keys out of the pocket of his damp jeans and walked over to his truck to hop up onto the plush gray leather seat of the extended cab. Turning the key in the ignition, he started the vehicle and put the gear into reverse, backing out of the spacious yard onto the paved driveway. The blaring of a horn and the screech of tires caused Devon to jerk down on his brakes. "What the hell?"

He looked to his right, outside his passenger window and was nearly blinded by the crimson red of the car, precariously close to his rear bumper. Angry because he knew she had been speeding, Devon jerked the emergency brake up, threw the truck into park and slammed out of the cab. As he stalked around the length of the truck, she unfolded her tall, curvaceous frame from the car. Devon came to a sudden halt in his tracks.

Electricity whipped between them like a bolt of lightning. The attraction was instantaneous. Their eyes traveled each other's bodies, taking in everything. Desire coursed through their veins like fire!

Chloe was mesmerized by his magnificence. This caramel-toned brother, with his strong, muscular physique, was more attractive than many of the male supermodels she'd worked with. He was fine, reminiscent of Taimak from *The Last Dragon.* She wanted to touch the soft waves of his freshly cut fade; she longed to look deeply into his deep-set ebony eyes and see into his soul; she could visualize him inhaling of her perfume with his long, wide-bridged nose; she wanted to feel the smoothness of his square jawline against her cheek; and oh Lawd, she wanted to be kissed with those soft, supple lips.

Chloe was overwhelmed by him. She actually felt breathless.

He was an African warrior. He was divine. She had never felt such an intense instantaneous attraction to someone before. Not even her initial awareness of Calvin had been this strong. Even in anger, his sexuality was electrifying, his eyes blazing, his stride like that of a sleek cougar. She let her eyes roam over him again and all she could say was, "Damn!"

The calendar did her no justice. This woman was exquisite. Her cat-shaped eyes captivated him, and her full, luscious lips enticed him. The deep bronze of her skin glowed healthy and appealing, begging to be kissed, massaged and licked. Her breasts were full and heavy, straining against the cotton tank she wore. Even though she was thinner than his usual taste, her body was still that of a seductive and alluring woman. His heart hammered hard against his ribs as a vision of their bodies, naked and sweating, entwined on the sloped hood of her car, flashed in his head and he became aroused. This woman spelled trouble with a capital "T," and Devon knew he had to keep his distance from her. She was hot and everyone knew that when you played with fire, you got burned!

"This isn't New York or the Indy 500. You could've killed yourself or—"

"Or what," she said sarcastically, as her desire for this man quickly fizzled. "Dent your precious truck?"

Devon forced himself to silently count to ten, calming himself. Now was not the time for anger. This woman, with her blazing angry eyes, was his client, and it would not be good business to curse her little butt out. And he meant "little butt" literally. What size was she anyway, a four? "Or," he said, only slightly sarcastic, his deep voice appealing with a southern drawl. "You might hurt one of the kids that live on this bend."

Chloe detected the change in him, the dissipation of his anger, and so she let the imaginary chip on her shoulder fall. "I apologize and you're right, I was driving too fast."

They were only six inches apart and the sexual tension was still there between them, thick and heavy. Chloe had to remind herself, with some difficulty as she looked at his handsome face and sculpted body, about her last fumble in the game of love with Calvin. No matter how fine he was, she didn't need to complicate her life with an "involvement."

"Look, it's too hot to be angry." Chloe outstretched her hand. "I'm Chloe Bolton and you're?"

"Devon Jamison," he drawled as he eyed her smooth hand

warily, before finally clasping it into his large, callused grasp.
"If I had known you were arriving in town today, we could
have scheduled an appointment to go to the site together."

Chloe looked down at their entwined hands, two shades of
brown mingled like a mosaic. His index and middle finger
rested lightly on the tender inside of her wrist. She shivered
with a rush of desire. Funny, she hadn't even known that was
one of her hot erogenous zones. She removed her hand as
though it had been near fire, afraid she would get burned.

"It was at the last moment. I was supposed to travel for
another month but I just couldn't wait to see how the house
was coming along. I hope that isn't a problem."

"No, of course not. How long are you in town for? You're
probably anxious to get back to your traveling."

Chloe looked at him with a curious expression. "I've
booked a suite at the Grand Royale in Charleston until the
construction of my house is complete. I guess you can say
I'm here to stay."

He was shocked to say the least. She really *was* moving to
Holtsville! But why? His eyes took in the flashy car, her scarlet
manicured hands, the two-hundred-dollar DKNY shades, and
the two-carat diamond stud earrings. She was wealthy and famous, and he could tell she only enjoyed the finer things in life.
Like staying at the most expensive hotel in Charleston for two
months. A big-city girl all the way. What could she possibly
want in a small town? A brief image of Elissa flashed in his
mind. He saw the two women as one and the same, although
this was the first time he met the beauty face to face.

"Will the house be finished by the end of next month?"

"Yes, we haven't suffered any major setbacks. We're right
on schedule—"

"Vonnie! Bring that girl in the house and offer her something to drink. You *were* raised!"

Chloe turned to look at the owner of the strong, feminine
voice. A petite, older woman dressed in a white cotton dress
stood on the wraparound porch, her hands on her narrow hips.

Her salt-and-pepper hair was pulled into a neat French roll, with a pretty, makeup-free face, even with the prominent wrinkles. She waved "hello" at Chloe with a smile.

"That's my grandmother. Just call her Miss Lil; everyone around here does." As she waved back, he studied the woman. He wasn't quite sure what to make of her. "Pull your car in behind my truck."

He crossed back around the truck and hopped up into the cab. After she pulled her car in behind him, onto the driveway, he walked over to her car door to meet her. "Since you're around today, why don't we meet in our office and I can answer any questions you have."

"My intent had been to call tomorrow and set up a time to come to the site. But if you're sure that I'm not inconveniencing you, we can meet today."

"Not at all." Actually, he would have preferred to foist the task off on his brother. Being around her made him nervous.

As they walked toward the house, he hoped she didn't turn up her nose at their home. He knew it was no comparison to her apartment in New York, or the luxury hotels she stayed in during her travels. If she showed any outward signs of disrespect to the home his loving grandmother had taken over caring for ever since she moved back into the house where she raised her own family, then he swore to toss the model out on her skinny butt. House or no house.

Chloe was charmed by the exterior of their sprawling three-level home, reminiscent of the old plantation homes of the eighteenth century. The large porch had a large wooden swing and a rocking chair, the whitewash was fresh and bright like it had been recently painted. The dark trim was the perfect contrast for the shutters, especially with the brightly colored flowers in the small boxes at each glass-paned window. She immediately felt comfortable here; it was the epitome of a country home.

"Hello Miss Lil, it's nice to meet you."

Lillian figured that in her eighty-seven years on this earth, she had become a good judge of character on her strong instincts alone. This beautiful and tall woman, who resembled her best friend Tessa so much, stood before her almost shyly. She was pretty but not conceited, confident and not arrogant, and she didn't take any stuff. She saw that from the way the beauty had stood up to a formidable Devon. The eyes were the mirror of the soul, and Lil liked what she saw in the girl's cat-shaped depths. Kindhearted, friendly and drug-free. The eyes of a drug abuser were sickly and yellow, and her eyes were bright white and clever. That dispelled all the negative thoughts Vonnie had of her being an airhead and a drug addict. Lil liked her on the spot. This was Tessa's grandchild.

"Nana Lil, this is Chloe Bolton." Devon spoke from behind her, and Chloe felt his warm breath on her neck as he spoke. She stepped up away from his closeness. *This brother could get to be irresistible,* she thought as she shivered with awareness.

"Nice to meet you, Chloe. I remember when you were just an arm baby, but now you grown up to be so pretty, just like Tessa." Lil stepped forward and hugged Chloe, the top of her head only reaching the model's shoulders.

Chloe hugged her back, only slightly surprised. "You knew my grandmother?"

"Knew her?" Lil scoffed as she released her. "Tessa and I were the best of friends, since childhood and right up until her and Odis's passing."

Sadly, Chloe thought of her own friendship with Anika and could only imagine the grief she would feel if she ever lost her. "I wished I could have known them."

Lil sighed, "Well I know they are proud of you and smiling from heaven. Well, come on in."

Chloe stepped into the house behind the older woman. The smell of lemon and pine assailed her nostrils pleasantly. It was a home filled with love of family. The walls were filled with photographs of the twins as children and with their parents. Their degrees from North Carolina State hung prominently and with pride.

Devon leaned in close to her ear, again from behind her. "I know it's not what you're used to, but we love it. It's our home."

Confused and startled, Chloe turned to set him straight, but Miss Lil called for her to come into the kitchen. She looked at the sardonic expression on his handsome face with a frown before following her down the narrow hallway into the brightly lit kitchen. Large and airy, it was well-used and probably a family meeting ground.

"Have a seat baby." She opened the refrigerator door. "Iced tea or lemonade?"

"Lemonade please, thank you." Chloe took a seat at the round oak table in the center of the kitchen.

"Nana, I'll be upstairs. If you'll excuse me Ms. Bolton, I'm just going to shower and change." He retraced his steps down the hallway. Soon they heard the sounds of him running up the stairs.

Chloe sipped from the glass of iced lemonade Miss Lil sat before her, letting the cool sweetness wet her throat. "Fresh squeezed? It's delicious."

"Thank you kindly." Lil sat in the chair across from Chloe. "So Vonnie . . . I mean Devon, says you won't be moving here permanently. I know Holtsville don't compare to New York and all those other places you've been to, but it's a good family-oriented place filled with hard-working people who can be a bit nosy at times. Plus, we take our family land very serious here and I know your grandparents would love for you to be living here on the land they worked so hard for. I would also love to get the chance to know my best friend's only grandchild."

Chloe nearly choked on her drink when Lil first started talking. "Devon said . . . what?"

Lil watched the other woman's shocked expression. "Devon said you weren't moving here permanently. You didn't say that?"

Miss Lil had this way of calling a person baby that would soothe the soul, but Chloe was angry about his assumptions and nothing would soothe that. She'd never spoken to the man, so how could he be so presumptuous about what she would do? Or was he just a habitual, bold-faced liar? "Miss Lil, I did not say that because you see, I'm here to stay. Devon was . . . mistaken."

Devon stepped out of the shower in the adjoining bathroom of his suite of rooms, which took up the entire third floor. The hot steam swirled around his naked, muscular form like a fog. Water trickled down his handsome, almost beautiful face, down to that little pocket of his collarbone, continuing down its wet journey to the deep valley between his hard, square chest. It followed the rugged, zig-zag pattern of his washboard abdomen to disappear in the ebony, curly bush of his groin.

She looked down her nose at your house, man, he thought as he toweled dry. He remembered that little Miss Diva was downstairs in his living room. He had noticed how she looked around the living room when she first entered the house. He hated to see what hideous decorating would be done to the house when construction was complete. Visions of massive crystal chandeliers and garish furnishings caused him to shudder with disgust. Elissa had spoken of her own dreams of a mansion filled with glamour and servants. Devon laughed as he tried to imagine himself sitting and waiting for someone to bring him a glass of water, in his own home. Never! Not when he could get off his behind and get it for himself!

He wouldn't be surprised if she did turn out to be one of those heroin-thin models. How could a woman survive being that thin? She couldn't possibly eat, or worse yet she might eat and then force herself to vomit. Bulimia. Black women weren't meant to be chocolate replicas of Twiggy, no matter how pretty the face. Well, okay, so maybe she wasn't *that* thin but he liked a woman he could hold on to. Another lesson he learned about himself from his relationship with Elissa, who was also thin. In his opinion, Chloe Bolton would be much prettier if she gained fifteen or twenty pounds.

Whoa! He stopped his thoughts immediately. It shouldn't . . .

no, it *didn't* matter to him what size she was, or how that related to the type of women he found himself attracted to.

"Vonnie . . . I mean Devon. Deshawn's pulling up in the yard."

Nana Lil's voice reached him faintly through the closed bedroom door. He walked naked to the hamper in his closet to toss in the gray towel he had been drying off with. He pulled out a casual outfit from the many clothes hanging in his walk-in closet. He was anxious to grab Deshawn and escort their beautiful client over to the office. The sooner they got this impromptu meeting over with, the sooner she would be back in place in her suite at the ritzy Grand Royale in Charleston. And the sooner that happened, the better!

Deshawn maneuvered his gray Ford F-150 pickup truck, like his brother's, to squeeze past the flashy red BMW in the driveway, to park in his usual spot, next to his brother. He eyed the vehicle before climbing the steps onto the porch and into the house.

He removed the hand-tailored lightweight Tommy Hilfiger navy blazer he wore, laying it on one of the two green leather recliners adjacent to the fireplace. He was so glad to take it off in the sweltering summer heat. His sweat-soaked back felt like someone had thrown a cup of water onto him. The only reason he had even gotten up and pulled on the monkey suit to go to church at all was to try and hook up with this pretty, dark-skinned girl that he saw there last week. Deshawn would go to *any* lengths for the sake of love, or was it lust? Well, whatever it was, he was determined.

"Nana Lil, whose car is that?" He yelled out.

"It's mine."

Deshawn looked up from his wrist, where he was removing his gold watch, to see the face that matched the soft, husky voice. He was *always* interested in meeting a new lady. He

froze for a second and then laughed, "Damn . . . oh, sorry.
'Scuse me, but you look just like—"

"Chloe Bolton, right?" She stepped forward, a soft smile
on her lips, her delicate hand outstretched. "Anyone ever tell
you that you look like Devon Jamison?"

He took her hand, enjoying the feel of her soft palm, inhaling the flowery scent of her perfume as he laughed at her
joke. "Ha . . . ha . . . ha . . . that's funny."

"Yeah, I thought it was." Chloe laughed at his feigned sarcastic expression. "Anyway, I *am* Chloe Bolton. You must be
Deshawn."

Reluctantly, he released her hand, at a total loss for words.
He considered himself a connoisseur of women, and this
woman was truly ranked with a fine, exquisite wine. The best.
As he looked directly into her smiling eyes, he gave her his
most charming and irresistible smile. When she smiled in return he said a silent, "Thank you, Jesus!"

They were identical, but Chloe saw the difference in their
personalities immediately. This one's eyes were bright, friendly
and charming, unlike the brooding, angry looks of his brother.
Instantly, she felt more comfortable around Deshawn, less on
her guard.

Lil walked out of her bedroom, which was directly off the
living room, holding a photo album. She sent him upstairs to
get his brother and to change. Quickly she showed Chloe the
few pictures of her grandparents in the album. Chloe gasped
with pleasure at the pictures of her mother as a chubby, an-
gel-faced toddler. Tears nearly spilled onto her cheeks when
Lil gave her a small, faded picture of a younger and slimmer
Adell, holding her as a baby, with both of her grandparents
looking on lovingly.

Lil had been saddened by hearing the news of Adell's passing
from Chloe, and the picture had instantly popped into her memory. She knew Chloe would love it and she did. It was the only

picture of both her mother and her grandparents that she'd seen. Moved beyond words, she could only whisper a heartfelt, "Thank you."

Lil patted the younger woman's hand to comfort her. "You will stay for dinner, Chloe?"

It was more of a statement than a question, but Chloe still attempted to decline. "No, thank you. I wouldn't want to intr—"

Lil waved a thin hand, prominent with large veins. "Child, please, you need a good home-cooked meal. If you don't get some meat on dem bones you'll snap in half like a dried twig."

Chloe smiled at the way Miss Lil sucked her teeth. She watched as she closed the photo album and moved back to the kitchen. The woman had more energy than the little pink bunny on those Energizer battery commercials. When Chloe followed her back into the kitchen, she found Lil mashing a pot of boiled and peeled potatoes with butter and milk. Her stomach betrayed her and growled in hunger . . . loudly.

"See there," Lil waved her spoon in Chloe's direction. "You hungry, girl."

"Are you sure Deshawn . . . or Devon won't mind?"

The older woman threw a "say what?" expression over her shoulder. "This may be their house but since I moved back in here, I've been running this show. If Lil invites someone to this table, then they're invited."

Chloe looked down at her slim, gold Movado watch. It was three P.M. and her ride back to Charleston would take a half hour. She preferred to make the trip during daylight. Figuring that she still had plenty of time, and reluctant to leave, she accepted.

She offered her services to Miss Lil, but the elderly woman refused profusely with a hearty laugh. "Baby, please, and have you break one of those nails in *my* gravy? No, thank you, just drink your lemonade and relax."

Chloe hid a smile behind her manicured hand. It was obvious that Lil thought she was inept in the kitchen. She didn't bother to correct her. Suddenly the hairs on the back of her neck stood on end and Chloe knew, before turning around, that it was Devon who had walked up behind her. She looked over her right shoulder and their eyes met briefly before they both looked away.

He walked past where she sat to enter the kitchen. "Ms. Bolton, as soon as my brother comes downstairs we can all walk over to the office." His tone was so professional and he was all business in his red polo T-shirt and baggy stonewashed jeans.

"Devon, Chloe accepted my invitation to dinner, which is ready. You'll have to have your meeting after the eating is done." Lil said this in a no-nonsense tone, as she sat heaping bowls of food on the table.

He whirled in shock to look at his grandmother and then whirled back, almost comically, to look at Chloe. She sat innocently sipping lemonade. Finally he turned back to Lil. "I'm sure Ms. Bolton has other plans that we don't want to keep her from."

She handed Chloe four warmed dinner plates to set out. "I'm sure she wouldn't have accepted if she had other plans, Vonnie."

"Devon," he corrected, almost off-hand. "We don't want to force Ms. Bolton to eat here."

Each time Chloe opened her mouth to speak up for herself, one of them spoke first, acting as if she was not present as they spoke of her. "I—"

"This girl needs a good home-cooked meal and she'll get one today . . . right now . . . right here."

Devon started to continue his unwarranted protests, but his grandmother shot him "the look" that let him know he was doing something she didn't approve of. When Devon was a child "the look" would immediately cease all wrongdoing. Although it didn't hold the same power now, he let his beliefs slide, knowing his grandmother would hate for him to argue with her. Honestly, he didn't know if he could stomach Ms. High and Mighty forcing herself to eat their common food. Just because he was building her house didn't mean he had to eat with her. Right? Right.

Chloe stood to set the plates on the table and silently wondered what his problem was. He was beginning to pluck her nerves with his assumptions. Yes, he was fine, but he was also turning out to be a pain.

He turned to face her, his handsome face expressionless and blank. "Ms. Bolton, I guess we will have to reschedule our meeting after all. I've made prior plans. Is that a problem for you?"

"If you've got plans, bro, go ahead. I'm sure I can . . . handle Ms. Bolton." Deshawn stepped into the kitchen, obviously overhearing the conversation.

He winked at Chloe, and she instantly smiled in return. "Yes, Mr. Jamison. Don't let me keep you from your plans. I'm more than confident that your brother can fill me in on all the details."

Chloe pretended to dismiss him and took a platter of hot buttered biscuits out of Lil's hands to set on the already crowded table. Deshawn took a seat and began to fill his plate. Lil stood over the sink, a glass of water in her hand, as she took her medicine. Each effectively ignored Devon.

He eyed the golden fried chicken longingly. His empty stomach yelled, *Sit down fool, you're hungry.* Instead he left the kitchen through the back door.

Chloe watched him go and felt suddenly at ease enough to pick up the juicy piece of fried chicken with her fingers, instead of the knife and fork she had been using.

Devon entered the restaurant with its dark green and maroon decor. He spoke to the patrons inside as he took a seat at a booth near the entrance. Donnie's Diner had been around for twenty-five years and was a landmark in Holtsville. But if one were to pay attention to the dim interior, the grease-stained walls and ancient, chipped wood furnishings, one would think it was more than a century old. The little diner needed renovations . . . badly, and Devon decided to try and persuade the owner/chef to allow Jamison's to do the job, at a fair price. He was sure that if Donnie ever washed the walls, the building would fall apart because dirt and grease were truly its glue.

He looked around after he placed his order with the waitress, the voluptuous Poochie. The portly white sheriff and one of his deputies were leaving with two take-out containers in a white plastic bag. To think, when Donnie first wanted to open the diner all those years ago, he had to get a petition with enough signatures before the all-white town council would allow the diner to open within town limits. It was the large black population that had supported him with signatures and patronage.

Cyrus, the town gossip, was holding court and talking animatedly with his usual crew listening intently. He was telling somebody's business, Devon knew. Unfortunately his voice carried over to where Devon sat.

"She *is* in town. I saw her for myself and Lawd, was she pretty. Y'all remember how cute Tessa was as a young woman, when we all sniffed around her skirts before Odis won her heart?"

The other older men all agreed. "Well her grandbaby is just as easy on the eyes."

Devon's food arrived, with an inviting smile from Poochie, which he ignored as he forced himself to tune out Cyrus and his friends' conversation. The last thing he needed was to hear them fawn over Chloe Bolton. His whole intention for being here was to get away from the woman. With a sigh, he started to eat his food.

Unfortunately, the food's quality mirrored the interior. Everything was edible but not any comparison to his Nana Lil's cooking. Donnie's baked macaroni and cheese had way more macaroni than cheese. The collard greens were mostly stems and he could distinctively taste the burnt skin under the gravy of his smothered chicken. The diner catered mostly to the bachelors and widowers of the small town. It was easy to see why. They couldn't do much better themselves.

"It can't be that bad Dev . . . or is it?"

He looked up from his plate to find his childhood friend

and secretary, Alicia Jenkins. His frown turned to a reserved smile. "Worse."

Devon stood up, waving a hand toward the empty booth seat across from him. She took the seat, sliding her petite, pear-shaped frame onto the booth. "I just came from Walterboro shopping and I saw your truck. Miss Lil ain't sick, is she, 'cause I know she throws down in the kitchen on Sundays."

Devon pushed his plate away, resigned to not eating until he went home, and that would be well after he thought *she* was gone. "No, she's not sick. I just felt . . . like . . . some . . . Donnie's, that's all."

The words were forced and Alicia knew her friend of nearly thirty years. "Word's out that Chloe Bolton came into town today."

A vision of her filled him at the mention of her name. He shook his head, as if to remove the image. "Yes, she did. First class in her convertible BMW. She's out to the house now. Nana Lil invited her to dinner."

"Oh," was all Alicia said.

"Anyway, Shawn's meeting with her after dinner." He sipped from his glass of raspberry iced tea, the only good part of his meal.

Something was up and Alicia knew it. For one, Devon was having Sunday dinner at Donnie's when she *knew* that Miss Lil had cooked. Two, the supermodel was finally in town and having dinner with Deshawn and Lil. Third and lastly, Devon was leaving a meeting to Deshawn alone, when he didn't appear to be doing anything more important instead.

Something was definitely up.

Alicia was well aware of Devon's less-than-complimentary opinion of the celebrity. On many occasions in the office, he had said how they were just a step above strippers, using their bodies to sell products. Deshawn, on the other hand, was like a kid in a candy store about the prospect of the grand Chloe Bolton moving down the road from him.

Alicia didn't know how she felt. From a distance, she en-

vied the beauty and fame of the supermodel. What woman
wouldn't? But seeing her face to face every day for any length
of time was a different matter. Chloe Bolton. She'd seen her
commercials, her face filled the fashion magazines, her beauty
books were bestsellers, her life was detailed in the gossip rags
and television shows. She was big time.

What did she want in a small town like Holtsville? Family
or no family, Alicia couldn't see herself being supa dupa rich
and *moving to* Holtsville. Most young people were rushing to
get away.

She looked down at his full, uneaten plate of food. "Look
here, I know you're hungry. Come to my place and I'll make
you something good to eat, friend."

Devon looked at her. "Naw, that's okay. You don't have to
cook for me."

"Oh. Okay then, I'll see you tomorrow at work." She
scooted her ample bottom over on the seat and stood up, walking past him to leave the restaurant. Suddenly, she turned.
"Chicken and dumplings?"

Devon jumped up and dropped a ten-dollar bill on the table
to handle his check and a tip. "It's on."

"That was good Al. Thanks."

Alicia stood, taking a mock bow, before picking up their
plates from the small round kitchen table to sit in the sudsy
water in the sink. She quickly washed up the few dishes before
joining him in her pastel-colored living room. He sat slouched
on her mint sofa, flipping through the channels of her nineteen-inch television. She smiled at the sight of him, big and
muscular, crouched on the small piece of furniture.

"What's she like?" Alicia asked suddenly.

Devon glanced toward her before turning back to the television. "Who?"

"Who else? Chloe Bolton."

"Exactly as I expected. Just imagine Elissa to the one hundredth degree," he laughed shortly as Alicia made a face.

She remembered Elissa well from the few visits she made to Holtsville. The woman had been quick to criticize and even quicker to lift her finely arched brow in reproach. Elissa had not enjoyed her visits, except for the time she wasted trying to change Devon. Nana Lil loved everyone and even she had admitted to Alicia how she had to bite her tongue to keep from telling Elissa to climb off her horse, in less-than-favorable terms.

Alicia was willing to admit, to herself anyway, that her own reasons for not wanting Elissa around went far beyond the woman's high saddity ways. Alicia had burned with jealousy of her. Not because she was going to college, nor because she was slender, pretty and well-dressed, but because Elissa had what Alicia wanted most in the world . . . Devon's love and devotion.

His distant and aloof manner had attracted Alicia like a moth to a flame. Ever since she was old enough to recognize that boys were good for more than playing hide-and-seek and tag, she had loved Devon.

Even now as she watched him, her heart ached for his love and her center throbbed for a touch she had never experienced from him. Both he and Deshawn were her very best friends in the world, but she wanted Devon as her lover. She let her eyes caress him, because her hands could not. Secretly, she envisioned the physical loving they could bring each other. She dreamed of him spending the night in her bed, and not her couch, as he had in the past as a friend. They could share passion in her bed, and love in their hearts for each other for the rest of their lives.

Four

"Chloe, there's nothing like the Carolinas at night. Ain't nothing can beat it!"

"Nothing Mama?"

"Unh-uhn. Not a thing."

"Not even the smell of lilacs?" the little girl asked, knowing it was her mother's most favorite thing in the world . . . besides her, of course!

"No, baby girl, not even lilacs." She smiled down at her daughter, her treasure, with her head resting lightly on her lap as they sat on the fire escape to get away from the heat of their apartment. "Down south the night skies are shades of deep blues and purples with millions of stars that look like fireworks on the Fourth of July."

The little girl lifted her head from her mother's lap to look up at the dark New York sky. "More stars than up there, Mama?"

Adell sucked her teeth. "Baby girl, that up there ain't nothing compared to a starry Carolina night."

She gently pushed her child's head back down on her lap, using her finger to trace the zig-zag pattern of her tight braids. "At night the air fills up with crickets, frogs croaking and owls hooting—"

"All that noise?" she giggled.

Adell laughed, and it resembled the light tinkling of a bell. "Ooh, you city kids are a mess. If you can sleep

*through the noise of this city, a few crickets and a 'hoot'
ain't gone block your sleep none."*

*"Naw baby," she sighed. "Ain't nothing like the Caroli-
nas at night. Not a thing!"*

"You were so right." Chloe's voice was like a husky echo
into the night. As she looked up into the sky, the stars reflected
and glistened in the depths of her eyes. Feeling near tears,
Chloe purposely let her gaze fall down coming to rest on
where she parked her car in the garage behind their house.
She left the window where she stood and crossed the hard-
wood floor to climb into the queen-sized bed. She enjoyed
the feel of the cool crisp sheets against her naked skin. Her
first night in "the Carolinas." Not exactly what she expected,
but pleasurable nonetheless.

What a day, she thought, as she shifted to find comfort in
the strange bed.

Nana Lil was a trip. She had kept Chloe and Deshawn
laughing all through dinner. She made Chloe feel like a real
family member when she called her "baby" and spoke of the
close friendship she shared with Tessa.

And Deshawn was so charming and funny, a real ladies'
man who was a harmless flirt. She thought of the twenty-five
dollars she won from him on a bet they made as they watched
a WNBA game on television. The Houston Comets went on
to beat the New York Liberty just as she predicted.

And Devon. Well, she really hadn't spent enough time in
his company to judge him, so she just pushed all thoughts of
the brooding man from her mind. As long as he did his share
to make sure her house was built as expected, then nothing
else mattered.

With a sigh, she turned over in the bed and reached to turn
on the lamp that sat on the night stand.

THUD!

Her hand accidentally knocked something onto the floor with a loud echoing noise. "Damn it!"

She sat up straight in bed and successfully turned on the lamp, basking the attic room in hundred-watt brightness. Chloe sat on the edge of the bed, looking down at the ceramic figurine on the floor. Luckily she hadn't broken it.

She reached down to pick it up and place it back on the table. Her intention had been to check the time on her watch. It was after midnight. She lay back down in the bed, pulling the sheets over her. The smell of lilacs clung faintly to the material and Chloe felt a pang of grief as she thought of her mother.

Devon pulled his truck into the yard and parked it in front of the house, not bothering to pull into the three-car garage in the back. As he passed the swing on the porch he thought briefly about his nightly ritual of lounging on it. It was his time to think and be in solitude, but he was tired and so he passed on the idea.

The house was quiet as he climbed the stairs in the darkness. He stopped at his brother's door but his lights were out and the distinct sound of a snore filtered through the oak. With a laugh, he jogged up the rest of the wooden stairs to his suite of rooms on the third floor. Not bothering to turn on the light in his bedroom, he undressed in the dark, leaving his clothes in a pile on the floor before climbing into his unmade bed.

Alicia's dumplings were lying heavy on his stomach and he kept tossing and turning to find comfort.

THUD!

Devon jumped up out of the king-sized bed. *What the hell was that?* He looked up to the ceiling, as if he could see through the wood and plaster to the attic above. He stood quietly, listening for another sound. Nothing. But he *knew* he heard something.

He reached back down into his discarded pile of clothes for his boxers and pulled them on. Not quite sure what he would find, if anything, Devon left his bedroom and turned right to walk the short distance to the stairs leading to the renovated attic room.

He flung the door open wide and flicked the light switch on the wall to bask the room in brightness. Shock widened his eyes at what he saw. The shock turned to a hot rush of desire.

Chloe sat in the middle of the bed, clutching the cotton sheet to her obviously naked body. Once her eyes adjusted to the sudden light, she saw Devon, or was it Deshawn, standing in the doorway in nothing but his snug cotton boxers.

"What the hell are *you* doing up here?" he barked.

Devon. It was definitely Devon.

Chloe pulled the sheet up higher and eyed him. "I think the better question is what are *you* doing up here . . . in those?"

She let her eyes fall meaningfully down to his Calvin Klein boxers, with a perfectly arched brow raised.

"I heard a noise and came to—" Devon stopped when he realized that he was explaining himself to her. "My head must be messed up because I thought this was *my* house."

"Look Mr. Jamison. I'm sorry if I scared you—"

"You didn't scare me," he balked.

She raised her brow again, this time in disbelief. "Okay, whatever. Your family invited . . . no insisted, that I stay here until the house is built. I appreciated the invitation and I accepted it. Of course I offered to pay for room and board—"

Devon laughed harshly, and shook his handsome head in amazement. "I *know* they didn't agree to take money for you staying here! This isn't a boarding house."

Chloe rolled her eyes heavenward. "No, they refused my offer, I just—"

"If my family offered for you to stay here, it certainly wasn't to bring in money." His nostrils flared in anger.

She was really getting tired of him cutting her off, and she was confused by his anger. "Look, I wasn't trying to offend anyone, I just—"

He slashed his hand across the air. "We're not living off

multimillion-dollar modeling contracts, but we hardly need to treat our home like a hotel, motel, Holiday Inn."

The sarcasm dripped from his words, and he said the word "modeling" as if it was vile.

Her confusion turned to white-hot anger. "Look, what's your problem?"

He snorted in anger. "I don't have a problem. The problem is when someone mistakes what we call hospitality in the South for a chance to flash money."

She watched in wide-eyed shock as he flicked the switch down, turning off the lights, and slammed the door behind him, leaving the room shaking in his quake.

"What the hell was that about?" she wondered aloud to herself, her voice whisper soft in the darkness.

"This isn't New York . . ."

"I know it's not what you're used to, but we love it. It's our home."

"Devon said you weren't moving here permanently."

"We don't want to force Ms. Bolton to eat here."

"We're not living off a multimillion-dollar modeling contract, but we hardly need to treat our home like a hotel, motel, Holiday Inn."

Comments Devon made swirled in her head, coming back to her at once as they ran together, colliding in her head.

"This isn't New York . . . I know it's not what you're used to, but we love it. It's our home . . . Devon said you weren't moving here permanently . . . We don't want to force Ms. Bolton to eat here . . . We're not living off a multimillion-dollar modeling contract, but we hardly need to treat our home like a hotel, motel, Holiday Inn . . . This isn't New York . . . I know it's not what you're used to, but we love it. It's our home . . . Devon said you weren't moving here permanently . . . We don't want to force Ms. Bolton to eat here . . . We're not living off a multimillion-dollar modeling contract but, we hardly need to treat our home like a hotel, motel, Holiday Inn."

He was moody and argumentative, high-minded, arrogant and . . . and . . . and fine! To see him half naked was to desire his muscled body. The strong masculine lines appeared to be sculptured in granite. His broad shoulders, hard chest and ridged stomach. The narrow hips and thick, strong and muscular thighs and calves. Her cheeks warmed thinking of how his maleness strained against the cotton material, large and daring even at rest.

Chloe sighed, the image of him clearly etched into her memory. She accounted it to hormones. It would take both hands and a couple of toes to count the months since she'd been intimate with a man. This very physical attraction she had for Devon was all because she needed to physically be with a man. That was all there was to it.

Then why didn't she feel the same attraction for Deshawn? They *were* identical twins, and except for their temperaments, she couldn't tell them apart physically.

She tried to force him out of her thoughts as she lay quietly still in the bed, letting the sounds of the Carolinas waft through the windows to lull her to sleep. But she was very aware that he lay in the room just beneath her.

Devon flew back down the stairs, passing his own floor, to come to a halt in front of Deshawn's closed door. It was late and his conscience said, *This can wait until morning; don't wake him up.*

Then he thought about how he had just argued with a beautiful woman in his boxer shorts. He opened the door. Deshawn lay in the middle of the bed on his stomach, his head buried under a pile of pillows. It was the exact same position Devon found himself in when he awoke in the mornings.

He placed his foot on the edge of the bed, pumping it up and down. They both slept light and Deshawn jumped up immediately, startled. "Dev, man are you crazy? What you wake me up for?" His voice was groggy and hoarse with sleep as he reached over to turn on the lamp on his nightstand.

Devon paced by the side of the bed. "What did you invite *her* to stay here with us for?"

A big goofy grin spread across Deshawn's handsome face. "Did you think I would let the opportunity to have that heavenly body under this roof pass and not take it?"

At Devon's unmoved attitude, his face became incredulous, as if to say, *Why don't you understand?* He sighed. "Anyway, Nana Lil invited her while I was in the office working on the draft for the Devane's room addition."

"Did you finish it?" Devon stopped pacing, immediately becoming focused on business. At his brother's weary nod, he said, "Thanks, man. I meant to work on it today."

"No problem." Deshawn wiped the sleep from his eyes. "Look, I know you have your bad assumptions about her, but she's a nice person. Nana Lil loves her and she can keep her company. She's here now, so try to keep your judgments about her to yourself."

He turned off the lamp and settled back down on the bed. "Oh, and shut the door on your way out. Night Dev."

He did close the door on his way out, and he retraced his steps back upstairs to his bedroom. He stepped out of his boxers again and lay down on the bed. Sleep eluded him.

Visions of mocha skin contrasting with white cotton plagued him. The gentle curve of a full breast outlined in an erotic shadow behind the sheet. Smooth thin material following the contour of a shapely long leg.

Damn her!

The construction of her house would take at least another month and a half, if not two. During that time she would be living up above him in the attic. He groaned as he remembered that there wasn't a bathroom up there. Since his was the closest, that meant she would have to use his.

He just knew she would spend hours enclosed in there. If

she hung up wet silk stockings to dry he would explode, and he better hadn't see one drop of makeup on his sink.

He growled in frustration. He felt foolish that a part of him was excited about knowing she was just up above him.

Damn!

Chloe stretched lazily in the bed, feeling rested and renewed. Once she had finally settled into a sound sleep, it had been the best night of rest she had had in a long time. She felt like she had enough energy to run five miles.

Checking the time on her watch, she was stunned. It was twelve-thirty in the afternoon. Never had she slept past seven, even if she was ill or she got in late. Always she was up and awake before seven. Her mother was country born and bred, and it was her ritual of rising early that had been instilled in Chloe. It was her body's natural alarm clock.

She stretched her long limbs again before pulling her naked form from the bed. Thank the heavens that she had washed her underclothes out last night before she went to bed. She would have to drive into Charleston today and get her clothes from the hotel.

She was in Holtsville, South Carolina, a far cry from the fast pace of New York City, the glamour of France or the vintage beauty of Italy. But she didn't question her choice, because it felt so right!

She couldn't wait to explore her new surroundings and try to see this small part of the world through her mother's eyes. Chloe wanted to feel the same love for the small town as her mother had.

But right now she was in need of a shower.

When Nana Lil had invited her to stay, she had told Chloe to use Devon's bathroom downstairs. With his attitude toward her, she had been more than a little apprehensive, but what choice did she have? Last night when she washed out her lacy briefs and brassiere, she had noticed the two entrances into the bathroom, one from the hall and the other connected directly to his bedroom. She made a mental note to always lock both doors.

She pulled on the thin cotton robe Nana Lil lent her and grabbed her lingerie from the windowsill where she laid them last night to dry. The house was quiet as she descended the short flight of stairs and entered his bathroom. His presence still hung heavy in the room, with its masculine tones of smoky gray and blue. The faint smell of his sporty cologne remained. A glob of toothpaste was dried to the faucet. She picked up the damp towel flung carelessly over the tub and removed the bar of soap being melted down by the shower dripping hot water.

The man was a slob. He had to know she would be using the bathroom. Surely he could have left it better than this pigsty.

She found a sponge and liquid cleanser in the cabinet beneath the porcelain sink. Quickly she straightened his mess before locking the doors and stepping into the shower.

Immediately she envisioned his naked form, wet and lathered with soap. It was almost as if she could see him standing there in the shower stall in front of her. His strong hands massaged his chest with circular motions, moving down to the densely curled hairs surrounding his long, thick flesh—

Whoa!

Chloe gasped at her erotic imaginings as the image faded into the steam filling the shower, but not before he raised his head and smiled at her with a roguish wink. Her nipples were erect and aching, just like the bud between her thighs. She dropped the soap and reached down to switch the water to cold. After the initial jolt, which caused her to jump back, Chloe stepped under the jet spray. The cold gush of water cooled her.

From now on, Chloe muttered to herself, as her body temperature became normal, *I'll take a bath.*

After she finished her shower, she rushed back to her room and dressed in the clothes she wore yesterday. Without her supplies she had to forgo the pampering she usually gave her body with her luxurious body kit. With a brush she had in her purse, Chloe removed the tangles from her weaved hair and pulled it into a tight ponytail.

Downstairs she found Nana Lil on the porch, sitting in the rocking chair as she peeled potatoes. "Good morning Nana Lil."

"Good afternoon, ain't it?" she said with a spunky wink at her.

Chloe smiled, taking a seat on the wooden swing, tucking her bare feet beneath her. "Something in this country air got me going. I never slept so late in my life."

"It'll do that to you."

She put a foot down on the porch and pushed off, causing the swing to rock gently. "Thank you again for inviting me to stay here until my house is done."

Lil nodded, her attention on the spud in her hand slowly peeled of its skin. "When are you going to get your clothes?"

"Now is as good a time as any."

"Mind if I tag along? I can use a road trip, and then maybe we can stop at the Piggly Wiggly on our way back."

"Of course, but can I ask one thing?" She stood and took the bowl to carry into the house. "What's that?"

Lil laughed. "It's the supermarket. Child, you got a lot to learn about the South."

Devon took a much-needed break, glad the construction of the roof was now complete . . . ahead of schedule. He climbed down the ladder. The site was filled with the sounds of saws, hammers banging, and welding as their crew continued to work throughout the house.

Glancing down at his leather-banded watch, he saw that it was nearly four o'clock. He crossed the grassy land to where his pickup truck was parked. The cooler on the bed held a few cans of soda and spring water floating in the melted ice water. Devon picked a bottle of water.

His stomach growled in hunger. This morning before they

left for work, Nana Lil had set out steaks to thaw for dinner. His mouth actually watered at the thought of her frying and smothering the steaks in gravy, accompanied by mashed potatoes. He was starving, having worked through lunch. As soon as he got the word that the electrician's crew was finished for the day, he would wrap up work.

He saw the electrician and his small crew packing their supplies and called out for his team to finish up for the day. Within the hour Devon was heading down the road, just a short distance from home. He couldn't help but think of what awaited him, or rather whom.

Chloe.

He still couldn't believe that she was living with them. Could he stand a month of her royal highness? He didn't think so. But he *had* to stand her because his grandmother had spoken and there were no arguments to be won with her.

The house was empty when he got there. Deshawn was supervising the completion of the Devane's room addition in Summerville, and there was a note from Nana Lil saying she drove into Charleston with Chloe.

The only smell coming from the kitchen was the faint odor of lemons. No steaks, no mashed potatoes. Nothing. He didn't even bother to look in the fridge. His culinary skills went as far as barbecuing on the grill outside. But a barbecue without potato salad, buttered corn on the cob, baked beans and catfish stew was not worth it.

So he grabbed an orange from the bowl on the table and went up to his bedroom. A long hot shower would loosen up the tightness in his shoulders and kill some time until his Nana returned. Quickly he undressed, leaving his dusty jeans and T-shirt in a pile with his underclothes and boots. He crossed the floor to the door adjoining to the sitting room of his suite.

His entertainment center was kept there, because he believed his bed was for two things only: sleeping and sex, not lounging around watching TV.

It was a quarter to five as he turned on the television,

before retracing his steps through his bedroom to the door leading into his private bathroom. He turned the knob, but it wouldn't budge. It was locked!

"What the hell?"

Naked, and not caring a bit that he was, Devon strode with long purposeful steps out of his bedroom and into the hall. He barged into the bathroom, and halted in his tracks.

This wasn't how he left it this morning. It was spotless and the faint scent of pine mingled with the spicy scent of his soap. His towel hung neatly on the rack behind the door and the bar of soap sat neatly in the dish above the sink.

It had to be her. Chloe.

This morning he had forgotten that he had to share the bathroom with her. Obviously she hadn't liked the way he left it. She also had locked the door leading into his bedroom and forgotten to unlock it when she was finished.

Her naked and wet body, lathered with foamy soap suds in his shower, sent a wave of desire through him. With the freedom of no clothes, his malehood lengthened and hardened where he stood. Growling, he jumped into the shower and turned the cold water on full blast, hoping to freeze the vixen from his memory. He directed the spray toward his groin area, eventually easing the burning hardness of his loins. In frustration, he showered quickly and left the confines of the shower, wrapping a gray towel around his waist.

He was rummaging through the top drawer of his dresser for a pair of boxers when the female voice on the television mentioned Chloe's name. His hand paused midway in the air as he turned to look through the open doorway at the big-screen television in the next room.

"This is your entertainment reporter Ericka Sloven out of Los Angeles. I have the latest scoop on supermodel diva Chloe Bolton. Reportedly she will build a home on land left to her by her mother, who passed away nine years ago after a battle with breast cancer. Her luxury apartment in New York has not been put on the market yet, so insiders are unsure of where she will reside now that she's retired. Chloe's publicist would neither deny nor confirm the story. I've followed Ms. Bolton's ground-breaking career for years. If her retirement last year, while still highly in demand, was not shocking enough, now a move to Nowhere, South Carolina. It's completely out of character for the beauty. I'm so shocked I'm speechless and that's a first for me! Ta-ta for now darlings."

Devon watched the images of Chloe flash onto the screen: Chloe on the runway; at a party; clutching the arm of a man; on the cover of *Vogue* magazine; standing among her celebrity peers. Each shot as beautiful as the last.

Long after the news segment went off, the words were in his head. Words that rang so close to his beliefs. Chloe Bolton in Holtsville, South Carolina . . . shocking.

Devon laughed shortly at the thought, as he angrily jerked on a pair of cotton boxers. Why was he angry? He didn't even know why himself.

Was it because she had scrubbed his bathroom spotless? *No, that's something I should've done myself.*

Was it because of the crap he heard on the news? Nowhere, South Carolina, indeed. *Nope.*

Or was it because his body was drawn to her, completely ignoring the logic of his brain? Bingo. *Thoughts of her make me feel like a horny teenager, and I don't like it.*

Five

After he got dressed, Devon left the house and crossed the short distance to the office. He playfully gave Alicia a light tap on the back of her head as he passed her. "Why are you still here?"

"I wanted to finish up these requisitions that have to go out tomorrow morning. And your messages are on your desk." She swiveled in her chair to look at him. "I was just about to beep you. You have to sign these when I'm done."

When she placed the form before him on the desk, he read them quickly before scrawling his signature on the appropriate line. A copy of Chloe's blueprints were still unrolled on his drafting table. He was amazed at the irony of the entire situation.

He hadn't cared for her living down the road from him, or even in the entire town, for that matter. Now here she was living in his house, sharing his very private bathroom, sleeping nude in the room above him—

Devon sat up straight with a start. *Sleeping nude?*

Where did that come from?

Well, she had been very naked under that thin sheet last night. Her brown round nipples strained against the cotton, yearning to be massaged, and kissed, and bitten . . .

"Excuse me, boss."

Devon focused on Alicia, who was looking at him with an odd expression. "What, Alicia?" he snapped impatiently.

"For the twentieth time: What are you thinking about?" She raised an eyebrow at him.

Devon cleared his throat and pulled his chair closer to his drafting table. Was he supposed to tell her of his erotic daydream about Chloe Bolton? A very naked Chloe Bolton.

Oh, hell no!

Instead he mumbled, "Nothing."

"Well that nothing had you staring into space with a big goofy grin on your face."

Devon ignored her, pretending to study the plans he had nearly memorized. Eventually she turned back to her desk, muttering under her breath.

"Oh Dev, I almost forgot. I met your houseguest today." She turned back around to study his reaction carefully.

Knowing she was scrutinizing him, Devon remained stoic. "Big deal. You didn't ask for an autograph, did you?" His tone dripped with heavy sarcasm.

"Yeah, whatever Devon." Her eyes were narrowed in speculation. *"An-y-way,* more of the special order materials for her house arrived today. They're in the storage area with the rest of it. The copies for the orders are in her file."

"Thanks Al. You're a gem."

"Even though I'm not a supermodel?" she asked, the question less innocent than it seemed.

"Especially because you're not a supermodel." He stood and walked over to the metal cabinet to pull out Chloe's bulging manila folder. "Believe me, you as a woman and her as a woman are two entirely different things."

The rest of Devon's words became unimportant to Alicia as she focused on: *You as a woman and her as a woman are two entirely different things.*

Hell, didn't she know it? She didn't need Devon of all people to remind her of it. Jealousy of the woman burned her until her ears felt like they were on fire. She looked over at Chloe's calendar on the wall by Deshawn's working area. Alicia knew that could never be her in the playful shot, capturing the beauty in a bright floral tankini on a white sand beach.

Bah!

She wished she could yank the offending thing off the wall and tear it to shreds. It was a constant reminder of everything she wasn't and would never be. Everything that she was afraid Devon would eventually want, especially with them both living under the same roof. The idea of her living down the road had been bad enough.

You as a woman and her as a woman are two entirely different things.

She had finally met her this afternoon when she popped over to visit Nana Lil. They had been preparing to ride into Charleston. The woman, Alicia grudgingly admitted, was as naturally beautiful as she was in full glamour mode on television. Chloe was every man's fantasy and every woman's nemesis. And now she was living in Devon's house. She sensed trouble with a capital "T."

"Uhm, Devon, I'll see you tomorrow, okay." Quickly she gathered her purse and left the building, barely giving him time to say good-bye.

You as a woman and her as a woman are two entirely different things.

She drove home in silence, her thoughts full. As soon as she was inside her small, two-bedroom cottage, she stripped off all her clothes and walked into her bedroom. Naked, she stood in front of her full-length cheval glass mirror.

She was honest at what she saw in the reflection. The small breasts, small waist and significantly larger bottom half of her short frame didn't compare to Chloe's tall and shapely slender frame.

You as a woman and her as a woman are two entirely different things.

She let her mind drift to Devon's tall, muscled frame and good looks. As her want of him rose, she watched as her brown nipples hardened in the reflection. Aching to release the building need, she hurried to climb into her bed, using her hands to massage the bud between her legs. With her eyes closed, she thought of him, dreamed it was him . . . wished it truly was him pleasuring her. One day she *would* have the real thing . . . Devon Jamison.

"You're where? . . . Doing what?"

Lil held the phone away from her ear at Devon's loud and shocked exclamations. When the line went quiet again, she replaced the phone to her ear. "Lower your voice," she scolded in a no-nonsense tone.

"Where's Ms. Bolton?"

Lil glanced over across the living room of the suite where Chloe lay on her belly, being carefully massaged. Her eyes were closed and she seemed perfectly relaxed. "Chloe's right here having a Swedish massage. I'm having one after my avocado facial. Anyway, we decided to stay in the suite tonight and we'll be home in the morning, so you boys better grill those steaks yourself . . . yes Vonnie, I will . . . okay . . . bye-bye."

Chloe opened one eye to glance over at Nana Lil, her heart hammering in her chest just knowing Devon was on the phone.

"Whoa, Ms. Bolton, you suddenly got so tense around your shoulders." The masseur began to gently knead her back. "Just relax."

She tried to relax, but it was hard when she thought of Devon's constant anger and derision toward her. And on top of that she discovered that Olivia had left three messages for her last night. She returned her call to discover that she had been nominated for the fashion industry's Female Model of the Year award for the work she did last year before she retired.

Olivia's enthusiasm had been off the charts, but at this point in Chloe's life she didn't want to have such a visible link to the profession she'd recently retired from. The televised event was being held in New York and Chloe knew she would attend. Never would she be so ungracious as to not show up.

Now she would have to find the right outfit and hairstyle. *God, images.*

Well the ceremony wasn't for another few months so at least she didn't have to worry about it . . . for now.

"Please, just relax."

Just relax, she mimicked his words to herself. *That's easy for him to say.*

Devon was lounging in one of the matching green leather recliners in front of the television in the living room. He was watching the local weather report. The bright light of Deshawn's lights flashed against the far wall as he turned his truck into the driveway. Minutes later his heavy footsteps carried him up the stairs and into the house.

"What's up, big brother?" he joked, referring to the fact that Devon was born six minutes before he was. Nana Lil liked to say that he bullied his way out first.

"Nothing, what's up with you?"

"We finished up at the Devane's. They're very pleased and I deposited their check for payment, making me very pleased." He stretched his own tall frame into the other recliner.

"Make sure you have Alicia drive out and take pictures for our portfolio." His gaze was fixed on the television. "Looks like a one hundred percent chance of rain tomorrow and Wednesday."

Deshawn reached over and plucked the remote from his brother's fingers with a smile. "Where's our resident beauty?"

Devon snorted in derision. "She and Nana Lil are spending the night in Charleston in her penthouse suite at the Grand Royal. As a matter of fact, when I spoke to her she was having an avocado facial and Chloe was having a . . . a . . ." He struggled to remember the term. "A Swedish massage."

Deshawn whistled. "That's something I would love to be a fly on the wall to see. Chloe Bolton butt naked on a table. Good lawdy!"

"You *would* say something crude like that," Devon drawled.

"Did Nana Lil sound like she was having fun?" Deshawn laughed out as he watched the seventies sitcom he had turned the television to.

"Yeah," Devon admitted grudgingly.

"So that's why I don't smell dinner cooking." He shut the TV off. "How 'bout dinner at Donnie's?"

Devon's stomach grumbled in response as he glanced over at his twin. "It'll beat a blank, which is what we have. Let's go."

Deshawn laughed as they stood, and he clapped his twin on the back. "Oh, and bring your wallet. It's your turn to treat."

The sun was nowhere to be seen among the gray and cloudy skies. The rain was pelting against the car, resembling the hollow beating of a drum. Chloe steered the sports car off the main road. Cyrus waved from the window of his storefront, and she blew the horn twice briefly in return.

She steered the car carefully on the wet roads, headed for the house. Lil yawned and Chloe knew she had to be tired. After their glamour session in the suite, which lasted three hours, they had found the nearest mall and had gone shopping with Chloe disguised in shades and a baseball cap.

She smiled when she remembered Nana Lil's expression when she paid two hundred dollars for a Donna Karan blazer, which was marked down. Chloe knew she had splurged, but she could afford to spend the three thousand dollars she did. She had even pleaded with Nana Lil to allow her to purchase a pearl watch that she saw her admire. She even found three Basic Reality tailored shirts by Toni Smalls, a black designer that both she and Anika loved. They were already on the way to be shipped to her best friend in New Jersey.

After returning to the suite they ordered room service: Alaskan salmon and asparagus for Chloe and grilled skinless chicken breasts for Lil. They had sat up all night trading funny stories and watching old movies on cable.

This morning they went exploring antique shops and rummage sales. Chloe had found a beautiful mahogany rocker said to be dated to the early 1800s, and a glass and steel curio cabinet that she planned to use in the kitchen. Both items were to be delivered this Monday morning and she planned to ask Deshawn if she could keep them in their storeroom behind the office until her house was finished.

After a late lunch they returned to the room and packed up the clothes Chloe had brought with her. Much to the manager's distress, and her pleasure, she checked out of the hotel.

Now at nearly five P.M. she turned the car onto the smoothly paved driveway. Both Devon's and Deshawn's pickup trucks were parked in front of the office along with Alicia's small compact.

Lil reached into her purse and pulled out a plastic rain cap to cover her hair. "Ain't nothing but rain," she said when she saw Chloe hesitate to get out of the shelter of the car. "Just pretend it's a shower."

She watched as Lil left the car and calmly walked in the rain onto the porch. Chloe dashed out behind her, and although she moved as quickly as she could, she still got drenched in the pouring rain. The white cotton tank dress she wore clung to her body and Chloe couldn't help but shiver from the chill in the air before she entered the house.

Lil was on the phone in the living room. "Hello Devon . . . oops, sorry Deshawn. When the rain lets up some y'all come and get Chloe's luggage and our packages out of the car." She paused, obviously listening to the person on the other end. "Yes, I had fun Shawnie, but will you get off this phone in this weather and just do as I asked?"

She hung up the receiver and looked over to where Chloe stood by the door. "We better change these clothes; we're both soaking wet."

"First I'll make a cup of tea to take up with me."

Lil removed her rain scarf. "You go ahead. As soon as I

change and warm these old bones I'll smother some chops for dinner."

Chloe walked into the kitchen as Lil entered her bedroom. She filled the flowered teakettle with water and placed it on one of the gas burners she turned on. While she waited for the water to boil, she searched for the tea bags and found them in the cupboard over the counter by the sink.

Once the kettle whistled, she hurried to make the cup of orange pekoe tea, adding lots of sugar and lemon the way she liked it. Turning to leave the kitchen, she carefully held the cup in the matching saucer, making sure not to spill any of it. Just as she reached the end of the short hall, Devon entered and they collided.

Chloe yelled out in pain as the cup fell to the floor, with a good bit of the hot liquid sloshing onto her right hand and wrist.

Devon swore before forcibly turning her body back toward the kitchen, headed for the sink. "Let me run cold water onto it," he ordered roughly.

The area was an angry shade of red and the cold water from the tap stung at first before becoming soothing. He stood directly behind her, his strong callused hands holding her wrist under the stream of water.

Chloe stood still. His body was too close to hers for comfort. Strong, muscled thighs pressed against the back of her legs. The touch of his fingertips was almost gentle against her wrist, and his breath fanned warmly on the side of her neck.

Why was she so attracted to this angry and brooding man? No, correction. This man who was angry and brooding just toward her.

"Next time be careful where you're walking with hot liquid in your hands."

Chloe was almost shocked by the anger in his voice. When wasn't he angry at her? But now she was angry, and he obviously hadn't heard of her infamous temper, which was legendary when awakened.

She whirled on him, the water on her hand flying wildly in his direction. "No, next time *you* be careful of trying to knock down someone carrying hot liquid. If you weren't so busy striding around this house with a huge stick up your ass and a chip on your shoulder, you would have been more careful."

Hazel eyes flashed angrily as she faced him, her hands on her hips, her stance firm. She didn't care one bit that his hands clenched into fists at his sides, or that he frowned so deeply that his eyebrows connected into one burrowed slash on his forehead.

"A stick up my ass?" he roared.

Chloe lifted her chin in defiance. "No . . . a *huge* stick, you bully!"

"You're an airhead that shakes what *little* ass she has on a runway for money." He looked pointedly up and down at her slender frame, as if to emphasize his point.

Twenty devils flew down her spine and she marched straight up into his face until her nose was touching his square chin. One slender finger poked into his hard, muscled chest. "Well this *airhead* with the little ass strutted her stuff until she made herself worth twelve million dollars last year alone. And then this little *airhead* donated nearly forty percent of that twelve million to charities. Now, did *you* bang enough nails last year, you hammerhead hick, to make twelve million dollars? I . . . don't . . . think . . . so."

Anger like he never knew filled him. All of his opinions and accusations were confirmed about her just then. She called him a "hick," obviously a snide reference to his southern upbringing, of which he was proud. Then she bragged on the millions she made for being an overpaid, underweight, untalented, no-account model. Hell, he'd seen better-looking, and a hell of a lot more voluptuous, women right in Holtsville.

He wanted her out of his sight. Now!!

But first . . .

"Who would pay a twig like you money to model anyway? I've seen better-looking faces on horses!"

Her eyes widened in shock and he knew he hit home . . . her vanity.

Chloe was shocked. He called *her* ugly!

"You . . . you . . . pig!" She stomped in frustration, close to tears but refusing to show it.

"You crackhead." His expression said, *so there*.

Chloe nearly fainted at his accusation. "A what?" She exclaimed. She felt like clawing at his neck and choking him until his head exploded.

"What's going on in here?"

Lil was the voice of reason in their heated, insult-filled argument. And the interruption was well-timed, because it was about to get real nasty.

"Nothing Nana Lil," Devon muttered, his eyes locked with Chloe's in a battle of wills. "Just stay away from me, Ms. Bolton."

Chloe eyed him back, not willing to be the first to back down. She poked him in the chest, enunciating each word. "You hurry. . . . up . . . and . . . build . . . my . . . house . . . Mr. Jamison."

She used her arm to try to move him aside when she walked by him, giving him round one as she broke the stare. Nana Lil's eyes were concerned. "I'm sorry Nana Lil."

She left the kitchen and was halfway down the hall before she suddenly turned and marched back into the kitchen. Devon was still standing where she left him, his hands on his narrow hips as he took deep and even breaths. "While I'm here, let's both try very hard to stay away from each other. If nothing else we have one thing in common . . . neither of us likes the other."

Chloe whirled dramatically out of the kitchen and flew up the stairs nonstop until she was in the comfortably decorated spacious attic room. Angrily, she snatched up a pillow and began to choke it, pretending it was Devon.

Back in the kitchen, now dressed in her one of her loose-fitting flowered caftans, Lil calmly walked over to the sink and turned off the running water. Devon growled and threw his hands heavenward in exasperation, before leaving the kitchen to stomp his way up the stairs to his own suite of rooms with a final slam of the door that vibrated through the house.

Lil shook her head before beginning to make preparations for dinner. A smile touched her lips at the way Chloe stood up to Devon. Seconds later she was howling with laughter until her sides ached.

Their heated argument, which had raged hotter than the summer weather, created tension in the entire household for the next two weeks. Dinner was always a strained affair as both Chloe and Devon pretended the other didn't exist at all. Any discussion on the house was handled by Deshawn.

Several times Chloe had offered to return to the hotel, but Nana Lil had looked hurt, and Deshawn had asked, "for what?" so simply that Chloe forgot about the idea. Besides, she got a childish thrill out of spiting Devon, just because she knew he didn't want her there.

The last time she spoke to Anika, her friend had jokingly advised her not to argue too harshly with him because country people were known for inbreeding, which probably meant he was mildly retarded. Chloe knew Anika said it more to make her laugh than because of any actual belief in the old myth.

To hell with Devon, she thought any time her mind crossed the argument, which seemed to be every other five seconds of the day.

Chloe concentrated all her efforts on shopping for more furnishings for her house, with the help of Nana Lil. The two women became very close, even though Chloe knew from his grunts and his frowns that Devon didn't like it one bit. As if Chloe would willingly do anything to hurt the sweet older woman that she had come to think of as a surrogate grandmother.

And Lil was just as fond of her. She proudly made the introductions whenever Chloe met someone new in the small town. It wasn't long before Chloe was on a first-name basis with nearly everyone she greeted. The entire town was curious about their celebrity. Cars with curious passersby drove by and then had to turn around and drive by again because the road was a dead end. Bold visitors, who knocked right on the door, were a constant at first. She also had to refuse several offers from local newspapers for interviews. A local cable station's "Dream House," which showcased unique homes built in the area, had also offered for her to appear on the program, but again she declined.

More and more each day, as she walked or drove through the small community, she felt she was home. She began to understand the love and wonder her mother had for her home town. And Cyrus was her frequent tour guide, even directing Chloe to the small cemetery where her grandparents were buried, as he had promised. Life moved at a leisurely pace, and she loved it.

One bright and sunny afternoon, Chloe was at the house alone. The twins were at the site and Nana Lil was at her social club meeting at one of the member's houses. She felt bored and contemplated calling Anika, but she knew she was busy at work and didn't want to interrupt her for nothing.

Briefly she thought about strolling over to the office to talk to Alicia, but she just as quickly scrapped the idea. The woman's friendliness always seemed false and forced. She immediately picked up that the woman didn't like her. Chloe knew Alicia was jealous of her beauty and her wealth, although she made sure to flaunt neither.

Well, except for the night Devon and she had argued, but he deserved that. She still seethed when she thought of him telling her a horse looked better than she did! *Was he blind?*

Sighing, Chloe left the house to sit on the swing. Warm sun rays kissed her bronzed skin as she rocked. The mystery novel she was reading lay open next to her, forgotten as she enjoyed the sun and dreamed of moving into her house.

"How ya doing, Miss Chloe?"

Her eyes snapped open as she turned to see who was yelling to her from the paved road. A smile replaced the frown as she recognized Cyrus walking in the road. Every day he closed his store at noon to walk because his doctor told him he needed the exercise.

"Hello Mr. Dobbs. How are you?" she called back, using her hand to shade the sun from her eyes.

When she saw him turn to walk into the yard, she got up and walked down off the porch to meet him in the driveway. Chloe thought his wiping his brow was more out of habit than necessity as he removed his handkerchief from the back pocket of his overalls. "Getting some exercise?" she asked.

"Yeah, yeah," he chimed as he placed the cloth back in his pocket. "Just a little exercise for my heart. I'll walk down to the dead end just past your house and back as always."

"Mind if I join you? I haven't seen the house since my first day here."

He laughed and whipped out his handkerchief again. "I would've minded if you hadn't offered."

Slowly they walked together and Cyrus, being a hopeless but lovable gossip, filled her in on all the latest news of who was sleeping with whom, who was cheating on their spouse, who had brought what new item, and any other bit of info he could remember. She only slightly recognized some of the people he spoke of, but she listened anyway.

They both heard the sound of the tires on the road before seeing the rust-colored pickup truck turn around the bend. It obviously had to be leaving from Chloe's land, since there was only a dead end beyond her house.

"Oh, that's Wilson. He just drove down there to get a look at your house is all. That man is nosier than me," Cyrus snapped before taking out his handkerchief to flag him down. "I'm going to get this ride back. You coming?"

"No, I still want to see how the house is coming along."

The truck slowed down in front of them. It was an older man Chloe had met in town before. Cyrus hopped into the cab and she waved as they drove off. She continued on with her walk, enjoying the scenery.

Never before had she seen such densely wooded areas. The scent of pine was heavy in the air from the trees, and the creatures of the forest called out to her as she walked the road. She was careful to look out for snakes as both Nana Lil and Deshawn had warned her to.

Within minutes she saw the beginnings of the cleared area and heard the sounds of construction as she neared the site. She smiled and clasped her hands when she saw how much progress had been made in the two weeks since she had last been to the site. The walls were in place and the roof completed.

Excitement filled her as she walked closer. An urge to pick up a hammer and join in the work filled her, but she of course squashed the absurd idea. She knew absolutely nothing about building a home.

Her steps faltered when someone called out Devon's name and a shirtless, muscled figure climbing a ladder to reach the roof turned in response. Her womanhood jumped in response, and she hated herself for it.

Even after their angry arguments with his hurtful insults, and the weeks of ignoring her, Chloe still found the stubborn idiot to be one of the most attractive men she had laid eyes on. As she watched the hard contours of his body, she could forgive him anything!

Six

Devon had pushed his loyal crew hard for the past two weeks, all in a rush to get that woman out of his house and into her own as soon as possible. Under normal circumstances he would be pleased with the progress, but this "situation" he was in was far from normal.

He found Chloe's constant presence in the house to be insufferable. Anywhere he turned, she was there or some reminder of her presence was left behind: the smell of her perfume after leaving a room, or the scent of her soap in the bathroom. He had to leave his own bedroom when she would take a shower, not being able to take knowing she was naked behind the one door connecting the two rooms.

He had to share every meal with her, and put up with those inane conversations she and Deshawn seemed to enjoy about absolutely nothing. Or she would be downstairs watching television, laughing at a sitcom or actually crying during a drama. Or she was on the phone with her friend from New Jersey for hours at a time. He would have to stalk upstairs to his room to get away from her constant presence. She grated his nerves, and he found her to be as aggravating as fingernails dragged across a chalkboard.

Yet he couldn't deny the way his heart pounded when she entered a room or the disappointment he felt when she left a room just because he entered it. And it irked him how Deshawn and she were as thick as thieves. Many times he found them sharing a joke that would send them both into a fit of laughter, or she would turn to Deshawn to ask questions about the house, completely ignoring him.

Even though he didn't talk to her, he still noticed a lot about her. Yes, some of it even surprised him and made him begin to rethink his opinions of her. She loved to read and many times she could be found huddled in a corner or on the porch, her head buried in a book. And the emotions she felt at what she read were always easily readable on her face. A brief smile . . . a frown . . . or even a tear, all depending on the mood of the story she was reading. And he was completely floored when one of the books he eyed her reading was *The Miseducation of the Negro* by Dr. Carter G. Woodson. Beneath the glamour and beauty was an intellect.

She loved to eat. He had honestly thought she had been starving herself to stay so thin, but he now believed she could easily eat him under the table. It didn't help that Nana Lil was serious with her mission to "put some meat on her bones." And she wasn't embarrassed by her healthy appetite as she spoke of the years she had to watch what she ate as a model. He remembered well the first time they all ate dinner together. Easily she had put away three pieces of cornmeal-battered croaker and cole slaw and an extra helping of seasoned french fries. He thought she would eat properly with a knife and fork, but she dug in just like they did and even sucked tartar sauce from her fingers, a move that had sent blood rushing to his head.

And she could curse like a sailor when angry enough, and only if Nana Lil was out of earshot of her. Late one night he was sitting in the chaise lounge in the corner of his bedroom, reading Zora Neale Hurston's *Their Eyes Were Watching God,* when he heard her stumble while getting out of the shower. Who knew such foul language could fly out of such a pretty mouth?

Everyone in town loved her. Younger girls looked up to her because of her fame and celebrity status, women wanted to be her with the beauty and wealth, older women wanted to adopt her as their grandchild because of her kind nature and friendly demeanor, and the men wanted her for . . . well, obvious reasons.

Yes, Ms. Chloe Bolton was turning out to be quite an enigma.

Devon was just climbing down from the roof where he had been inspecting it again, when he spotted her standing by the driveway. He nearly fell off the ladder, because it was such a shock to his senses to see her standing there so suddenly after she had just been in his thoughts. He let his gaze rest on her momentarily. How could he deny what all the men in the town thought and talked about? She was beautiful.

He had only told her she resembled a horse to spite her in anger. Her hair was long around her shoulders with tendrils caressing the side of her face. The bright lime tank and khaki drawstring shorts she wore could not hide the slender yet curvaceous figure underneath, hinting at the shapely figure that could bloom.

He turned away and finished climbing down the ladder, quickly striding to his pickup truck. Just before he reached his vehicle he passed a group of men from the plumber's crew sharing a private joke. The words "what I wouldn't give" and "riding all night long" filtered to him. He paused in his steps to listen.

"I saw a picture of her in one of the sports magazine's swimsuit issues. She wasn't wearing nothing but a thong and a smile, with her hands covering her breasts. Lord, it was like looking at a *Playboy* magazine in the bathroom!"

The men all laughed and snorted.

"She's just as pretty as her pictures," one of the men said.

Another nudged him playfully. "Why don't you ask her out?"

They all laughed again, knowing he never would.

"She's probably a wild one in bed. Think you can handle it?"

Devon's blood boiled in anger and some other emotion he refused to name. He whirled on them like a tiger about to pounce. "Your boss is paid by me to have his crew do the plumbing, not to dream. Move it," he roared.

He knew he had been hard on them, but he didn't care. It seemed as if everywhere he went Chloe Bolton was the talk of every man, and frankly he was sick of it.

Chloe was just about to walk closer to the house when she saw nearly all the men on the site stop working to stare and wave in her direction. She had even seen Devon look her way from where he had stood on the ladder. Her heart had jumped into her throat when she saw him almost fall, but he had corrected himself and climbed down easily.

When she heard him yell at a group of men standing near his truck, she immediately assumed he was mad because of the distraction she was causing among the men. She was just in the middle of deciding whether to wait until the crew left to inspect the house or to enjoy her right as the owner of both the land and the burgeoning house to visit whenever she pleased. She chose the latter.

Some of her bravado faded when she saw the murderous look Devon threw in her direction before he stomped up the stairs into the house, pulling his T-shirt as he went. But then she got angry. Who was he to make her feel unwanted on her own property? Just how much of his bullying was she going to take?

After two weeks of smoldering over their unfinished argument, Chloe was ready to do battle with him and this was the perfect chance to throw down her gauntlet. She marched toward the house, unaware of the tantalizing sight she made with her eyes blazing in anger and her hair billowing in the air behind her. The long strides she took emphasized the toned muscles of her thighs, and her breasts bounced, straining against the thin material of the cotton.

She ignored the whistles and catcalls of the men as she took the brick stairs by two. Only one man was on her mind . . . Devon Jamison. Once she laid her eyes, and preferably her hands, on him, it was on!

"Devon!"

He saw her coming from where he stood, and he hated the way his loins tightened at the impressive sight she made. She marched as if going to war. He couldn't help but wonder what she was stirred up about. It wasn't until she yelled his name like a banshee that he realized that *he* was her target.

"Aw hell," he muttered. He wasn't in the mood for another battle with the woman.

Before he could dash and hide from her, she appeared in the doorway of the living room where he was. She looked very out of place among the wooden framework. With much more cool than he actually felt, he glanced in her direction and then purposely glanced away, a clear dismissal.

"I don't know what crawled up your rear end and died, but you need to get it out and get over it!"

Devon almost laughed as he pretended to measure the window frame, his back to her. But he didn't allow it to fall from his lips because he knew it would only ignite her anger further. "What can I do for you, Ms. Bolton?"

His voice was calm, too calm, and Chloe was spoiling for a fight. "You can stop making me feel like I'm not wanted on my own damn property. What are you trying to do, hide shoddy workmanship?"

His body tensed and Chloe felt a perverse moment of triumph that she had hit a nerve. But then his shoulders relaxed and he faced her with the most polite and complacent expression. "Jamison Contractors has a fine reputation for building quality homes. We welcome any of our homeowners to visit the site as long as no harm could possibly befall them."

He sounded like a commercial! He wouldn't rise to the

occasion and he wouldn't argue back. She felt like she was near the breaking point with anger, and he was so calm and cool. She wanted to get some reaction out of him after two weeks of him acting as if she didn't exist. She wanted him to stop treating her like she was invisible.

She *was* Chloe Bolton!

Okay, no, she didn't head trip often but he was one of the first men to be totally blasé toward her. And this was one time she wished her beauty and fame worked in her favor. The man was a definite blow to her ego.

"In fact, Ms. Bolton, I'll walk you through now if you like."

She was more than surprised at his request. Devon Jamison was *offering* to be in her company. And with the offer he effectively took away her reason for being mad in the first place. But the last thing she wanted was to be in his company. When it came to Devon Jamison she was *always* in a foul mood. "No thanks, I'll have Deshawn walk me through when he has a chance," she said with a snooty air.

Devon instantly got angry at that. "Look, if you have designs on seducing my brother . . . forget it!"

Chloe's full bottom lip dropped in shock. "Designs on Deshawn?" Her voice was incredulous as she faced him. Sure Deshawn flirted shamelessly with her, but she didn't take him seriously. She doubted if Deshawn ever took himself seriously. They were friends . . . nothing else!

Devon was almost as shocked as she was by his accusation. Never before had the thought entered his mind, but the woman had a way of bringing the worst out of him. He knew Deshawn was slightly infatuated with her, but what they had was obviously a friendship that was purely platonic. He had made the comment just to be spiteful because it had irked him when she made it clear that she would much rather be in his brother's company than his.

But why should he care?

Well, he couldn't back down from the comment now and look like a fool. "Just do as I said."

"Go to hell, Devon Jamison!" she yelled.

"I'll see you there."

"Idiot."

"Witch!"

She quelled the urge to walk over and kick him, and instead stormed out of the house, wishing there was a solid door to slam. Deshawn walked from behind the house just as Chloe descended the steps. "Hey, Deshawn."

"You and that brother of mine arguing again?"

She sighed. "I don't want to talk about it."

"My brother didn't pick on you, did he?"

She looked away from his friendly gaze. "Actually I started it, and I *don't* want to talk about it."

"I didn't know you were coming today."

"Neither did I. It was spur of the moment."

He looked up at the burgeoning structure. "Whatcha think so far?"

"I love it," she said with honesty, patting the hand he had placed on the metal railings. "I really would like a closer look at it, if I'm not too much in the way."

"Tomorrow is as good a time as any.

Chloe nodded in agreement. "Okay, I'm gonna head on home now."

"You want me to drop you off?"

"No, I'll walk, but thanks. I'll see you later."

She waved after she passed him and walked slowly down the driveway, eventually disappearing around the bend toward the house.

Devon watched her with narrowed eyes as she spoke to his brother, and when she reached out to touch his hand, his gut clenched, imagining the smoothness of her palms upon a man's skin. He knew it was as soft as a baby's bottom and could be as sensual as a lover's touch.

Thoughts of her forever intruded on his thoughts, but he refused to give in to the temptation. Not even if she had gained a few pounds that made her shorts look all the more inviting as she walked out of his line of vision.

Deshawn's eyes also watched her, unaware that he and his twin were doing the same thing . . . undressing their houseguest with their eyes, although Deshawn was a bit more roguish in his perusal. He considered himself a connoisseur of women and this woman was top of the line.

Only her constant offer of friendship kept him from getting too close to her. Besides, he'd rather have her as friend. He was not interested in a serious relationship with anyone. So he kept thoughts of him and Chloe wildly making love on the floor in his dreams.

Chloe closed the mystery novel she was reading in her attic room and checked the time on the watch on her slender wrist. It was six-thirty P.M.

She had seen both Devon's and Deshawn's trucks parked in the back about an hour ago, so she knew Nana Lil would be calling everyone down for dinner soon. She could have easily helped her prepare dinner, but Nana Lil would not let her near her kitchen. She swore Chloe would burn something, not season it right, or break a nail into the food. She shook her head with a smile. *If only she knew.*

Chloe decided to have a quick shower before dinner and moved quickly around the spacious area gathering her bath essentials. She knew Devon's routine and he always showered as soon as he got in from work. The bathroom they shared should be free and clear. She removed her clothes and slipped into her navy blue cotton PoloSport robe before padding barefoot downstairs and into the bathroom through the hall entrance.

She had found it odd that the bathtub and shower curtain were completely dry, but she quickly turned the water on to the right temperature. She stepped into the claw foot tub and pulled the shower curtain closed. She longed for a hot bath, but she always saved that luxury for when Devon was away at work, not wanting to intrude on his time.

It crossed her mind, as it frequently did when she used the bathroom, that Devon was on the other side of the door in his bedroom. She knew he could hear the shower running and thus knew she was in there.

He probably wishes I would go down the drain with the water, she thought as she lathered her loofah with Pleasures perfumed bath gel. She laughed as she began to rub her upper torso with it.

Once she felt like she had touched every inch of her body with the loofah and then followed it with her wash cloth, Chloe rinsed off and remained standing in the shower, inhaling the steam as a sort of mini-spa technique she frequently used. She felt a pang of loneliness that she tried to push away.

After her debacle of a love affair with Calvin, Chloe had successfully steered clear of becoming involved in another relationship. The pain of Calvin's betrayal had scarred her deeply, and the wounds were just beginning to finally heal. She wasn't going to open herself up to be hurt again.

There had been many men who tried over the years, from the rich and famous like herself to the delivery boy from caterers during photo shoots, with everything else in between. She had been wooed by flowers to actually being kidnapped by a friendly but adventurous photographer in his loft.

All attempts failed.

So maybe it was a blessing in disguise that Devon hated her guts because never had she felt so instantly drawn physically to any man.

Why did he dislike her so?

Why did she want his body?

Who knew the answer to either question . . . only God above. And no matter how rich and famous Chloe was, that was one powerful connection she didn't have!

Devon slammed the cordless phone onto the base in anger. He'd been on the phone for more than an hour, along with Alicia, trying to find out what happened to the shipment of imported terra-cotta tiles from Spain. The tile was ordered six months ago for Chloe's foyer and hall, and should have been delivered yesterday. When Alicia had called the company to inquire about the shipment this morning, it was MIA: missing in action.

If the suppliers didn't find where the costly, handcrafted tiles had gone, then they would have to reorder. That would delay the completion of the house. That meant more months of Chloe living in the attic above him.

That was a no-no.

Could he take any more of her?

No!

She was clouding his thoughts, arousing all his senses, and filling his body with desire for her against his better wishes. He didn't want to want her. She was another Elissa, and he wasn't giving in to that again.

Besides, they always fought like cats and dogs or ignored each other—

Wait!

He refused to finish his line of thought. He refused to even rationalize or contemplate the relationship he had with Chloe Bolton.

Alicia jumped up and down excitedly in her seat, the phone clutched in between her ear and shoulder. He focused onto her side of the conversation as she jotted down information.

"And your name . . ." She scribbled it down on the notepad. "Well, Warren Berkeley, Jamison Contractors is holding you personally responsible for getting our shipment here first thing Wednesday morning . . . uh-huh . . . your number again . . . okay. No problem."

He sat up straight in his chair when he began to realize that Alicia had found the shipment. As soon as she hung up the telephone, Devon picked her petite frame up out of her chair and gave her a big bear hug with a kiss on the cheek.

Alicia melted on the inside from the feel of his body pressed into hers, and she wished it was one of promise, desire and love, instead of gratitude and friendship.

"Thanks Alicia, you're an angel."

She smiled and warmed under his appreciation. "Just doing my job, boss man."

"Well enough work for today. Will you stay for supper? I'll follow you home if it's late. I know how that car acts up on you." His mocha eyes searched hers.

What else could she say but a breathless, "Yes!"

"Come on, let's walk over together." He put his hand to her elbow, helping to guide her steps, after they cut off the lights and locked up the office,

They laughed over Devon's expression when she first told him the shipment was lost. Soon they entered the house through the kitchen entrance in the back. Nana Lil was at the sink taking her medicine, comfortably dressed in a cotton caftan of bright yellow. Her face warmed at the sight of them.

"Alicia's gonna stay for dinner."

She smiled with pleasure. "That's fine. As a matter of fact I'm gonna put you to work."

Devon nudged Alicia playfully with his arm. "While you women do your job fixing dinner, I'll go shower."

Lil sucked her teeth and Alicia rolled her eyes heavenward. "Careful I don't get barefoot and have a baby right up in here!"

She used both of her hands to push him out of the kitchen, with a playful swat at his backside. Devon raced up the stairs and almost collided with Deshawn, who was just stepping out of his room.

"Hey slow your roll, Dev."

He did slow his tracks, but only momentarily. His skin felt like it was itching from the day's worth of dirt on it, and he wanted to take a shower . . . bad. "Problem solved with the shipment of tiles."

Deshawn threw a thumbs-up signal as he descended the stairs.

Devon finished climbing the stairs, stripping off his work clothes as soon as he shut his bedroom door behind him. He balled the soiled items up and threw them into his laundry hamper. Naked, he walked over to the closed bathroom door and listened.

No sound of the shower running and the door was unlocked. He thought he had made sure it wasn't occupied by their houseguest before he opened the door and walked in.

Chloe stepped out of the shower, the warmth now gone. She felt so refreshed and her flat stomach growled in hunger. Mentally she prepared herself to ignore Devon. She swore not to let him get to her. She reached for her towel but before she could get a grasp on it, the door swung wide open.

They both froze in surprise as their eyes roamed freely over each other's naked forms. The same electricity crackled between them as at their first meeting. The desire was so hot they both felt like they stepped in the very bowels of hell, but this could only be paradise . . . the Garden of Eden. A man and a woman that were meant for each other . . . destined for each other . . . wanting each other. Their minds said no but their bodies said yes, and eventually how could they resist?

Devon's eyes clouded with desire, missing no details, capturing everything for memory. The slender neck with a mole above her collarbone; shoulders that rounded above long shapely arms; beautiful pendulous breasts with round aureoles that oddly were large, with her nipples hardened into tight buds. Her waist was small with a strawberry shaped birthmark on one of her curved hips above long, shapely legs. The triangular bush that hid her rawest femininity was curly and black. He had a desire to play in it.

How could his body help but react.

She was divine!

Chloe let her eyes devour every bit of the muscled man she saw, achingly aroused by the sight of his malehood surrounded by curly hairs, hardening and lengthening before her very eyes. Her pulse raced and her very center throbbed with desire for the thick, lengthy piece of him. His body was lean and hard, with his muscled neck and powerful chest. A desire to lick the contours of the washboard hardness of his abdomen filled her. She wanted to be held with his strong, sculptured arms and have her legs entwined with his.

Jesus!

Only seconds passed, but it seemed an eternity. No words were spoken, but none were needed.

Devon turned and walked out of the bathroom, closing the door firmly behind him. He was surprised to find that his hands and body trembled with desire for her. His swollen member still stood erect and curved away from his body. His heart raced, his chest felt light and his stomach burned like hell.

"Damn," he swore. "She probably thinks I walked in on her on purpose."

Then he became embarrassed. The woman saw him naked,

for goodness sake! And his body had betrayed him in front of her. How could she not think he was a pervert?

He knew she had left the bathroom because he heard the door leading to the hallway close firmly, probably done intentionally so that he knew for sure that she was finished.

Why didn't she lock *both* of the doors? If she had, he wouldn't be sitting on the edge of his bed with an erection, desiring a woman that was exactly the type of woman he didn't need!

Chloe was prowling back and forth across the attic floor. *Why hadn't I locked that damn door leading to Devon's room?*

She growled in frustration and embarrassment. The man had seen her stark naked and she'd seen . . . every glorious bit of him.

How was she gonna face him now?

The informal seating arrangement for dinner did not help things for either Chloe or Devon. She had been the last one down to dinner and when she entered, her eyes had immediately met with Devon's. They held for a few seconds before they both looked away.

Chloe couldn't help but wonder if he caught a flashback of seeing her naked, and she flushed with warmth. Heat rose from her toes to her ears with embarrassment. If she had been Caucasian, she would have been beet red.

Nana Lil sat near the entrance with an empty chair to her left, then Deshawn with Alicia sitting near the back door and Devon next to her with another empty seat to his left. If she sat between Deshawn and Nana Lil at the circular table, then she would be across from Devon. The only other available seat was directly next to the man. She didn't know which was worse, sitting next to him or across from him, able to look directly in his face.

"Hello Alicia," she greeted the other woman as she took her seat next to Deshawn.

"Hi." Alicia smiled at her, obviously forced, before turning her attention back to Devon.

Chloe studied the woman as dinner progressed and saw the love that she had for Devon in her eyes as they spoke. It was evident in the way she used every opportunity to touch him, and how most of her attention was focused on him. It was hardly the behavior a best friend would show.

Was the adoration reciprocated?

Chloe studied him beneath lowered lashes. This would be hard because Devon was not one to show emotions, so who knew? Sure, right now he appeared as if he treated Alicia like a little sister, but maybe he didn't show sexual affection in public. He was definitely not the extrovert that Deshawn shamelessly was with his constant but harmless flirting.

Why did jealousy burn her looking at Devon lean his handsome dark head toward Alicia?

When Alicia playfully rubbed Devon's cheek, Chloe was so startled by the bold move that she dropped the fork she held in her hand, sending it clattering noisily to the floor.

All eyes immediately were on her.

"Clumsy I guess," she weakly explained as she retrieved the utensil.

"Devon, reach behind you and get Chloe another fork." Nana Lil jerked her head in the direction of the kitchen drawers.

Devon did as asked and when he handed the fork to Chloe their eyes met again. She swore she felt the spark of electricity between them radiate through the metal.

They both thought of what happened between them upstairs.

Chloe's breath caught in her throat when she thought she saw desire in his eyes. Under his scrutiny she nervously licked her lips and her heart stopped when his eyes dipped down to watch the innocent act.

Deshawn stood up from the table, the sound of his chair scraping against the floor, bringing the revealing moment to a sudden halt. "That was good Nana," he sighed as he patted his rock-hard abdomen.

"Don't forget to thank Alicia. She mixed the potato salad up for me and baked the cornbread." Nana Lil smiled warmly at her.

The men complimented her, but spitefully Chloe thought the cornbread was dry and the potato salad bitter. She *knew* she could do a lot better.

Deshawn walked over to the sink, letting his plate slip into the hot depths of the sudsy water, before moving back across the kitchen to lean down and kiss her wrinkled cheek.

"Shawnie, you eat too fast. Your stomach's gonna hurt again," she said, as she swatted him away playfully.

"I know Nana Lil." He smiled and winked at her. "But I have to see a man about a dog." He used the popular phrase in the South for when a person didn't want to exactly tell someone where he really was going.

Nana Lil laughed. "More like a woman about a pussycat," she said with her usual bluntness before taking a bite of food.

Devon nearly choked on the limeade he was drinking. Alicia reached over to clap on his back, as she also laughed. Chloe's mouth hung upon, not quite sure she would ever get used to Nana Lil's bluntness, before she also joined in the laughter around the table.

Deshawn held up his hands. "Ha . . . ha . . . ha. Real funny," he said dryly. "I'm going to play cards."

Devon stretched his lean, muscled frame in the chair, his movements only hinting at the strength he held. Two sets of eyes watched him and both women could only force themselves to look away. "Going to Charlie's?"

Charlie's was a small wooden shack at the end of a dead end road where mostly the men of the small town gambled, playing pitty-pat, poker or bid whist. Charlie would hold tournaments for money and always sold steamed sausage dogs, potato chips, sodas and bootleg liquor.

Deshawn grabbed his keys from the hook by the back door. "Yeah, you wanna ride with me?"

"Naw, I'll come by after I follow Alicia home."

Chloe didn't miss the way Alicia looked like a cat who just swallowed a fat rat. She wondered if they had a rendezvous planned. It was only a little after eight; why did he have to follow her home? Would they make love at her house before he went to Charlie's? Or would he spend the night?

The thought of it made her seethe with jealousy because she was honest in admitting that she wished Devon and she would climb the stairs together, to sleep in the same room and make love in one bed.

But she knew that there was a better chance for a snowball in hell!

Nana Lil complained of a splitting headache and retired to bed early, leaving Devon, Chloe and Alicia to clean up the kitchen. It was a simple task that turned out to be very tiring for Chloe. Alicia made sure of that.

First she tried to talk her out of helping.

Chloe had just scraped the food out of all the plates and was about to start washing them in the sink when the other woman shook her head. "Don't worry about those. I'm sure Devon and I can handle it," she said as she came over to stand next to Chloe by the sink.

For a few moments their eyes locked. "I don't mind helping. I usually help Nana Lil after dinner anyway," Chloe insisted, turning her attention back to the sink.

Alicia reached for the dishcloth in Chloe's hand. "I said don't worry about it," she said peevishly.

Chloe forced a tight smile and snatched the cloth back. "And *I* said I don't mind, but thank you for the offer . . . Alicia."

She knew the woman wanted to be alone with Devon, who

was watching them with a confused look on his face. *He probably thinks we're crazy,* she thought.

Round one went to Chloe as she washed the dishes, but the other woman was determined.

"Devon, remember when we were nine and we washed that stray dog?" she asked from over where she was wiping the table off with a damp cloth.

Devon grinned and shook his head as he dried the dishes Chloe handed him. "Yeah, we all ended up wetter than the dog and poor Shawn . . ."

". . . fell in the tub," they said in unison, before laughing.

And so it went for the remainder of the ten minutes it took to finish straightening the kitchen back to Nana Lil's usual neatness. They reminisced over their lives growing up in Holtsville so much that someone would have thought they hadn't seen each other in years. Needless to say, Chloe felt left out, just as she suspected Alicia wanted her to.

Chloe finished scrubbing the casserole dish and then dipped it in the half of the double sink filled with rinse water before handing it to Devon. "That's all the dishes. I'm gonna read on the porch awhile."

She left the kitchen quickly and dashed up the stairs to retrieve the book she had been reading earlier. When she came back downstairs, the lights were off in the kitchen. She assumed correctly that they were gone.

Before she went outside she looked in on Nana Lil and saw that she was sleeping comfortably. The nighttime southern air was alive with the sounds of creatures and the scent of blooming flowers. Chloe settled into the rocking chair, folding her feet under her as she began to read. She was resolved not to let herself think of the embarrassing bathroom incident, or how good he had looked naked, or about what he and Alicia were doing at her house.

Easier said than done.

* * *

Devon's thoughts were filled with Chloe as he drove the dark, winding country roads. Just this one time he let his mind wander, not forcibly pushing the thoughts away. Tonight at dinner he had felt that piercing stare of hers on him several times, even though he didn't acknowledge her. He wondered for the hundredth time what she had been thinking.

Then when he handed her the fork and their eyes had met, he swore he saw desire in the honey-brown depths. He hated to admit the pleasure he felt at even believing she could want him. Her expression made him believe she was as attracted to him as he was unwillingly attracted to her.

Yes, on a purely physical level he wanted her. But women like Chloe would never accept that. Before he met and lived under the same roof as she for three weeks, he had thought her lacking in morals, believing the rumors. But she wasn't a drug addict or an airhead. Everyday living with her had reshaped his opinions concerning her until he didn't know what to think, because he still saw many similarities between her and Elissa.

It was lust! He lusted for her like a horny teenager, until he could smell her when she wasn't even in his presence. He wanted to bury himself between her thighs and hear her moan his name with that husky voice of hers. He wanted to see those honey-colored eyes blaze with desire for him. Those eyes seemed to haunt him in his dreams with their intensity.

His desire for her was evident from the bulge straining against his jeans. Thoughts of her naked body inflamed him, and there was only one way to douse the flame. But he didn't want to get burned.

When he pulled into the driveway, having decided not to go to Charlie's, he saw her lone figure huddled in the rocking chair on the porch. Devon assumed she was still reading.

He parked in the back, but walked around the trail leading to the front of the house. When he stepped onto the porch, he had expected her to look up from the book, but instead her head stayed down.

He felt nervous in her presence. He wanted to apologize for what happened between them today, although it wasn't entirely his fault. With shame, he realized he hadn't ever been gentlemanly enough to apologize to her. *He* had been the one to walk in on *her* regardless. "Chloe."

As he got closer he saw that her eyes were closed and her breathing was slow and easy. She was asleep. "Chloe," he called her name again, louder this time.

She would have a nasty crick in her neck from the way her head was nodding down toward her chest. He smiled when her perfectly heart-shaped mouth opened and she snored lightly. Unbelievable. The glamorous supermodel snored in her sleep.

She *was* beautiful. Long, curled lashes rested against her healthy bronzed complexion, her mouth slightly ajar as she breathed. Her auburn hair was loosened from the braid she wore earlier, and her hair spilled over her shoulders. A loose strand lightly touched her cheek as the night air floated past. The temptation to stroke the hair from her face surprised him.

Innocence and beauty, intelligence and curiosity, were all personified with her. Devon knew that the anger he had toward the beauty was really meant for himself for falling under her spell, exactly what he didn't want to do. He knew he was wrong for that.

No, he didn't love her, but he did want her so badly that it was driving him over the edge. Did she want him too, or did he imagine the desire he saw in her eyes tonight?

He called her name again but she did not stir. He couldn't let her sleep on the porch even if it was a warm summer night, and she looked as contended as a babe in her sleep. He bent down and gathered her easily into his muscled arms, expecting her to be jarred awake, but instead she snuggled close to his chest with another short snort.

As she breathed deeply in her sleep, her breath fanned against his neck, her breasts pushed softly into his chest, her buttocks curved against his hand as he carried her into the house and up the two flights of stairs. The simple gentlemanly act was pure torture for him.

He stooped in front of the attic door, twisting the doorknob and pushing the door open with his foot. A scent, her scent, filled the space, assailing his senses. It was a delightful mix of perfume and this woman in his arms.

Reluctantly he laid her gently on the bed, upon which she immediately curled her body into a ball. He chanced only removing her sandals, and he covered her with a thin blue coverlet that matched the lavender and blue decor of the spacious attic room, which was the same length as his entire suite.

She sighed in her sleep and then snored again. Devon smiled and gazed down at her serenely sleeping figure framed by the bright moonlight streaming through the open window. He left the room, closing the door softly behind him.

In his bedroom he stripped in the dark and climbed into bed. Having her in his arms tonight was more pleasurable than he liked. He knew the hunger he had for her was occupying too much of his time, and the changing opinion he had about her wasn't helping him any.

"Damn," he swore into the silence of the room as he climbed beneath the covers of the bed. He knew tonight would be the worst night of sleep he ever had. He knew he would be haunted with visions of cat-shaped, honey-colored eyes and a heart-shaped beauty mark.

Seven

The next morning Chloe woke up drenched in sweat and fully dressed. The last thing she remembered was sitting in the rocking chair last night, reading. She leaned her head back against the pillows and looked around, still slightly groggy with sleep. How in the devil did she get up two flights of stairs, kick off her sandals, get the coverlet from the window seat and climb into bed without remembering it?

Had she been *that* tired?

Did she sleepwalk?

Had someone carried her to bed, and if so, who?

Probably Deshawn after he came in from Charlie's. Lord knows Devon would have probably let her sleep outside during a rainstorm. It was way too thoughtful an act for *him*.

Besides, he probably spent the night at Alicia's, she thought nastily, as she climbed out of bed.

Chloe walked over to the window. Already the heat was stifling and she knew it was going to be a scorcher. In all haste she peeled the sweat-drenched clothes from her body, letting them fall into a heap on the floor. She pulled on her robe and left the room. This time when she entered Devon's bathroom, Chloe made sure to lock both doors, although she was sure Devon would probably hesitate before walking into his bathroom again. She took a leisurely bath, trying to force herself to stay focused on neutral thoughts.

But she couldn't help but be reminded of the embarrassing

incident yesterday, especially being back at the scene. During her modeling career she had found herself scantily clad in front of a roomful of people, male and female, but under Devon's hard gaze she was filled with embarrassment. But she was resolved to try and put it behind her. It happened, it was over and there wasn't anything either Devon or she could do about it but get over it. Accidents happen all the time. The naked body was a beautiful and natural thing, not something to be ashamed of, right?

Although the way Devon's shaft had hardened in front of her seemed unnatural. His . . . uh, maleness was certainly the most . . . uh . . . impressive she'd seen . . . ever. He had nothing to be ashamed of, that's for sure!

This time when she stepped behind the curtain into the tub, her vision of Devon lathered in soap was much more realistic with oddly remembered details. A scar on his left shoulder blade, a light birthmark on his left muscled thigh.

Yes, yesterday had been very revealing. Surely now Devon knew details of her body intimately, more so than any man had in a long time. Chloe literally shook her head to remove the short lived event from her thoughts.

After a long hot bath, she dashed back upstairs wrapped in a towel. Because of the heat, Chloe decided to forgo a bra, and she pulled on a pair of Calvin Klein thong bikinis. She dressed in a white cotton tank and a white tennis skirt with a fresh pair of white and silver Air Nikes. She pulled her hair into a tight ponytail with a gray scrunchee.

She glanced down at the new platinum and diamond watch she'd bought. It was seven A.M. Too early for any stores to be opened in Charleston to shop. There was *nothing* to do.

With a sigh she grabbed her car keys, just in case she decided to go for a ride, saving herself the need to climb the three flights of stairs. When she got downstairs Nana Lil was sitting in one of the recliner chairs watching a local morning news program on the television.

"Morning Nana Lil. How's your headache?"

She looked up at Chloe with a smile. "Good morning. My head's feeling much better after I rested last night," she lied. "Would you like some breakfast?"

Chloe shook her head. "No, thanks. I'm not hungry."

Lil started to fuss but stopped herself. Chloe was a grown woman and if she wasn't hungry then so be it. Besides, she *did* have another headache and just didn't feel like nagging. "Shawnie said to tell you to come down the road as soon as you were ready."

She smiled in pleasure, her eyes bright. "Then I'll go now. I'll see you later, Nana Lil," she yelled over her shoulder before dashing out of the house.

The older woman waved her off and turned back to the television. Chloe decided to drive the short distance because of the heat. She lowered the top of the convertible, hopped in and put the key in the ignition before backing out of the driveway. Moments later she turned onto her land and parked next to Devon's truck. She didn't see Deshawn's truck and thought maybe he parked in the back of the growing structure.

Once again most of the men turned and waved as soon as they noticed her. She waved back and smiled as she looked around the many heads busy at work. She didn't notice Deshawn anywhere, or even Devon for that matter.

Two jeans-clad men strode past her. "Morning," they both spoke.

"Good morning, fellas, have either of you seen Deshawn?" She flashed them her famous brilliant smile.

The slender one with freckles and slender build blushed beet red, nodding his head toward the house. "He's in the master suite at the end of the hall."

She didn't bother to remind him that it was her house, built to her wishes, thus she knew very well where the master suite was located. Instead she thanked him and walked toward the house. She found him hammering in the walk-in closet, squatting with his back to her. "Hey Deshawn. I'm here for my tour," she said as she entered the room.

His body stiffened noticeably before he stood and turned to face her. "Sorry to disappoint you, but Deshawn had to go and pick up Alicia. She's having car trouble again."

Her heart hammered in her chest when she realized it was *him,* and she knew it was him before he even spoke. No one, not even his identical twin, moved like Devon, with barely contained strength. So he hadn't spent the night at Alicia's, or else Deshawn wouldn't have had to pick her up. She would have driven in with Devon.

His eyes were intense as they watched her, and Chloe became nervous under the scrutiny. "I'll just come back when Deshawn gets back. Tell him to call down to the house."

She turned to leave, ready to flee from his powerful presence, but his deep-timbred voice stopped her. "Is there something I can help you with, Chloe?"

Nervously she turned but did not look at him, instead looking at an invisible spot on the floor. "Deshawn was going to give me a tour of the house."

"Checking for shoddy workmanship?" he asked dryly, reminding her of her sarcastic crack at him yesterday.

Chloe jerked her head up to look at him, thinking that *he* was spoiling for a fight this time. She was surprised to see the hint of humor in his obsidian eyes. "Look, I'm sorry for that. I was in a bad mood yesterday."

He waved off her apology. "Forget it. I've had a few days of perpetual bad moods myself." Devon took a deep breath as he watched her, finding it funny that she couldn't look him in the eye for long. "Uhm, look, Chloe we need to talk."

She crossed her slender arms across her ample chest, the diamonds of her watch glistening in the sunlight. "About?" she asked, her voice trailing off.

"Yesterday."

She squeezed herself with her arms. "I already apologized for jumping at you."

He shook his head. She wasn't going to make this easy. "You *know* what I'm talking about, Chloe."

And of course, yes she did know exactly what he was talking about, but she remained silent and instead gathered the
courage to look him in the face.

Mistake . . . big time.

His eyes were intense and direct. She could not look away.

He let his eyes lock with hers and felt surrounded by shades
of hazel. He wanted to see those eyes blaze with desire.
"Chloe, I should have apologized then for barging in on you.
I thought the bathroom was empty or I wouldn't have ever
walked in on you like that."

His voice was deep and sincere. She hadn't once believed
he had barged in on her on purpose to cop a free look. Why
would she? The man detested her. But she was moved by his
apology and knew it was heartfelt.

"It was an honest mistake, just an accident. I should've
locked both doors and I'm sorry for that. It really was no big
deal—"

"No . . . big . . . deal," he scoffed, his voice incredulous.
"Thanks for the blow to my ego."

Her cheeks felt hot when she realized he thought she was
referring to his male member. Her mouth dropped open, her
hazel eyes were round. "That's not what I meant . . ."

Devon threw his head back, laughing. Chloe liked the
sound of it, rich and throaty. It was also the first time she
could remember him laughing in her presence. Humor made
his face even more open and handsome. "I *know* you didn't
mean it that way. I was just kidding, Chloe."

She raised one finely arched brow. "Don't be so sure I
didn't mean it that way."

It was her turn to laugh when he abruptly stopped laughing
to look at her. She held up both of her hands. "Just kidding."

"Look, I'll show you around, at least until Shawn gets back.
Just let me finish this up first."

He turned back to his squatting position and began ham
mering the nails he retrieved from his leather tool belt into
the beam running along the interior of the closet.

A vision of Devon naked and lean, squatting in the same position, with only his tool belt and construction boots on, flashed briefly in her mind. Laughter bubbled out, filling the empty room with reverberations of it.

Devon stopped hammering and turned on his haunches to cast her a piercing stare. When she ducked her head, avoiding his eyes and covering her grin with her hand, his instincts told him that she was laughing at him.

Did he have a hole in his pants, a foreign object hanging out of his nose? What the hell was so funny?

Chloe chanced another look in his direction. With him still squatting, but now facing her, the vision changed to his male anatomy swinging between his thighs, his tool belt and boots still in place. Her lips sputtered with laughter again, resembling the tinkling of bells.

Devon stood up, his hands on his narrow hips, causing Chloe to double over in laughter, tears filling her eyes. "Okay, Chloe, what's so funny?" he demanded, his expression impatient.

Chloe tried to swallow her laughter but failed to keep a straight face. "Nothing. I'm sorry Devon," she sputtered, bursting into laughter again.

"I fail to see anything humorous," he drawled.

She laughed so hard she snorted and her head began to pound. "If you saw . . . what I saw . . . you'd laugh too," she said, as she tried to catch her breath.

So she *was* laughing at him. "What did you see?"

She took deep calming breaths through her mouth. "I just imagined you naked and hammering with nothing on but your tool belt and your big old construction boots!"

Chloe howled with laughter when he looked down at himself and then back up at her. He didn't find the notion of himself naked to be comical at all. He raised a brow at her, his handsome face serious. She sure hadn't been laughing yesterday in the bathroom when her eyes had gotten wide as saucers at seeing his "endowments."

He started to tell her a few things, like:

Why was she thinking of him naked anyway?

or

Why hadn't she laugh yesterday?

or

Would she like for him to show her just how serious the sight of him naked could get?

But instead he gave her a stern look with his piercing black eyes. "Anyway, let's start in the living room."

Devon walked past her out of the master suite, slipping his hammer into a leather rung on his tool belt. When he heard her cough back another round of laughter behind him, he actually smiled. Okay, the thought of someone naked in boots with a tool belt *was* hilarious.

An unspoken truce developed between them.

Eight

A month had passed since Chloe first moved to the Carolinas. The September heat was nearly as sweltering as July's, with the only relief to be found after the sun went down in the late afternoons. She had truly begun to think of the small town as home. It was a connection to her mother and the generations of Boltons before her. Frequently she could be seen driving by on the main road leading to Charleston in the new 2000 Lincoln Navigator SUV she bought after turning in the convertible sports car she had been renting.

Always a hopeless shopaholic, Chloe truly took shopping to new heights. It had become her new pastime. But she still secretly yearned for the newest fashions from New York and Paris. Her weaved tresses were done with an infusion technique and Chloe doubted she could find anyone skilled enough with the process in the area. Plus, she missed Anika's wry brand of humor. Okay, so there were some things to be found in New York that she couldn't do without.

She was cruising at seventy miles per hour down Highway 17 from Charleston when she thought of the upcoming Fashion Awards, to be held in New York. The televised event was just under two months away and she knew she *had* to attend. The only upside was that while she was in town she could get some serious shopping done, get pampered at the Estee Lauder spa, get her weave redone by Tahia at The Hair Solution, and spend some quality time with Anika.

Smiling, she picked up the cellular phone from the console, quickly dialing Liv's private business line with her right hand as she drove the SUV with her left hand easily.

"Talk to me."

Chloe smiled at Liv's usual greeting, but hated the harsh coarseness of her voice. "Hey there darling. Guess who?" Chloe said in an awful imitation of an exaggerated southern drawl.

"Hello stranger. How are you?"

Chloe could imagine her with a cigarette between her index and middle fingers. "I promised I would keep in touch and I haven't spoken to you since I returned your call about the Fashion Awards."

Liv laughed. "Yes, and I'm glad that you called today. I wasn't so sure you were still going to make an appearance."

"I really would prefer not to, Liv." Chloe paused as she swerved around a dead raccoon in the road. "But I have no choice."

Liv's voice became animated. "Do you realize what a coup this will be? Why not win the award and announce that you're returning to reclaim the top spot?"

Chloe shook her head, nervously biting her bottom lip before she spoke. "No, Liv. I wasn't happy being in the business anymore."

"You can't hate me . . . for trying."

Chloe knew that during that pause Liv was surely lighting up another cigarette. "I could never hate you, Olivia."

Another pause. "Regardless, you must know that this will be a big event for you. Chloe Bolton . . . one year later . . . how does she look now? . . . yadda yadda yadda. Just promise this old woman that you'll come into town at least one week before the event." Another pause. "The world's gonna be looking at you. You'll need the right outfit, hair and makeup."

Chloe knew she was right. For too long she had lived in front of the cameras to go only halfway with her appearance now. "I will be in town one week before then, Liv, I promise."

"Good. There's one more thing, hon."

A big wad of bird crap landed on her hood. "What's that?" she asked absentmindedly, knowing her paint could be ruined if she didn't get the mess removed.

"You'll also need the perfect date. Let me set something up."

"Liv, you know I never liked publicity dates." Her voice was firm.

"Okay then, are you seeing someone? Has Calvin finally won your heart again? Maybe a big strapping southern buck with spurs?" Liv laughed.

Again she bit her lip. "No, I'm not seeing anyone."

An image of Devon filled her mind, but Chloe shook the image away. *Why had she thought of him? Well, he certainly was a strapping southern buck, minus the spurs.*

What would she do for an escort? Maybe she could just go alone. She would ask Anika, but sitting through an awards show was not her best friend's type of thing, and besides she saw the awards show as the justification of parading men and women around as life-sized Ken and Barbie dolls. Maybe she should just let Liv set up one of her infamous celebrity publicity dates. It wasn't like she had never done it before; she just didn't like it. But it was just someone to pose with for pictures, and then the night was over and everyone went their separate ways.

"All right Liv, do it. But don't get anyone over the top. If Dennis Rodman shows up at my door—"

Liv was pleased. "I'll get right on it and I'll call you with details, hon."

Chloe felt like she resigned herself to a fate worse than death. "Okay Liv. Call me at the number I gave you."

She ended the call and replaced the phone on the console's base. The Lincoln Navigator was headed down the main strip in Holtsville under her steering. This was the town's downtown area and it was only the length of two metropolitan blocks. It really would take some getting used to.

The downtown area was made up of one small bank, an even smaller post office, Cyrus's two-pump gas station with a small store, a second-hand store, a moderately sized brick church, a police station, a video rental store and a small diner. It left a lot to be desired. A whole lot.

She turned off the main road and drove the rest of the distance to the Jamisons' in reflective silence. With every vehicle that passed her, the drivers waved or blinked their lights in greeting, and she did the same in kind. In New York, a driver was lucky to get a look of indifference as acknowledgment, if not an angry glare or an expression that said, *What are you staring at?*

Chloe looked over to her left at the local day care center, where toddlers were loudly playing behind a fenced yard filled with swings, jungle gyms, merry-go-rounds and slides. She loved children, especially babies and toddlers. Their innocence captivated her and she allowed a sharp wave of regret to fill her, that she had never slowed down in her career long enough to have children of her own. But then who would she have had them with?

Many times during her relationship with Calvin they had discussed marriage and a family. In fact he had even proposed putting the wagon before the horse. Calvin had a way of waiting until her defenses were down, like while making love, to beg her to have his baby, to fulfill his dream of seeing her round with his child. *First comes love, then Chloe with a baby carriage, next comes marriage?* It's no wonder the nursery rhyme didn't go that way.

Now, in hindsight, Chloe thought he probably didn't want something as committing as a child, but only a chance to make love to her without a condom, something she had never allowed him to do during their entire relationship. When she thought of him in bed with another woman, she was glad she had not made that allowance for him. Maybe she'd seen the signs of his infidelity all along.

A child with Calvin would have been the last thing she

needed now, especially since she couldn't stand the sight of the man. What type of environment would that have been for a child to grow in? Then again, maybe Calvin would have pulled a dip move like her own father, who had left the heavy weight of being both parents, single provider and single disciplinarian on her loving mother.

Chloe didn't think of her MIA father very often. How could she? She hardly knew much about him, and had never met the man. She could still remember the night, so many years ago, that she had asked her mother the question so many fatherless children do . . .

"Mama, why don't I have a daddy?"

Adell looked up from the crossword puzzle she was doing in the back of the TV Guide, her reading glasses perched on the end of her nose. She looked down to where her eight-year-old daughter sat on the floor at her feet, reading. Chloe's eyes were so large and hesitant in their clear hazel depths, as if it was a question she wanted to ask for a long time, but had just worked up the nerve to actually ask.

Stalling for some time before she answered the question she had known would one day be asked, Adell slowly closed the TV Guide and removed her glasses. Chloe waited patiently, her eyes never wavering from her mother. She truly wanted to know where the faceless man who was her father was. Why didn't he want to be a part of their family? Why didn't he care that he missed her first words, her first steps and her first day of school? Did he know how pretty she was? Didn't he want to do the things daddies did with their children, like Anika's dad? Didn't he love her? Why didn't he want her?

Adell smiled lovingly at her child, just the faint hint of tears in her hazel eyes. "Come sit next to Mama, Chloe," she said, her voice husky, barely above a whisper.

And as she gathered Chloe's thin frame to her ample side, she realized her mistake. She knew then that she should have told her daughter all the details about her father. But how could she make an eight-year-old, even one as bright as Chloe, understand about falling in love with a man and being filled with such pain when he leaves her and the baby he doesn't want that she has to push all thoughts of him away? There was no way to explain that to a child.

So instead of answering Chloe's question directly, which would mean telling her the horrible truth, she tried to captivate the inquisitive child with stories of the man she yearned to know. Adell knew that her evasions could not last forever. But she wanted to spare her child the searing pain of rejection that she found difficult to deal with herself. Adell tried to never out-and-out lie to her child.

"Chloe, when I was eighteen I left from my home with my parents in Holtsville. As much as I loved it there, I knew there was no real work for me. So I accepted my Aunt Loreen's offer to come stay with her, here in New York, until I got a job."

Chloe glanced up at her mother. She knew all this. She wanted to know about her father, but she dare not be disrespectful. When she focused back on the story she noticed she had missed some of it, but nothing concerning her question.

"I was so proud of my first apartment, Chloe. Twenty-one and living alone for the first time in my life. The apartment building wasn't much to speak of, but I put every spare cent I had into making my place look good, and it did. In fact I used to try to keep the front of the building and the hallways clean. Some of the other tenants looked at me like I was a fool."

She laughed then, remembering, and Chloe smiled too. "Then about two or three months after I moved in, on a

Saturday, I went downstairs to work on that little four-by-four dirt patch in front of the building. I wanted to plant some flowers." She sighed then and closed her eyes with a faint smile. "I was knee high in dirt, face smudged with a head rag on, when I hear this deep male voice say, 'You're too pretty to be in dirt that way.' I turn around and it's my next door neighbor Terrence Gilford. Lord, he was fine. Tall and kind of a smooth caramel complexion, just like yours, with a slender build and big feet."

They both laughed at that and Chloe's heart raced with excitement!

"And he could dress. Well, I noticed him since the first day I moved in but I never thought he noticed me . . . until that day I was planting the garden."

Adell lowered her head until the side of her face touched the top of Chloe's plaited head. "And do you know what he did, Chloe?"

Chloe shook her head no, anxiously awaiting her mother's next words.

"He rolled up the sleeves of the shirt he had on and got right down in the dirt with me planting those flowers. I was so impressed by him. And after we finished in the little garden, if you can call it that, we went upstairs to his apartment and drank lemonade and talked."

"Terrence was twenty-seven and a musician. He played the trumpet and knew everything about every song you could name. His apartment was filled with crates of records from the floor to the ceiling, and there were posters and pictures of him with famous singers he played with or got an autograph from. He grew up in Harlem, but both of his parents died in an accident. His birthday was August thirteenth, a Leo. He was an only child, just like you and me, Chloe.

"We would sit on the porch just outside his first floor apartment and listen to jazz playing from his old record player through the window. Or he would play his trumpet

*for me. He was so romantic and loved to play tricks on
me, and he was forever reading . . . just like someone else
I know."*

*"Me Mama?" Chloe asked, looking for some piece of
him in her.*

Adell nodded. "Yes, he loved to read just like you."

"Did you love him, Mama?"

*"Yes, baby, I loved him with all my heart." Her voice
was hoarse with pain.*

Tears blurred Chloe's vision and with good judgment she
pulled her SUV over onto the side of the road. Even today her
father's betrayal stung. Those same questions she had as a child
remained unanswered. As she got older she realized that her
mother had filled her with all the details on her sire, but always
succeeded in avoiding directly answering those questions.

With age and wisdom she had eventually answered them
herself. He wasn't dead, he never showed his face, never
called . . . he didn't want her. And that hurt and affected her
more deeply than she was willing to admit.

Now here she was, her loving mother gone, her best friend
a thousand miles away, her grandparents gone, and with a
father who might as well be dead because he had never been
there for her.

Chloe hated the tears, but looking at the children in the
playground had opened up all these feelings she thought she
had long buried. She dropped her head on top of her hand
on the steering wheel. Soon they were soaked with her tears,
and she just didn't have the strength to drive.

So she let the tears flow freely. Her body shook and never
had she felt so alone in her life.

Devon headed down Highway 17 from Walterboro, on his
way back from a trip to the hardware store to pick up the

eight boxes of nails they needed. He could have sent anyone to purchase them, but he felt like a ride. The wiring and plumbing were complete, allowing the interior walls, ceilings and floors to be installed. The house would be finished within the allotted time, if not sooner.

With a sigh he decided to stop at the diner and pick up lunch for the crew. Devon picked up the cell phone from off the seat, where it carelessly lay, and dialed Donnie's. He wanted to get back to the site ASAP, so he placed an order for something that could be made fast . . . ten club sandwiches with fries. The sandwiches were about the only thing Donnie made that was good.

In another ten minutes he would reach Holtsville and the order should be at least halfway finished. Devon tapped his strong fingers against the steering wheel as the radio played a new rap song by Method Man of the Wu Tang Clan. He smiled as he remembered how Deshawn and Chloe had blasted the song on her SUV's radio while they washed the rather large vehicle. Soon their good intentions went when Chloe started a water fight with his brother.

He had watched them from where he sat on the porch, his eyes squinted against the sun. Of course he had thought it hilarious when they doused each other at the same time, Chloe using a bucket of water and Deshawn the hose.

How was he supposed to know that they would both turn on him, quickly soaking him right where he sat? What could he do but join in and get some revenge? It was the most fun he had had in a long time, and the sight of Chloe's T-shirt soaked to her skin, revealing a skimpy lace bra, hadn't been half bad either.

The diner was just ahead on his right and Devon swung his truck into the parking spot easily. Leaving the truck running, he jumped out and walked into the small diner. It was empty except for the cashier/waitress Poochie and Donnie. He glanced at his watch, seeing that it wasn't quite time for the noontime rush.

"Hey twin," Donnie called out from the window separating the kitchen from the patrons' dining area. It allowed him to look out at his patrons but pretty much cut any ideas of someone looking into the kitchen off completely.

"Twin" was also many of the townspeople's way of addressing Deshawn and him, since they couldn't tell the two apart.

"What's up Donnie?" he yelled back. Eight white Styrofoam containers sat on the counter, so he knew the order was almost complete.

"Hello there Poochie," he addressed the voluptuous woman behind the register as he reached in his back pocket for his wallet.

"Hey there." She started to ring up his bill on the register, but her eyes kept darting back up to Devon's face. "Which one are you anyway? Not that it matters, you both look so damn good!"

Devon looked up from the money he was counting. The invitation was obviously there in her dark eyes. There was a time he would have gotten her number, taken her on a date or two, and enjoyed himself between her voluptuously thick thighs. But, oddly, his taste had moved on from the woman's light complexion, full heavy breasts, ample derriere and wide hips. Thus Poochie's ample good looks enticed him for but a brief moment and then waned, while the desire he had for a slim, sharp-tongued woman of dark bronze would not subside.

Feeling devilish, Devon gave her his best imitation of his twin's wolfish and charming grin, the dimple in his cheek deepening. "I'm Deshawn," he drawled with a wink.

She took the money he offered to pay the bill, letting her hand lightly caress his fingers. "Well of course you are. I can see it now. You're much cuter than the other one."

Devon nearly choked on his laughter. Was she for real? They were totally identical! Playing along, he said, "That's what the ladies always say. Why don't you give me your number."

He swore she actually swayed on her feet before tearing off one of the receipt tickets and pulling a pencil from deep in the valley of her ample cleavage. Devon had to admit that that move even made him swallow over a sudden lump in his throat.

Poochie licked the tip of the pencil in a seductive move, her tongue moist and pink, before writing her number down without moving her eyes off of him. "You make sure you call me." Her voice was low and husky as she kissed the ticket, leaving a lush pink replica of her pouted lips on the paper.

"I sure will."

Donnie came out of the back carrying the last two containers. She reluctantly looked away from him to help bag the orders, eventually handing the five plastic bags over to him with a smile. "Bye, Deshawn."

Devon waved and left, gratefully putting the bags on the seat next to him. He laughed as he put the truck in reverse and then pulled into traffic.

He turned off the main road and headed home, his mind imagining Deshawn's face when he gave him Poochie's number. He had just come around the bend past the day care center when he saw Chloe's SUV parked on the side of the road. He knew it was her because who else could afford the luxury vehicle, and her personalized license plate, "CHLOE," helped a whole lot.

Concerned, Devon flipped down his signal light and pulled off the road behind her. He turned off the truck and jumped down to the ground. At first he thought it was empty, but as he walked briskly forward he saw that she was slumped onto the steering wheel.

Moving fast, Devon yanked open the driver's door. He heard her whimpers before she even looked up at him with tear-filled hazel eyes. Her face was wet, and tenderness for her filled him.

"Come here, Chloe. What's the matter?" He reached in and

swung her easily onto the ground to stand in front of him. Wordlessly he pulled her body into a tight embrace against him. Her frame still shook with tears.

Chloe couldn't stop crying and she thought, with a wry sense of humor, that it had to be hormonal. Lord only knew she didn't want to be an emotional mess in front of anyone, especially Devon. And on the side of the road, no less!

She let her body be calmed by the soothing way he swayed back and forth, rocking her like she was a baby. But even in her emotional haze she was well aware of the feel of Devon's muscled thighs against hers, the feel of both of her palms against his muscled chest beneath the thin white T-shirt, and the heavy masculine scent of him as she smelled the column of his neck where her face lay.

Her back tingled where his hands were wrapped around her and she was comforted by the feel of his chin resting on top of her head. She couldn't remember the last time anyone had held her.

Devon was busy feeling like a heel.

Why?

Because even though his intention had been to comfort her when she was obviously in need, his body was fast becoming aroused by the feel of her body so near to his. Somehow he knew it would feel this good to have her in his arms. But he knew now was not the time to press his erection against her, so he moved his lower half away from her.

Chloe took deep breaths to calm herself until the flow of bitter tears finally subsided. Reluctantly she raised her head from the warm hollow of his neck to look up at him. "I'm sorry. It's just one of those days, I guess." The explanation sounded weak even to her own ears.

Devon looked down into those haunting hazel eyes with their odd cat shape. He knew if he allowed himself, he could get lost in their bright depths.

"Are you hurt?" he said. It was a question he realized he should have asked when he first approached her.

Chloe shook her head, unable to look away from him. "I'm fine."

"Wanna talk about it?"

Instinctively she knew from the concern in his eyes and from the tender way he held her that he would listen. She thought talking about it would just open up the dam of tears again. "Rain check?"

Devon smiled. "Anytime."

Was this caring man comforting her when she felt at her lowest the same man she had been at war with for weeks? Hard to believe, but true. "Thanks, Devon."

He felt the faint breeze of her breath against his lips. Her mouth was open and moist, so inviting. How could he help but want to feel those lips against his own, to want to know the taste of her tongue? Damn, he wanted her! It was driving him insane.

Chloe shivered in desire and she nearly fainted in pleasure when she saw the same attraction for her in his eyes. Devon wanted her!

When he growled low in his throat and lowered his head toward her, never had Chloe felt so desired. She leaned her face upwards, rushing to experience the kiss she yearned for as she enjoyed the hard pounding of his heart against her hands.

Their mouths were just an inch apart, so close they breathed in the air between them slowly. Chloe's eyes were closed in anticipation.

Devon released her suddenly and stepped back, his expression remote and closed. She felt waves of bitter disappointment and almost toppled forward with her lips hilariously puckered. She caught herself from falling and stared at Devon with amazement. Had she imagined that he was going to kiss her?

No, definitely not. He changed his mind . . . that's all.

"Are you feeling better, Chloe? I picked up lunch for our crew and I don't want it to get cold." His tone was neutral as he looked at her. Gone was the light of desire in the obsidian depths of his beautiful eyes.

Chloe nodded and got back in her SUV, closing the solid door firmly behind her. She started to say something, anything, but what was there to say? So instead she waved and forced a stiff smile before pulling the vehicle back onto the road.

Devon watched her drive around the next bend until her vehicle disappeared out of his sight. "Damn it," he swore, using his hand to massage his jaw, an obviously nervous gesture. He kicked the ground, causing dirt to fly up around him, and he threw his hands up in exasperation.

Growling in frustration, he paced in front of his pickup until his erection eased. Once in control, he got back into the cab of his truck. Okay, he wanted to kiss her . . . badly, and she wanted him to kiss her. "Why the hell didn't I just do it?" he asked himself as he started the truck and steered it back onto the road.

Chloe parked the SUV in one of the spots in the garage behind the house. She wasn't given the chance to fret over what had happened, or rather what almost happened, between Devon and her. Just as she stepped off the running board and walked around the vehicle to retrieve her packages from the back, a large silver delivery truck passed by on the road.

"Ansa" was emblazoned on the side and Chloe knew it was special cabinets that she had ordered for the kitchen. Rushing, she flew into the house, yelling a quick hello to Nana Lil before dashing up the stairs. She pulled off the scarlet tank and capri pants that she wore, carelessly throwing the clothes onto a pile in the middle of the bed.

From the heavy mahogany trunk at the foot of the bed she pulled out a pair of faded and well-worn Versace stonewashed jeans and a crisp white T-shirt. It was only when she began to pull on the jeans that she realized she had put on a few pounds. Chloe had to struggle to button the now snug denims. She did some leg bends to loosen the fit some before walking over to look at her reflection in the round cheval mirror in the corner of the room. She studied her newly blossomed figure from all angles in the mirror.

Her derriere was definitely more round and her hips more curvaceous, but still slender. She liked it and immediately pushed all thoughts of dieting away.

After pulling her hair into a ponytail, Chloe sat on the end of the bed to slip her bare feet into her sneakers. Moments later she jogged downstairs. "Nana Lil, I'm going down to my house," she called out over her shoulder as she moved toward the front door.

"Chloe!" Lil's shrill yell stopped her in her steps.

When she turned back to peek her head through the front door, it was to find Nana Lil walking out of her bedroom with her orthopedic shoes in her hand. "Wait for me. I wanna see how this house of yours is coming along for myself."

It took just a few moments for her to put on her shoes and get her purse. Chloe helped her up into the SUV before rushing around the front of the truck to hop up into the plush leather driver's seat.

She backed out of the driveway, looking over her left shoulder as she did. "I saw the delivery truck go by with the cabinets and shelves I ordered for my kitchen," she said. Her husky voice was filled with excitement as she steered the vehicle easily. "I can't wait to see them."

Nana Lil smiled in understanding and reached over to lightly pat her hand on the steering wheel. "I just know they're lovely, baby."

Chloe flipped on her left turn signal as she slowed down in front of the site. All of the men were scattered about the property. Some sat on the porch, on the hoods of vehicles, or just on the grass, as they ate the lunches Devon had spoken of. His truck was pulled alongside the delivery truck, and she saw both him and Deshawn conferring with the driver.

She had to admit that the site of Devon was impressive enough, but Deshawn and he standing close together was overwhelming. All three of the men turned in the direction of the SUV as Chloe pulled into the driveway and parked next to his truck.

Nana Lil clapped her hands together in pleasure as she studied the structure through the windshield. "It's already so beautiful and it's huge. I'll have to be sure to visit often so that you're not lonely in that big ol' house of yours."

Chloe smiled. "You're welcome anytime, as long as you promise to bring those lemon cookies of yours that I love so much."

She laughed in pleasure. "That sounds like a plan."

They left the vehicle and walked over to the delivery truck where the men were. The driver and another man were about to unload the crates holding her cabinets and shelves. Devon and Deshawn both looked at their grandmother in surprise.

Deshawn spoke first. "Nana Lil, what are you doing here?"

"Can't an old lady get out of the house? I didn't know I was on house arrest, Shawnie."

Chloe was amazed as always that the old woman could tell them apart, and she seemed to be the only one able to do so. If she wasn't aware what color T-shirt Devon had on, then she wouldn't have been able to tell them apart so quickly. She had to remember to ask Nana Lil how she did it every time.

"Hi fellas." Chloe waved briefly, purposely focusing her eyes on the men at work unfastening the straps that secured their cargo during transit.

She was nervous just being near him, and she became quiet as one of the twins directed the men to carry the boxes into the house and leave them in the kitchen. Nana Lil's constant chatter was not enough to bring Chloe out of her reverie.

Devon had been so close to kissing her; she had seen it in his eyes. She was certain now that he wanted her but he didn't *want* to want her. He had fought the desire to kiss her and then became distant. It wasn't as if she wanted to want him either. She was firmly resolved not to get involved with anyone, but if he had kissed her back on the side of that road she knew she would have gladly given in to the passion. Her body was drawn to him, overruling what her head tried to remind her about getting hurt.

Of course she thought a big part of her "problem" was that she hadn't had intimacy for nearly three years. She was a normal woman with needs. Maybe she had denied herself pure physical pleasure for too long.

But sex had never been uppermost in her mind, not until she met this brooding southern man. Chloe wanted him . . . badly. She considered giving a man her heart the same as giving him the power to hurt her, but what if she gave her body without the heart being involved at all . . . was that the same thing?

Shaking her head, Chloe forced the thoughts out of her head as she noticed that the delivery men were taking the last of the shipment into the house. The twins were standing together, still by the delivery truck laughing at something, and their grandmother was talking to one of the crew members about his ailing aunt.

She was anxious to see the black wrought iron and glass cabinets and shelves that she knew would give the kitchen a unique and modern flare. When she discovered that the California-based company also had a round kitchen table with matching chairs, all made of the same textured glass and rimmed in the same iron as the other pieces, she had immediately ordered one along with some other items she wanted for the house. Those items would not arrive until the house's completion.

Quelling the desire to run into the house and claw the crates open with her nails, she looked over toward Devon when someone touched her elbow lightly. Chloe turned to see the burly, dark-complected driver standing nervously in front of her, an invoice clutched in his hands. "Yes?"

"Excuse me, Miss Bolton, but would you autograph this for me?"

Chloe flashed him her smile and held out her hand for the paper. "Sure, no problem . . . Jaleel." She had paused to read his name off the white label of his striped uniform shirt.

He handed over the paper and a pen from his back pocket, his eyes on her face as she scribbled out a note and signed her first name with flair. "You're even more beautiful in person."

"Thanks, Jaleel."

She handed him the paper and pen back, but he stood there a moment longer. Chloe gave him a friendly but questioning smile.

"I'm sorry for staring." He folded the paper and placed it in his shirt pocket. "Thanks again."

Chloe waved to the men as they hopped back into their truck and reversed out of the yard. Both of the twins were looking in her direction, with Devon frowning considerably.

She fought the urge to childishly stick her tongue out at him, instead walking past them to enter the house. The only thing on her mind at the moment was her cabinets.

Devon had just counted to ten to try to diffuse the anger he felt. Every pair of eyes on the site were focused on Chloe's derriere swishing in a hypnotic motion in those tight jeans she wore.

Why would she wear those things to a site filled with men?

They were all dumbstruck by her. The driver, Jaleel, had been about to drool as he stood looking at her, and she had the nerve to smile, showing every tooth in her pretty head. A pleasurable vision of him putting Chloe over his knee and spanking the seat of those tight jeans for being such a temptress brought a huge grin to his handsome face.

"She really wows 'em, huh?"

Devon turned to look at his brother, who was also wolfishly

eyeing her as she entered the house. "Yeah and she enjoys every minute of it."

Deshawn was about to make some lascivious comment about her "attributes" but Devon walked away before he could. He really wasn't in the mood to hear his twin go off on one of his "Chloe Bolton is a goddess" speeches. Instead he told the men to finish up lunch and get back to work, before walking up the stairs and into the structure.

He heard his Nana Lil's and Chloe's voices echoing throughout the empty house before he reached the kitchen.

"The boys have really done a good job on this house, although I knew they would . . . they always do." The pride in her voice was clearly present.

"I wish one of your boys would hurry up and finish opening these crates so that I can see all of it." Chloe's voice was sardonic and Devon could imagine that left eyebrow of hers arched.

He stopped dead in his tracks when he reached the doorway of the kitchen. Chloe was bending over to look into the crates, her behind up in the air wiggling as she moved about.

How could he help but imagine her in the same position, but naked, with himself standing closely behind her filling her with his hardness?

Shaking off the image, he entered the large kitchen. "Careful of the nails on the crate, Chloe."

She hated the way her insides melted at the sound of her name gliding off his lips. "I am being careful, but please hurry, I want to see if they're as nice as they were in the catalog I ordered them from."

Deshawn and the other crew members began to file into the house. Chloe and Lil moved back out of the way as Devon and an impressively muscular man named Horse used crowbars to finish opening the crates, careful not to break the cargo inside. Soon all four sides were opened and lying on the floor. The packing material had already been removed when Devon and Deshawn inspected the cabinets and shelves to make sure they hadn't been broken.

Chloe walked up close to see them. They were perfect. Already she could imagine them on the walls, filled with her dishes.

"Thanks, Horse." Devon handed his crowbar over to the other man.

"No problem, boss man." The giant of a man took the tools and left the kitchen through the area where the sliding patio doors would be installed.

That left Lil, Devon, Deshawn and Chloe in the kitchen. "Are they as nice as they were in the catalog?" Devon's voice was low and only slightly mocking.

She shivered from the feel of his husky voice so near to her ear. Turning her head she looked over at him. "Nicer."

Their eyes met and held.

Nana Lil's eyes widened in surprise as she watched the two. Her thin lips shaped the letter "O" as things began to crystallize in her head, and she saw something she hadn't even noticed before. She smiled in pleasure. "Shawnie, why don't you show me around this mini-mansion of Chloe's."

Deshawn was yanked out of the kitchen by a surprisingly strong Nana Lil. The sound of her voice echoed throughout the house as she bombarded him with questions.

Chloe and Devon both laughed, finally looking away from each other. "Nana Lil's like a child sometimes with all the questions she asks," Devon said to fill the silence.

Neither was aware that she had purposefully left the two alone. Devon began to clear up the stray packing materials, shoving them into a heavy-duty garbage bag from a box in the corner. Wordlessly, Chloe began to help him and they worked with only the sounds of construction echoing throughout the house.

As he watched her, he wanted to ask Chloe about her breaking down on the side of the road, but he didn't want to pry or to open whatever bad feelings she had been having,

so he left it alone. She bent over again near him to pick up
something. His eyes devoured her, and his hand actually itched
to touch the soft plump derriere she was waving in his direction.

"What possessed you to wear those jeans, Chloe?" He
meant to sound disgusted but instead his voice came out low
and husky.

Chloe stood up and whirled to face him. Self-consciously
she looked down at herself. *They are mighty snug.* "What's
wrong with . . . my jeans?"

Her own voice was indignant until she looked up into his
face and saw the desire in his eyes, causing her voice to trail
off slow and soft.

They were just inches apart. Nervously, her heart hammered
against her chest. She licked her full lips with the tip of her
fleshy tongue. His eyes darted down to watch the innocent,
but nonetheless sexy, move.

He broke.

With a hungry growl, he pulled Chloe to him, dropping
the plastic garbage bag to the floor. All he could say was
"damn," as he lowered his handsome head to taste of the
sweet nectar of her lips.

Initially their kisses were short, breathing in the air between
them after touching their lips together briefly. Devon used his
tongue to lick the tender contours of her mouth and they both
shivered with desire. She was as sweet-tasting and fulfilling
as the juiciest and sweetest fruit. He felt like he could kiss
her for an eternity.

Chloe moved her hands around his narrow waist and down
to grasp his hard buttocks, wanting to touch as much of him
as she could. She felt pleasure when she heard him moan at
the feel of her hands as she massaged him. He deepened the
kiss, wanting and needing more as he drew Chloe's tongue
out to suck on it gently as his hands moved to massage the
fullness of her breasts beneath her T-shirt. Her breasts were
as soft and smooth as he imagined, and he got a rush from

feeling the divine pair in his hands. They were perfect twin peaks of chocolate distraction. Her nipples strained against the thin material as he teased them with his fingertips.

She used her hands to press their lower bodies together, the feel of his length of hardness against her stomach sending wave after delicious wave of pleasure through her body. He was man personified to the littlest detail. Everything there was about a man that women cherished, he contained. The physical power, inner strength and resilience and still, yes, tenderness as he kissed her sweetly, seeming to worship her lips.

The growl he released was barbarian as he offered his tongue to her. She sucked it deeply, as he had done hers.

Sweet Jesus! They both knew it would be good, but not this explosively good.

Devon felt the stickiness of his member against his boxers. He was near a climax just from kissing this beauty in his arms! Chloe felt as though her undergarments were drowning in the moisture he created.

The sound of Nana Lil's voice nearing the kitchen broke them apart, their breathing ragged, hearts racing, mouths still damp from their intense kiss. Chloe felt dizzy from the sudden loss of him, touching her hands to her swollen lips as she watched him walk over to the open space in the wall where the patio doors had yet to be installed.

"I'm sorry, Chloe. That shouldn't have happened. It was a mistake," he said raggedly before walking out of the house.

She didn't feel bereft at his words of regret over what just happened between them. She didn't care, because at that moment she had seen but a glimpse of paradise, and she wanted more. He didn't know he made a very big mistake in allowing them to kiss each other.

When she had told Anika of her growing attraction to the man, her best friend had told her to go for it. And she did. At that moment she decided she wanted Devon in her bed, if not her heart, and she was going to have him.

Nine

Nana Lil's wise eyes took in Chloe's swollen mouth and lazy eyes with a knowing smile. *Well, well, well,* she thought. *My Vonnie and Chloe. Who would've thought it?*

Chloe saw the look the older woman gave her, but said nothing as she pretended to study the cabinets. Now, anytime she used them she would remember the kiss they shared.

Just kissing that man had brought her closer to an earth-shattering climax than any man had with ardent lovemaking. The brother was fierce, and he made her feel even fiercer in her own prowess as she remembered his primal response to her.

"Well Chloe, what in the world are you going to do with a big kitchen?"

Chloe looked over to where Lil was studying the design of the room. "You know, I *can* cook."

She snorted in disbelief. "Sure baby. Hey, I was thinking we would throw something on the grill, maybe even invite over a few friends. Whatcha think?" But before Chloe could answer, Lil started making plans. "We'll have to go to the supermarket and get some things."

Lil dug in her purse and pulled out a small notepad and a pencil. "Here baby, make a list."

She tried to jot down everything the woman said, but Nana Lil was rattling off things so fast that it was a wonder to Chloe that she didn't run out of breath.

"That should do it. Got everything?"

At Chloe's weak nod, Lil took the pad and pen back, shoving them into her purse. "We'll have to work fast. Let's go to the house now and call everyone who's invited. Then we'll pick up Alicia from the office and go to town."

Chloe inwardly cringed at the mention of Alicia's name. She would much prefer to make the twenty-mile ride without Alicia's sour personality, but she loved the older woman and would do anything for her, including spend an afternoon in the company of someone she couldn't stand.

"Well, let's go tell the boys."

Chloe smiled at how fast Nana Lil could move her frail frame. At times the woman seemed to have more energy than a toddler who had eaten a ton of candy. When she did saunter outside, Lil had already informed the twins, and was on her way over to Chloe's SUV. She was on a mission.

Chloe paused on the porch to look over toward where Devon stood about fifty yards away. He was on his cell phone and whomever he was talking to made him smile. His straight, even, white teeth gleamed as the dimple in his cheeks deepened.

He looked up and saw Chloe looking in his direction. Immediately he looked away and turned his back to her. With an arched brow, she left the porch and headed straight for him. Whomever he was talking to, it wasn't a business-related call. Why would he have to walk away from the crew to talk if it was? And as she neared him, the low huskiness of his voice really clinched her beliefs.

Was it Alicia?

Who knew? But it was definitely a woman.

"De-von," she sang loudly in a sweet tone, making sure that whoever was on the phone would surely hear her. "Who are you on the phone with?"

He whirled around, his eyes wide with surprise, or was it shock. "Uh, I'll call you back. Okay . . . bye."

The phone beeped as he disconnected the phone call. "Can I help you with something, Chloe?"

She flashed him *her* smile. "Yeah, I have this itch that needs to be scratched."

Devon watched her with a confused expression. "Huh?"

Chloe laughed as seductively as she could, letting her hand rest lightly on his chest. "I sure hope you're clumsy because I can go for another one of those mistakes of yours."

She leaned in, as if to kiss him, and Devon immediately leaned back. His eyes were dark and stormy, but she honestly didn't know if it was from desire or anger. "Look, Chloe, I don't know what kind of game you're playing, but cut it out. You're acting . . . odd. I'm sorry for pouncing on you in the kitchen, it was a . . ."

She laughed, knowing he started to say "mistake." He quickly changed it up. "It was an act of bad judgment," he said firmly instead.

Chloe straightened and flashed him her smile again. "Yeah, whatever. I'll see you later, Devon."

He watched as she walked away, his eyes dipping down to watch the movement of her hips in those jeans of hers. The sight of her snug in them had driven him so wild earlier that he had to kiss her.

It had been good, too good. Now he wanted more.

And if he wasn't mistaken, Chloe was flirting with him. If she kept that up, how could he deny himself *and* her? He was going to have to keep his distance from her.

What was she up to anyway?

Sighing, Devon dug in his back pocket to retrieve the number he had gotten from Poochie earlier. He walked over to where Deshawn was measuring something on the porch. "Someone told me to give you this."

Deshawn closed the measuring tape he was using and reached for the slip of paper his brother was handing him. "Who gave you this?"

Devon sat down on one of the steps. "Poochie from Donnie's."

He thought of the thickly framed girl with the light complexion and pretty face. "Oh yeah?" He trailed off in pleasure.

Devon nodded. "Yup."

"That girl has got a body on her!"

Devon agreed. "She sure does. You gonna call her?"

Deshawn looked at his twin like he was crazy. "Does a dog chase cats?"

Devon laughed, the sound of his voice deep. "A girl like that will have you *wide* open."

"I wouldn't give a damn, if it's as good as it looks."

People were everywhere, on the lawn, on the porch, in the backyard, and the music blaring from Deshawn's portable radio mingled in the air with their voices. Battery-operated outdoor lights hung from the trees to give off more illumination as the sun began to descend. Three tables were set up, laden with food, beside the driveway next to the huge barbecue pit. Nana Lil, with Alicia's help, had really gone all out with potato salad, tuna salad, catfish stew, corn on the cob, baked beans, deviled eggs, garden salad with homemade vinaigrette, lemon meringue pie, strawberry shortcake and sliced melons. The twins had grilled the ribs, steaks and chicken to perfection.

Chloe sipped on a cup of limeade punch where she sat on the front porch. Her eyes never strayed far from Devon, and several times she would find him looking at her as well. She could still remember the look on his face when she first joined the party, walking outside onto the front porch. His eyes had lit upon her, his mouth open in what could only be surprise.

She had been pleased because she put a lot of time into her appearance. After a long bath this afternoon, she had massaged mousse and gel into her hair, causing it to dry into a mass of curly and crimped hair that surrounded her face. The silk white sun dress she wore was a Donna Karan and maybe too dressy for the simple barbecue in the yard, but she wanted to draw his attention. She wasn't aware that she drew nearly every other man's attention at the party as well.

The halter top of the dress clung to her bare breasts, tying around her slender waist before falling in drapes with a full skirt around her knees. Strappy white sandals completed the outfit with a full makeup job that took her thirty minutes to complete.

The reaction on his face had been well worth all the effort!

Devon hefted the platter of raw meat, covered by aluminum foil, up into his arms and took the walkway around the house. He entered the kitchen through the back entrance, stopping in surprise at finding Chloe already there, leaning against the counter, eating. "Hi Chloe," he said, purposefully keeping himself from looking directly at her. "Why are you eating in here?"

Chloe wiped her mouth with a paper napkin, careful not to remove too much of her lipstick or foundation. "I felt like everyone was staring at me."

Devon laughed as he slid the platter onto a cleared shelf in the refrigerator. "The way you scarf down food I can see why you wouldn't want an audience."

"I don't scarf down food," she balked, rolling up her soiled paper napkin to throw at him playfully.

He dodged the ball and caught it easily with one hand, throwing it into the trash can near the door. "You're not good at baseball. Better stick to your day job."

"Ha ha. I don't have a day job anymore, remember." Chloe sat her plate on the counter and turned to wash the greasy liquid from the barbecued chicken off her fingers.

Devon gave in and let his eyes trail from her long shapely legs to her curvaceous hips, over the smooth caramel of her back and shoulders. Damn, she looked good!

She turned and caught his eyes on her, just before he

quickly looked away. *You can run but you can't hide.* "Devon, would you pass me a beer please?"

His eyes widened in shock. "Since when do you drink beer?" he asked as he opened the fridge and got out the beer, along with one for himself.

"I drink beer," she said indignantly.

"I would've thought you were more of a Moët drinker myself." He twisted off the top and walked over to hand her the bottle.

"You know, before I was rich and famous I grew up in the Bronx, lower middle class in a small two-bedroom apartment with my mother." She took a sip of the cold beer. "I wasn't always able to afford Moët, or even Alizé for that matter, Devon."

He nodded, digesting the info. "I never thought of it like that."

"That's okay."

They were companionably silent for a few seconds. "Your hair's different," he said. "I like it that way."

"Thanks, Devon." Chloe looked up into his obsidian eyes. "I thought you would. That's why I did it this way."

"For me?" he asked doubtfully.

She nodded. "And the dress. Do you like it?" She spun in front of him, causing the dress to rise up like a parasol around her waist, showing the skimpy black thong she wore underneath.

Devon's loins flamed with desire. "Chloe." His voice, deep and resonant, was like a warning as he watched her tease him.

Not to be deterred, Chloe placed the beer on the counter next to her plate and stepped closer to him. "And the perfume. It's Trésor by Lancôme. I bought it today. You like?"

"Chloe, what are you up to?" His voice was tight as he fought for control.

She laughed huskily and leaned back to look up into his warm eyes. "I told you before, I want my—"

Nana Lil walked into the kitchen from the front hall and

they jumped apart. She smiled. "Didn't know you two were in here. Just need some more salad dressing. Excuse me for interrupting."

"You weren't interrupting anything, Nana." Devon's voice was strained.

"No, nothing at all, Nana Lil," Chloe piped in.

Lil stooped to get a bottle of her homemade vinaigrette from the door of the refrigerator. She pulled air between her teeth and shot them a knowing look. "Yeah right, whatever."

She left the kitchen. "Carry on," her voice floated back into the kitchen before they heard the front door firmly close behind her.

"I have to get back to Angela," he said, reminding them both of his date, who was probably outside looking for him.

Chloe nodded slowly. "Okay but while you're with Angela . . . think about this."

She stepped back close to him and wrapped her arms around his neck, pulling his head toward her. With deliberate slowness, she licked his lips and pressed her body into his. Moaning, he deepened the kiss and took the lead as he let his hands cradle her waist, before lifting the skirt to massage the softness of her buttocks.

"I want you, Devon Jamison," she moaned against his lips before moving away reluctantly. She left the kitchen through the back door without another word, leaving him totally stunned.

The night deepened in color and only a few guests had taken their leave. Chloe was glad Alicia had finally headed home. She had a feeling the woman just couldn't stand to see Devon with another woman. It didn't bother Chloe one bit; it was an obvious ploy on his part to try to distance himself from her. In all the weeks she had been living in the house she had never heard or seen or accepted a phone call from *any* woman, especially anyone named Angela. It was as if the woman just appeared from nowhere. Who cared? Just because he danced with the woman and sat next to her to eat, his eyes remained on Chloe. She made sure of that.

Anytime she found him looking at her, she would blow him kisses, lick her lips, lift her skirt to show the long, shapely expanse of her leg, or shake her breasts at him.

No one else noticed because she stood off from everyone else by her SUV in the driveway. It offered the perfect cover from everyone . . . but Devon. A couple of times he smiled or raised his drink in a toast to her performance.

Devon promised himself that he would think real seriously on that idea of spanking Chloe after she pulled another one of her tricks and blew him a kiss. She was so hidden behind that damn big SUV of hers that only he seemed able to see her from where he stood by the tall hedges.

"Devon? De-von!"

He brought his attention back to his date. She was looking at him with darts to kill in her eyes. He hadn't spoken in months to the petite beauty he used to date sporadically, but he had invited her to the barbecue tonight to help him resist the desire he had for Chloe. It wasn't working. "Yes Angie?"

She rolled her eyes and stood to gather her purse from the bench where she sat. "Do me a favor, huh?"

He glanced over her head to where Chloe was sucking on her index finger. "Huh Chloe . . . I mean Angie."

Angela punched him in the chest. "Did you just call me Chloe?"

Devon laughed guiltily. "No baby. Hell no," he denied.

"Go to hell, Devon." She marched off from him and climbed into her VW Cabrio, reversing out of the yard with an angry squeal of tires against asphalt.

He didn't even try to stop her. Setting his beer bottle down on the bench, he strolled over to where Chloe was . . . or had been anyway. When he reached the other side of her SUV, he didn't see her anywhere. Where did she go that quickly?

Chloe walked into the house through the back door and raced up the stairs. She paused at Devon's door before walking in on impulse. Boldly she stepped out of her thong bikinis and left them on his pillow before leaving the room. She dashed up the rest of the stairs to her room.

Once there she untied the straps of the dress around her waist and neck, letting the dress fall to a silky white puddle around her feet. Kicking off her sandals, she climbed naked into bed and waited for the barbecue to end. Her center was wet with anticipation and she only hoped Devon was as ready as she was, because there was no turning back now!

"Praise God for paper plates and aluminum pans," Nana Lil said as she threw the pan that had held the barbecued meats into the heavy-duty garbage bag.

It was ten o'clock and the last of their guests had finally left. Lil had gladly separated the remainder of the leftover food among the guests to take home with them. Neither she nor the boys cared for leftovers.

Deshawn rolled the huge barbecue pit back into the back-yard, freshly cleaned by him. He placed it under the heavy tarp back in the small storage house. Devon followed behind him holding two of the folded tables above his head with strength.

"Shawn, get that last table for me?" He put them against the wall of the storage house and covered them with tarp also, leaving it rolled up for Deshawn to put the last table next to them.

He walked up onto the back portion of the wraparound porch. Leaning down, he kissed his grandmother's cheek. "Go to bed, Nana Lil. I know that's where I'm headed. Everything's in order."

She nodded and leaned over the railing to dump the filled garbage bag into the large plastic trash can next to the bottom step. "Anyone see Chloe?"

"She went upstairs earlier and never came back down." Deshawn walked up with the table on his strong shoulders. "Probably sleeping.

Or hiding, Devon thought as he followed Lil into the house.

"Dev, I'm going to Charlie's. Wanna ride with me?" Deshawn called out as he closed the door of the small storage house.

Devon shook his head from inside the kitchen, standing at the door. "I'm gonna turn in early."

"All right, but don't be mad tomorrow if I win all the money. You know how it is on a Friday night." Deshawn climbed into his truck and pulled out of the yard.

Devon closed the door and locked it. He turned off the lights downstairs and called out good night to his grandmother before climbing the stairs. Just before he walked into his bedroom, he looked over his shoulder to the short flight of stairs leading to Chloe's attic room. The lights were out. He shook his head as he thought of her antics before he entered his room.

In the darkness, he undressed and climbed into bed naked, as was customary for him, not even seeing the underwear until he turned onto his side and laid his face on the pillow. The sweet, intimate scent of a woman surrounded him. The softness of the silk touched his nose and cheek. Sitting up, he reached over and turned on the light. He was startled to see the lacy black thong. It was the same one *she* had on tonight.

She'd been in his room and left them . . . unless she was still in here. Grabbing up the underwear he checked the entire suite, not finding her anywhere. *What kind of game was she playing?*

Sinking down on the foot of the bed, he lifted the panties

close to his face and inhaled deeply. The mix of perfume and her womanly scent intoxicated him. His malehood hardened between his legs, standing tall, heavy and erect against his stomach.

She was trying to drive him crazy!

"Why settle for those when you can have the real . . . thing?"

Startled, he dropped the panties and looked up to see Chloe standing above him. He hadn't even heard her come into his bedroom. The sheer white lacy teddy she wore pushed him beyond the brink of control, and with a hungry growl he pulled her down, lowering her to the bed beneath him.

Ten

Chloe's heart nearly burst with success as Devon opened her legs with his knees and lay his naked body on top of her. She let her hands caress the sculptured definitions of his back as he kissed her with passion and pressed his lengthy hardness onto her body. She felt lightheaded and breathless from his seduction.

Devon lost all rationality on why this was all wrong, with Chloe writhing beneath him in his bed. His hands held her face as he kissed every inch of it, finally letting his mouth rest on top of hers, open and waiting. With deliberate slowness he sucked her lips, enjoying her moan of pleasure, before he plunged his tongue into the sweet warmth.

Their tongues danced between them, lightly touching and dipping away, enjoying the teasing game. It was erotic and drove them both wild. Wanting him to taste more, Chloe pushed him off of her onto his back and slowly got off the bed.

She was glad the lights were on as her eyes devoured the sight of his hardness. Lightly she gasped in shock as he massaged the length of himself in a hypnotic rhythmic motion as he watched her strip out of the teddy.

Pleased at his sharp intake of breath at seeing her totally bared of clothing, Chloe lay on the bed next to him, their eyes never parting. She pulled him back on top of her with a delicious sigh.

Devon kissed her quickly before moving to nuzzle her neck, sucking on the hollow there, inhaling her sweet scent, leaving telltale love marks. Down he moved to taste her breasts, reveling in the tightness of the nipples he dreamed of. Enthralled by them, he lightly gripped one with his hand and licked lightly at the bud with the tip of his tongue. He looked up at her to gauge her reaction, pleased to see her head thrown back in pleasure and her eyes closed as she whispered his name in passion.

Moaning, he closed his mouth over the nipple, hot and wet as she arched her back and used her hands to press his head closer to her.

"God yes, Devon," she moaned. "Please . . . don't stop."

He did as she demanded, wanting to please her, and he took as much of the tasty full breast as he could into his mouth. Her hips arched upward nearly knocking him off of her. "You like that, Chloe?" he asked hotly, his eyes enjoying the sight of her face rapt with delectation.

Bringing his other hand up, Devon held both of her breasts, moving back and forth between them with his tongue, sucking and nipping the buds the way she begged him to. He moved to lie on the side of her, using one of his hands to move her left leg open over his hip. He slid one arm beneath her head to reach for her right nipple, teasing it between massaging the full globe. With his other hand he played in the curly hairs between her luscious thighs, before moving down to touch her slick, wet core.

"Damn it's wet, Chloe," he moaned against her breast. It throbbed beneath his fingers as he massaged it deeply.

Chloe's moans were loud and rough in the quiet of the room. The combination of him tasting one breast, fondling the other and teasing the bud of her womanhood was driving her mindless with passion.

"Touch me Chloe," he begged, moving his head to suck her neck as he continued to drive her insane with his touches.

She reached down and took him into her hand, using the

same rhythmic motion she saw him use on himself earlier. She reveled in the feel of the hot and hard throbbing mass in her hands. He strained his hips off the bed toward the pleasure she brought him. He growled in the rawest of pleasure.

"Damn," he swore loudly, feeling his own release nearing. "No baby, no more. It's too soon."

She pushed him onto his back and moved to lick a trail from his ankles, to kiss behind his knees, up to trace her tongue on his muscled thighs. She only rubbed her face against his hardness and moved to stick her tongue deeply into his navel.

He bucked in pleasure.

Chloe licked the contours of his muscled abdomen, letting her full hanging globes tease his hardness as she did. Up she moved to taste his nipples, and his hands shot up to hold her head, letting his fingers tangle in the wavy tresses of her hair as he massaged her scalp. "Suck my chest," he begged hoarsely.

And she did, missing not one inch with her mouth nor her tongue.

She moved on to suck his neck and Devon let his hand move over her body, massaging her back and shoulders, groping the fullness of her buttocks. Wanting him to touch her core again, she put her knees down on each side of his hips. "Touch me," she begged urgently against his nipple.

As soon as his fingers felt the hot wetness, Devon moaned and rolled her beneath him. In return he tasted every inch of her body, even her toes. When he moved to kneel between her open legs, Chloe held her breath in anticipation. Would he? God, she hoped so!

And he did.

Devon used his fingers to open the brown lips, exposing the pink fleshy bud to him. Lightly he licked it with his tongue and Chloe quivered in pleasure, her hands clutching the pillow she lay on, her hair spread like a halo around her head.

"Feel good?" he asked, his voice deep and husky and showing the effects of their passion.

She nodded anxiously, unable to form words. He laughed huskily and took the bud into his mouth. He lay flat on the bed between her legs as he suckled the very essence of her desire. He pleased them both in the rawest of passionate acts. Over and over she moaned his name in a voice she didn't even recognize as her own, flinging her head back and forth in abandonment.

The feeling got so good that she tried to move away from him, but Devon used his arms to wrap around her thighs, locking her in place as he growled and used all of his tongue to wildly please her. He laughed again at how she bucked beneath him. He knew he was pleasing her the way she deserved. The way he had dreamed of pleasing her for many nights.

So aroused was she that she grabbed her own breasts and massaged them, teasing the hard nipples with her own fingertips. Devon's head exploded with wanting her. Never had he had a woman so free and uninhibited in his bed. He wanted to give her release. He wanted to taste of it, knowing it was as sweet as ambrosia.

Devon sucked Chloe's bud, the scent of her heady. Her body went still and then she began to tremble and he knew that soon he would taste of her nectar. He watched her closely, his mouth filled with her, as her eyes widened in shock and pleasure. She moved her hands from her breasts to his head, pushing him to her.

"I'm coming," she gasped, lifting her hips off the bed toward his mouth.

He did not relent, even as she bucked wildly beneath him. Her sweet nectar exploded and he sucked deeply, not missing a drop! Her release went on for long, earth-shattering moments until she moaned and whimpered like a baby.

"Was it good, baby?" He asked unnecessarily.

Chloe nodded and pulled him up to lay between her legs.

He kissed her deeply and she tasted herself on his lips and tongue.

"I need you, Chloe," he moaned as he moved his hand to remove the condom he got out of his dresser from its package. Watching him roll the prophylactic down his hard length pushed her further over the edge. She whimpered as he slid his hands beneath her to lift her hips. With one deft stroke he entered her. They both gasped in pleasure from the connection.

Devon became still. "Chloe, it's so tight, baby," he moaned against her neck, his eyes closed as he tried to adjust to the feel of her sheath around him.

She writhed beneath him and Devon gave in, stroking his hardness inside of her like they both wanted so badly. He moved so deftly and with such strength that the bed squeaked beneath them, but neither cared.

Over and over they moaned each other's name, as Chloe moved beneath him in one united rhythm.

Devon used his hips to stroke the sweet sides of her before stroking back up the middle. She was so perfectly snug around him. His heart pounded and nothing but thoughts of pleasing her was on his mind, and it showed in his actions.

He lifted his head up from her neck and looked down into her eyes, cloudy with passion.

She moaned as she flicked her tongue against his lips.

Sweat drenched them as his strokes became deeper, stronger and faster. "I can't hold back, baby," he moaned against her lips as he gave into his own powerful release.

He growled like a bear, stroking her as his climax filled her with each spasm. His release went on for long moments, and Chloe continued to move her hips up off the bed, even as he hoarsely begged her not to. Finally spent, Devon kissed her fully on the lips before moving to lie on his back. He pulled her to lie in his arms, still enjoying the feel of her body next to his. His heart hammered against his chest and he felt hers doing the same.

Chloe shut her eyes, snuggling closer to him as she let her leg drape over his. Never had she felt so satisfied in her life. She had been blind with passion. She knew it would be good . . . but *that* damn good . . . never!

They both said "Damn" before falling into a deep and exhausted sleep in each other's arms.

Eleven

Chloe smiled into her morning cup of tea, nearly two weeks after their first explosive night of passion together. She was still feeling the physical effects of their lovemaking last night in the bathtub. Even now she felt herself wet with desire as she thought of the fervor they shared in each other's arms every night.

They shared the most incredibly satisfying intimacy ever.

But she was still dealing with Calvin's betrayal and Devon had Elissa. Chloe felt no jealousy for the woman Devon had once loved. Nana Lil had been the one to tell her about the woman. She remembered the conversation well.

Chloe's house would be finished by the deadline, and she had asked Nana Lil to ride with her to Hilton Head Island. She wanted to stock up on linens, dishes and other necessities for the house. She had discovered that Hilton Head catered to wealthier society more so than Charleston did, and she was sure to find the top quality products she wanted. And she had. Her checking account nearly two thousand dollars smaller and her SUV filled with packages, Chloe and Nana Lil headed home late in the afternoon.

"You know, Elissa would've loved to be your friend," Nana Lil said suddenly.

"Elissa?" Chloe asked as she slipped her Dolce & Gabana shades on to cut the glare of the sun through the windshield.

"She's Devon's ex-girlfriend," Lil said so matter-of-factly

as she used the electronic controls on the door to adjust the seat until her small thin frame was comfortable.

Chloe nearly ran off the road. Of course, Devon had had girlfriends. That was not anything to fret about. But instinctively she knew there was more to the story surrounding Elissa than any other woman Devon had dated. "Why would you say that, Nana Lil?"

"Elissa would've loved going with you to all those stores with those expensive things." Nana Lil looked over at Chloe. "I mean really, Chloe, thirty dollars for one plate? I don't care if it is rimmed in eighteen-karat gold."

Chloe was patient with her as the older woman switched gears on her, speaking of the Ralph Lauren flatware and linens she had purchased. "Anyway, like I was saying, going to all those stores and whipping out your credits cards or checkbook and buying whatever you want without blinking an eye. And all those people recognizing you and asking for autographs and pictures. Elissa would've *loved* that because she was always putting on airs like she could and would do those things. That's why Devon broke up with her snooty behind. You can't take a steak-and-potatoes man and make him . . ." She turned to Chloe. "What's that we had for lunch?"

She smiled as she drove. "Lobster caesar salad with avocado, asparagus, basil croutons and lobster coral dressing."

"Well that." Lil sniffed. "Do you know I overheard him tell Shawnie that she wouldn't even let him kiss her after she put on her makeup, and that she always had to be on top so that her hair wouldn't get messed up."

Chloe laughed at the face Lil made. "I don't know about this Elissa, but I'll take steak and potatoes any day."

Lil gave her a serious and hard look. "You're not like Elissa. You have what she wanted and don't even flaunt it. She wanted what you have, but didn't have it and wanted to pretend like she did. She expected Vonnie to do the same thing." Lil sighed. "No, you're not like Elissa, but remember that it might take Vonnie a little while to realize that."

Chloe remembered she had asked her what she meant, but Lil had just given her a look that said, "Ask me no questions and I'll tell you no lies."

As remnants of that conversation faded into the distance one phrase stuck out. *No, you're not like Elissa, but remember that it might take Vonnie a little while to realize that.*

Chloe stood up from the table and moved to the sink to wash her cup and saucer. "Elissa had hurt Devon and Calvin hurt me," she said aloud softly to herself as she rinsed the dishes and set them in the dish rack on the counter. "Neither one of us wants to be hurt again."

Although their late night rendezvous were getting to be habit forming, the secrecy of sneaking to his suite once everyone was in bed only heightened the experiences they'd shared. They both had agreed it would be best to keep what went on between them private. The town was full of gossip-mongers and, frankly, it wasn't anyone's business.

The house was quiet. The twins were down working on the house with their crew, of course. She had dropped Nana Lil off to her friends to finish a quilt they were working on together, and Alicia was over in the office.

She had just settled on the couch in the living room to start a new hardcover by Terry McMillan when the doorbell rang. Setting the book on the chair, she rose to answer it. Chloe groaned audibly when she saw the résumé clutched in the plump elderly woman's hand standing before her.

"Hello Ms. Bolton. My name is Maddie Connors."

Chloe's hazel eyes widened as the woman rushed to speak before Chloe could even open her mouth. She talked so quickly that her words seemed to run together. "I know they said you were turning away all the people who've been here so far, but I thought I'd try anyway. If you'd just read my résumé and references, you'll see how qualified I am as a housekeeper and cook."

The woman paused to take a deep breath, her voluminous

chest heaving up and down with the effort beneath her "I Love S.C." T-shirt.

Chloe gave the woman a friendly smile. "I'm sorry Mrs. . . ." She looked down at the résumé. "Mrs. Connors. There's been a mistake, just like I've explained to the other twelve women who've stopped by this week. I'm not in need of the services of either a housekeeper or a cook."

Madeline's plump face became confused. "But Alicia—"

"Alicia?" Chloe cut the other woman off. Her voice hardened.

She nodded, looking crestfallen. "Yes, Alicia said you asked her to put an ad in the paper for help because you couldn't boil water and had never cleaned a day in your life. I guess we thought we would get a jump on the position before it was advertised."

Chloe breathed deeply, trying not to direct the anger she felt at this innocent pawn in Alicia's game. She forced a smile to her lips. "I'm sorry Mrs. Connors. Alicia was mistaken, but if I change my mind I will consider you."

Madeline stomped her foot in anger. "I don't know why I listened to that girl. Ever since she was a little girl she's told a lie quicker than a gnat can lick his own ass!" She cut her round eyes over toward the office building, where she knew Alicia was. "Ms. Bolton, you have a good day and I'm sorry about the mix-up. I feel foolish coming here."

Chloe felt sorry for her. "Would you like to come in for a cup of tea, Mrs. Connors?"

The woman shook her head and turned back to look at Chloe. "No, but thanks for offering. I best be getting on home now. My ride's waiting. Good-bye."

Chloe watched as the woman walked down the steps and got into the passenger seat of an old, battered pickup truck. She waved as the truck passed on the road. Before it was out of sight she was already marching with long angry strides over to the office.

Alicia initially looked surprised when Chloe stormed in,

slamming the door behind her. The woman's expression turned to one of pure dislike.

"Why are you telling people that I'm hiring a cook and housekeeper?" She put her hands on the woman's desk and leaned down in her face, her voice cold with an angry edge to it.

Alicia leaned back in her chair from the anger she saw. "I didn't tell anyone that. I could care less what you do down that road," she said flippantly, her voice showing more bravado than she actually felt.

"Liar," Chloe shouted. "Mrs. Connors just told me you told her that."

Alicia shrugged. "I didn't."

"You know what, just keep my name out of your mouth," Chloe warned her, her hazel eyes stormy green with fury.

Spitefully, Chloe looked her over behind the desk, from the disastrous bob haircut to the pink hued makeup on her pecan complexion to the bulky sweatsuit she wore to hide her disproportionate shape. She felt like offering her a free copy of one of her beauty books.

Her eyes showed disapproval at what she saw. "You really should use the extra time you have to talk about me to do something with yourself. You look a mess. Maybe Devon *might* pay you more attention if you'd pay some to yourself."

Alicia stiffened in anger and embarrassment. Tight-lipped, she snarled, "I guess you think he wants you. All your money and fame, Ms. High and Mighty Supermodel, wouldn't make Devon want you!"

Chloe started to tell her just how much Devon wanted her, but instead said mockingly, "I'm not the one lusting undercover for him, you are!"

She turned and walked to the door, "Just remember, you little dwarf, keep my name out of your mouth or I'll fill it with a slap."

She slammed the door after she stepped out of the office, missing the hate-filled daggers Alicia's eyes threw at her.

Filled with embarrassment and anger, Alicia jerked back her chair from the desk and stalked over to Deshawn's work area to snatch down the calendar. Viciously, she tore it to shreds, wishing she could get the real version out of her life just as easily.

Chloe walked back over to the house, still seething in anger. She wanted to yell out in frustration. She had never done anything to that idiot, so why did the woman instantly dislike her? Her mother had taught her not to begrudge the next person anything. If she wanted the same, then get out and work for it. It was insane to hate someone because they had money.

She went in the house and retrieved her novel, resolved not to let that woman's venom ruin her day. She gently swung on the porch swing as she read. The sun was up, but the weather wasn't very hot. A nice breeze drifted by every so often, offering a refreshing reprieve from the warmth. She finally became so engrossed in the novel that she didn't break in her reading for a solid two hours, and only then because she heard Alicia's car door slam.

Chloe's mouth widened in amazement when the woman childishly flipped her the bird as she backed out of the yard. Maliciously, she hoped the woman backed her car into one of the ditches running alongside the road, but then she changed her mind. Sometimes the bad people wished on others came back on them two-fold.

Her stomach growled in hunger and she realized how the hours had passed. Folding the page of the book where she had stopped reading, Chloe closed the book and went into the house. She had just finished making a sandwich from the leftover ham Nana Lil cooked last night when she heard the front door open and close.

In a flash Devon strode down the hallway to the kitchen, took the saucer and glass of lemonade out of her hand and set them on the counter. With a devilish smile he pulled her slowly into his arms.

Chloe laughed huskily in surprise, very happy to see him and be near him. "Hello there."

His response was a low growl as he captured her lips with a full kiss that shook her in her shoes. He deepened the kiss and captured her tongue to suckle. She was breathless when it ended, her eyes glazed and lazy with released desire.

"Nana Lil went for her quilt making?" he asked, his voice hoarse as he massaged the small of her back.

"Where's Deshawn?" she asked huskily, nodding in response to his question as she rubbed her hips into him.

"He went to see if Poochie could get off work early." They kissed again, brief but satisfying. "I don't see her car. Did Alicia go to lunch?"

"A few minutes ago."

"So we're all alone."

"Uh-huh!"

"Let's go!"

He smacked her soundly on the behind as she ran past him to fly up the stairs to his room. He was right on her heels. She was already stripping out of the ecru embroidered peasant dress she wore, letting her wedges fly as she kicked them off.

Devon quickly undressed as well, his eyes never leaving Chloe. "I've been thinking of you all morning, Chloe."

Naked, she climbed onto the bed. "Yeah?" she asked playfully.

He nodded and climbed between her open legs. Already the scent of her desire was in the air and driving him wild. He took a hard nipple into his mouth and she arched her back for more.

Chloe was hot with desire, but not crazy. "Why . . . are . . . you . . . home . . . so . . . early?" she asked breathlessly, reaching over to his night stand to remove a condom. With ease, she removed it from its wrapper and sheathed him.

Devon lifted one of her long shapely legs and put it around his waist, with Chloe wordlessly lifting the other. "I've got a surprise for you."

"What?"

"Later, Chloe."

"What's my surprise, Devon?" she whined.

"Later," he moaned against the soft chocolate globes. "I've got something else for you now."

"What's that?"

"This." He entered her and they became lost in the passion.

Chloe rolled her sweat-drenched body off of Devon. Her heart raced from their lovemaking. She looked at him where he lay sprawled on his back, his eyes closed as he breathed raggedly through his mouth.

"We have the most incredible sex, Devon," she gasped, reaching down to pull the sheet over their naked bodies.

He moaned in response, already beginning to fall asleep.

Chloe laid her head against his sweat-dampened shoulder. Soon she felt herself drifting into an exhausted slumber as well. Suddenly she sat up in the bed, the sheet falling around her waist, baring her breasts.

How could I forget? She shook him. "Dev . . . Dev! Wake up."

Devon opened one eye and looked up at her. "What?"

"My surprise, what is it?"

He stretched his tall muscular frame in the bed. "All right, all right. Get dressed."

Chloe hopped out of bed with more energy than she had a few seconds ago. She gathered up her clothes into her arms, carrying them with her toward the bathroom.

Devon looked at her in surprise. "Where are you going?"

She looked back with a saucy wink. "To take a shower. Coming?"

His eyes took in her curved naked form and hurried to jerk off the jeans he had just put on. "No doubt."

* * *

Thirty minutes later Chloe climbed into the cab of Devon's pickup beside him. He headed in the direction of her property and Chloe looked at him in confusion. Moments later he turned into her driveway and she gasped in surprise. A large red bow was on the front of the house and she knew without him saying that the house was complete.

She turned and faced Devon, the pleasure evident in her face. "It wasn't supposed to be completed for another two weeks."

Devon said nothing at first, moving to get out of the truck. Chloe followed and did the same, coming to walk beside him. "Deshawn and I put in a lot of extra time with a couple of men from the crew. It was just a matter of getting the painters, plumbers and electricians in earlier than originally scheduled to finish up their parts of the job."

It was perfect and Chloe loved it instantly, just as she had when the architect took her ideas and returned to her with this unique design on paper. Now this sprawling one-level structure was a reality.

Devon touched her elbow lightly. "Come on, let's go inside."

He moved to walk into the house, but Chloe stopped him with a soft touch of her hand on his back. He turned, a questioning look on his handsome face. She flung herself at him, wrapping her arms tightly around his neck. Leaning back, she looked up into his face. "How can I thank you for building my and my mother's dream house?" she asked, her voice whisper soft.

Devon saw the hint of tears in the hazel depths and pulled her slender frame closer to him. Feeling she needed her spirits lifted, he joked, "Your cashier's check for payment will be thanks enough."

He was rewarded by the muffled sounds of her laughter where her head was buried in his neck.

* * *

Deshawn followed Poochie's voluptuous figure into the small brick house where she lived with her mother. The interior of the house was cluttered and messy with the stagnant smell of uncirculated air. Clothes were strewn everywhere, and they literally had to walk over them to get to her bedroom.

It was not in any better a state. The sheer curtains at the windows were dingy with old age, and dust layered as a film against the windows. The lilac and pink decor was hidden by the piles of clothes on the rocker and the print rug in the middle of the floor. Dishes with hardened remnants of food were piled on her nightstand.

The room looked like a hurricane had blown through it.

But Deshawn saw none of this as she used an arm to swipe the clothes off her bed to float in the air like confetti before sinking to the floor. His attention was entirely focused on her climbing onto the middle of the bed, not even noticing the dingy sheets.

She smiled and turned onto her knees with her full behind up in the air in his direction, her sneakered feet hanging off the bed. Laughing huskily, she hitched her short jean skirt around her waist, exposing the thin white thong bikini she wore.

Deshawn whistled. "Damn, girl."

Poochie lowered herself down onto her elbows. Reaching behind her, she lightly patted her buttocks. "Come and get it," she purred, pulling the thong material to the side with a long taloned finger painted bright fuchsia.

Her idea of foreplay was none at all. Deshawn discovered that the first time he took her to bed, the night of their first date . . . one week ago.

She had blown his mind . . . among other things!

She was younger than he by four years, but in the time since they started cavorting she had taught him a few things in bed, and that was saying a lot. Ah, who knew an ice cube could work such wonders?

Devon had been right to warn him. Poochie did have his

nose wide open. The woman was a clawing, scratching, licking, growling tigress in bed . . . or in the car . . . or on the diner's kitchen floor.

Chloe was a rare jewel to be treasured and dreamed of, but Poochie . . . well, she was a very soft and very willing reality. Deshawn unzipped his jeans, releasing his hardened member. He didn't even lower his pants; Poochie liked it that way.

After rolling a latex condom onto his hard length he walked behind her, putting both of his hands on the softness of her derriere and guiding himself into her wetness with one hard thrust from behind. Oh yes, Poochie was his very willing and eager reality.

Alicia parked her car behind Chloe's expensive SUV, tempted to run into the back of it. She knew if she did that she couldn't afford the repairs if she was discovered, so she withdrew the idea. Alicia walked into the office. She still boiled with anger from her earlier confrontation with Chloe.

Had she been so obvious with her love for Devon that Chloe had noticed? Who else suspected?

"I hate her," she muttered as the lunch of roast beef and mashed potatoes threatened to purge. She had to admit that the woman had surprised her with her forthrightness. Never would Alicia have thought that Chloe Bolton had that much spunk. She thought the twig would have really clawed her eyes out!

"Maybe Devon might pay you more attention, if you'd pay some to yourself."

Alicia pulled out the round compact from her pocketbook, opening it to look at her reflection. She saw what she always saw, surely not as bad as Chloe had put it.

Would she tell Devon?

She could see the woman doing it just out of spite. Alicia knew she couldn't allow that. Closing the compact, she leaned back in her chair, thinking. What if she went to Devon first and told him Chloe had picked a fight with her and said hateful and spiteful things. Devon's opinion of the woman should help him believe what she would tell him, plus he was *her* best friend. Surely he would pick her side against that walking skeleton?

Resolved to tell him as soon as possible, Alicia grabbed her purse and left the office. She would go to the site and tell him immediately. Then maybe she'd invite him over for dinner, and well . . . who knows? Tonight might be the night for her to finally make her move on Devon. Waiting for him to do so was driving her insane.

Alicia got into her car and soon was headed left toward Chloe's house. She pumped the brakes, slowing the car down. Only Devon's midnight blue truck was parked in the yard. There was no sight of any of the other crew members, not even Deshawn. She then remembered they were rushing to finish the house before schedule, and judging by the bow on the front of the house and the lack on any work being done, they must have accomplished that goal. But they didn't tell her they would be finished today.

The flash of someone walking by the living room window caught her eye. *Probably Devon,* she thought as she turned her car onto the driveway, the engine of the car loud and grinding.

Another figure walked past the window and she saw that whoever it was, was definitely slimmer in build and slightly shorter than Devon. At first she assumed it was a member of the crew. Who else could it be?

A scream of disbelief froze in Alicia's throat, and her eyes widened as she slammed on the brakes. Her stiff body jerked forward against the steering wheel. From where her car was, just a few feet away from the house, she could clearly see that it was Devon . . . and Chloe!

And at that moment he was kissing her with the same intensity and fervor that Alicia prayed he would one day show her. She watched them, filled with pain, her hands clutching the steering wheel as Devon unbuttoned Chloe's dress and lowered his head to capture one of her exposed breasts in his mouth.

Alicia's throat tightened in raw pain and shock as tears blurred her vision.

Tears of unrequited love.

Tears of pain.

Tears of disbelief.

Tears of embarrassment.

Tears of pure hatred . . . for Chloe.

Unable to take any more of seeing her worst fears shown real, she jerked the car into reverse with stiff movements. Her entire body shook, tears streaming down her cheeks. Alicia pulled off down the road at an alarming speed, trying to outrun the scene she just left, but failing miserably. Forever the sight of Chloe in Devon's arms would be etched, like a hot branding iron, into her memory.

"Maybe Devon might pay you more attention if you'd pay some to yourself."

Frantically she drove on, having to swerve wildly to miss a dog crossing the road. People she passed turned to watch her with confusion and fear clearly etched on their faces. Angrily, Alicia swiped at the bitter tears that continued to stream down her face. With a squeal of tires she turned the car into her small, dirt-packed yard. She barely turned off the car before she jumped out and ran inside her small cottage house, leaving the car door wide open.

"Maybe Devon might pay you more attention if you'd pay some to yourself."

Flinging her petite frame onto her bed, she clutched her pillow to her chest and let the bitter tide of tears flow freely. Her moans of agony were muffled as she bit down on the downy mass in frustration.

Maybe it wasn't Devon but Deshawn, she thought wildly, searching for an answer. For one brief moment the pain lifted from her chest and the tears eased, until she remembered that Deshawn was involved with Poochie from the diner.

No, she was sure. No matter how much she wished it wasn't true, it had been *her* Devon with Chloe. The pain swallowed her whole like a tidal wave and the tears built up in the back of her eyes until they stung. "Why, Devon?" she moaned into the pillow. "Why her? Why not me?"

When had it begun?

Why hadn't she known?

When had his disgust and dislike for Chloe Bolton turned to lust?

And that's all it was, Alicia knew. Just lust, pure and simple. It was not the love she had for him. Love that still blossomed in her heart.

How she hated that woman.

Why couldn't she stay in New York? Why did she have to move to Holtsville?

These questions and many more plagued Alicia as late afternoon became early evening. The sun descended from the sky and darkness began to settle around her small cottage. Never once did she move off the bed.

Even now, hours later, as the tears had finally waned and numbness had settled in, the image of Devon and Chloe replayed like a scratched record, over and over and over again. Hatred for the supermodel burned her gut. Her mind worked overtime for a solution on how to get rid of Chloe Bolton.

The phone rang loudly in the darkness of the bedroom. Alicia wanted to ignore it and wallow in her hatred and self-pity, but it continued to ring persistently. Rolling over onto her stomach, she reached for the telephone on the nightstand. "Hello," she croaked, her voice strained from the tears that had racked her body.

"Hello . . . Alicia? What's up, girl? You sound like hell!"

Alicia grimaced at how loud Tara, her sister, was talking into the phone. She had a viciously pounding headache and her eyes were swollen and nearly closed with a tight and gritty feel. "I was taking a nap," she lied. "You woke me up."

"I just wanted to check up on you. I heard how you were speeding on Willow Lane. They said you looked upset. What's up?" Tara's voice was filled with concern for her younger sibling.

Inwardly Alicia groaned. Small-town busy bodies didn't miss a thing. "Who told you they saw me speeding, Tara?"

"They asked me not to say, and it's not important anyway. Were you speeding like a bat out of hell?"

"No, they're lying," she lied.

Tara was quiet a moment. "Okay, then forget it. I heard Chloe Bolton's big house is finished. True?"

Alicia's lips tightened at the mention of her nemesis. Hatred boiled. "Yeah."

"I know she'll be pleased. That house makes five of mine!"

Alicia bit her bottom lip. "Yeah she's pleased, so she can stop complaining about Nana Lil and the twins' house," she lied easily, wanting to tarnish the perfect image of Chloe.

"What?" Tara exclaimed, her voice shrill as she waited for more details.

"I overheard her on the phone with her big-time friends from New York laughing at the house and the people from town." Alicia's heart raced as she continued to weave her lies like a vicious and deadly black spider. "I even heard her talking about doing drugs."

Tara gasped in shock, "No!"

"Yes, but Tara, you didn't hear it from me."

"Well, of course not. I sure didn't."

Devon looked down at Chloe's sleeping form, huddled in a ball. Their bodies were padded by the impromptu bedding of comforters on the wooden floor of what would be her private gym. They had enjoyed each other's bodies in every one of the rooms of the house before coming to this room last, to watch themselves couple in the mirrors running along the walls.

His appetite for this woman was infinite. He never seemed to get enough of being with her. Even now, after long hours of physical delight, the sight of her nipples now soft and flat in her sleep made his loins tighten in hunger.

She had dispelled all the misconceptions he had had about her. Never once had she looked down her nose at his hometown or its occupants. She never complained about all the things the small town lacked in comparison to New York, although he was sure it must have crossed her mind. Both he and his brother liked designer clothing and traveled to Charleston and Hilton Head to purchase their wardrobe themselves.

Sometimes when he looked at her, he saw just a beautiful woman with a kind heart and good nature, not the glamorous supermodel that had blossomed in front of the camera. Especially when she wore her long hair in those two ponytails she loved so much.

At odd times during the day he would think of little things about her. The way she closed her eyes and wiggled in her seat when she ate a bite of something delicious. Or the way she snored when she was deep asleep, something she vehemently denied when he told her about it. Or especially the way her eyelids became lazy when he stroked deep inside of her.

Chloe.

Where is this headed?

Surely incredible sex between two consenting adults could not last long if that's all the relationship was based on. So where was this headed? Neither of them had spoken of it, but he knew that he had no thoughts of any other woman since the first night they shared together.

Did that mean something?

Physically he was drawn to her, but he knew it was best to keep his distance emotionally. He doubted she would remain in the small town for long. He still saw some similarities between Chloe and Elissa. Devon had to admit that he just didn't believe she would actually move to the small town, regardless of what she proclaimed. Eventually this phase of her life, to fulfill her mother's dream of building the house, would pass and she would seek out her jet-setting life of wealth and glamour. She was only in her mid-thirties and once she finished focusing all of her time on decorating the new house, what did she plan to do with her time all day?

Chloe snorted in her sleep before turning onto her side to snuggle closer to Devon's chest. He was lying on his side watching her, his head propped up on his hand. She didn't awaken, but smacked her full lips in contentment, the sheet draped over her naked form.

She *was* exquisitely beautiful; he could well see why she had been so wildly acclaimed as a model. Okay, yes, he was more than a little cocky about having one of the most desired women in the world in his bed, acting like she couldn't get enough of him. And he felt very protective of her.

Chloe Bolton.

She'd walked the runways, posed for magazine covers and layouts, did TV commercials, guest starred in music videos and movies. She was named one of *People's* "Fifty Most Beautiful People" six times, and her name had stayed at the top of the list of most sought-after models. Bestselling beauty books. Endorsements. Wealth, fame and glamour.

Devon looked down at her, focusing on how good her breasts felt pressed against his chest. Leaning down, he nuzzled her neck, inhaling her sweet unique scent. He let his hand slide under the sheet to caress the deep curve of her waist before dipping down to grip the fullness of her derriere.

Chloe stretched her long limbs, awakened by the most wonderful sensation as Devon's head dipped to capture one of her hard nipples in the wet warmth of his mouth.

"Aren't you ever satisfied?" she moaned playfully as he rolled onto his back carrying her with him.

Letting the sheet fall to her waist, Chloe rose to a sitting position atop him. The base of his hardened length pressed

against her core. His hands moved up to cup her full voluminous globes, teasing her nipples with his thumbs. In just
seconds, he was covered with protection. Her eyes glazed with
desire as she rose up on her knees and held his hardness
straight up with one hand. Slowly she squatted down on him,
smiling at how his mouth formed an "O" from the pleasure
of surrounding him with her sheath.

Chloe said nothing as she rode him, just letting her eyes
feast on him and his reactions to her. She moved her body in
a snake-like motion, her hands on his chest and his hands
clutching at her waist tightly.

Their eyes remained locked and Chloe lowered her upper
body down onto her elbows, letting her breasts hang in his face,
her hips still grinding into him. He didn't move. He didn't have
to. She knew how to please him. They shuddered together in
release and Chloe fell onto his chest in exhaustion. Her leg muscles quivered from exertion. Devon rubbed the total expanse of
her soft back, still deeply planted inside of her.

"You ever rode a horse, Chloe?" he asked as he placed a
kiss on the top of her sweat-drenched hair. "I think you're a
natural. We'll have to see if you're as good on a real stallion."

Chloe laughed lightly and then playfully bit his chocolate
nipple before moving her hands to his sides to tickle him. "I
must be a jockey the way you just got to the finish line so
quickly."

Devon whistled. "Give me about a twenty- or thirty-minute
nap to build up my protein and we'll see if you're still brag-
ging."

Nearly one hour later they gathered up their quilts and
dressed in the darkness of the unfurnished house. Hunger
forced them out of hiding. Neither said so, but both were
reluctant to leave their haven, knowing when they got home
that they would have to part and sleep in separate rooms.
Neither admitted that they would miss the other, even in sleep.

Twelve

Devon did actually hold Chloe up on the horseback riding after that following Sunday afternoon. They drove to the small town of Lamberg, just ten minutes outside of Holtsville. A friend of Deshawn and Devon had a large stable of more than fifteen horses there.

That morning after breakfast, with Nana Lil off to church and Deshawn gone to sniff behind Poochie, Devon made the offer to Chloe, who had excitedly accepted.

It would be another week before she could officially move into her house because small details, such as making an appointment for the electrical lines to be laid underground, had to be taken care of. She was more than willing to spend time with Devon alone as the time neared for her to move into her own home alone.

They drove in silence in his truck, the local rhythm and blues station playing on the radio as he drove with speed and efficiency. Chloe was surprised and pleased as Devon's hand moved off the steering wheel to grasp her thigh with warmth and strength. That simple move marked the start of a fun, carefree and surprisingly romantic afternoon for the couple.

Devon selected a powerful black stallion named Thunder for himself, and an equally swift gray mare named Butterfly for Chloe. They rode at a leisurely pace around the acres of lush green plains that the horse farm provided. The trail they followed was well-marked.

As the trail narrowed through rows of trees, Chloe nudged the mare forward to take the lead single file. Devon let his eyes lazily caress her. She sat comfortably in the saddle and moved as if one with the animal.

The trail widened back into an open field and Devon trotted up to ride beside her. "You ride well. Where did you learn?"

"Egypt," she said with a wink as she turned her face to look at him.

Devon looked surprised. "Egypt?"

"Yup." Chloe nodded, her beautiful hazel eyes squinting to block the sun glaring brilliantly in the sky. She longed for one of her many pairs of designer sunglasses. "This sports magazine shot their annual swimsuit issue in Danir, Egypt. The Sheik Rahmeed of Danir graciously offered the entire entourage use of the apartments in one wing of his palace. The invitation included free use of his stable of horses." She laughed as she remembered the trip. "A couple of the girls were excellent in the saddle, but I knew nothing about horses, period. I mean we didn't exactly have them grazing around the Bronx when I was growing up."

He smiled. "So one of the other models taught you to ride?"

Chloe looked off to some faraway spot in the distance as they rode. "No, uh . . . actually the sheik did."

"The sheik?" His deep southern voice was mocking.

"Yes. He offered his personal services to me, along with his two soldiers flanked with automatic rifles who would then unload an entire tent with picnic preparations." Chloe laughed as she recalled the events. "It really was exciting being courted by a wealthy, dark and handsome sheik. Especially when he graciously invited me to share his life as wife number eight in his harem."

Devon doubled over in laughter, careful not to fall off the horse. "Harem . . . wife number eight."

He continued to laugh until he saw her hurt expression. Reaching for her reins, he brought both of their horses to a complete stop in the middle of the green field. "I'm sorry baby, it was funny."

Leaning over, he kissed her full on the mouth, and Chloe's pained anger subsided. Taking her reins back, she walked the mare ahead. Devon soon followed behind. "You say he was tall, dark, handsome and filthy rich. His courtship was exciting. So why didn't you marry him?"

Chloe looked back at him in shock and saw that his expression was serious. Sighing, she answered him, "When I decide to marry a man I want him to have the kind of love for me where I'm the only woman he could ever love. I want every bit of energy not used by his heart to pump life into his body, to be given to me. I need that man to be my man and mine alone, because I plan to give him all of those things in return. Fidelity, honesty, trust, passion, laughter, tenderness, protectiveness, children, family, 'til death do us part . . . and love."

Chloe's eyes clouded as she thought of Calvin. She had foolishly thought she found that man, when instead she had a boy disguised in a man's body. Shaking her head slowly, Chloe laughed low and husky. "I can never seem to find the one man with all those qualities. There's either passion with no fidelity, or . . . tenderness and laughter with no passion, or passion without love."

The body but not the heart.

Sadly, she realized fully that the last phrase quantified her relationship with Devon, but she didn't expound on the point. "I guess my limits are set too high and are unrealistic, huh?"

Devon now rode alongside her and looked over at this regally beautiful woman, seeing yet another dimension to the complexity of her. He was awed by the feelings she shared with him, moved by the sincerity of her words, and pained by the hurt that lurked in the depths of her beautiful hazel eyes. She was looking at him now, waiting for an answer and the desire to have her in his arms filled him. Not for sex, but just to comfort her.

But he just lowered his head, his voice husky and low, barely above a whisper. "No Chloe, your limits are what you deserve."

They rode in silence, each deep in their own thoughts, until Devon nudged his stallion in front of Chloe's mare. "Follow me."

Chloe did follow closely behind his horse at a gallop as they crossed the grassy area, veering off the marked trail. He slowed as they came to a tightly knit area of trees resembling a dense forest. She doubted that the area could even be breached, until he did just that through a small clearing. It could not be found by anyone who didn't know it was there. Curious, she followed behind him.

They followed the dense trail for nearly an eighth of a mile before it suddenly opened to a splendid grove of cottonwood with a glen beside a small clear pond. The grass was thick and emerald green, and the flowers were a mosaic of lavenders, ruby reds, topaz and amethyst with scabiosa, daylilies, mums and vines of clematis.

Chloe gasped in shock and surprise as she dismounted and handed the reins to a waiting Devon. He then loosely tethered them to a tree along with his own reins. She turned to question him and instantly found her open mouth filled with the heat of his tongue, and her body wrapped tightly in his arms. Giving in to the pleasure he gave, she wrapped her arms around his neck and held him just as tightly. She felt as if her heart was about to burst with pleasure.

Slowly he broke the kiss, raising his head from hers only a fraction. "You really are beautiful and amazing, inside and out," he said huskily, his hands trembling as he traced the side of her face with his index finger.

As Chloe closed her eyes, leaning her face toward his hand, she sighed, "Thank you."

So few people in the business had realized or even cared that yes, she had an inner beauty that was as treasured as her outward appearances. His compliment was simple perfection.

Devon lowered his hand to slowly raise her T-shirt over her head. He undressed her, each shedding of clothing exposing some exquisite part of her body to his eager eyes until she stood naked, proud and unashamed before him. "Chloe," he whispered in awe, before lowering his head to tenderly kiss every inch of her upturned face.

With a guttural moan he lowered her to the ground, her body blanketed by the plush layers of sweet emerald grass. Trembling, she watched him as he stood and removed his clothing. Her eyes devoured the tantalizing sight of his sleek, muscled physique. It was a body sculptured from years of hard work, and she appreciated every bit of her African warrior.

She felt totally complete as he lowered himself to the ground and gathered her into his arms, handling her like a precious jewel. She felt anxious but safe as she watched him slowly enclose his hardness with a condom. Now they both were protected and able to enjoy their rapture. They made love with slow intensity that shook them both. Their warm bodies touched, his hardness inside of her sweet softness. No words were spoken, but they both felt the new heightened awareness of one another as they pleased each other. Their bodies molded in a perfect fit. It was like they were made for each other. Like Adam and Eve in the Garden of Eden.

Together they climaxed, he with a deep moan against her breast and she with a sigh of his name as she stroked the hard expanse of his back. Their arms were tightly wrapped around each other as if they were afraid to let go. Their hearts were pounding, bodies damp with perspiration, feelings of tenderness and some other emotion surrounding them with a warm glow.

A long time later, arm in arm they walked to the pond a few feet away, naked and unashamed. Slowly they slipped beneath the cool wet depths. They swam, enjoying the feel of the water on their skin, never venturing far from each other.

Like children, they laughed and played around, splashing water and chasing one another.

The afternoon passed at a leisurely pace for them as they dined on the roast beef sandwiches, fresh fruit and bottled spring water that Devon had surprised her with from his saddle bag.

Neither bothered to dress in their secluded haven as they lay on a blanket he also brought along, but had been too eager earlier to retrieve. The horses were their only witnesses and who would they tell? They talked, with Chloe answering many of the questions that Devon had pondered concerning her and her career. She spoke with false bravado about the death of her mother, although the pain was still etched in her beautiful face. And her voice was resigned as she filled him in on her career: how she had been discovered, her accomplishments and finally how she had begun to feel weighed down by the work she once loved. Briefly she spoke of an ex-boyfriend, Calvin, but offered no real details.

Devon admitted to himself that the feeling stirring in his gut was jealousy at the thought of her with another man.

And then he talked about his life growing up with a twin and the tricks they used to play on people, especially unsuspecting girls after puberty hit. He obviously cared for his parents deeply as he spoke of their deaths. He spoke of college and struggling to rebuild the business their father began with pride.

He didn't mention Elissa, and Chloe didn't let on that she already knew about his first true love. She took the omission as meaning he was still too deeply hurt to even speak about her. Not that she had given him many details about Calvin, either.

They both laughed as they watched as others passed on the marked trail, secluded by the dense area of trees. They dressed slowly, packing up the remnants of their cold lunch. Chloe untied her horse and mounted easily. Devon did the same and rode up beside her.

"Chloe."

She turned at the softness of his voice saying her name. He had picked a long-stemmed brilliant scarlet daylily and handed it to her with a boyishly charming smile. He said nothing and just rode off in front of her. The flower was named so because it would last for only one day when cut, but was beautiful nonetheless. Chloe inhaled its fragrant scent. The simple and sweet gesture moved and confused her.

It was after four when they pulled into the driveway. Chloe grimaced at seeing Alicia's compact parked behind her SUV in the driveway, looking even more battered and beaten next to the luxury of the Navigator.

"Won't it look suspicious that we've been together all day?" she asked innocently, knowing they had agreed to keep their business just that . . . their business.

Devon hated the anger that rose in him as he thought for a brief moment that she was ashamed of being with him, but when he looked into the depths of her cat-shaped hazel eyes he saw no hint of it there. Besides, they had both agreed to keep this between just them.

Laughing, he leaned over for a brief taste of her sultry full lips. "We've been shopping for antique furniture in Charleston."

They left the truck and walked into the house. Alicia was lounging on the living room couch, the venom in her eyes obvious as she glared at her. Chloe was startled by the pure hatred in the woman's dull brown depths.

Nana Lil walked into the living room, wiping her frail slender hands on a plaid dish towel. "Where'd you two go off to?"

"Charleston."

"Hilton Head."

They both spoke simultaneously and glared at each other before looking away. Devon answered, "We went shopping for antiques in Charleston."

Nana Lil gloated. "Yeah right, pee on my head and tell me it's raining."

Her laughter remained with them even after she walked back into the kitchen.

"Devon, can I talk to you?" Alicia rose and came to stand by him, placing her hand on his arms. Pointedly, she looked at Chloe. "In private."

Chloe wanted to shout "hell no" into the woman's face but instead she swallowed her irritation and smiled sweetly and falsely. "I'll just go upstairs."

Alicia waited until Chloe's retreating figure disappeared up the stairs before she turned back to him. "Let's walk outside."

Devon yawned and looked down at his friend. "Alicia, can't this wait? I really would like to go see what's happening at Charlie's after I shower."

"No, it can't," she insisted.

Sighing, he let her lead him out of the house and onto the porch, where he flopped onto the swing. "So what's up, Al?"

He listened patiently, his handsome face serious and expressionless as he focused on her as she spoke of the argument she and Chloe had. This bit of information surprised him but he didn't show it.

Alicia carried on, her voice condemning as she lied easily, accusing Chloe of looking down her nose at her and picking the argument. For good measure, she voiced her opinions of Chloe, using many of the same terms Devon had found himself using . . . before he really knew her.

"The woman ain't nothing but trouble." Alicia feigned tears, causing her voice to quiver as she saw no visible reaction from him. "I know I'm not a famous supermodel, Devon, but I never did anything to that woman. I was a big fan of hers and look how she makes me feel like I'm nothing compared to her."

Devon immediately rose to pull Alicia's petite frame into his arms. This was his friend and she seemed very upset. "If you two don't get along, then it's best to keep your distance from one another, right?"

Alicia stiffened. That definitely was not what she wanted to hear.

He patted her back in an act of comfort. "Don't cry, Al. Regardless of who it is, never let anyone know they've hurt you."

She leaned back and looked up into his handsome face. She was disappointed by the friendly love she saw there. "We all should've listened to your warnings about her. I just wish she would get the hell out of Holtsville, just like you . . . right?"

How did he feel about everything Alicia just told him? He didn't know, but he did know that he was in no rush at all to see Chloe leave him.

Chloe descended the stairs, her eyes widening as she saw Devon wrap Alicia's frame into his arms through the windows looking out onto the porch. She knew if it was at all possible, her smooth bronze complexion would become green with envy. Fuming, she stomped down the rest of the stairs and into the kitchen.

"What's wrong, Chloe?"

"Nothing, Nana Lil." She took a seat at the table, drumming her nails on the polished wood.

Lil eyed Chloe as she stirred a pot on the stove. "I didn't feel like cooking a big dinner, but there's some smothered chicken and rice if you're hungry."

Distracted, Chloe nodded. "Thanks."

She's probably telling him about our argument earlier this week, Chloe was thinking as she again glanced down the hall at the front door.

Lil watched with amusement as Chloe jumped nervously when the front door opened and closed, turning her attention to the salt and pepper shakers as if nonchalant. She shook her head and her thin shoulder shook with restrained laughter.

Devon walked into the kitchen alone, his eyes resting briefly on the back of Chloe's head before moving to his grandmother.

"Where's Alicia, Vonnie?"

"She, uh, went home." He raised a brow at the stiffness of Chloe's back. He thought he heard her mutter "good riddance" under her breath.

"What's that, Chloe?" he asked.

Chloe scraped the chair back noisily, moving to stand. Stiffly she faced him, still angry at seeing Alicia in his arms.

Nana Lil smelled trouble about to brew, and she was not in the mood to hear one of their explosive arguments with one of her headaches coming on. "Time out children," she said, holding up her hands.

They both watched as she fixed a glass of water. "Go to your corners, come out strong, and good night."

Lil left the kitchen and soon the firm shutting of her bedroom door was heard.

"I suppose she told you we argued earlier this week," Chloe snapped as she again faced him.

Devon nodded slowly as he leaned casually against the archway, his arms crossed on his massive chest. "Yes she did."

"I also suppose that she told you I instigated it." Her voice was nasty.

"Yup." He started to smile at the incredulous look on her beautiful face at his answer.

"And I suppose you believe that, don't you?"

Oh no, I'm not falling into that trap. "Why don't you tell me what happened? I wasn't there."

Chloe sighed, feeling like a child being questioned by her parent. She explained to him about what caused the argument.

"Are you sure Alicia did say those things?"

When Chloe jerked her head up to glare at him, he knew he said the wrong thing. Inwardly he groaned.

Angrily, Chloe stepped closer to him. "I wouldn't expect you to rationalize the truth." Her finger angrily poked into his chest as she spoke through clenched teeth. "You can't even see that the little flat-chested dwarf has the hots for you, you dope."

His face became shocked as he looked at her. "Now you're being ridiculous. Alicia is my friend. Can't a man have a female friend?"

Chloe threw her hands up in exasperation. "Can you see the nose on your face or is that invisible to you too?"

With that she gave him an angry shove and flew down the hall and up the stairs to her room. She was steaming with anger, but she was also disappointed that their beautiful day was spoiled.

Sighing heavily, he pushed his large muscled figure off the wall and left the house, not even bothering to shower. Some gambling and a cold beer at Charlie's was what he needed right now.

Badly!

Thirteen

It had rained all night and the trees glistened with moisture as the newly risen sun shone brightly upon the trees. The scent of woods, pines and wildflowers was in the October air. Unfortunately the front of the land was muddy and unsightly, unlike the perimeter where the grounds had not been cleared. Chloe glanced down at her Movado watch, her slender body draped across the three-seater wrought iron swing she had installed onto the porch just yesterday.

It was seven thirty in the morning.

One week ago she finally moved into her dream house, just one week after it was completed. The house had passed county inspection, and the electricity, her unpublished telephone line and cable services were all installed. Full insurance coverage was paid up. This house was hers.

The small town of Holtsville had bustled with activity as the trucks began to roll in earnest with her furniture deliveries. Because of her careful planning, Chloe knew where she wanted every piece of furniture to go in the large house. The twins had brought the items she had in their storeroom on the back of their pickup trucks. She had done the interior decorating in every room and was overwhelmingly pleased with her results.

Sighing, she sipped from her cup of herbal tea before walking through both the black wrought iron screen door and the carved wooden door to enter her inner sanctum. She smiled with pride at what she saw.

The foyer, with the multicolored terra-cotta tiles on the floor, circled out like a rising sun. The only decorations she put in were deeply stained mahogany side serving tables on either side of the front entrance. Neoclassic, gold-framed African motif paintings adorned the bright white walls and a large modern chandelier hung from the center of the domed ceiling. The navy, maroon and gray hues of the tiles were a treat to the eyes, by themselves and she hadn't wanted to distract from that.

To the left through a large domed archway was the oval-shaped dining room. To the right of the foyer was a similar entrance leading into the sunken living room decorated in shades of navy blue, powder blue and white with silver accents. Straight down the middle of the semicircled foyer was a long, wide hallway where the tile continued.

Chloe closed the front door and walked down this hallway, the walls framed with photos of herself, her mother and Anika. To the left was the brightly lit yellow-and-white kitchen of her dreams, but she passed that archway and the two doors leading to the guest rooms on the right to come to the end of the hall where her indoor pool was the circular centerpiece of the house.

The hall divided around the glass-enclosed pool, with the hall to the left leading to her master suite and the other to the sauna and gym. Two doors were on either side of the circular room.

As she did every morning, Chloe swam ten laps in the heated oval pool, allowing the mediterranean blues and sea greens of the tiles to soothe her. Here she had placed poolside chaise lounges of deep royal blue around the pool. Silver racks held royal blue, emerald green and white folded plush towels. A clear plastic minibar stocked with fruit juices, spring water and soda took up the back wall. There was enough room to hold a party in there poolside, especially with the built-in stereo system. And the glass ceiling was retractable by remote controls, allowing in fresh air if she pleased.

Once done with her laps, Chloe pulled her sleek dripping wet body out of the pool and stepped into one of the mini-showers located in the corner of the rooms to rinse off the chlorine. She pulled on one of the thick terry cloth robes lining the walls on silver hooks, slipping it on as she left the room through the door to the left to cross the circular hallway to her master suite.

Chloe was momentarily blinded by the white-on-white decor as the sun glared though the vertical blinds of her windows. Crossing the plush white carpet, she entered her bathroom. It was nearly half the size of the entire spacious master bedroom. Here the white decor continued with silver accessories, like the makeup table and the etagere in the corner.

She removed her robe and the skimpy white bikini she wore, throwing them into the white wicker clothes hamper next to the octagon-shaped individual shower stall. Under the hot jet spray she showered, making sure to get all the chlorine from her skin and hair, before leaving the cubicle to wrap herself in a plush white bath towel. She contemplated sitting in her personal home sauna in the corner, but decided against it, instead leaving the bathroom to pad barefoot into her bedroom. Vigorously she wiped her damp hair with another towel. From beneath the material she caught sight of her king-sized bed sitting in the middle of a white circular platform in the center of the room.

Chloe wished Devon was lying there waiting for her, but he wasn't. They hadn't shared any real time alone since they argued that night about Alicia, and after such a romantic, unbelievably sensuous time at the pond. She still shivered with desire when she thought of the precious moments they shared that day.

Neither of them seemed to want to be the first to approach the other, for that was a sign of weakness. But she missed him so, and to see him as he helped her move in, and not speak to him or touch him or kiss him had been pure torture. Several times their eyes had met and held before one would look away, no words spoken between them. That had really bothered her, so she tried not to think of him.

Chloe walked over to one of her two walk-in closets. Anika, to her eternal credit, had shipped the rest of her clothing from the New York apartment. It really boosted her wardrobe and she had endless selections to choose from.

It had rained last night but the sun was now shining brightly, so she wanted to dress comfortably because she had a lot of running around to do for the day. Chloe chose a cotton Nike dress with short sleeves and a rounded collar with matching sneakers. After lotioning her body with Pleasure, she pulled on her black cotton sports bra and thong before slipping on the dress and sneakers.

After pulling her wet wavy hair into a scrunchee, she threw her personal items and wallet into her duffel sack. Chloe glanced down at her watch. It was a quarter to ten in the morning. Sighing, she retraced her steps to the front door, pausing to activate the alarm system she had installed on the house, before leaving and locking the door.

Within minutes she was seated behind the wheel of her SUV, grimacing at the mud on her sneakers before she pulled out of the yard. On impulse, once she caught sight of the large white house, Chloe turned the large vehicle into the driveway next to Devon's blue truck.

"Well, hello stranger," Nana Lil called from the porch as she walked out of the house.

Chloe hopped down to the ground with a smile. "Stranger? Deshawn just dropped you down to the house yesterday, Nana Lil."

Lil winked. "I know. You sure look pretty. Where ya headed?"

"Grocery shopping. You all are still coming to dinner tonight?"

"Yes," she said hesitantly, her expression pained. "You sure you won't be needing help?"

Chloe laughed. "No ma'am. Do you need anything from the store?"

"No. Don't think so."

Just then Devon walked out onto the porch. He didn't appear to be surprised to see her, so Chloe knew that he knew she was outside. "Hello, Devon" slipped so easily from her mouth that she hated herself for it.

His eyes were obsidian pools as he stared at her. "So you're speaking to me again." He nodded. "Hello, Chloe."

Lil looked from one to the other before walking back into the house without another word.

Chloe shifted nervously under his scrutiny. She missed him and she wanted him back in her life. No, it hadn't been in her earlier plan to need him, but she did. Funny, as she looked at him, with his handsome self, she couldn't quite remember why they had even been mad at each other for a brief moment. Coughing nervously, she asked, "You will come tonight for dinner?"

He said nothing, instead jiggling the keys in his hand as he descended the stairs to walk over to where she stood wringing her hands nervously. "And *you're* supposed to be cookin' this dinner?" he asked, his deep voice playfully mocking.

She stiffened in indignation and raised a finely arched brow. "Yes I am. I *can* cook, you know."

"This I'll have to see." He leaned down to touch her mouth with a feather-light kiss before hopping in his truck to reverse out of the yard.

Chloe battled herself, forcing her body not to turn and watch him drive off. Her lips still quivered from his kiss and her nipples had hardened into two tight buds beneath her dress. Literally she shook it off before she climbed into her SUV with a sexually frustrated groan.

She drove to town, pulling into the small parking lot of the Piggly Wiggly grocery store. Once she parked, Chloe grabbed a shopping cart that had been abandoned in the spot next to hers.

Chloe went up and down each aisle placing whatever item she wanted in the cart. Occasionally she waved and smiled at people she knew from Holtsville. She came to the aisle with the paper products: magazines, paperback books, stationery and greeting cards. On impulse she slowed the cart in front of the section holding the many magazines. Leaving the cart, her eyes scanned the rows until they lit on the glossy and colorful magazine covers she had once graced: *Elle, Vogue, Mirabella, Ebony, Essence, Glamour* and *Mademoiselle.*

Lia Montague, Chloe's once biggest competitor, smiled from the coveted *Vogue* cover. She had to admit that it was a good photo of the woman's pale Swedish beauty. Liv had already informed her months ago on how Lia's popularity had soared among the industry upon Chloe's retirement.

The woman was also nominated for the award Chloe was up for. *She'll probably win,* Chloe thought as she studied the cover picture, now holding the thick glossy magazine in her hand. To her it almost looked as if the smile on Lia's face was one of triumph, as if saying "I'm going to finally beat you."

Placing the magazine back where she got it, she moved on, first grabbing the recent issue of *Essence* to read later. She finished her shopping, her cart now completely filled with groceries. Moving into the shortest line, she brought the cart to a stop and opened the magazine to browse while she waited.

Soon she was in her SUV, her groceries stored safely in back, headed homeward down 17. Chloe couldn't wait for the chance to finally prove to everyone that she could throw down in the kitchen, and she also wanted to show off her hand at interior decorating in her dream house. It would take careful planning to make sure everything would be fixed around the same time, but Chloe knew she could pull it off.

As she passed their house, she noticed that Devon's truck was not parked there, and Alicia's compact was in its place.

Not stopping, Chloe steered the vehicle up the road to her house. Before turning in the driveway she pulled on the other side of the road on the right and hopped out of the vehicle to retrieve her mail out of the plain white mailbox. She carried the bundle of envelopes along with her copies of the *New York Times* and *USA Today,* not even bothering to glance through them as she got back in the SUV.

"I really do need to call some landscapers," she said aloud to herself as she surveyed the land surrounding the house. It looked three times as bad with the torrential rain last night turning everything to slick mud.

Parking on the left side of the house by the large sliding glass door off the kitchen, she deactivated the alarm by the keypad after she entered the house. Chloe began to unload her packages from the vehicle to the kitchen's smooth, black-tiled counters.

She truly loved how the skylight in the center of the room allowed the sun's rays to beam into the kitchen. At night the stars twinkled just as brightly. As she unpacked the groceries and put them away in the appropriate storage areas, Chloe threw her stack of mail and newspapers onto the glass and wrought-iron table that matched her cabinets.

The cabinets.

Chloe smiled because they were a constant reminder of Devon and the first kiss they shared in this very same spacious room. That kiss had been just a sample of the chemistry they created whenever they were together. Whether arguing or making sweet love, the sparks always seemed to fly.

Leaving the kitchen through the arched entrance on the other side of the massive room, Chloe turned down the hall and headed back to her suite. Quickly she made her bed and changed into an oversized gray T-shirt and black leggings, leaving her feet bare before walking back out to the kitchen. Using the remote, she turned on the black, nineteen-inch television in the corner on a swivel wall mount. After settling on one of those television magazine programs, she had just taken a seat on one of the stools at the black marble island to start peeling potatoes when the phone began to ring. Reaching behind her Chloe picked up the cordless phone from its base on the counter.

"Hello."

"Hey Chloe."

A wave of pleasure went through her at the sound of Devon's voice. *Maybe he's ready to really apologize.* "Hello Devon."

He laughed. "Sorry, baby girl, this is the other twin, the cute one with the dimple in the left cheek, not the right."

So is that how Nana Lil knows them apart?

Chloe laughed, even though she was bitterly disappointed. "What can I help you with, Deshawn?"

"Just wanted to know if I could bring a friend with me tonight."

A brief mental image of the voluptuous girl flashed in her mind. "Sure you can. You do mean Poochie right?"

Deshawn laughed, the sound so familiar to Chloe because of its likeness to Devon's laugh. "Maybe," he said vaguely.

"Whatever, Shawnie," she said with a smile. "I'll see you both at six o'clock, okay?"

"All right . . . oh, and Chloe?"

"Yes?"

"Do I need to bring Alka Seltzer?"

She disconnected the line, cutting off his laughter.

Devon could not take his eyes off of her as she guided the small group of five on a tour of the house. His breath was taken away, as if seeing her for the very first time. Her hair was pinned up with a riot of curls, a few strands slipping loose to caress her cheek and the nape of her slender, graceful neck. The blue-beaded, three-strand choker she wore emphasized her delicate collarbone and soft, rounded shoulders above the midnight blue strapless dress she wore with allover floral embroidered lace overlay. Her curvaceous frame gave the A-line dress new definition as it hugged her, stopping just above her knee with a scalloped edge to showcase her long shapely legs and delicate ankles in the strappy matching sandals she wore.

She was stunning.

Reluctantly, he drew his attention away from her as he realized how intently he had been staring at her. For the first time he looked around at his surroundings. So far he had to admit that she had done an excellent job of decorating the uniquely structured house. None of the haughtiness he had originally believed he would see was evident. Everything was clean, unique, uncluttered, but yes, expensive and elegant.

It was in the game room that he was truly impressed as an avid sports fan. The walls were, as he knew, painted a deep rich navy, and large autographed sports jerseys were on white backdrops in silver frames. The football, basketball and baseball jerseys had to be worth a small fortune, with big-time athletes like Michael Jordan, Randall Cunningham, O.J. Simpson, Isiah Thomas, Magic Johnson and Ken Griffey Jr. A large seventy-inch projection screen television took up most of the space on one wall, surrounded by a cream leather sectional with navy and bright yellow pillows. Two pool tables were in the middle of the room underneath aluminum bell hanging lamps. Arcade games, a dart board and a state-of-the-art entertainment center including a retractable movie screen also were to be found and enjoyed.

Cyrus planted himself on the sectional and turned on the television. Deshawn challenged Devon to a game of pool, and Poochie fawned over Chloe's collection of celebrity snapshots alongside another wall. Lil went bustling after their hostess, who went to check on dinner.

Chloe was shaking with bad nerves. Not because of the dinner but because she had felt Devon's eyes on her since he arrived. And God, he looked so fine is his lightweight linen suit. Her thoughts were so filled with Devon that she didn't even see Nana Lil behind her until she had already reached the kitchen.

"Need any help, baby?"

She looked up from the pot she was stirring. The aromatic scent of all the delicacies she prepared was in the air. Chloe nearly toppled over in her stilettos as she moved quickly around the island to block Nana Lil from getting any closer to her pots. "No, thank you. I'll call when it's time to eat."

She grabbed her shoulders and steered the older woman back toward the hall. "Well ain't nothing smelling burnt," Lil said in lieu of a compliment.

Once she was sure Nana Lil had walked back to where the rest of her guests were, Chloe began to carry the serving bowls into the oval-shaped dining room through the archway connecting the two rooms. She had chosen a cranberry and cream decor, picking up the mahogany in the tile of the foyer and hall. The contemporary dining room set consisted of a long rectangular beveled glass tabletop with two creamy marble pedestal bases, large enough to seat eight comfortably. The alternating cranberry and cream Parsons chairs of jacquard fabric gave the room a real elegant and contemporary feel without having her guests feel uncomfortable.

Soon the table was laden with all the dishes she prepared, and Chloe looked at the results with pride. Even her table setting with gold utensils and a beautiful floral centerpiece was wonderful. Using the intercom system installed in every room of the house, Chloe called everyone to dinner.

The sound of their voices echoed down the hall as they began to walk into the dining room. They all took seats and Chloe was vindicated by the gasp of shock and amazement that she saw on their faces.

"Good bread, good meat, good Lord, let's eat," Cyrus said as he eyed the spread of food hungrily.

Well, well, well, Nana Lil thought as she inhaled the tantalizing aroma of the food. *I hope its all as good as it looks.*

Deshawn's stomach grumbled noisily in hunger as the delectable aromas clouded his senses. *Damn, little Chloe sure did out—* He lost his train of thought as Poochie began to massage his inner thigh.

Devon was too shocked to think or say anything. He looked over to where Chloe stood. She gazed at him with a look that sought approval, still looking so beautiful after cooking such a big dinner, as she nervously bit off the lipstick from her full bottom lip. Well, Devon felt a piece of that old heart of his fall in love.

Baked macaroni and cheese perfectly browned and creamy with four cheeses in it. Crispy and golden fried chicken seasoned to perfection. Candied yams. Swedish meatballs. Smothered pork chops. Shrimp gumbo. Collard greens. Homemade biscuits and cornbread. Peach cobbler and sweet potato pie. Mouth-watering.

Every last bit of it was delicious!

Chloe smiled at the sound of people enjoying good food. Lips smacked, forks scraped on plates, and serving spoons hit the sides of bowls for second and third helpings. She had warmed under their endless compliments.

"I told you I could cook, Nana Lil," she mused. "My mother taught me. I knew how to make most of these dishes before I was twelve."

Chloe glanced at Devon, who sat to her immediate left. He was eagerly sopping up the spicy shrimp gumbo with a soft buttery biscuit. When he looked up at her, his handsome face became sheepish. She said nothing, only raising one arched brow at him as if to say, *I can't cook, huh?*

"Sure there aren't some catering tins hidden in the garbage, Chloe?" Deshawn called from down at the other end of the table where he sat.

"Go ahead and look." She waved her hand toward the entrance to the kitchen.

"No need, no need," he acquiesced with a wink, earning him a hard pinch from Poochie.

Devon reached for her hand and held it inside of his warm grasp on top of the table. Chloe was surprised and moved by the simple gesture. It was the first outward sign of affection that Devon had made toward her in front of his family.

"Dinner was delicious, baby." He leaned over and kissed her full on the mouth.

Chloe's soft gasp of surprise was mingled with the other reactions:

Nana Lil sighed with pleasure.

Cyrus choked on the cobbler he was chewing heartily on.

Poochie snapped her fingers with a decisive, "You go girl."

Deshawn whispered, "Well I'll be damned."

Chloe looked into Devon's eyes and saw something in the depths that took her breath away. She knew then that their relationship had just moved to a new level.

Memories of Calvin's betrayal lurked and because of it, quite frankly, she didn't know how she felt being on the next plateau.

Chloe and Devon stood arm in arm on the lit porch as Deshawn pulled off in Poochie's car with Nana Lil and Cyrus in the back seat. After the car disappeared from their view, he leaned down and kissed the back of her neck. He had wanted to do that all night.

"God, I've missed you, Chloe," he moaned, his voice deep with emotion.

He held her tightly from behind and Chloe closed her eyes, caught up in how it felt to be in his arms again. Yes, she had missed him as well and she told him so, but that didn't resolve their earlier argument. It had kept them away from each other, unable to satisfy the need they created in one another for nearly two weeks.

It wasn't that she was jealous of Alicia, nor did she even contemplate him being involved with her any longer, but she wanted him to believe her. "What about Alicia?" she asked, as she stepped sideways out of his embrace.

Devon's face clouded with confusion. "What about her?"

Twirling, she looked at him and saw his face. He truly looked perplexed, as if he didn't know what she spoke of.

Devon wiped his hand over his eyes. "Chloe, you're my woman and she's my best friend. This is a helluva fix y'all got me in."

"A fix?" Chloe spat. "You're in a . . . fix, Devon?"

"Yes," he yelled. "You want me to be angry at her. She wants me to be angry at you. Why don't you two like each other anyway?"

"What . . . were . . . you . . . mad . . . at . . . me . . . for anyway?" She accentuated each word with a poke of her index finger into his chest. The poking was her trademark when she was mad.

"I wasn't mad. I thought you were mad at me and I know how quick you are to jump up in my face . . . just like now," he said with emphasis. "So I gave you time and space to cool off and get over it."

She stared long and hard at him. "Well you know what, Devon?" she asked, her voice showing the hurt feelings he caused. "You underestimated the time . . . big time."

He watched her walk past him and into her house, softly closing both the wrought-iron gate and solid wooden door behind her.

"What the hell did I do now, Chloe?" he asked aloud although he was well aware she could not hear him.

No one got him to deal with his emotions like Chloe, not even Elissa, whether it be anger, humor, passion or tenderness. Depending on her varying moods, she drew a similar response from him instantaneously.

Like tonight, when he kissed her he hadn't thought about it first. Just looking at her wanting her guests to eat with pleasure, and knowing she put so much time and money out for his family, had filled him with the overwhelming need to kiss her right then.

Why fight the feeling, right?

Once the initial shock and surprised reactions of his friends and relatives had passed and the dinner moved on, he had felt as though a heavy weight had been lifted off his shoulders. The Chloe that he discovered all along was a woman for him to be proud to have in his life.

Who cared about what anyone thought or said!

Devon actually waited, his stance akimbo, as he looked toward the house. A faint shadow of her tall curvaceous figure passed by the dining room's long windows. He guessed that she was finishing up clearing the dining room, having refused everyone's offer of help.

Sighing, he fought and won over the desire to knock on the door, wait for her to open it, pull her into his arms and kiss away her anger. Instead Devon released a long, drawn-out sigh before jogging down the steps. Soon he was in his truck and pulling out of the yard, not even aware of the shadowed figure standing to the window as he drove off.

Fourteen

As he neared home he noticed Poochie's car was parked next to his brother's truck. Not in the mood to see them horny as teenagers around each other, especially with his lady mad at him, Devon headed toward Charlie's. It was Friday night and as he turned down the short dirt road he saw that the small yard in front of the structure was filled with cars and trucks.

Parking next to his friend Terrence's purple pickup, Devon spoke to the few men who stood talking outside the small one-room wood house before walking in. One lone lightbulb hung in the middle of the ceiling and four square tables were set up in front of the makeshift bar where Charlie made his sales. The room was stifling hot with all the men crowded inside.

He moved through the crowd, speaking to everyone, as he finally neared his companions Terrence, Sean and Luther. "What's up?" he greeted them.

"Drove down to see Chloe Bolton's house. Looks good Dev."

Devon nodded his thanks to Luther, a tall brawny man who was usually loudmouthed and boastful. He didn't really care for him but kept his opinions of the man to himself, instead choosing to stay out of his company. He just turned his back to him and spoke with Terrence.

"Haven't seen you out in a while?" Terrence motioned for Charlie, a wizened old man, to sell him two beers.

Devon accepted the can offered him by his friend, taking a long swig from it before answering. "We wanted to finish the house up early. We cut two weeks off the completion date."

"I sure as hell wouldn't be in a rush to get a rich and famous supermodel out of my house," he joked.

Ignoring that, Devon asked him about his work. Terrence went on to fill him in on the labor disputes at the paper mill where he worked. It was halfway through this conversation that Devon heard Chloe's name mentioned by Luther.

It was on that conversation that he now focused his attention.

"I ain't surprised at all to find out she does drugs. My girl tells me that the paper she read said the woman was broke and couldn't even afford to pay for that big house—"

"You know, Luther," Devon interjected, his voice cold and hard. "A grown man should have better things to do with his time than gossip like a woman."

The warning was clear in his voice and any other man would have been wise to heed it. Luther was a braggart, though, and didn't want to be embarrassed in front of the large group of men, all of whom had overheard.

Devon appeared relaxed in his stance, but his hand tightly clenched the beer can until it began to bend inward. All conversations in the one room had ceased. At that moment all eyes were riveted to where the two men stood.

"I wasn't talking to you, Dev." Luther looked the other man in the eye. "What do you care what I have to say about that rich bitch—?"

Devon dropped the beer and swung his fist into Luther's face in one swift move, landing a solid, jaw-cracking blow. His opponent fell backward, almost landing on Sean, who quickly sidestepped, allowing him to crash with a thud to the dirt floor. Dust swirled up around his large frame.

Luther jumped up quickly and lunged for Devon. The rest

of the men would have allowed them to have at it, but Charlie raced from behind the counter to jump between them. He didn't want them to tear up the place.

"Stop," he yelled, putting a hand on each man's chest as they squared off.

"If I ever catch Chloe's name in your damn mouth I'll knock the hell out of you again!" Devon pointed his finger toward Luther, his eyes menacing.

"You must be tapping them boots the way you're acting."

Devon lunged for him again, right over Charlie's slight frame. The older man pushed hard at his chest with both hands, showing more strength than Devon would have thought he had. "Cut it out, Devon Jamison."

Lord knows the people of Holtsville loved gossip and a good fight. Right in front of their eyes they both were unfolding. Many were agreeing with Luther about Devon obviously being involved with the beauty. That bit of gossip would spread through the small community like a bad rash.

"Just remember what I told you, Luther," he warned before pushing his way through the crowd and leaving the shack, slamming the hopelessly erected door on its rusted hinges. He hopped into his truck and turned on the headlights. It was when he moved to turn the key in the ignition that the dull throbbing of his right hand registered in his brain.

"What damn paper?" he muttered as he remembered Luther's words. He winced as he turned the key and started off down the short road.

Chloe loaded the last plate into the state-of-the-art dishwasher conveniently located in the island. Once started, the machine was so quiet she couldn't even tell it was running. She grabbed a handful of dishtowels and the bottle of window cleaner to wipe down her kitchen table, just as she had in the dining room. The mail still lay there where she left it in a bundle this morning.

Setting the roll of paper towels and glass cleaner down on the table, she picked up the bundle and removed the rubber band. She immediately recognized the bright colorful front page of a well-known and unfortunately successful gossip tabloid paper, *The Star Gazer.* Slowly Chloe's eyes widened in shock as she read the bold-lettered front page:

SUPERMODEL CHLOE BOLTON'S DRUG HABIT LEADS TO BANKRUPTCY
Story on page three (Photos of southern hideaway included)

An obviously doctored photo of Chloe looking haggard, tired and seemingly strung out on drugs was on the cover beneath the caption. Numb with shock, she slid down into one of the chairs at the table. Against her better judgment she slowly flipped the pages to the story inside:

Nearly one year to the date of her retirement the truth has been finally revealed on why Chloe Bolton's no longer on top. Insiders close to her reveal that she had to retire because her contracts with her modeling agency and Ashanti Cosmetics were not going to be renewed, at their request. It seems her long history of drug use was brought to their attention. The insider, a close friend to the strung- out ex-supermodel, reveals that Chloe has been addicted to cocaine for well over eight years now, since the death of her mother . . .

Chloe closed her eyes against a wave of pain that swallowed her whole. She fought back the tears that threatened to fall, pressing herself to continue reading. She wanted to be aware of all the lies. Skipping past some information on her accomplishments before her supposed tragic downfall, Chloe read on.

The home is on twelve acres of land that she luckily inherited upon her mother's death. Chloe now resides in the small town of Holtsville in South Carolina.

Sadly the stunning beauty's drug use has drained most of her financial resources. A friend close to Chloe confirms that the model plans to sell her luxury apartment in New York to offset some of the hefty bills she's accumulated over the years. Her friends fear she'll overdose on drugs from the constant abuse.

The modest home in the southern small town is reported to be going on sale and the profits used to pay the builders. The friend states, "She can't even afford to decorate the house she's so deeply into the drugs and doesn't care. But once the home is sold, where will she live?"

The rest of the words blurred as bitter tears racked Chloe's body. Angrily she flung the paper to the floor and stumbled out of the kitchen and back to her bedroom, where she flung herself onto the king-sized bed. Her body trembled as she cried angry, bitter tears that scorched her cheeks. She hugged one of the many down pillows, burying her face in its soft depths and not caring about the makeup that smeared against the white Egyptian cotton.

She had removed herself from the spotlight and now this! "Lies," she moaned with a wailing cry. "Nothing but lies."

The sound of New York life was alive and busy. Tall skyscrapers with brightly lit windows beaconed against the black velvet sky. Cars were bumper to bumper on the city streets below. People moved briskly on the cemented sidewalks.

A lone figure watched this from the window of his luxury apartment. Everything about him spoke of a wealthy New Yorker from the cut of his loose-fitting black Versace leather pants and boots to the Giorgio Armani charcoal velvet coat and matching knit sweater he wore. Urban wealth and sophistication was personified in the expensive modern furnishings of his home and the arrogance evident in his stance.

Sighing, he looked down at the gossip rag clutched in his hand. Angrily he crossed the marble floor of the living room and entered his private office. He noticed none of the mahogany and gray decor as he strode to the phone.

Quickly he dialed the number, the phone ringing just twice before someone answered. "Turner Investigative Services."

"Yes, Turner. I know it's after hours but I have a job for you. I need you to locate Chloe Bolton for me in . . ." He paused to skim his eyes over the article again. "Holtsville, South Carolina. I want the phone number ASAP."

"I can get the address for you as well," the man offered, eager for the work. "And detailed directions if you need."

"Yeah, you do that. Although I have no intention of traveling to some backwards town in South Carolina. Anyway, contact me when you have the information. I will of course pay you well for your services."

He hung up the phone, not even waiting to see if Turner had any questions. Cal felt that there was no reason the P.I. should have any; his instructions had been clear and succinct as to what he wanted. And in the end he always got just that . . . whatever he wanted.

He *wanted* Chloe!

It angered him that she chose a life in a small southern town. Here in New York, and in all the countries they used to travel to together, were the luxuries they could well afford. He had chosen the wealthy supermodel as his life mate and it would have happened if he hadn't been caught in bed with another woman, whose name he could only vaguely remember. She had been only one in the long line of women he'd cheated on Chloe with.

He looked down at the rag in his hand again. Calvin did not believe its claim of her being strung out on drugs and near penniless. Chloe abhorred drugs and was way too intelligent to lose her millions of dollars. No, they were all lies and he knew that. But it proved that she needed him to protect her.

Turner Investigations was a resource he could have used a long time ago to get personal information on her, but he hadn't wanted to go that route to win her back. Well, now was different. He would get her back and keep her this time.

"What the hell?"

Angry, Anika snatched the tabloid magazine *The Star Gazer* off the supermarket rack where she stood in the express line to pay for her groceries. When she stopped off to the supermarket around the corner from her house, it certainly had been to get something to fix for dinner, not to be shocked beyond belief by the lies boldly printed on the front page of a rag!

She didn't even bother to read the story inside; it only expounded on the lies in the headline. Swearing loudly, and not caring that she drew odd looks from the cashier and the other patrons in line, Anika began to dig into the oversized mahogany Coach drawstring bag on her shoulder, shoving all the useless items she carried in it aside in search of her cell phone.

"Damn," she swore loudly. "Where's that damn phone of mine?"

When the cashier shot her another odd look, Anika pierced her with a stare. "Do you have a problem?" she asked nastily.

The woman instantly looked away.

Anika dropped the square red carrier holding her items onto the floor and pushed past the people in line ahead of her to leave the store. Her heart ached for Chloe, knowing the bitter lies would hurt her friend's feelings. Anger burned her and she wished she could get *her* hands on the throat of the writer of that trash or whoever else was involved.

Using the remote that swung off her key chain, Anika deactivated the alarm on her car. The cell phone lay carelessly on the passenger seat. Avoiding the rising October night winds, she quickly got into the driver's seat and dialed Chloe's number. Pushing the neon-lit SEND button, she anxiously awaited as the phone rang with no answer. Eventually the answering machine came on.

"Chloe, this is Anika. I don't know if you've seen *The Star Gazer* yet but they have one helluva piece of trash story on you in that rag. I know how this crap always upsets you and I want you to call me as soon as you get this message . . . anytime. Let me know you're okay. I think you ought to sue their sorry asses. Uhm, Chloe just call me."

Anika pushed the END button on the cell phone and let it drop back to the leather passenger seat. Her appetite was now gone. Turning the key in the ignition, she started the car and drove the short distance home.

Hopefully Mister Devon was worth more to Chloe than a good lay because right now she needed someone to support her. Anika knew that *he* was what Chloe wanted and needed.

Alicia smiled as she fingered the yellow receipt of the check she deposited in her bank account. "Fifteen hundred dollars more than I had two weeks ago, that's for sure," she said with satisfaction.

Calling *The Star Gazer* had been more profitable than she could ever believe. Effectively she had killed two birds with one stone: she ruined Chloe's reputation to run her out of town, and she made some money. The pictures she supplied from the twins' portfolio had given her an extra bonus.

Too good to be true.

They had been more than willing to listen as Alicia had posed as a "friend" over the phone. And she had made sure everyone she knew had heard about the story in the paper, although she let on to no one that she had sold it to the gossip rag. She would not let that get back to Devon.

And she did this all for him . . . well, for them, really.

Tomorrow she planned to "drop by" for a visit to her

friends, just to innocently mention the article to check their reactions.

Oh, Chloe knew about it. Alicia made sure of that when she slipped a copy of the paper into Chloe's mailbox today. She laughed as she imagined the woman's distraught face.

How she hated her and now she got her revenge!

Fifteen

Chloe heard the phone ring but she ignored it. The pain and betrayal was the same as the first time she had been the subject of the gossip rags. She had been just a few days shy of eighteen and still remarkably innocent, even after three years under her belt in the business. She was now in her early thirties, just one year after retiring from a lucrative career. She was successful, independent, mature and intelligent, and it still hurt like it did all those years ago.

Adell knocked on her daughter's bedroom door. Chloe didn't answer but she knew she was in there. Trying the doorknob, she found it unlocked, and she slowly entered the room. Her heart broke to see her only child's slim figure balled into a fetal position in the middle of her bed, her body shaking with tears.

As any mother would, Adell wished she could carry all of the burdens that rested on her child's shoulders. "Chloe baby," she called out, coming to sit on the side of the bed.

"Honey don't shut me out. I would fight the world for you . . . if I could." Tears glistened in her own full eyes as she laid a comforting hand on Chloe's designer-jeans-clad leg.

Chloe still did not look up from the pillow she squeezed tightly to her body. Adell knew then that she had not pre-

pared her young innocent child for the pitfalls of becoming famous and stepping into the public eye. How could she really when she didn't understand the phenomenon of it herself?

She had still raised her daughter in the same manner before she began modeling, even after they moved out of their small apartment and Chloe gained supermodel status. Adell wanted Chloe to remain grounded, so she knew she had to be blunt to toughen this child-woman of seventeen. Chloe had to learn to battle on her own and not hide.

"Honey I'm sorry 'bout those lies. You and I, and all of the people who know you and I mean really know you, don't believe a word of that trash in those papers or on those TV gossip shows." Adell paused, struggling to find the right words. "Do you know what my Mama, your Nana, always told me? That as long as people have tongues in their mouths there would be those who lied, and that I shouldn't let it break my spirit because they lied on Jesus Christ. Until the ends of time there are going to be mean and spiteful people who'll keep on lying. She told me to always hold my head up high and be proud with the truth and ignore the lies. Let 'em roll off your back like water."

Leaning over, she reached for the pillow covering Chloe's beautiful face. "Chloe baby, there are jealous and evil people out there who will break you . . . if you let them."

She smiled down at Chloe's tear-streaked face, so like her own when she was around the same age. "We live in a nasty world filled with people who love negativity. It makes them feel better about themselves. That's why those gossip rags sell. They don't want to hear about Chloe being a sought-after supermodel and straight-A student about to graduate from high school top of her class. They don't care that you volunteer almost all of your free time to the homeless shelters and women's clinics in your neighborhood. Honey, those things are the truths for you to be proud of.

"You sit up, wipe those tears and show them liars that you don't care. You're greater than them. So just let them lies roll off your back like water, Chloe."

"Mama," Chloe moaned, her eyes burning with tears. "I need you. I need you so much."

Let them lies roll off your back like water, Chloe.

Her mother's words, more than fifteen years old and still wise, replayed in Chloe's mind. No, Adell wasn't here now but all of her life's lessons that she passed on to her daughter remained.

Let them lies roll off your back like water, Chloe.

Chloe got up out of the bed, resolved to not let those foolish lies break her spirit. She was not a drug addict, she was nowhere near poverty and the home built on her family's land was beautifully furnished and completely paid for. All of it was stupid and foolish lies that were easily provable as such. She would have found them funny . . . if she felt like laughing.

Slowly she undressed, letting the expensive custom evening dress from Biba bis fall to the thick white carpet in a pool of midnight blue. Naked, she walked into her bathroom and ran steamy water into the double-sized claw-foot tub. She dropped in a handful of freesia-scented bath beads and lit the numerous Paddywax scented candles around the room before dimming the lights.

Chloe slowly stepped into the bath, letting her skin adjust to the steaming water before finally sinking beneath the scented depths with a sigh. Her head hammered from her earlier crying and her face was tight with the residue.

Let them lies roll off your back like water, Chloe.

"You are so right, Mama," she whispered, sure that from where her mother was in the heavens above that she could hear her. "I'm going to let them lies roll off my back just like water. I'm better than those liars. I *will* hold my head up with pride for everything I've accomplished."

Gone were the tears and, yes, some of the hurt had subsided, replaced by resilience. Now just the anger remained because the longer she rested in the warm depths of the water and inhaled the soothing aromatherapy, the more her thoughts were clear. They no longer jumbled and they began to crystalize.

Something very succinct had brightened in her thought process like a lightbulb . . . a very big and bright thousand-watt lightbulb. Chloe sat up straight in the tub, water flying everywhere.

How did *The Star Gazer* get photos of the inside of her house?

Devon turned into the driveway with his left hand as his right continued to throb like the devil. He was more than glad that Poochie's car was nowhere in sight. Parking, he reached across his chest to turn the key in the ignition with his good hand.

He wiggled the fingers of his injured right hand. At least it wasn't broken. Sighing, he hopped out of the truck and walked up the stairs into the house. No sooner had he closed the door behind him than his grandmother walked into the living room carrying a bowl of ice and an Ace bandage.

Deshawn called from the kitchen, "How did you get in a fight without me?" before he too walked into the living room.

Lil pushed him down onto the sofa as she sat beside him and examined his hand. "Great goodness, Vonnie," she exclaimed softly.

"How'd you know—"

"Charlie called me," she interrupted him before he could even finish his question. "Said it was with that jackass Luther over Chloe. True or not?"

Her voice was no-nonsense as she settled his hand into the

bowl filled with ice cubes and cold water. Devon winced before answering, his voice tight, "I don't wanna talk about it."

Deshawn bit noisily into an apple as he peered down from where he stood behind their grandmother's seated form. "Well this is a small town and even if *you* don't want to talk about it, everyone else will."

Another noisy bite.

Devon leaned back against the blue plaid sofa, his eyes closed. His hand was nearly frozen and still throbbing. He thought of Chloe, wishing it was she tending his hand. He could see her face so clearly, masked with concern, her hair flowing around her, the sweet scent of her surrounding him as she nursed the hand he injured defending her honor.

Deshawn took another noisy bite, his mouth filled with the sweet crisp fruit. "If I heard him bad-mouthing Chloe I would've knocked him on his—"

"Shawn!" Nana Lil shouted, cutting him off before he could release the obscenity.

"Sorry Nana."

"Charlie also told me about that article about Chloe in one of those tabloid papers."

Devon sat upright, his voice exasperated. "What paper?"

The squeal of tires and the flash of lights turning into the yard precluded any further discussion. A car door slammed and before anyone could move to the window to see who their visitor was, the front door flew open like a hurricane blew it.

Chloe stepped into the house, dripping wet and clothed only in a thin cotton robe that barely concealed her nakedness. Water pooled from her hair down the back of the robe. Her chest heaved in anger, and a crumpled colored newspaper was clutched in her grasp.

She looked as if she'd fallen in a pond.

Devon thought she never seemed more beautiful than when she blazed with anger, especially with her skin glistening from the water, her beautiful cat-shaped eyes flashing, and her breasts heaving up and down in a rather hypnotic rhythmic

motion beneath the thin cotton material that clung to them.
He could see the outline of a plump nipple.

Suddenly he realized that if he could gaze upon the nipples
he loved to taste, then so could his brother. One glance at
Deshawn's bemused expression as he ogled Chloe confirmed
his suspicions. "Deshawn," he warned, his voice deep with
an edge.

"What?" he asked innocently, glancing briefly at his
brother before returning to his leering.

"Chloe baby. What's wrong?" Lil swooped the afghan from
the back of the couch and brought it over to put around Chloe
where she still stood by the door. "You're soaking wet."

"I was in the tub when I realized that Alicia sold pictures
of my house to this . . ." She held up the balled paper
clutched in her fist. "To this . . . this tabloid garbage. She
probably sold them the lies as well."

"Alicia?" Devon and Deshawn both exclaimed in
astonishment and immediate disbelief.

Nana Lil looked skeptical as well. "Chloe, let me see this
mess everybody's talkin' 'bout."

Lil took the paper from Chloe and straightened out the
crumpled pages as best she could before slipping on her reading glasses.

"Alicia?" Deshawn repeated again. "Why would you think
she would do a thing like that, Chloe?"

Chloe looked to Devon, ready for his skepticism or outright
disbelief of her accusation of Alicia. He met her stare but
said nothing, knowing full well that the topic of his best friend
was a very sore subject between them. But even if he did not
say so, he did not believe Alicia would do what she was accused of and Chloe saw that in his eyes. She stiffened in
anger.

Lil snorted in derision, her wise graying eyes bright with
anger. "Well that's the biggest bunch of bull crap I ever saw.
Chloe's no more on drugs than I am. And the way this girl
shops, how in the world could she be broke!"

"Drugs?" Devon barked, breaking his stare with Chloe.

Deshawn grabbed the paper and read the entire article aloud. Chloe hated the stab of pain she felt in her gut as she heard the vicious lies about her. Devon saw it and felt his anger rise as Deshawn neared the end of the article.

Chloe wrapped the blanket closer around her body and turned to gaze out the window at the starry night.

"Is this the crap you punched Luther about?" Deshawn balled the paper up and threw it solidly into the wastepaper basket across the room. "Too bad you didn't break his damn jaw."

Chloe's eyes rounded with surprise as she whirled to face Devon. It was then she saw his hand resting in a bowl of ice water. "Devon, what happened to your hand? Who did you hit? What did this Luther say about me?"

The questions flew out of her mouth like automatic gunfire as she rushed to kneel by Devon's feet. Gingerly she reached out to touch his injured hand, causing the blanket to fall from around her shoulders. "Oh Devon," she whispered, and felt tears rising again.

Nana Lil walked over to pat Chloe's shoulder comfortingly. "He's okay, baby. Why don't you dry his hand and then wrap it tight with this Ace bandage?"

Chloe took the white hand towel and Ace bandage Lil offered her, immediately getting to work on his hand as instructed. The concern he imagined was clearly etched in her beautiful face as he watched her closely. He felt comfort as the sweet scent of her rose for him to inhale and her hair floated forward off her shoulders.

He was still so angry about the lies told on this beautiful woman that he didn't even feel the pain as Chloe tightly wrapped his hand. He would gladly injure it again if he could get to the one who hurt his woman!

To think months ago he would have believed the crap. "I'm sorry Chloe," he whispered, deep and low enough for just her ears. "I don't believe one word of it. You know that."

Chloe looked up at him, her eyes hesitant. "Do you believe me about Alicia? Honestly Devon, do you?"

When he didn't answer, Chloe shook her head before lowering it to finish her task. Hurt assailed her slender frame. "Chloe—" he began.

Her head shot up and he saw the pain in the honeyed depths. "I have no reason to lie or accuse someone unjustly. I would never do that."

After tightly wrapping his hand, Chloe moved away from him. He felt lost. Devon watched as she retrieved the newspaper from the wastepaper basket, her curvaceous body outlined by the lamp beneath her robe.

"Deshawn, please go to the office and get your portfolio." she asked, her voice determined.

"What does that have to—"

"Please Shawn."

Unsure of her purpose but still willing to honor her request, Deshawn left the house.

"Chloe, I saw the pictures of your house in the paper. But do you understand why it's hard to believe Alicia's involved in this mess?" Nana Lil spoke from where she leaned against the back of the recliner. "She's a dear friend to the family. Alicia and the twins have been the best of friends for years, since they all were children."

She held up her hand when Chloe's face tightened in anger. "Hold up, Chloe. I also don't believe you're lying . . . just mistaken. Maybe someone else got into the house before you moved in and took the pictures."

Chloe said nothing as she wrapped her arms around herself, avoiding Devon's gaze, which she felt intently upon her. Deshawn re-entered the house carrying the large black leather-bound portfolio under his arm. "Here it is, Chloe."

She nodded. "Please find the pictures Alicia took of my house for the portfolio when the house was first completed.

Devon rose, coming to stand next to his brother, as did Nana Lil. Deshawn flipped to the two pages, easily found since her house was their last project. Chloe remained where she stood, the tabloid in her hand opened to the color layout displaying photos of her home.

"I think you will find that the photos in this rag are the exact same pictures in the portfolio. I remembered them from when Deshawn showed them to me." She stepped up and placed the open tabloid onto the open pages of the portfolio in Deshawn's hands.

"I'll be damned," Deshawn whispered.

"Oh, Alicia, why?" Lil turned away from the incriminating evidence.

The photos were exactly the same, just as she knew they were. Only Devon, Deshawn and Alicia had access to the precious portfolio chronicling Jamison & Jamison's achievements. Obviously if they weren't the ones to turn over the photos or the negatives, then Alicia had to be the culprit.

Just then the lights flashed against the walls again as a car turned into the yard. Lil moved to look out the window. She lowered her head with a pained expression. "Lord help us all," she murmured dryly before moving to open the front door.

Alicia flew in with quick strides, heading straight for Devon with wide, frantic eyes. "I heard about the fight at Charlie's. What happened, Devon?"

She looked back and forth between Devon's and Deshawn's identical faces, both expressions cold as they looked down at her. It was then she knew something was terribly wrong.

Sixteen

"Didn't I warn you what would happen if you didn't keep my name out of your mouth?"

Alicia turned at the sound of Chloe's voice closing in behind her and immediately felt the sting of a hard slap across her mouth. Chloe moved to grab at the woman's neck, her eyes blazing with murderous rage.

Devon stepped quickly between them and wrapped his arms around Chloe. She struggled against his strength, clawing and twisting to get at Alicia. "Let me go, Devon. Let . . . me . . . go!"

He didn't flinch when she directed the angry blows on his chest. Turning, he saw that Deshawn had Alicia similarly detained. "Girl, I'll stomp a mud hole in your little behind," Alicia yelled over Deshawn's shoulder as she tried to be freed from his strong hold as well.

Lil stepped between the two couples. "I will not have fighting in this house. Now stop it . . . both of you . . . now!"

She gave both women a hard stare, brooking no room for argument. She was an elder and when she spoke, she expected and deserved to be listened to. They both immediately quieted down, though they shot angry glares at each other from around their captors' bodics.

Lil faced Deshawn and Alicia, moving sideways so she could look into the woman's face. "I just want to make it clear that I am very disappointed to see that you have such a mean and evil spirit in you, Alicia."

She feigned innocence, making her face the picture of confusion. "Nana Lil, what did *I* supposedly do?"

Lil held up a thin hand. "Just stop it. Haven't you lied enough?"

She turned to Devon and Chloe. "Take Chloe in my room."

He immediately swung her up into his arms easily and strode with her across the short span to his grandmother's bedroom, right off the living room. Once inside, he lowered her to the floor and closed the door behind them.

Chloe moved away from him, offering him the view of her backside and an icy cold shoulder. She felt his warmth as he neared her and stiffened when he reached out to touch her. "Don't," she spat.

Devon rubbed his hands over his eyes. "Look, I'm going out there to see about Alicia. We'll talk as soon as we're all done out there."

Chloe flung herself onto the edge of Nana Lil's quilt-covered bed. "Whatever, but I hope you know that if not for Nana Lil I would have clawed her eyes out."

"I don't doubt it," he muttered before leaving the room and closing the door behind him.

Alicia twirled to look at him. "Dev, I know you don't think I had anything to do with this?"

He took the paper that she wiggled in his face. "Alicia, how do you explain these pictures being the same exact ones in the portfolio?"

She felt panic as her eyes looked into the hardened, chiseled features of Devon's handsome face. His eyes blazed with anger and mistrust. Even though he allowed for an explanation, everything about him said she had already been tried and convicted. Alicia knew then that she had gone too far. Gone were her friends, replaced by these two brooding strangers. Yet both of the twins looked at her as if *she* had changed.

"I'll go check on Chloe." Lil crossed the living room and

walked into her room, allowing a brief glimpse of Chloe's robed figure before she closed the door behind her.

"Why'd you do it, Alicia? Chloe told me you disliked her but I didn't believe it. How can you hate her so much to sell lies to a gossip rag to hurt her?"

Alicia's mouth widened in mock indignation. "Devon how could you believe—"

"Cut it, Alicia." He slashed his hand up in the air in anger. "I thought you'd be woman enough to admit to what you did."

Tears filled Alicia's eyes. Her best-laid plans were going painfully awry as Devon eyed her with contempt. She felt swallowed by the pain. "I can't believe my best friends would think this of me. Has she turned you against me? She hates me—"

"I can see why she would," Deshawn interjected wryly from where he now stood by the staircase.

Her ready tears and pleas moved neither of them. What she did was treacherous and deceitful. Those were traits neither of them found they wanted in a person they called a friend, or an employee.

"Look Alicia, because you took advantage of your job to obtain the photos, we're going to have to let you go." Devon became saddened and wearied by the whole affair. "I'm sorry Al, but you brought this on yourself. Chloe is our client and this could jeopardize future projects because of your lack of respect for our client's privacy."

Alicia's tears dried up and her face twisted in anger. She looked from Devon to Deshawn and back to Devon again. "I'm fired?" Her voice was incredulous and hoarse.

"Yes Al," Deshawn answered from behind her.

She nodded and looked down at her hands, which were trembling with anger. "Oh I understand. You had a choice to make, either me or the rich bitch. With friends like you two, who needs enemies?"

Devon saw the hatred for Chloe and maybe even himself as he looked at her. He could hardly believe that this evil, twisted-faced shrew in front of him was his childhood friend. "Look, just calm down, Al."

"Calm down?" she yelled, stomping her foot in frustration. "I hate her. Why couldn't she just leave town? She's got your nose so wide open that you'd turn your back on your friend. You're whipped, Devon!"

"That's enough, Alicia," he warned.

"Just go home, Al," Deshawn said wearily before walking over to slump into one of the recliners in front of the television.

"She's a damn coke fiend," Alicia spat as she shoved Devon's chest.

He grabbed her hands and pushed them down to her sides, before releasing her. "And you're jealous."

She laughed bitterly to disguise the hurt his words caused. "Oh yeah? Jealous of what?"

Devon's eyes raked up and down Alicia, his intent clear. "It's pretty obvious."

Alicia's eyes filled with hurt and real tears. He instantly regretted the words because right now she resembled the girl he grew up with. "Alicia—" he began.

She slapped him hard across his face. "I hate you, Devon!"

His face stung from her attack. "Get out, Alicia. Stay the hell away from Chloe. If you attempt to harm her in *any* way, I will make sure you regret it."

"Chloe . . . Chloe . . . Chloe," she mimicked in a high-pitched voice. "This is all her fault."

Devon eyes glittered with anger. "Chloe and I are together. I don't give a damn who doesn't like it, and that's including you . . . for whatever reasons you have."

She stiffened at his words. "She told you that I was in love with you, didn't she?" Alicia spat. "And y'all just laid up in bed together and laughed at me, right? Well I got the last laugh, didn't I?"

"Get the hell out of my sight. You'll never find a man to

love an evil witch like you." He turned his back and walked into Nana Lil's bedroom.

She was weak with grief. Devon was completely lost to her now. Tears flowed bitter streaks down her cheeks, collecting at the edge of her face before dropping to wet her T-shirt. "What have I done?"

Deshawn felt pity for their friend as her legs seemed to give out beneath her. He moved just in time to catch her before she fell. But at the touch of his hands, she angrily slapped them away.

"You turned on me too, Deshawn. So stay away from me." Alicia forced her body to move as she walked stiffly to the front door under his watchful gaze.

"Look Alicia. Are you gonna be okay?" Deshawn asked, but the door had already closed quietly behind her with a click.

"Nana Lil, can I talk to Chloe alone please?"

"I think that's a good idea." She exited the bedroom, leaving them alone.

Chloe flung her arms around a surprised Devon's neck. He immediately pulled her tight against his chest, burying his face in her neck, fresh with the scent of soap. He enjoyed the feel of her body through the thin cotton material.

"Oh Devon. We heard every word in here." She leaned back to look up into his eyes and saw the mixed emotions in them. "I'm sorry. I know Alicia's your friend, but what she did was despicable. You did what you had to."

Devon nodded before planting a brief kiss on her upturned mouth, his one good hand freely roaming her body with gentle massages. "I know. It's just that I didn't know she could be so vicious."

"Where's Deshawn?"

He shrugged. "Probably somewhere eating something," he said wryly, and they both laughed.

"Did you really beat someone up for little ol' me?" she asked sweetly, feigning weakness.

Devon slapped her soundly on her behind before tightly gripping the full swell. "If you were there you would've done it yourself. You've got one helluva swing."

"Yeah, so you better watch out, especially with only one functioning hand."

He raised a brow in mock indignation. "I'm shaking in my boots, baby."

"I love that," she sighed, just as his hands grasped her.

"What . . . this?" He massaged the soft fullness of her buttocks.

"No," she answered quickly, laughing at his shocked expression. "I meant when you call me baby."

"You are my baby . . . baby." He lowered his voice as he nuzzled her earlobe. "I'm sorry about all of this. If I had just listened to you I could have prevented—"

"Ssshhh," Chloe silenced him. "I wish it hadn't happened either, but it did and I'll just have to deal with it like before."

"Before?"

"Uh-hum." She filled him in on her first tango with the treacherous tabloids.

"Damn," he swore when she was finished. "You were just a kid."

Chloe nodded, her head against his chest as he rocked their bodies in a slow and gentle motion that could lull her into falling asleep on her feet and in his arms. They remained that way, simply enjoying the warmth and comfort of one another. In each other's arms they felt they could battle all challengers and win.

"Why don't you sue?" Devon asked, his own voice dragging like he was near sleep himself. "Make them print a retraction. All of the lies can easily be proved false."

"True, but I think I'll follow my mother's advice."

"And what's that?" His mouth kissed a trail from her earlobe to the base of her neck as he struggled to lift her robe up around her waist with his uninjured hand.

Chloe gasped in pleasure when he began to explore her intimately with his fingers. "Let . . . it . . . roll . . . roll, uhm let . . . it . . . roll . . . off . . . oh, my . . . wow!"

He laughed low and husky against her neck, enjoying the havoc he wracked on her senses. "What's that?" he asked as he lifted her leg around his waist and delved his fingers into her wetness.

"I said . . . let . . . it . . . roll . . . oh, just . . . forget it." She grasped both sides of his face with her hands and kissed him, deepening it with her tongue. His moan of pleasure was just as loud as her own.

Baam . . . baam.

They jumped apart as someone knocked loudly on the bedroom door. "You two are mighty quiet in there. Whatever it is you're doing, don't need to be done in my room!"

They laughed as Lil's voice floated through the solid wood. Chloe retied her robe just as Devon opened the door. Lil walked in, sniffing the air.

"I don't smell anything, so I'm guessing I knocked just in time. Now scat. I'm gonna watch TV."

Devon and Chloe left the bedroom hand in hand to enter the living room. Deshawn was nowhere in sight. "Wait here," he ordered, before running up the stairs.

Chloe's eyes caught the tabloid hanging halfway out of the wastepaper basket with the rest of the trash where it belonged. She felt much stronger knowing she had this family, especially Devon, behind her with support. Her heart swelled with affection for them as she thought of their immediate defense of her.

Devon walked back down the stairs carrying a small duffel bag. "Let's go."

Chloe feigned innocence. "Where?"

He pulled her in his arms and kissed her thoroughly. "We can finish what we started in my bedroom upstairs. I'm sure you remember how that was, keeping ourselves from screaming out each other's name too loud. Or, we can hop in your big SUV and shake the rooftops at your place. What'll it be?"

Chloe winked, her breathing still ragged from his kiss. "Race you to the big SUV?"

Seventeen

In just two days the tabloid's lies had made it to radio and television media everywhere. They were having a field day with it, especially with the fashion awards just two weeks away. Chloe's answering machine was filled with calls from her concerned friends, many of them members of the famous and rich elite like herself. And Anika called every morning and evening with the brash advice for her to tell the world to kiss her rear end.

She couldn't bear to have the television or the radio on for too long. And she was tired of the whole circus, praying for when some other unlucky celebrity would become embroiled in calumny, leaving Chloe's scandal but a forgotten memory to the gossip hungry.

The small town of Holtsville was of course ripe with the news, although overall they were very supportive and not believing of the lies. For that she felt even closer to the town's people.

Sunday morning Chloe reluctantly left Devon lying on his back, his head under the pillow, asleep in bed. Thankfully his hand had recovered from its injuries and last night he had spent the night showing her just how adept his hand was again.

Chloe picked up his gray Nike T-shirt from their pile of discarded clothes on the floor and slipped it over her naked figure. In the bathroom, she cleansed her face and brushed her teeth before padding barefoot out of the room and down the long curved corridor to the kitchen.

The sun's rays blasted through the clear glass of the skylight, warming the large kitchen. Within minutes she had their breakfast on. Ham steaks fried in the cast iron skillet, fresh peeled potatoes sliced with green onions and bell peppers cooked on another eye in a similar pan, and a bowl of six eggs sat mixed in a bowl ready to be scrambled. She settled on browning thick slices of Texas toast over dealing with making homemade biscuits.

Using the remote, Chloe turned on the television in the kitchen, which was also equipped with cable, and turned to the *Bobby Jones Gospel Show* as she settled on one of the stools surrounding the island. Her thoughts were filled with the latest turmoil in her life, and they seemed endless.

She was scheduled to leave for New York at the end of the week and she hadn't yet worked up the nerve to tell Devon. Instinctively she knew he wouldn't like her returning to what he called "sin city." Every time the path in front of them seemed smooth, a large hurdle would appear.

First, she had to get past her own hang-ups and realize that it was okay to have this man in her life. Then, they argued about Alicia and that kept them apart for two weeks that seemed an eternity. And then they argued again about Alicia the night of her dinner party. And now this.

But she had to tell him because she *was* going. His dictating her moves was not a part of her plans for them, but he did deserve to be told. Chloe knew she might as well get it over with. "I'll tell him today," she promised herself out loud as she flipped the ham steaks. "It's only for two weeks. I'll tell him today."

"Something smells good."

Chloe turned to find Devon groggily walking into the kitchen, clad only in Calvin Klein boxers. He looked just as good as the handsome, muscled models of the notorious

Calvin Klein ads. He rubbed his eyes and stretched before coming over to look down at the food cooking.

"Good morning, baby."

"Morning."

He leaned over and kissed her cheek. "I would kiss that sexy mouth of yours, but . . ."

"Morning breath," they said in unison and laughed.

"I'll go shower and brush my teeth." He walked out of the kitchen.

"Breakfast will be ready in a few minutes, Devon," she called after him.

When he emerged back into the kitchen, now clad in a tank and matching nylon sweat pants, he pulled Chloe away from the stove and kissed her thoroughly. "Now that's a good morning."

Dizzy with desire, Chloe's step faltered when he finally released her and took his seat on one of the stools. Inhaling deeply for breath to strengthen herself, she set a plate of food in front of him, along with a carafe of orange juice and a saucer of the buttered Texas toast before serving herself.

Devon whistled at the sight and smell of the food. "Damn, my baby can cook."

She smiled in pleasure. "Thanks."

"So what do you want to do today?" he asked as he dug into the home fries on his plate, now soaked with ketchup.

"I don't know, what do you want to do?"

He took a large gulp of his juice. "Whatever you want to do."

She knew he was trying to get her mind off the media frenzy swirling around her, and she adored him for it. After thinking about it, she said, "Frankie's Fun Park."

Devon nearly choked on his juice, looking at her in surprise. "You want our first date to be at Frankie's?"

"Second date."

"Huh?"

"Our first date was when we went horseback riding."

Nodding, his eyes met hers as they both recalled that day by the pond. "You really want to go to Frankie's?" he asked after a while.

At her nod, he returned to eating. "It's nothing like Disney World in Florida, so don't get your hopes up. But if you want to go, then Frankie's it is. We'll leave at eleven o'clock."

"Eleven it is." She glanced at the round digital clock on the wall. "That gives us another whole hour. What shall we do to pass the time?"

Suggestively he wiggled his eyebrows, and Chloe knew they both had loving on their minds.

It was four o'clock when Chloe and Devon walked out of the small amusement park arm in arm. They had ridden all the water rides, played the video and arcade games, and laughed at each other's antics until they were tired and ravenous. Many times during the day they had resembled the hordes of children surrounding them as they frolicked together.

It was the most fun she had had in along time. Probably because it was time shared with Devon. Just as Chloe suspected, her relationship with Devon had stepped to another level, something that she hadn't wanted to venture into when she first seduced him, yet couldn't seem to avoid. It was as if everything was following a logical course of events. But she told herself that she hadn't fallen in love, so the power was still hers.

"Where do you want to go to eat?" he asked as they climbed into Chloe's SUV with Devon driving since he knew the Charleston area better than she did.

"Wherever you choose is fine, but I would love some chicken quesadillas."

Devon glanced over at her. Again she amazed him with her simplistic requests from him. It was as if she was a normal woman, and not a mega-rich celebrity. "Mexican it is," he said, as he started the engine.

The spicy scents from La Hacienda could be smelled outside as he parked. Chloe's stomach grumbled loudly in protest to its emptiness. She wished now she had accepted Devon's offer to eat at the amusement park, but she wasn't a fan of hot dogs.

"Hungry?" he asked wryly, having heard her stomach's growl, before shutting off the Navigator.

Chloe pinched his arm playfully before climbing out of the vehicle. "You shouldn't fool with me when I'm hungry."

He laughed as he came around to walk with her into the restaurant. "Believe me, I know. Remember, I've seen you eat plenty of times."

For this he got a soft pat on the back of his head.

She saw, with relief, that the other patrons were dressed casually, ensuring that Devon and she wouldn't feel out of place in their jeans and T-shirts. They were seated within minutes and supplied with laminated menus.

Chloe already knew what she wanted, so she looked around the restaurant as Devon studied the many selections. The decor was dark with wood paneling and maroon carpeting, but the walls were lined with sconces, allowing small amounts of light that gave the entire restaurant a cozy, warm atmosphere. A light Spanish love song played in the background and the tantalizing scent of Spanish delicacies was in the air. All of it combined for a warm, welcoming atmosphere. Hardly Tavern of the Green in New York but she liked it just the same.

"Can I take your order?"

Chloe looked up at the pretty, honey-complected waitress standing at their booth looking at Devon, who was still looking at his menu. Rolling her expressive eyes upward, Chloe cleared her throat. "I'm ready even if he's not," she said sweetly with a false smile.

The waitress reluctantly turned to her and Chloe felt satisfied when the young woman's eyes widened in recognition of her. "I'll have a double order of the chicken quesadilla appetizers and a frozen margarita with salt."

Chloe truly enjoyed the woman's star-struck expression as she handed over her menu. "You're Chloe Bolton!" she said in a reverent tone.

Devon cleared his throat. "Now *I'd* like to order," he said wryly.

The waitress turned to Devon, interest still in the depths of her eyes but definitely not as intense. "I'm sorry. Go ahead, sir."

Chloe looked at the woman as Devon ordered. Gone was the look of adoration. She jotted down his request for a bowl of three-bean chili, followed by seared chicken and Spanish pilaf, with nonalcoholic sangria.

Devon handed over his menu and the waitress left the table. "You forgot to order something for your ego."

"Ha ha," Chloe chanted sarcastically.

Obviously Devon had seen the silent challenge between the women, followed by Chloe's look of triumph when her opponent backed down. She took a sip of her ice water. "Not ego . . . confidence, thank you very much."

"It doesn't hurt your . . . *confidence* to be a famous supermodel?" he asked smugly.

"Not one bit."

They both laughed at her honesty.

"Do you miss it?" he asked suddenly, his obsidian eyes serious as he watched her across the booth's square table.

"Honestly?"

He nodded before taking a sip of the drinks the waitress sat on their table.

"My life just a year ago was hectic. I own a wonderfully luxurious apartment in New York, which I spent a total of thirty nights in since I've owned it. I lived out of Gucci and Samsonite luggage in five-star hotels across the globe. I have a best friend I love like a sister whom I see five times a year, tops." Chloe paused, looking off toward the busy highway through the window, her eyes distant. "I have a few people that I can truly consider friends, and they happen to be comedians, designers, musicians and other models, but a lot of people I found myself surrounded by just wanted to say they hung out with someone famous. The work was not always easy. The schedules could get very hectic with photo shoots at odd times of the morning or in extreme weather situations or . . . confining and uncomfortable clothing . . . all to get the perfect shot.

"The partying I was never into. Out of ten invitations I'd receive a month, for some club or restaurant's opening, or a charity event or movie premiere, I would go to like two, tops. And that was only if Anika went along with me." She paused again as the waitress brought their food. "Any spare time not working I would volunteer at charities in my old neighborhood, which I miss, or I would visit schools, or just chill out at home reading. My life outside of work was really boring because I didn't have time to develop it. Anika says I don't take advantage of my star status enough."

"Boring? Minus the celebrity friends, traveling across the globe and being lusted after by men everywhere?" he asked, his voice amused as he tasted the chili.

"Of course," she said with a beguiling smile that made his heart jump.

"You still haven't answered my question. Holtsville is a helluva lot different from New York and Europe. Do you miss it all?" He hoped his voice didn't betray how important her answer was to him because it spoke of his biggest fear concerning Chloe.

"No, I don't," she said with honesty. "Holtsville is my home now, and the only drawback is not having Anika around and maybe the shopping. I really wish you could meet Anika. She is one of a kind. She says what she wants when she wants, she takes no shorts, she's beautiful and so funny with the quirkiest sense of humor. I really miss her so much."

"Isn't she ever going to visit you? I could meet her then."

Chloe cleared her throat. Now would be the opportune time to tell him about her trip to New York, but she chickened out, afraid of his reaction. "She wants to meet you. I've told her all about you."

Devon looked surprised. "Oh, and what did you tell her?"

"Now that's none of your business, Mister Jamison." She turned her attention to her food with a wink.

Devon lowered his eyes. She looked and sounded so sincere about moving to Holtsville. Could she really turn her back on New York? Why didn't he believe her? More importantly, was he ready to admit to himself why the thought of her leaving Holtsville bothered him so?

The Carolina sky was deeply ebony in color and star-filled, with a brightly glowing full moon as Chloe leaned against Devon's chest. His muscled arm was securely around her as he drove them home. Almost as if instinctively, his fingers lightly traced circles on her arm and Chloe felt her nipples tighten in sharp response.

During the entire drive from Charleston, they rode in companionable silence, intensely aware of one another. Chloe really had had fun today with Devon, seeing a more carefree and playful side to him that she thought only existed in his rascal twin. They had talked all through dinner and Chloe had shared her never-voiced plans to increase her charity works with all the time she had on her hands.

Her wish was to create a foundation in honor of her mother. The foundation would benefit inner-city communities such as the one she grew up in and still loved and supported financially. This was very important to her and there were many issues in these communities that only money could address.

That admission had earned her so much respect from Devon, and he wondered if he would ever know how deep her character was. They had both shared so many bits of information about each other, expanding their knowledge of one another beyond what they already knew.

Her favorite color was maroon, his forest green.

She loved fried eggs on toasted bread with jelly and butter, while he favored lima beans and cornbread. They both frowned in dislike at the other's choice.

Her all-time favorite movie was *Love Jones* starring Nia Long and Larenz Tate. His was *Cooley High*. Both could live with that.

They both loved jazz . . . Miles Davis, Thelonius Monk and Wynton Marsalis. But they both also loved hip-hop.

Each claimed to be the supreme best at playing Scrabble. A challenge was given, and the winner would be declared after a game.

She loved flowers, especially perennials. He admitted to designing the landscape of their property.

It had been a day filled with new discoveries.

Devon smiled as he also remembered their day together. This woman beside him was an irresistible mix of city girl sophistication with down-home charm. Could this uptown beauty be his down-home girl in disguise?

October nights in South Carolina were a lot chillier than Chloe would have thought. She adjusted her central heat up to seventy-two degrees before crossing the Persian rug to where her answering machine and telephone sat on a long marble table behind the couch. The red light blinked, signaling she had messages. Actually, five messages according to the digital counter display.

Chloe pushed the PLAYBACK button. Her outgoing message played first. "Hey, this is Chloe. You know the routine."

Beep.

"Chloe . . . Chloe . . . pick up." There was silence and then a dry hacking cough. "This is Olivia. I guess you're not home. You never are. Anyway there's been a change in your escort for the awards ceremony. Call me back for details and I hope you're feeling better about that tabloid bull."

Beep.

"Hello Chloe. This is Warren Atkinson." Chloe recognized the reserved and authoritative voice of the president of Ashanti Cosmetics. "I know that you are officially retired, but I have a business proposition that I believe would be beneficial to both Ashanti Cosmetics and you. I understand that you'll be in New York next week. This would be an opportune time for you to meet with the board of directors. Please call my assistant, Evelyn, to set up an appointment at your convenience to discuss this offer."

Chloe raised a finely arched brow from where she sat on the couch, her legs crossed under her. Business proposition. She didn't have time to ponder that bit of news as the machine continued.

Beep.

"Chloe, this is your best friend in the world. The diva to top all divas. I can't wait for you to get your country-sounding behind back to the Big Apple this week. Call me."

Beep.

"Cat . . . how are you, baby?"

Chloe stiffened at the sound of Calvin's smooth baritone voice. She rolled her eyes heavenward in irritated exasperation. "How in the hell did he get my number?" she muttered as she eyed the machine as if it were the vilest of creatures.

"I saw the tabloid article on you and of course I know they're just ludicrous lies. I hope you haven't let them break your spirit in that backwards boonies you've chosen to hide in." There was pause. "God, Cat baby. I miss you. Damn, Cat, I love you and you know I do. Call me and let's talk."

Chloe shook her head, ignoring the supposed passion in his voice. "He probably believes that too," she muttered incredulously.

Beep.

"You think you're so damn smart. How did you turn my

friends against me? You know damn well that I didn't sell nothing to *The Star Gazer*. Are you that . . ."

Chloe sighed wearily as she recognized Alicia's voice. Was the woman insane? She just wished Devon had come back here with her, instead of deciding to stay home tonight. Then he could hear his little buddy playing on the phone.

". . . insecure about your screwing around with Devon. You're only using him and I'm gonna prove it. I love Devon too much to lose him to a black Barbie with about as much brains as a rubber doll. If you know what's good for you, you'll leave him alone."

The line, thankfully, disconnected and Chloe laughed at the woman's craftiness. She still spouted her innocence on the message while slandering her, so that if Chloe decided to tell the twins about it then they would hear her basically still defending herself.

"*I* have no brains? *I* would've been smart enough not to use the photos from the portfolio at my job, you nitwit," she said to the empty room before unfolding her tall slender frame from the plush couch to leave the living room through the rear entrance. It led into the game room and Chloe continued to fuss as she walked. "The little elf left a trail back to herself and she says *I* have no brains."

She laughed harshly into the air as she briskly strode through the game room and went through the next rounded archway into the wood-paneled sauna off the gym. "I'm not the one moping behind a man who does not want me, yet *I* have no brains!"

In the sauna there were two entrances. She took the one to the left leading to the pool. Chloe barely took the precious moments to remove all her clothes, her watch and sneakers before plunging beneath the warm depths of the circular pool.

She felt weighted down by all the activities going on in her life simultaneously. Relentlessly, she swam laps until she forced herself to slow down before she caught a wicked and painful cramp. As she allowed her body to gently float on the water, she reviewed her life.

A little twit country bumpkin was hell-bent on revenge because she was currently involved with the man the little troll secretly desired. Alicia's selling of photos, and possibly the story, to the tabloid proved she was capable of anything. So now Chloe felt she had to be on her guard about the woman's activities concerning her.

Directly because of Alicia's foolishness, Chloe was in the midst of a media frenzy about her being a drug addict and near poverty. She could only imagine the barrage of questions she would encounter once back in the Big Apple. The paparazzi were a lot more forceful than what she encountered in the genteel South.

Then, her philandering ex-boyfriend was still hot on her heels for a reconciliation she did not want. He was now in possession of her private and unlisted phone number. He might even have her address. She knew all too well how persistent and seductively convincing he could be. She had to be on her guard for whatever attempts at a loving reconciliation Calvin had planned for her.

Liv was constantly trying to convince her to give up retirement, telling Chloe of the offers she still received for her once-top supermodel. Liv actually believed the tabloid story helped to boost Chloe back into the minds and hearts of her fans. And of course Liv had a hand in her next dilemma; how else had they gotten her number?

The president of Ashanti Cosmetics was calling her personally at home to offer a business proposition. The company had always been very obliging to her needs as their spokeswoman, and somehow she knew their proposition would be irresistible. She would of course honor their request for a meeting because of their past working relationship, but she had to be on her guard not to relent and accept the offer. No matter how inviting.

And lastly, she knew that if she didn't guard her precious

heart more carefully, she could easily find herself falling for Devon, going beyond her unspoken rule of the body but not the heart.

Eighteen

Monday morning dawned bright and early for Chloe, but she wished the sun had never risen. Longingly she turned on her side to clutch Devon's pillow to her, wishing that it was truly him. With a groan she threw the pillow to the floor.

Why did the man have to be so obstinate and stubborn?

Last night he had surprised her by driving down to her house. She had been pleased and touched when he told her he missed her and followed his impulse to see her immediately. After making glorious love, they showered and sat towel-clad in the steam room, something Chloe had to talk him into for nearly twenty minutes before he agreed. It was as they sat, sweating and inhaling the steam, that she finally got the nerve to tell him about her upcoming trip to New York.

With a grimace, Chloe recalled the brief and highly disappointing conversation.

"Uhm Devon, we need to talk," she began as she watched his muscled form, clad only in a loose-fitting towel, stretch out on the wooden bench along the wall of the steam room.

He bent one leg up on the bench and put his arm over his eyes. "About?"

Chloe watched him closely from where she sat on the bench opposite him. "About . . . uhm . . . me leaving for New York Sunday.

She saw his body tense for one brief second before he regained his relaxed composure. "Are you coming back?"

His voice revealed nothing and Chloe didn't know what to think. "Of course I'm coming back, Devon. Holtsville is my home now."

She moved to sit next to his feet, letting her hand slide from his muscled thigh to up underneath the towel he wore. He tensed at the feel of her hand.

"Have fun," he said shortly as he sat up suddenly, causing Chloe's hand to fall softly to the bench. "Look, I better be getting back home. Nana Lil wasn't feeling well and I wanna check on her."

Chloe immediately felt the distance he put between them as he wordlessly left the steam room. "Damn it," she swore, her voice whisper soft.

She shut off the steam and left the room as well, letting the swirls of steam escape out the opened door. He was in the bedroom, almost fully dressed when she reached him.

"Devon."

He looked up from tying his sneakers as he sat on the edge of the bed, where they had made passionate love just minutes before. "Yeah?"

Confused, Chloe came to sit down next to him. When he made a move, she reached out to clutch his arm. "Devon, I'm going to miss you," she said, her voice husky as she touched the side of his handsome face. "Gonna miss me?"

His smile was obviously forced as he turned his head to look at her. "How long will I be missing you for?"

"Just two weeks."

Just two weeks! his mind screamed. But he just nodded. "Okay. Look, I'll call you when I get in the house."

With that he stood and strode from the bedroom. Soon the sound of the front door closing reverberated throughout the quiet house.

He didn't call and neither did she. Last night had been the worst night of sleep of her life. He had been so distant and nonchalant. So blasé about it. For God's sake, he didn't even ask why she was going back to New York, or give her a chance to tell him.

Chloe had wanted to share the unexpected pleasure she was beginning to feel at her chances for winning the award. Of course she knew she shouldn't have prolonged telling him. But obviously he didn't care, right?

Childishly she kicked her feet up in the air under the covers in frustration. "Men . . . are . . . so . . . so," she struggled for the right word. "So infuriating."

Sighing, she forced herself to calm down. God she missed him. Deshawn and he were supposed to lay the cement for her walkway and patio today. Would they show?

Oh, who knew?

Devon walked out of his bathroom, toweling off the water beaded on his naked body from the long shower he took. He looked down at his bed and envisioned Chloe lying naked and writhing beneath him. They had shared many long, steamy nights of passion in that very same bed. Ever since she moved into her own house, sleeping in it had never been the same for him.

"Damn," he swore, angrily flinging the towel onto the floor.

Last night when she told him she was leaving for New York, his immediate reaction was to forbid her to go. But he knew forbidding Chloe Bolton to do something was akin to talking to a wall.

Yes, he would miss her.

No, he didn't want her to go.

Yes, he had been filled with relief when she said she would return in two weeks.

No, he wasn't positive she would return.

He *knew* she was itching to get back to New York. All along he had doubts about her moving to Holtsville permanently, and this only confirmed those suspicions for him. She said only for two weeks. Then why was she going at all?

Last night he had to get out of her house, so sure that he was on the verge of making a fool out of himself by trying to talk her out of going. He felt that if she got caught up in her life back in New York, she would see what Holtsville lacked and not return.

Right now he just couldn't fathom his life without Chloe in it. "Damn," he swore. He was in deeper than he thought.

When he and Deshawn turned into her yard, her SUV was not parked there. He ignored the look of confusion Deshawn shot in his direction as they exited the vehicle. They started mixing cement and stones at nine A.M., and by noon they were well into the job.

Chloe still hadn't returned and Devon was more than a little curious about where she could be. They had finished laying the cement for the walkway leading to the back of the house and were hammering the planks for the patio when Deshawn stopped.

"Think Chloe will mind if we grab something to drink?" Deshawn asked, wiping the sweat from his forehead with the back of his hand.

"Naw. I could use a break myself."

They walked over to the glass patio doors. Thankfully, she had left them unlocked and the alarm disabled. Once they entered the kitchen Devon was assailed by her scent hanging in the air. His gut clenched in reaction to it.

Deshawn reached into the double-door black-faced refrigerator and pulled out two bottles of fruit punch. He handed one to his brother before opening his own to take a healthy swig from it. Devon did the same.

"Where *is* Chloe, Dev?" he asked once his thirst was quenched.

Devon shrugged. "Who knows? Probably shopping."

"Let's get back to work." He winked at his twin as he threw the now empty bottle into the glass recycling bin Chloe kept for Cyrus to collect once a week. "I wanna finish up as soon as possible. Poochie's gonna practice CPR on me."

"How's everything going with Poochie?" Devon asked as he pitched his own empty bottle into the bin.

Deshawn smiled wolfishly and Devon shook his head. "I meant besides the sex, Shawn," he said, his voice sardonic.

"Besides the sex?"

At his brother's nod, he pondered the question. What did Poochie and he have besides explosive sex in odd places? They didn't talk about much. They didn't go out to dinner or anything of that sort. Ninety-nine percent of their time together was spent having sex and the other one percent was spent *planning* to have sex. Poochie was an attractive girl with a fun and high-spirited outlook on life, but Deshawn never even considered a serious relationship with her.

They had nothing besides sex, unlike his twin and Chloe. Although neither seemed to know it, they were crazy about each other. Whenever he saw them together he actually felt the chemistry that radiated between them. They were destined for each other, but they just didn't seem to know it.

No, he couldn't compare how he felt about Poochie to what he saw growing between Devon and Chloe.

He saw that his brother was still waiting on an answer and he was honest with it. "We don't seem to have anything but great sex. How are things with Chloe and you?"

Devon had never held too much from his twin and he wasn't going to start now. He shook his head, obviously troubled. "As well as can be expected. She's leaving for New York this weekend and I don't want her to go."

"Is she coming back?"

Devon shrugged. "She say's she'll only be gone two weeks."

"Why don't you want her to go?"

His brows lifted. "Because . . ."

Deshawn walked over to playfully nudge his twin's head. "Because you're worried she won't come back."

He looked over at his twin. He couldn't lie to him even if he wanted to. "Exactly."

Deshawn studied his brother. "She's not Elissa, you know."

"I know that—"

"Then stop putting all that garbage you had with Elissa onto Chloe." Deshawn shrugged. "She'll be back. Believe me, she's just as anxious to be up under you as you are her, big brother."

"Whatever," he said, dismissing the subject. "Let's walk out the front. It's quicker."

They left the kitchen and walked up the hallway, getting to the foyer just as the phone rang. Deshawn was reaching for the front door when Chloe's answering machine clicked on after the third ring.

"Hey, this is Chloe. You know the routine."

Beep.

"Cat baby, this is Calvin. Why haven't you called me back yet?"

Devon's steps halted and he stopped himself from walking out the front door as his twin had just done.

"Damn, Cat, I miss you. I'm glad you're coming back to New York this week and getting the hell out of the boonies with those hicks. I can't wait to see you."

Devon's body was rigid with anger, jealousy and yes, fear. Even through the phone lines he heard the wealth and prominence in the man's voice. So that's why Chloe was going to New York, to meet up with her old lover.

"We need to talk, Cat. Call me."

The man's voice was urgent as he pleaded with *his* woman.

"Aw hell."

Devon looked away from the entrance to the living room to see Deshawn still standing on the porch, his expression grim as he obviously overheard the message as well.

"Well Shawn," Devon said tightly, barely able to control the anger, raging jealousy and betrayal he felt. "Now we both know why Chloe's headed home. To hell with her!"

Deshawn wiped his mouth. "Man, you don't know what that call's about. Talk to Chloe first."

Devon gripped the doorknob so tightly that his hand ached, but not nearly as deeply as his heart. "To hell with Chloe just like I said, and let *Calvin* finish paving her damn patio. I'm out of here."

Angrily, he brushed past his twin. Deshawn understood the emotions raging in his brother right now. He also knew there was no reasoning with Devon when he was angry, so he didn't even try. Instead, he closed the front door and walked onto the porch.

Just as he moved off the last step, Chloe's SUV whipped into the yard. Deshawn looked heavenward, wishing like hell that he wasn't here to witness the scene that he knew was about to go down.

Chloe pulled the SUV in directly next to Devon's navy pickup truck, her eyes taking in Deshawn's pained expression and the angry glare Devon shot in her direction before he got in the driver's seat of his pickup. Something was up.

This morning she had finally pulled herself out of the bed and called Anika at work, knowing her blunt best friend would help her make sense of her life. And Anika, being Anika, told Chloe to stop moping behind a man who was behaving like a little boy. Not exactly comforted by her friend's brash advice, Chloe had driven to Saks Fifth Avenue on King Street in Charleston and gone on a major shopping spree.

Leaving her three shopping bags in the vehicle, Chloe got out and walked over to where Devon sat stoically in the driver's seat looking forward. His profile seemed to be cut from granite.

"Hello Devon," she said cautiously.

He turned his head and gave her a cold, angry look that froze the blood in her veins.

"What the devil is wrong with you?" she asked, now angry for his unexplained contempt of her.

"Look Chloe, I advise you to just get out of my face or—"

"Or what?" Chloe yelled as she yanked open the truck's door. "Or what, Devon, huh . . . what?"

Angry, she continuously asked, "Or what, Devon?"

He eyed her with open hostility.

Deshawn dashed toward the truck, coming to stand beside Chloe. "Look, both y'all acting childish. Now stop this before you both say or do something you'll regret later."

Devon laughed harshly, his eyes steadily on Chloe. "Too late. I regret the day I got involved with her."

Chloe didn't know if the hot stabbing pains in her chest were from hurt or anger. For one brief moment the pure confused pain she felt shone brightly in the depths of her eyes.

Devon fought the urge to pull her into a tight embrace and kiss away the words he just said. He saw the hurt he caused her flash in her eyes. But what about the pain she caused him? She was going to New York to meet her lover, for God's sake. "Make sure when you get to New York you tell Calvin I said 'Hello.' "

Chloe's gasp of shock mingled with Deshawn's heavy sigh of regret.

"What are you talking about, Devon? You know damn well I don't want Calvin." Her voice was weary.

"Funny," he spat. "I couldn't tell that from his message. Look, go to New York and have a damn ball. I . . . don't . . . care anyway."

What message, she thought to herself, but she said, "I'll do just that Devon."

She turned, nearly knocking Deshawn over as she ran into the house, tears now freely streaming down her cheeks.

Deshawn shot his brother a resentful look. "You sure screwed that up big time."

"Shut up Shawn," he mumbled.

* * *

Chloe slammed and locked the doors behind her. Tears welled up in her hazel eyes again, but she refused to let them fall. If Devon wanted to act like a donkey, then let him.

He had said something about a message from Calvin and she wanted to see just how much of this disastrous afternoon was Calvin's fault. Just as she reached the table where the answering machine sat, Chloe heard the squeal of tires as Devon and Deshawn left. Obviously he was so disgusted with her that he wasn't going to finish her patio and driveway.

"That's professional," she muttered nastily as she pushed the PLAYBACK button on the machine.

"Hey, this is Chloe. You know the routine."

Beep.

Her anger soared after she listened to Calvin's message. *That Calvin! Why can't he leave me alone?*

Okay, she had to admit that her ex-boyfriend did make it seem as though they were going to meet up in New York. But, Devon should have asked questions first before jumping to conclusions. It's like Anika always said, when you assume you make an *ass* out of *u* not *me*.

To think, he thought so little of her. This wasn't how it was supposed to go when she first set out to bring Devon into her life. He wasn't supposed to be able to hurt her. She wasn't supposed to be sitting in the middle of her living room floor numb with hurt, embarrassment and anger. Slowly the boundaries had begun to fade and she had missed it.

Bitter tears began to fall down her cheeks, and Chloe wrapped her arms around her knees, hugging them to her chest as she rocked. Even in anger, she missed the tall, bronzed and brooding man. Even now she had to fight the urge to run to her SUV, drive to his home and explain about Calvin. She wanted to throw herself at his feet like a sniveling idiot and beg forgiveness for something she hadn't even done.

She could not . . . no, would not let that happen.

Chloe quickly unfolded her body and grabbed the cordless

phone from the base. Within minutes her arrangements were made. Then she dialed Anika's private line in her office.

"Anika Fox."

"Girl, this is Chloe."

"What's up?"

"I'll be arriving in New York late this evening."

"Today," Anika shrieked. "What does country boy have to say about the early departure?"

"He can go to hell."

"Oh," was all Anika said, immediately understanding. "You'll be at your apartment?"

"Yeah, I'll just catch a cab from the airport." Chloe carried the phone with her out of the living room and into her bedroom, grabbing one of her suitcases out of the walk-in closet.

"I'll drive over as soon as I leave work."

"Uh, Anika, bring chocolates. Lots of 'em."

"That bad?" Anika asked softly, her voice concerned.

Chloe remembered the scene with Devon in the yard. "Worse."

Nineteen

Never had the environment around the Jamison household been so stilted. Usually the rambling three-story structure was filled with a comfortable silence, but now the quiet was tense.

Deshawn had filled Nana Lil in on Chloe and Devon's argument a week ago. Both now blamed Devon for the fact that Chloe was gone, although neither came right out and said so. He knew how they felt nonetheless, especially since his grandmother had stopped speaking to him at all and shot him hard looks every chance she got. Sometimes actions spoke louder than words.

It wasn't as though Devon was in a talkative mood anyway. He became even more withdrawn and spent most of his nights in his suite, especially when Nana Lil got the note Chloe left saying she had left for New York and would call her in a few days.

Devon just assumed that Chloe had run to her lover, anxious to be back in his arms, and he would admit to no one how deeply that thought hurt and angered him.

The Friday after Chloe left, word had already spread around town that she was gone, and speculation on why she left moved through the small community like a tornado. Devon didn't miss the odd looks he received, or the whispered comments, anytime he went near the main street in town. In fact, one afternoon he stormed into the house after a particularly harried session with Cyrus, who tried to command him to go get his woman.

But she wasn't his woman any longer. She was Calvin's now.

Devon groaned in exasperation when his grandmother threw a now familiar nasty look at him before turning back to the afghan she was knitting. Bah, everyone blamed him! Chloe left to be with another man, yet this was his fault?

"Let 'em be mad," he muttered as he stomped up the stairs and into his bedroom.

Right now, as he frequently did, he envisioned Chloe having a ball in the big city. A beautiful sparkle in that unique smile of hers directed at Wesley, winking mischievously at Denzel, pouting those full luscious lips at Tyson, being serenaded by Kenny Lattimore, or giving Calvin that lazy-eyed look she got when she was caught up in passion . . .

Devon punched violently at the air in an attempt to vent his anger as the images plagued him. He forced himself to stop thinking of her. For his sanity's sake, he had to forget Chloe. She was in New York, reunited with her ex-boyfriend, with no thought of him or Holtsville on her mind.

"To hell with Chloe," he muttered, reaching in his wallet to rip up the picture of her he had carried there. If only he could get her out of his blood, his dreams and his heart that easily.

One week back in New York, among the same fast-paced bright lights and hustle-bustle she had fled from, had Chloe anxious to run back to the small-town charm of Holtsville. Luckily the press was not aware she was back in town and she just thanked God for small favors.

She looked out of the bay windows of her luxury apartment. New York was bustling with activity at even seven in the morning. Everyone seemed to be racing, afraid to slow down or they might miss success or some other attainable goal. Sighing, she turned away from the windows to look around the same black and marble decor of her bedroom.

Funny, she had been away from the apartment for more than a year and did not feel a twinge of regret about it. She had been away from her house in Holtsville only one week and missed it so deeply that she actually felt pangs in her chest at the thought of it.

This was the most lived-in the apartment had ever looked. For the past five days she moped and lounged, in FUBU and thick socks, watching television, listening to music, gobbling up hordes of gourmet chocolate ice cream, and generally feeling sorry for herself with perpetual tears. Nearly every room looked like a disaster had hit and Chloe didn't care that it did.

Anika thought she was losing her mind and came by nearly every night after work to check on her. They did say that one of the first signs of someone going crazy was a complete change in their cleaning habits. Maybe Devon had succeeded in driving her insane.

She winced at the thought of him. Not being with him, and knowing she never would, hurt Chloe far more than stumbling upon Calvin's infidelity. Constantly she thought of him, wondered what he was doing, envisioned him spending his time dating beautiful southern women, and not caring that she had left. That last bit always sent her into a fit of tears, or into a fresh bucket of ice cream.

Plus she missed Nana Lil's bluntness, Deshawn's charm and Cyrus's sweet nosy nature. She knew they missed her as much as she missed them, even if Devon didn't.

Chloe looked over at the phone on the bedside table, peeking from beneath the navy blue sweatpants she had worn yesterday and carelessly thrown aside. She did promise Nana Lil in the note she left in their mailbox that she would call her. And she *could* check up on Devon, killing two birds with one stone.

Sighing, she walked over to the phone, flinging the sweatpants over her shoulder onto the dresser across the room behind her. Quickly, before she chickened out, Chloe dialed the Jamison residence in Holtsville, South Carolina.

The phone rang three times. "Hello."

"How are you doing, Nana Lil?" she asked, forcing gaiety into her voice.

"Chloe?"

"Yes ma'am. How've you been?"

"Hi stranger! You know, I'm gonna get you for runnin' off up that road and not coming to see me first."

Chloe closed her eyes against a wave of homesickness that hit her at the warm, deep southern accent in Lil's voice. "I'm sorry about that but things got a little hectic. How's everybody doing?"

"Shawnie's still sniffing around Poochie and Devon's grouchy as a bear woke up early from hibernation." Lil sighed. "You know, Chloe, just because you and Vonnie had a falling-out didn't mean you had to move back to New York."

"That's not the only reason I came to New York," Chloe assured her. "I was nominated for an award and the ceremonies are next week, here in New York. That's the original reason for my trip here; I just came a little earlier after our argument. At first I was only going to be here for two weeks and I told him this."

Lil sighed in pleasure. "Congratulations, sugar, and I hope you win. But why didn't you just tell Devon that's why you had to go back?"

The older woman's voice was obviously confused, but Chloe shook her head, ready to voice her protest. "Nana Lil, when I first told Devon about my going to New York he didn't care about why. Then the next day we argued over a message an ex-boyfriend left on my answering machine. A message that he overheard and misunderstood."

"Calvin?"

"Yes."

"Baby, it's none of my business, but are you back with him?"

"No . . . heavens no, Nana Lil," Chloe shrieked, slumping down onto the bed among the disheveled sheets and duvet. "I never told you, but I caught Calvin in bed with . . . another woman. That's why we're not together."

"Oh."

"So you see I have no desire to reconcile with him, although he is quite persistent in his attempts to win me back." Chloe rolled her eyes heavenward. "This is all his fault, but that still doesn't excuse the contempt Devon showed me. He truly hurt me, Nana Lil."

Lil clucked her tongue. "Deshawn told me about all that, but Devon must've been awfully mad and jealous to act in such a way."

"Maybe it's all for the best anyway," she said, her voice resigned. *A blessing in disguise.*

"Chloe, you and Devon need to talk and—"

"Nana Lil, I'd rather not talk about it anymore."

Lil heard the firm finality in Chloe's tone and let any further arguments she had pass . . . for now. "Okay, but I hope you both know what you're doing."

"Thanks."

"You're not ever coming back? What about the house?" Her voice was worried and saddened.

"I'm coming back home, Nana Lil, even though it will be hard." *I just don't know if I can stand living in Holtsville and not being with Devon.*

"Is the award show going to be on television?"

"Yes ma'am." Chloe gave her the time and cable station the ceremony was being broadcast on. "You're going to watch it?"

Lil laughed. "Of course. I want to see you win."

"I might lose," Chloe said seriously.

"Oh no baby, you'll win," she said with confidence that sent a surge of love for the older woman through Chloe.

"Thanks, Nana Lil."

"Oh, and Chloe?"

"Ma'am?"

"I give you and Vonnie one week to get it together. After that I'm butting in."

Chloe rubbed her fingertips over her eyes. "Nana Lil—"

"One week," Lil stated firmly. "Give me your number so that I can call and check up on you."

She recited the number. "I'll call you sometime next week, Nana Lil, okay . . . all right . . . I will . . . bye bye."

Chloe pushed the TALK button on the phone and flung it beside her on the bed amongst the jumbled linen. At least she wasn't the only one miserable. So Devon was in a foul mood and moping around the house. Good!

Maybe now he was regretting his behavior. Or maybe he still believed she was in New York with Calvin.

Bzzz.

That was the intercom. She knew it was Anika since her friend was the only person who knew she was in town early. With a groan she pulled herself up off the bed and walked to the intercom system in the hallway. "Yes Mr. Harrison?"

"A Mr. Calvin Ingram to see you."

Chloe saw a kaleidoscope of a hundred shades of red fill her line of vision. How dare he come to her home! How did he know she was in town? She knew that she should confront him once and for all and put a final end to his attempts at reconciliation, but she instead pushed the TALK button of the intercom system. "Mr. Harrison, do not allow him entrance and please inform him that I do not wish to see him."

She pushed the LISTEN button, but Mr. Harrison's end was quiet for a few seconds before he finally spoke. "Ms. Bolton, he has left as instructed, although he was not pleased to do so."

"Thanks Mr. Harrison."

Okay, so she wimped out. The only way to put an end to Calvin's interruptions in her life was to set him straight and stop running from a confrontation with him. But she just wasn't in the mood for it all. More important thoughts plagued her.

Chloe wasn't surprised when her phone began to ring a few minutes later. Quite sure it was Calvin, she cut the ringers off of all her phones, moving quickly throughout the apartment until silence reigned once again in her home.

Devon and Calvin were so different. Never could she imagine the aloof and quietly arrogant Devon behaving in the relentlessly obsessive way Calvin was. But then Calvin *had* been in love with her, or at least claimed to be. Devon had made no such admissions.

Although Chloe told herself that she didn't want to become absorbed in another man the way she had been about Calvin, when she reviewed her behavior the past week she knew she was very close to doing the same thing. She was near tears at every slow song she heard, moping around her unkempt house looking just as unkempt with constant thoughts of Devon. Hell, she even went and stood in her bathroom to watch herself cry in the vanity.

And that was just . . . pitiful!

Bzzz.

Chloe groaned. If that was Calvin she *would* call the police and let them deal with him, since she lacked the courage to do so. She left the den where she had just settled onto the sofa to watch television. Another intercom pad was located directly by the front door.

"Yes."

"It's Ms. Fox, Ms. Bolton."

"Send her up, Mr. Harrison."

Chloe left the front door slightly ajar and dragged herself back into the den. It wasn't long before she heard the click of Anika's heels on the marble floor after she closed the front door.

"Where are you in this oversized pigsty?" she called out.

"Den," Chloe yelled back.

Anika appeared in the wide archway. Of course she looked fantastic, wearing a bronze leather blazer, a ribbed silk sweater and matching wool pants with dark mocha leather ankle boots and gold accessories. Her solid curvaceous frame carried the suit well.

"All right Chloe, enough is enough. Sitting around here moping and going to pot proves what?"

Chloe barely looked away from the sixty-inch television. "I'm not moping, nor am I going to pot. I'm just . . . relaxing."

Anika swung her purse and leather portfolio onto the couch next to Chloe. "No, what you're doing is pining away for a man that you refuse to even admit that you're in love with."

That got Chloe's full attention, her expression one of total shock. "I am not in love with that arrogant, stubborn, pig-headed hick Devon Jamison," she shrieked angrily, completely overreacting.

"Who are you trying to convince? Me?" Anika asked, waving a well-manicured hand at herself. "Or you?"

Just then a video show Chloe was watching played "When Will I See You Smile Again?" by Bell Biv Devoe. Seconds later she was bawling like a baby.

"Good heavens," Anika moaned, looking heavenward for assistance. *Yet she says she's not in love!*

Anika reached down and plucked the remote control from Chloe's quivering hand, immediately shutting the television off with a decisive click. "You miss him, right?"

Chloe sniffed, only able to nod in response.

"Then call him."

Chloe sniffed again, and shook her head no.

"Well that's your life, live it. But I refuse to continue letting you sit around like this any longer." Anika pulled her leather blazer off and laid it on the back of the chair. "Now I took it upon myself as your sista-friend to schedule that meeting with Ashanti Cosmetics today at four P.M. Needless to say, you need to wash, change and do your hair. But first we're gonna clean this apartment up." Anika shook her head in disgust. "If it gets any worse the Department of Health will close this place down, and I'd gladly hang the 'Stay Out' notice on your front door myself."

"Ha ha, Anika. Real funny," Chloe said sarcastically.

Ignoring her friend, Anika crossed her arms over her ample chest. "I'm taking the day off from *work*. Oh, you're gonna get something accomplished today. So where do you want to start?"

Twenty

The fall and winter were never a busy time for Jamison Contractors, and Devon wished that was different now. With nothing but free time on his hands, he found himself constantly thinking of Chloe. Good thoughts and bad. He was very willing to admit that he missed her.

She had made him laugh, she'd given him passion in his life, and she'd made him stop and enjoy all the pleasure and wonders that he took for granted in the country. He smiled as he thought of how she never backed down from him in an argument, something many men couldn't say. She gave as good as she got. Just like a down-home woman.

Damn it!

Foolishly, he had begun to think that Chloe and he were building on something, that their relationship had moved beyond sex. God, he felt so stupid. With a growl he crumpled up the architectural design of a contemporary two-story house he was working on, just to kill some time.

Tossing the pencil aside, he looked around the renovated barn. The office was quiet, the phone only ringing once since he had been there and that had been a wrong number. Alicia usually came in every day like clockwork, and right now she would have had the radio playing or been watching those soap operas she loved so much.

Devon missed his friend. Or at least the person she had been before her jealousy of Chloe had eclipsed her. Or was it more than her feelings against Chloe, and instead her feelings for him?

Alicia hadn't denied being in love with him the evening they confronted her about the *Star Gazer* article on Chloe. Was a hidden love for him the motivation behind Alicia's hate campaign against Chloe?

It was still very hard for Devon to believe that. Alicia had never shown any inclination of amorous feelings toward him. She'd been like a little sister to both Deshawn and him. He couldn't imagine that deep down she had harbored feelings for him. Surely he would have seen some sign, or was he as blind as Chloe had accused him of being?

Devon thought back on all the nights he'd eaten dinner over at her house, or the few times he'd even slept on her couch overnight, or the many times she listened to him discuss other women he was involved with. That surely was not the behavior of a woman who wanted a man for more than a good friend.

Hell, he didn't know.

Sighing, he wiped his deep-set obsidian eyes and glanced at the clock on the wall. It was after five and once again he had no plans for the evening. Going to Charlie's didn't entice him, but it would be a way to pass a few hours. Briefly he contemplated calling one of his female friends, but just as quickly he rejected the idea.

What woman could wipe Chloe from his memory?

No one.

He stretched his tall, muscled frame and stood. Perhaps he should work on talking Donnie into renovating. They didn't need the money but a long day of physical labor would leave him too tired to do anything at night but sleep, and hopefully not dream.

As he turned off the lights and left the building behind him, he promised himself to ride out to the diner with a proposal for the surly, tightwad owner.

Already the sun was beginning to set, casting the skies in varying hues of graying blues as night approached. Devon walked over to the house and sat down on the swing. It had been so long since he had done his once nightly ritual of sitting on the porch long into the night, enjoying the solitude. Until recently his nights had been filled with loving Chloe.

Chloe.

What is she doing in New York? Is she still with Calvin? Is she dining out with celebrity friends? Does she miss me?

They were hundreds of miles apart, but with the differences in their worlds it might as well be a million. He was a fool to have believed she would enjoy quiet nights swinging on a porch watching the sun set and the moon rise, listening to the lulling sounds of night creatures, willing to take life at a leisurely pace.

"Coming in for dinner, Vonnie?"

Devon looked up in surprise at his grandmother standing in the doorway. "You talking to me now?" he asked laughingly, turning back to look up at the full moon now in residence in the darkening skies, framed by the outline of the tall pine trees.

Nana Lil said nothing, instead pushing the screen door wider open to walk out onto the porch. The door squeaked in the stillness of the night before closing with a swish. Devon moved over to make room on the swing for her. The faint scent of her lavender oil surrounded him, and Devon was hit with a sudden pang of nostalgia. He remembered being surrounded by that scent as a child when this strong, resilient woman would hold him close to her with love.

They swung in silence for long minutes, surrounded by the unique sounds of a country night, before Lil spoke. "I really miss Chloe, you know."

Immediately she felt him stiffen beside her, his face tightened with some emotion she couldn't identify offhand. Okay, she could tell now was not the time to stir her hand in the pot. He wasn't ready to listen yet, and she never wasted good advice on deaf ears.

"Vonnie, I'm going in my room. You and Shawnie's dinner

is in the oven." Lil stood and then impulsively pulled his upper body into her arms tightly. "I love you, Devon," she whispered huskily.

Devon closed his eyes, allowing himself to wish he was still a child and his Nana could kiss his troubles away. "Love you too, Nana."

She went into the house, the screen door squeaking close with a final bam against the frame. Devon remained swinging late into the night. He was comforted by his grandmother's faint scent, still clinging to his shirt, and haunted by a hazel-eyed temptress. If only everything could have turned out differently.

In the cool darkness of her room Nana Lil lay in pain quietly. The headaches were getting worse instead of better. She repositioned the folded wet cloth on her forehead, praying for some release from the sharp pain that radiated there. It was so intense that any movement of her body sharpened it.

Already she had taken three over-the-counter pain tablets, but that was twenty minutes ago and she wasn't feeling the effects of it yet. Sighing, Lil said a silent prayer to the Lord.

The black ribbon of the road was nearly empty, save for a few cars that passed Deshawn's truck. He ignored the sulking pouty looks interspersed with angry glares that Poochie shot in his direction as he drove them home from the hotel. Usually, whenever they were in a car together she lay clutched to his arm, or arousing parts of his body the way she loved to. Tonight she pressed herself to the passenger door so closely that he hoped it was properly closed or she would surely fall out.

Deciding to use his charm to get his way *and* stop her from being mad at him, Deshawn reached his right hand over the seat to grip her lush thigh in the tight jeans she wore.

"Don't . . . touch . . . me!" she shrieked. If it was at all possible, she pressed herself closer to the door. "I don't see why we couldn't spend the night in the room, and go home in the morning."

"Because Devon and I have an early morning job to do," he lied easily, with his best smooth-talking voice. "Baby, I have to get some rest so that I have energy for work in the morning. You know I can't lay next to you all night without making love to that beautiful . . . soft . . . body."

She looked cautiously over at him, the sound of his warm-honeyed voice disconcerting. He could see the edge begin to wear off already. For good measure he threw in his killer smile. As if by reflex, she smiled in return. Deshawn knew he had her.

Poochie scooted over on the seat and gave him a quick peck on the lips, which she would have deepened if Deshawn hadn't quickly avoided it by turning back his head to look at the road ahead of him. That didn't stop her from massaging his thighs.

He was more than glad when he pulled into the dirt yard of the house where she lived with her mother. Deshawn shook his head at the haphazardly hung venetian blinds in the windows. If she would just love to clean as much as she loved to have sex, their house would be spotless.

Anxious to get home to his own bed, Deshawn kissed her only briefly. "I'll call you tomorrow," he drawled.

Reluctantly, she opened the truck door, but turned to face him before she got out. "Too bad you had to work tomorrow because I've been practicing getting my legs all the way behind my head."

Deshawn visualized the daring move and was tempted to tell her to get in and head back to the Best Western. No, he seriously needed a break from all the sex they'd been having. And that was an odd thought for him!

"Save it for me baby." He leaned over and kissed her full lips lightly. "I'll have to just dream about it tonight."

Still displeased with the way the night turned out, but now charmed by her wily lover, Poochie left the truck with a wave before walking into the house.

Not that Deshawn noticed because he was already backing out of the yard before she got in the house good. He drove the remaining miles home in silence. That last go-round with Poochie in that chair had him drained, and he was more than ready to hit the sack . . . alone.

When he pulled into the yard, he saw that his twin was swinging on the porch. Deshawn glanced at the digital clock on the dashboard. It was 1:38 A.M.

He parked and got out of the truck, taking the steps up onto the porch two at a time. "What's up, Dev?"

Devon shrugged. "Nothing much."

Tired as hell but well aware that if his twin was sitting on their porch in the wee hours of the morning that something must be on his mind, Deshawn wearily sat next to him on the swing. "Can't sleep?"

Devon shrugged again. "Just enjoying the porch before winter sets in is all."

Deshawn nodded slowly several times, mulling that bit of information over. "Thinking about Chloe, huh?"

"Nope."

"Yeah, right." Deshawn pushed off with his foot, causing the swing to slowly glide back and forth. "Look, I know it ain't none of my business but I think you're wrong about her."

"Look De—"

"Wait, wait. Let me just say this." He held up a hand. "Before she moved here you accused her of being some sort of airhead heroin junkie with evil intentions toward Holtsville. Later you found out you were wrong. She told you about Alicia's rather obsessive crush on you, and you didn't believe it. Once again you were . . . well, wrong. She told us about Alicia selling the story and the pictures to the tabloid, and we sided with Alicia at first. Once again you, along with the rest of us, were wrong again. See a pattern developing?"

"This is different, Shawn," he snapped.

They swung in silence then, Deshawn believing that he was giving his twin a chance to absorb what he just told him. Instead Devon's mind was on one of his brother's earlier comments.

"You really think Alicia has a crush on me?" he asked, his voice incredulous.

Deshawn nodded. "Big time."

"Why?"

"I didn't really realize until Chloe brought it to my attention. Once I thought it over, I realized she was right." Deshawn slapped his brother on the back of his head lightly, receiving a nasty look in return. "Since we were kids Alicia, you and I have *all* been best friends. But as we got older Alicia seemed to get closer to just you. Think about it. Alicia would cook dinner and just call for you to come over. Or just call you to go to the movies."

"Exaggerating, aren't you, Deshawn?" Devon balked.

"I've never spent the night at Alicia's. Have you?"

Yes, he had.

Devon waved his hand. "Look, just forget about it. There's no need to worry about it now because Alicia moved to Florida anyway."

"Wrong again, big brother," Deshawn laughed with a yawn.

Devon looked over at him questioningly. "Now what?"

"Poochie told me tonight that Donnie told her that Alicia came into the diner looking for work." Deshawn pushed off with his foot again.

Devon stood suddenly, causing the bench to jerk. "I need to talk to Al."

He watched, bemused and tired, as his brother patted his pockets looking for his keys. Clearing his throat to draw Devon's attention, Deshawn asked, "Do you really think going to the house of the woman who has secretly loved you for years, at . . ." he glanced at his watch. ". . . two in the morning is wise?"

Devon's action immediately ceased. If, and only if, Deshawn and Chloe were right, and Alicia harbored a crush for him, then his twin was right. "She's probably asleep. I'll go tomorrow afternoon," he mumbled, ignoring his twin's knowing look.

Deshawn rose up off the swing, his eyes already drooped with fatigue. "I don't know about you but I'm headed for my bed."

"Good night."

"Oh and Dev?"

Devon looked up to see him paused in the door frame. "Yeah."

"Just *where* did you sleep those nights you stayed at Alicia's?" Deshawn asked before closing the front door behind him. The sound of his laughter filtered outside and rang in Devon's ears.

The next afternoon, Devon turned his truck down the small road Alicia lived on. As he neared her cottage, he saw that her compact car was indeed parked in the front yard of her house. They had been friends for a long time and he didn't favor the way their friendship ended. He felt he had to talk to her, find out her true motivations and come to some sort of understanding. He wanted to know if all of this was his fault. Had he led her on? Had he acted in a way to make her feel that way about him?

Sighing, he parked his truck next to her car and turned off the ignition. Deshawn had tried to talk him out of coming, telling him he should be more focused on trying to talk to Chloe. But Chloe left to be with another man, so he had no desire to talk to her. But he had to settle things with Al. Their friendship would never be the same of course, but he didn't want them to be hostile toward each other like their last meeting. He just hoped he wasn't making things worse instead of better.

* * *

Alicia heard a vehicle turn into her yard and moved from where she was looking through the want ads in Charleston's local newspaper to look out her living room window. She gasped in shock, surprise and pleasure.

Knowing she had but seconds to spare, Alicia raced to her bedroom. She decided to think positive about Devon coming to her house. To her that was a good sign. She was already well aware that Chloe had finally dragged herself back to New York.

This time she was going for it. For years she held back on expressing her love for him, and look where it got her. Nowhere. She just hoped he was as ready for her as she was for him!

"Alicia!"

Devon's eyes widened as he looked at the woman who stood in the doorway. It was Alicia, but just a new and better version of her.

"Devon? Hi," she yawned. "You got me up out of bed. Come in."

He stepped into the house behind her, immediately overwhelmed by the scent of peaches. "You're in bed at two in the afternoon?" he asked as he took a seat on the living room couch.

Alicia nearly grimaced. "Uhm, I'm not feeling too well," she lied easily as she eyed him. *God, he looks good!*

She sat back and crossed her legs, purposefully causing the satiny robe she wore to fall open, exposing her legs from the thigh down. She nearly jumped with glee when she saw his eyes dip down to look.

Devon quickly averted his gaze, more than nervous. Was Alicia trying to seduce him? He moved down on the sofa, away from her, putting more space between them. She certainly looked prettier with her hair cut in that new shorter style and makeup on.

Wait a minute!

Makeup on and she just got out of bed? He instantly smelled trouble, with a capital "T," especially as she began to swing the leg she had crossed, causing the robe to fan open and expose a thick smooth thigh and . . . !

He gulped nervously. She was naked beneath the robe! He was ready to say what he came to say and haul it out of there. Clearing his throat, he began, "Al, I came to talk about all the crap that went down last month. You and I were real good friends, and I just can't believe the person I know you to be would be so vindictive."

Alicia stiffened. She didn't want to talk about that, especially if he was about to defend Chloe. Quickly she thought of the best way to deal with steering the conversation away from a road she didn't want to travel. "Look Devon, let's be friends again. We'll both just apologize for whatever wrongs we've done to each other and move on from here, 'kay?"

He nodded slowly but was not satisfied. She still hadn't admitted to the wrong she did against Chloe, and if she didn't see fault in her actions how could he jump back into their old friendship again? "Al you called *The Star Gazer*—"

Before he could finish his sentence Alicia stood and untied the robe, letting it fall to a peach puddle of satiny material around her bare, newly manicured feet. Devon immediately turned his head. "Alicia, what the hell are you doing?"

She took a step forward as he moved to stand, using her hands to push him back down on the couch and straddle his lap. She trembled in anticipation, nearly dying from wanting him.

Devon grabbed the hands that were rubbing his chest. "Stop this, Alicia! Damn!"

The desire and love this woman had for him was in her eyes clearly now. There was no mistaking her actions or her feelings. How could he have been so blind?

She whispered, "I love you Devon."

Chloe had never told him those words. A vision of the slender temptress astride a faceless man filled his imagination. Jealousy ate him alive, anger at her leaving pained him, and her betrayal stung.

Alicia took his hands and guided them to her small, pert breasts. "Please Devon. I love you so."

With all the emotions raging inside of him, Devon lost good sense. Why should he fret over Chloe, a woman who didn't love him, who cheated on him and then left him for another man, when a very naked and willing woman sat astride him? Devon lowered his head, about to capture a breast in his mouth.

Alicia arched her back in anticipation and sighed with love, desire and victory.

Twenty-one

This is all so different from my last dinner party.

Chloe took a sip of Moët from her Waterford crystal flute, letting the chilled, expensive liquid fill her mouth to savor the taste, before she let it gently flow down her throat. Her eyes scanned the crowd of thirteen people mingling in her living room. The bartender was set up in the corner of the room by the wide bay windows, and her guests enjoyed any drink they desired.

Everyone was fashionably dressed in designer clothing varying from casual elegance, such as the Shaka King wardrobe some of the men preferred, to the traditional tailored suit look. The women were adorned with priceless jewelry. The air was heavy with "I'm rich, I'm famous and I know it."

Chloe stood alone by the entrance, her arms draped across her chest, her hand gently holding the expensive crystal flute. She looked stunningly beautiful in a silver leather halter and matching leather pants that clung to her curvaceous frame.

She was surrounded by music industry heavyweights, fashion industry insiders, and entertainment moguls of the black elite, but all she thought of was Holtsville. She missed the tranquil nights, clear, star-filled skies, acres of land with emerald green grass and wildflowers, and her beautiful house which she loved dearly. She would much rather be surrounded by Nana Lil and her brash and blunt personality, or Cyrus's nosy gossiping disposition, or Deshawn's roguish charm. And Devon, well she missed *everything* about that man.

What she wouldn't give to be swinging on her porch as she lay back in his strong arms, her head on his chest just watching the stars scattered in the sky.

This dinner had been Liv's idea, and Chloe had allowed her to plan the whole thing, from what to serve to whom to invite. The only people Chloe had insisted on being here were Anika, of course, and Jeffrey. It was just one night in Liv's preplanned week of events to get the buzz going about Chloe before the awards show tomorrow night.

Sighing, she took another leisurely sip of her champagne. Could Devon be here in her world of designer originals, expensive champagne, celebrity friends, glamour, wealth and fame? No, she couldn't envision it and not because he wasn't good enough, but because she knew he would not want to be around these people, some of whom she called friends. She smiled as she imagined Devon and Jeffrey in a conversation. Now that was hilarious!

The awards show was the next evening and originally her plans had been to return to Holtsville that Saturday. But within three simple weeks everything was different . . . everything had changed.

Needing to be alone, Chloe left the party and walked down the hall to her bedroom. Once inside she closed the door, the dark quiet of the room offering some comfort to her. Sighing, she crossed the plush carpet to sit on the bed, her flute of champagne still in her hand. This she sat on the nightstand next to the cordless phone.

Not once had Devon called, although she spoke to Nana Lil nearly every night. Chloe had honestly thought he would realize that he was wrong about her and call by now to say so. Obviously he still thought she was involved with Calvin. How could he think so little of her?

How could she still miss him and want him so?

At night, with all the lights off in the apartment and she

alone in bed in this room, she remembered their passion and actually shivered from wanting him. A wave of homesickness filled her. Needing some connection to home, she turned on the lamp and picked up the phone, quickly dialing the long-distance number.

The phone rang just two times before it was picked up.

"Hello."

Chloe gasped, her heart hammering against her chest, her breathing shortened. She knew without a doubt that the deeply masculine and solemn-sounding voice was Devon's!

It had been nearly three weeks since she'd heard that voice . . . his voice. She was instantly filled with a deep longing to be by his side again.

"Hello," Devon said again, his tone now clearly agitated. "Who would you like to speak with?"

But Chloe said nothing, unsure if he would burst into another angry tirade at the sound of her voice on the phone.

"Chloe . . . what are you doing in here?"

She whirled around, frantically waving her hand to silence Anika, who had just walked into the room talking loudly. Quickly she pushed the button to disconnect the line.

Had Devon heard Anika call out her name? If he had, then he knew it was her sitting on the phone wordlessly, like a child playing a phone prank. Chloe flushed with embarrassment. She could only pray Anika's voice had not carried across the large expanse of the room.

"Who were you on the phone with, Chloe?" Anika asked, closing the door behind her.

Chloe looked down at the cordless phone in her hand, still affected by the sound of Devon's deep masculine voice. "No one," she lied as she sat the phone back on its base.

Anika sat beside her on the bed. "Call him, Chloe," she said softly as she nudged Chloe's shoulder with her own.

There was no need to explain who "him" was. "No, Anika."

"You miss him, so call him. You're miserable without him and you love him to death."

"I do not love him," she said vehemently, refusing to admit to the feelings. She thought of Calvin's betrayal and how she had been blind to his affairs because of "love." Couldn't two people be involved without losing themselves to each other completely?

Anika shook her head in amazement, reaching for Chloe's discarded flute of champagne and taking a sip. "Chloe, I don't understand you, and frankly you're beginning to bug me."

Chloe's mouth dropped open in shock. "What—"

Anika held up her hand. "No, let me finish. I know that Calvin hurt you, honey, but that was four years ago now. And I know that you never really got over your father not being in your life. You're a smart woman, so I know you understand that you cannot judge every man by either of them."

"My sire has nothing to do with this."

Anika held up her hand again. "It's obvious that you feel the two men you gave your love to betrayed you, and you're afraid to open up your heart again. I'm sorry that your father never wanted to know your love and that Calvin betrayed it, but that has nothing to do with Devon, your feelings for him, nor the type of man he is."

She took Chloe's hand in her own with a firm grasp. "Honey, you have got to get over Calvin, and yes, you have to come to grips with your father not being in your life."

"You're wrong because I'm completely over Calvin."

"No you're not. You've been dodging this man for years, afraid to confront him the way that you need to to get him out of your life once and for all. If you would just stand up to him and stop running. Learn that it's okay to be in the same room with him and not have to leave, like you nearly did at your own farewell party." Anika looked her in her eyes, seriously. "Sometimes I think you're worried that he'll actually talk you out of your panties again. And the way you run from him, he probably thinks so too. And that gives him more of a reason to chase you. You have to show yourself and Calvin that you are so over him."

Chloe's throat constricted in pain. She knew that all her friend's words of advice were true. Tears welled in her eyes and she swallowed them back with anguish. All of it, the pain, the betrayal, the rejection, the jealousy, and the mistrust was fresh, as if it all happened just moments ago. Calvin and her faceless father had shaped her into a woman afraid to love a good man.

Chloe wrapped her arms around her body. She let the tears fall freely down her cheeks. Anika hugged her friend, aching with the same pain she knew she felt. "Baby, I can't force you to do anything. But you, my compadre, are so deep in love with Devon that it's just too late to try to fight it now. So you better accept it and swim with the current, or keep denying it and drown."

"Good night and thanks for coming."

Chloe waved to the last of her guests and closed the front door behind them. Even Anika had left due to an early morning appointment she had. But of course, before she left she squeezed Chloe tightly and whispered, "Prove to yourself that Calvin is nothing to you and then realize that Devon is everything to you."

Anika had a way of making everything seem so easy.

Chloe sighed, stepping out of her clothes just as her phone rang. On the second ring she picked it up. "Hello."

She stiffened at the sound of his voice before forcing herself to relax. "You're just the man I need to speak with."

The half hour it took for him to reach her apartment gave Chloe the chance to change into a bulky sweatsuit and compose her words. When the knock sounded on her front door she took a deep breath before opening it. "Hello, Calvin."

He smiled as he walked past her into the foyer. He obviously thought he had succeeded in his campaign to win her back. Chloe nearly choked at the idea.

"Needless to say, I was surprised by your sudden offer for me to come over, Cat." He removed his lambskin leather jacket of a buttery caramel. It perfectly offset the ivory mock neck sweater he wore with stone-washed loose-fitting jeans. Even the leather boots were the exact same color as the coat.

He always did have style, she thought, as she hung the jacket up in the small closet off the hall. She wasn't surprised at all to see Gucci on the label inside the coat.

"Calvin, I—"

When she turned to face him he pulled her into a tight embrace. Her lips were pressed down upon soft, once-familiar lips, her senses overwhelmed by the scent of his Joop! cologne.

She felt absolutely nothing. How could she when she instantly remembered the sight of him in bed with another woman naked and writhing beneath him. Chloe struggled to be free of his hold and his kiss. At least now she knew that his effect on her was far below what she had imagined all these years. Anika was right, she had been afraid that Calvin had the power to smooth-talk her into bed, but no more!

"This is not what I called you over here for, Calvin." With a hard shove of her hands on his chest, she pushed him away finally.

Just as quickly he took a step toward her again and grabbed her hand, pressing it to his erection. "Don't you see what you do to me?"

Chloe grabbed the fleshy sack beneath it instead, and he immediately jumped back as she started to tug hard. "Anyone with a skirt does that to you."

"Okay, okay. Truce?" he asked as he eyed the frozen, hostile stare on her face.

"Whatever," she answered flippantly.

Calvin threw his best smile on his handsome face. At one

time she would have given the world to see him smile at her like that, and he knew it. But she just grimaced in return. *This isn't working out like I planned.*

"I need to talk to you about you calling my house in Holtsville. How did you get my number, and once you did get it, why did you use it? I want you to stop harassing me," she finished firmly, walking past him to enter the living room where she took a seat on the sofa.

He followed, taking a seat beside her. "What's this crap about harassment? Surely that's too harsh a term for a man willing to fight to have the woman he loves back in his life."

Chloe shook her head in amazement. "It is when the woman doesn't want to be back in your life. How did you get my number, Calvin?" she asked again, staring at him hard.

"I hired a P.I."

"You what?" she exclaimed, her voice near a shriek.

"Hey, I was getting desperate," he explained with a shrug. "I love you, Chloe. A man's gotta do what a man's gotta do."

She shook her head in amazement. "You don't cheat on someone you love. You don't screw another woman in the bed you have shared with the woman you love. You don't lie. You don't disrespect her." She paused before continuing. "You know what, Calvin?"

"What?" he said in a silky charming voice, expecting more from her and about to get less.

"You are so stupid."

Chloe looked at the handsome man sitting in front of her. This man had once been her world, his kisses had moved mountains for her, but his betrayal had nearly destroyed her. He had delivered a crushing blow to her ability to love again. She might not be able to confront the other man in her life who had betrayed her more deeply than any man ever could, but she could finally face this one.

She knew for sure that she did not need or want him in her life in any way. And she was going to make sure he understood that.

"Calvin, I hope you realize that what I am about to say to you, I mean from the bottom of my heart. There is a better chance for a snowball staying frozen in hell than you and I getting back together. I don't want you, I don't need you. No, Calvin, seeing you does not make me want to run from you anymore. You have no effect on me. I do not love you and I do not care if you still love me. That's your personal problem that you need to deal with. Leave me alone. Do not call my house, do not come by any of my homes, and if I ever find out you have hired a P.I. to investigate my private affairs again, I will make your life a living hell."

She stood, ready to retrieve his jacket so that he could leave. His purpose in being here was served. He jumped to his feet and she knew without turning that he was about to touch her. "Don't, Calvin," she said with a firm voice that brooked no argument.

She left the room to retrieve his jacket, returning with it quickly. "Good night and good-bye, Calvin. I hope you can finally be mature about all of this."

Calvin accepted his jacket and slipped it on. He watched her intently as he did. What he saw hurt him. His Cat was lost to him forever. He knew then, as she stared unflinchingly into his eyes, that he had lost this incredible woman standing before him. He would regret that for the rest of his life. Before she could stop him he pulled her into a tight hug. "Good-bye, Cat."

She felt no reaction at all from his body being so close to her. He left with a brief kiss on her cheek. As the door closed behind him, she actually felt a large chapter in her life close as well.

Twenty-two

The two teenaged girls walked out of the high school where they were sophomores. They had just turned the corner to walk to the bus stop when a tall, muscular guy called out to them. They both stopped and turned to face where he leaned against the corner of the brick apartment building.

Chloe wasn't interested in a boyfriend, so she was happy when the leather-bomber-and-construction-boot-wearing boy turned his attention to Anika with his handsome grin. Chloe didn't trust men. How many times had she seen girls her own age or women like her mother struggling to raise a child by themselves? Men seemed only interested in the now and not the forever, especially when it came to their children.

Their bus pulled up and Anika's chubby face broke into a pretty smile before she ran behind Chloe to catch the bus. She yelled out her phone number to him just before the doors closed behind her. He was, of course, all the girls talked about on their ride home.

Anika didn't harbor the same ill feelings that Chloe had toward men, but then she had a father. So why should she?

Usually after school Anika came over to Chloe's to do her homework, but that day she went home in case Hakeem called. So Chloe did her homework and had chicken fried, *rice steamed and corn boiled in butter by the time her mother came in from work. She could see how tired her mother was, and she tried to help out by keeping their small apartment cleaned and by fixing meals.*

She thought of Anika's exclamation of being in love with Hakeem on their bus ride. "Mama, how do you know when you're really in love?"

At Adell's raised brow, the beautiful teenager rushed to explain about Anika. That only made Adell sigh as she thought over her answer carefully.

"You know you're in love when you meet a very special man. See, love is a feeling. It's about the affection and tenderness two people have for one another. It is the basis for many a good long relationship. A lot of young girls think being in love is only about that feeling. But love is so much more than just feelings. It's actions too."

"When you're in love you're unselfish, loyal and faithful. You have concern for one another's welfare, trust and respect. See, if a person says they're in love but doesn't show it, then it's just three little words. And it takes time to really fall in love. It's too special to happen too fast and still be real."

"But even if you're in love, don't ever let a man talk you into doing something you don't want to do. Love ain't about hurting and abusing. It's about feeling good. And if it's more bad than good, then it ain't love."

"Love is so very special, Chloe, and you'll know, baby, believe me. When the time comes, a man that is beautiful inside and out will make your heart race and make you feel special and worth loving. When you think of yourself down the line, that person is still who you want to share your life with."

"Please Chloe, don't forget what I've said. And I'll make sure I'll tell little Miss Anika the same thing when I lay my eyes on her."

* * *

Chloe smiled as she remembered her mother's words of wisdom. All of her words fit the way she viewed and felt about Devon. She knew it as she sat huddled in the dark in her plush armchair overlooking the New York City night. It was as plain as the nose on her face.

She picked up the cordless phone, dialing the numbers by the moon's light.

"Hello," Anika growled, half asleep and all angry.

"I'm sorry to wake you, Anika, but I had to tell you . . . you were right." She sniffed as tears welled in her eyes. "I am so deeply in love with Devon." Her voice was husky and soft, barely above a whisper as a lone tear raced down her cheek.

"Oh Chloe, welcome to the world of the seeing, for you are no longer blind, my friend," Anika said, her voice equally soft and filled with emotion.

Twenty-three

"Look this way, Chloe and Kyle."

Chloe plastered a false smile to her face and kept it there as she turned on her date's arm to pose for another round of photos for the paparazzi. Questions were of course asked about the article in *The Star Gazer,* but Chloe ignored them.

She was anxious to get inside and get seated. The constant flashes from the cameras were causing colored spots to float in front of her eyes. And the mundane and repetitive questions of the entertainment reporters were starting to sound like gibberish to her. On top of that, her arranged date with a popular R&B singer was a total disaster. He seemed to believe that the date included sex, and she swore if he groped at one of her private areas again she was going to deck him in his face.

They finally made their entrance into the building and were seated. He crossed his legs and slipped his hand onto her knee. Using her freshly manicured nails she pinched him . . . hard. She felt vindicated and pleased when he yelled out in pain and jerked his hand away.

"What's wrong with you?" he whispered in her ear angrily.

They were surrounded by reporters, celebrities and the elite of the fashion and entertainment industry, so she didn't want to make a scene. She forced a tight smile onto her face. "Don't touch me again, or next time I'll grab something that will make you sing high notes that you never knew you could!"

The lights of Radio City Music Hall dimmed. Latecomers rushed to their seats. The hostess for the 1999 Fashion Awards, a leading actress known for her trendsetting fashion sense, took her spot on stage. As the cameras began to roll, she began her monologue and Kyle again attempted to strike first base with Chloe.

All she could think was, *What am I doing here?*

"I saw a glimpse of Chloe," Nana Lil shouted excitedly as she pointed to the screen.

She sat on the edge of one of the recliners, and Cyrus sat on the other with his feet up on the built-in footrest. Deshawn lounged on the couch with Poochie, and Devon was upstairs, refusing to watch the awards show when Lil told him about it. As they all spotted the well-known singer sitting beside her, they all thought it was a good thing he wasn't watching. The man was obviously her date. Devon was in a bad enough mood and he didn't need to see that!

The audience clapped as the next two presenters were announced. Silence fell as the couple began to read the Tele-PrompTer. Chloe had to admit she was nervous as a cameraman stationed himself close by to point the camera at her as the winner for the award she was nominated for was announced.

Although the seat next to her was empty, Chloe was glad. Kyle had stormed out in anger an hour ago when she pressed her stiletto heel into his foot for groping her in the darkness of the auditorium.

"The winner for the 1999 Fashion Award for Female Model of the Year is . . ."

Chloe forced a neutral face for the television cameras pretending not to notice it directed toward her face. The male presenter, dressed in chocolate leather pants and a knit sweater, ripped open the envelope. He handed it to his female counterpart, an actress dressed in a silver pantsuit.

Chloe wanted to scream, *Just read the damn name, will you!*

"It's Chloe Bolton!"

The look of shock and excitement on her face was not faked. People sitting next to her clapped her shoulders in congratulations and hugged her as she stood and made her way down the aisle. She finally got to the stage amongst a standing ovation, and stood behind the podium clutching her award. This was a major feat to win after she had already retired. She was speechless and happy.

The Jamison living room erupted with applause and exclamations when Chloe's name was announced. Lil shushed them as Chloe moved to the podium and was handed her award. The camera swung to the audience as she received a standing ovation.

Devon closed the book he was reading. The excitement and applause reached him upstairs in his suite. Chloe had won. Against his better judgment he used the remote to turn on the television, flipping through the channels to the cable station where the award show was being broadcast.

His heart hammered in his chest as her smiling face filled the twenty-seven-inch screen. She looked beautiful and . . . different. She had cut off her hair. The extremely short pixie cut hairstyle framed her face and highlighted her large, cat-shaped eyes, high cheekbones and full mouth. The smoky makeup on her eyes and the shimmery lipstick were perfectly matched to the white lycra top she wore with a keyhole neckline and quarter-length sleeves. Snug copper leather pants and matching boots completed the look.

Chloe looked even more beautiful than ever. If only he could believe what his grandmother had told him. If only he hadn't misunderstood the call from what his grandmother called "a no-account harassing fool." But it was too late for "if only."

Chloe paused in her speech, having just thanked those in the business who helped her career, including Liv and Jeffrey. "Thank you . . . I would also like to take this opportunity to announce the launching of my new line of hair care products by Ashanti Inc., which will be simply named 'Chloe.' I have enjoyed a fruitful collaboration with Ashanti during my career, and I'm sure this new venture will continue that trend. I'm proud to state that all profits accrued on my behalf will be donated to several charities that I have been connected with in the past through the Bolton Foundation, which will be set up in my mother Adell Bolton's memory."

Applause again.

"Lastly, I have to thank a wonderful group of friends that I have, new and old. To my mother and my grandparents, who are all here in spirit, I love you all. Anika Fox, Nana Lil Jamison, Cyrus Dobbs, Deshawn Jamison and . . . Devon Jamison." She looked directly into the camera. "Devon is a very special man in my life. I miss you, baby. Thank you all for this award."

Nana Lil sighed in pleasure at Chloe's speech. She beamed with pride, as if she were her own grandchild. A commercial came on and Deshawn remarked on how beautiful Chloe's new looks were, earning him a sharp elbow from Poochie.

The doorbell rang and Deshawn jumped up to get it, a way to avoid Poochie's retaliation for his harmless comment. He opened the door to find Alicia standing on the other side.

"Hi Alicia," he said, confusion clearly etched on his face.

"Is Devon home?" she asked, not even greeting him.

"Yeah, he's upstairs." He stepped back out of the way as she flew past him up the stairs.

"What is that all about, Shawnie?" Nana Lil asked as he reclaimed his seat.

"Devon . . . what else."

Alicia opened the door to the suite at his gruff, "Come in."

Her eyes widened in shock as they fell on the suitcase opened on the bed. "Devon?"

He looked up and sighed when he saw her. "Look Al, I don't mean to be rude, but what are you doing here?"

Tears filled her eyes. "How can you be so cruel to me after what almost happened?"

Devon rubbed his hands over his eyes. "Coming to your house yesterday was a mistake."

"A mistake?" she wailed.

"Yes!" he shouted. "I was jealous because I thought Chloe was with another man. I thought I made all of this clear yesterday when I forced you off my lap and made you get dressed, Al. I don't feel that way about you and I'm just glad I didn't let jealousy push me to do something I didn't want to."

Her throat was tight with pain. Yesterday when he lowered his head toward her breasts, she had thought the world she wanted was finally hers, but suddenly he had jerked his head away and pushed her off of him. "I gave you time to think it over. That's why I didn't come over until tonight. I thought with a little time you would realize that we were meant—"

"To be friends, Al. Nothing more. And I'm not even sure that's appropriate any longer," he said firmly. "I'm sorry if I gave you any other impression."

He moved to his closet to snatch several outfits and then retraced his steps to the bed to place them in the garment bag.

"Where are you going?"

He zipped the garment bag closed and folded it over to snap. "New York."

Tears fell in earnest as pain clawed at her like a rabid dog. "Why?"

"Not that it's any of your business," he said, slipping the bag over his shoulder. "But I'm going to get Chloe."

Twenty-four

The insistent buzzing of the doorbell finally broke through Chloe's deep sleep. She had a rough night of sleep and was not in the best of moods because of it. She wished she could throw a blanket over the sun, but alas, morning was smiling her in the face, even if she wasn't smiling back.

Somehow, after her admission last night, she had thought Devon would call and say . . . something, anything. But after she got in from the celebration dinner at Fifty Seven, Fifty Seven with Anika, Liv and Jeffrey, who also captured a few awards for his innovative fashions, the phone hadn't rung. There had been only an excited message from Nana Lil and Deshawn on the answering machine, but no mention of Devon. She hadn't returned their call since it was so late when she got in.

The buzzer sounded again.

Probably Anika, she thought as she climbed out of bed and pulled on the full-length satin robe that matched her sheer nightgown. She left the room to enter the hall.

"Yes, Harrison," she said, her voice groggy with sleep and agitation as she spoke into the intercom.

"Sorry to bother you, Ms. Bolton, but the gentleman is rather determined to see you."

That damned Calvin! "Please inform Mr. Ingram that if he continues to harass me that I will press charges."

"Uhm, it's not Mr. Ingram, ma'am.

Confused she leaned her head against the wall. "Then *who* is it, Mr. Harrison?"

"A Devon Jamison."

Devon? Was here? In New York? Surely Harrison had made a mistake. But then she heard his voice in the background asking, "Is she home?"

Chloe flew out of the apartment and anxiously pushed the button for the elevator, unaware and maybe just uncaring that she was still in her night clothes and her newly cropped do was wildly disarrayed on her head. All she thought of was getting to Devon ASAP.

Devon paced as the doorman attempted again to reach Chloe's apartment, but he just kept saying, "She won't answer, sir."

Was Chloe that angry at him? But how could she be after what she said in her speech last night?

Both he and the doorman turned as the elevator doors opened. She ran at him and Devon took deep breaths as he caught her in his arms. Chloe wrapped her arms around his neck and inhaled deeply of his scent. Devon pressed his face into her neck, enjoying having this remarkable woman, his woman, in his arms again. They remained in the foyer that way, entwined and enjoying the feel of each other, for a long time.

Twenty-five

Devon looked down into Chloe's sleeping face. As always, he was amazed by her beauty and her passion. He loved her.

But he was curious about seeing this side of Chloe's life and that's why he wasn't sleeping as she was, after their hour of ardent and passionate loving. Devon got out of bed, careful not to wake her, and pulled his discarded boxers onto his naked frame. With one last loving glimpse at her, he left the bedroom.

Five minutes later he was totally floored! He had known Chloe was wealthy, but he had not imagined just how much wealth she had accumulated during her career. Enough to afford the expensively furnished luxury apartment. Enough to donate all her earnings from her new project to charities. Enough to earn numerous humanitarian awards for her efforts in fundraising in the past. Being in this apartment felt like being in a mini-palace to him.

It was so unlike the quiet charm of her house in Holtsville. It was so unlike the Chloe he knew at all. But this was *her* house. Obviously there was a lot about Chloe that he still didn't know.

"Devon?"

He walked back into the bedroom at her call, and went to sit on the bed next to where she lay. "Yeah, baby?"

Chloe smiled up at him, reaching to caress his square jaw. "I thought I dreamed it all."

"No baby, it's for real." He leaned down to kiss her lips. "I'm sorry for the way I acted that day in your yard."

"And you should be," she asserted, giving him a stern look.

"And *you* should have told me weeks ago that you were going to New York and why." He tapped the tip of her nose with his finger playfully. "It wasn't my grandmother's place to tell me, but she did."

"You should've given me a chance to tell you, instead of running home with a stick up your—"

"You shouldn't have run here to New York."

"You shouldn't have assumed I was back with my ex."

"He shouldn't have called you."

"You're right about that!"

Devon laughed and pulled her up into his arms. "Have I congratulated you on your win last night?"

"No."

"You know what?"

"What?"

"You should have called me sooner and told me you missed me, instead of telling me *and* millions of television viewers."

"That's all it took for you to come here?"

He nodded. "That and Nana Lil explaining to me about your ex and the awards show, like you should have."

"She's our own little cupid . . . God bless her!"

"I really missed you, Chloe, and I'm sorry my jealousy led to all of this."

Chloe kissed him full on the mouth. "And I'm so happy you're here, Devon."

He removed his boxers, kicking them off into a pile at the foot of the bed under the covers. With a groan he pulled her naked, curvaceous body to his and nuzzled the warm intimate spot in the hollow of her neck. His tender, warm kisses sent shivers of pleasure through her as she closed her eyes in sweet longing and gave in to his passionate loving.

And lovemaking it was. Slow, gentle and safe, with lots of tender kissing and stroking. Soul-searching stares and entwined limbs. Admissions of love in their eyes, although not slipping from their tongues.

Devon rolled to lay on his back, and Chloe straddled his strong hips, his hardened mass deeply implanted inside of her warm sheath. His eyes worshipped the sight of her breasts, full and heavy with dark aureoles and tightened nipples. She leaned down and lightly licked the contours of his full lips, letting her breasts lightly graze his hard-muscled chest, teasing them both.

Slowly and deliberately she rode him, grinding their hips into each other. Their eyes never parted and Chloe felt tears well in her eyes. They worked in unison as Devon raised his hips up off the bed to deepen each stroke within her. And he felt like he touched her very core. Deep inside of her gave him comfort like he had never known, and he wanted to stay there as long as he could. Chloe began to shiver with her first release, biting her lips to keep from screaming out.

"Scream. Yell if you want to. Don't hold back from me, Chloe. Come on baby."

He grabbed her hips with his hands and stroked deeper to hasten her climax. And Chloe did give in to the feeling, quivering from her toes to her soul. She sat up straight, her hands clutching wildly at her own hair. White blinding lights seemed to flash around her as he brought her release. She let out the scream she tried to bite back, and it was primal and hoarse.

How could he not give in to his own release as her reaction to the pleasure he brought her pushed him over the edge. Devon turned over, pinning her beneath him, and held her close to him in his arms as he stroked inside of a little piece of heaven. He planted his tongue deep into her mouth as she panted, kissing her as if he drew energy from her soul. His body stiffened with the first white-hot spasm of his release. He felt that they would have surely created a child from their explosive union if not for their use of protection.

"Chloe, I . . ." he bit his own bottom lip to keep from telling her how much he loved her.

* * *

Chloe had wanted to show Devon a little bit of New York. She crammed in more dinners in four-star restaurants, and front seats at Tony-award-winning plays into one week than he cared to remember.

Devon would have preferred to stay in her apartment cuddled in front of the marbled fireplace, just spending time with his woman. But he wanted to please her, and going out on the town seemed to make her happy.

Honestly, he had had it with rubbing elbows with the metropolitan's wealthy and famous elite. He had thought Chloe had said she had tired of it as well, when she was in Holtsville. But alas, as he feared, being back in her hometown had obviously awakened in her the desire to jet set. Devon planned to return to Holtsville, but he was beginning to doubt whether she would return with him. Not when she seemed so at home in this environment.

Tonight she made reservations for dinner at some fancy restaurant, when he would have been happy with some of her good home cooking. But he was fast realizing that his Chloe in Holtsville was far different than this Chloe in New York.

Chloe leaned over and kissed Devon's cheek in the back of the Lincoln Town Car Ashanti had provided for her twenty-four-hour use while in town. All of this week had been for him. He had never been to New York and she wanted to show him the best it had to offer.

She herself had seen more of New York's famous night life this one week than she had when she lived here. Chloe was hoping he wouldn't disdain the Big Apple as much as he had before, especially since she had to spend another month here to begin promos for the hair care line she was endorsing.

His opinions of the city mattered to her because she was hoping to ask him to remain here in New York with her, just until her promotional work was done. Then they would both return to Holtsville . . . together.

The Fifty Seven, Fifty Seven Restaurant and Bar in the Four Seasons Hotel was a deluxe dining experience. It was one of Chloe's favorite restaurants. Devon and she had been immediately ushered to their seat by the maitre d', and were given the red-carpet treatment. They had just ordered drinks, a margarita for Chloe and a rum and coke for Devon, when she spotted Calvin and a leggy beauty enter the restaurant.

She crossed her fingers, hoping that he would have enough class and taste not to make a scene. But Calvin wouldn't be Calvin if he hadn't headed in her direction as soon as he spotted them.

"Devon, here comes Calvin . . . my ex."

"Hello, Chloe."

"Calvin."

She gave him a nasty look but he was busy sizing up Devon, who was equally busy sizing up Calvin. "Devon baby, this is Calvin Ingram. Calvin, this is my boyfriend, Devon Jamison."

Devon stood and flexed his muscles in the Shaka King coat-length blazer he wore. He was obviously more muscular in build than Calvin and when Chloe eyed them both standing in front of each other, shaking hands with barely concealed hostile looks, she found Devon purely the superior man.

She breathed an audible sigh of relief when Calvin moved on with his date to their table. He hadn't even bothered to introduce the woman, not that either Chloe or Devon minded. "Sorry about that, Dev."

"No problem" were the words he said, but Devon was thinking, *What the hell did she see in that asshole?*

Devon had wanted to punch the pretentious uptight jerk in his face, but now was not the time nor the place for a show of male bravado. In the brief meeting he had immediately picked up on the man's superior attitude. How could his Chloe ever have been compatible with that snob?

Chloe immediately picked up on Devon's distant mood. He seemed to have something on his mind, as he frequently would get a faraway look in his eyes. She tried to engage him in conversation, but his mental attention was obviously focused on something else.

"Devon . . . Devon?"

She kicked him under the table.

He immediately jumped and howled out in pain. Several nearby people turned to look in their direction. "What, baby? Why did you kick me?"

"Because I'm tired of talking to myself." She watched as he leaned down to rub his bruised shin. "I'm sorry, but it was the only way I could think of to get your attention."

He gave her a look of total disbelief. "You could've tapped my hand!"

Chloe started to say something, but changed her mind, instead looking at him with an apologetic smile that lit up her face. "You're right, but tell me what's on your mind, Dev."

He looked down at his plate of grilled chicken that they both had ordered. "We need to talk, but it can wait until we get ho— . . . uhm, back to your place."

Chloe thought that over for a few seconds. "Well let's go *home* and talk . . . now."

He was more than ready to leave the glamorous establishment. When she reached in her small, beaded clutch purse, he cleared his throat. She looked up, saw his expression, and immediately closed the purse. When he first arrived they argued over who would pay for their dates, and they agreed to take turns.

Devon signaled for the waiter to bring the bill and slipped his gold card inside the slim leather billfold. Moments later he returned with the receipt for him to sign, and they left.

When they were back in the limo they were silent, each composing their thoughts, but they held onto each other's hand tightly in the space between them. The silence remained even in the elevator ride up to the apartment.

Once inside, Chloe dropped her purse and wrap on the plush sofa in the living room. "So what's up, Devon?"

"I thought you told me you moved to Holtsville to get away from the hustle and bustle of New York?"

"I did, and I still feel that way."

"So when are you going back home?"

She smiled when he referred to Holtsville as her home. "I never moved away. It's just that Ashanti had offered me an opportunity to make a lot of money for the community I was raised in, other needy areas and worthy causes, like the South Africans still feeling the effects of apartheid, or AIDS and cancer research. I wouldn't have come out of retirement for any other reason, if not the opportunity to help." She looked at him, her face showing how important this was to her. She only hoped he understood. "If other people had the fame and recognition that I have to make a lot of money in a short amount of time to help themselves, then I would have rejected the offer."

She spoke with such conviction that Devon wanted to kiss her, hold her . . . and love her.

"A part of that requires that I remain in New York for at least another month, and I'll be required to do some traveling in the months to come." The last words she spoke trailed off.

He removed his tailored jacket. "Chloe, I understand how important this *all* is to you." He waved his hand around the apartment. "But Holtsville is just as important to me, and I want you there . . . with me."

He sighed, wiping his hand over his eyes. "What about us, Chloe, huh? I can't take another day here. I'm ready to see Holtsville, South Carolina. So what about us?"

Tears filled her eyes. "Are you asking me to choose between making millions of dollars for charities, even if it means spending a little bit more time in New York than I planned when I retired, and having you in my life?"

"Don't cry, Chloe. Damn!" he yelled as he stalked to stand by the window. "Just admit you never wanted to retire. Admit that you love eating at expensive restaurants and having front row seats to hit Broadway shows. Just admit that dirty little Holtsville can't compete. Admit it!"

Chloe flinched as his voice rose in anger. "Devon, you really don't think that about me, do you? Because if you do, then you don't really know me at all."

"For you to drag me around in the midst of New York night life, then you don't know me at all either, Chloe."

Silence reigned after that, and it was deafening. Chloe blinked back the tears pooling, in her eyes. Devon continued to stare out at the city below. Even at close to ten P.M., the streets were filled with fast-moving people and slow-moving cars.

"So you're leaving me this time, Devon?" she asked quietly, sniffing back the tears.

His heart ached to hear the pain in her voice. "The choice is yours, baby. I'm leaving tomorrow and I would love for you to come home with me."

Chloe let the tears fall. "That's so unfair, Devon," she whispered, but she was alone. He had quietly left the living room.

That night they slept on opposite sides of the bed, each afraid to reach out for the other. Neither would be able to stand the rejection they believed they would get. But both wanted to be in each other's arms. It was the worst night of sleep either of them ever had. So close . . . yet so far.

Chloe awoke to an empty bed. Frantic, she searched the entire apartment, but she knew already that he was gone. To her the feeling was akin to abandonment. She was intelligent enough to know that she was wrong to project her anger at her father onto Devon, but she did it anyway. *How could he ask me to chose?*

She found the note on the bedside table. In her earlier haste to search for him, she hadn't even noticed it.

Chloe,

I realize I was wrong to ask you to choose. So I made the choice for both of us. This week in New York has made me realize that it's for the best. This wasn't easy for me to do, so please don't think so. I will miss seeing your beautiful face, so seeing you on T.V. will have to suffice. I honestly don't believe you have any intention of returning to Holtsville. I'm sorry I couldn't face you but that would've made it hard for me to leave. You will be in my thoughts forever.

Devon

P.S. Tell Anika that it was great finally meeting her.

Chloe shook her head in disbelief as she read the note again and again. Did he think he was being noble? No, she wouldn't have left with him today, but she had no intention of moving to New York permanently again, regardless of what he thought. But now how could she return to Holtsville, knowing Devon would not be in her life because he didn't want a relationship that would have to be long distance at times? Obviously he didn't think she was worth it.

Imagine how foolish she would have felt if she had admitted to him that she loved him with every fiber in her being. Chloe balled up the paper and threw it across the room in anger, where it bounced off the wall. She *tried* to tell Anika that, for her, loving a man was all about disappointment.

Twenty-six

Devon turned his truck into the yard with Deshawn directly behind him in his. They had just finished up their first day of renovating Donnie's Diner. Deshawn, with the help of Poochie, had talked the belligerent owner into modernizing the restaurant while Devon was in New York three weeks ago.

They entered the house and were engulfed by the acrid smell of smoke. "Nana Lil," Deshawn yelled out, running to check her bedroom.

Devon dashed into the kitchen, where a pan of grease sat on a lit eye on the stove, the source of the smoke filling the house. He rushed toward the stove to push the pan off the hot eye. Smoke was everywhere, and it began to sting his eyes and throat.

When he began to cough, he moved to open the windows. It was then that he noticed his grandmother's prone and lifeless body on the floor by the back door.

"Deshawn!" he yelled out before he fell to his knees by her, huddling her body into his arms. He nearly fainted with relief when he felt a pulse at her wrist. It was weak and thready against his fingers, but thankfully present.

Deshawn flew into the kitchen, and if it was at all possible for a black person to blanch, he did. Their eyes met over her body. Fear was in the depths.

* * *

"Why didn't she tell us she was having these headaches for weeks?" Deshawn whispered to his brother over their Nana's sedated figure in the hospital bed. "We could have gotten her to the doctor before the aneurysm ruptured and caused the stroke."

"I don't know, Shawn. You know how stubborn she is," Devon whispered back. "I just thank God that she's alive."

They had to talk quietly because the doctor had placed their grandmother on aneurysm precautions. She was to have complete bed rest with the head of her bed elevated slightly. Her room was to remain dark, without the intrusion of television, radio or even reading materials. Hot or cold beverages and caffeine products were cut from her diet. And her visitors were very limited. She was sedated to help her comply with the restrictions because she was at risk for another rupture or rebleeding of the aneurysm. Surgery to correct it was being postponed until her condition stabilized. They both prayed she pulled through and would return home with them soon.

"Y'all don't have to talk over my body like I'm dead."

They both jumped slightly at the sound of her weak voice. Deshawn recovered first. "Don't talk Nana Lil. The doctor wants you to relax and remain calm."

Lil felt so very tired and drained, but she wanted so badly to go home. She hated hospitals. "I'm so tired, babies," she groaned, her eyes floating closed under the effects of the sedation.

They both were filled with dread. Never had they heard their strong and resilient grandmother complain. Devon had to force himself to smile at the weak and frail woman lying in the bed. It was hard to believe that she was the same vibrant woman they left at home this morning. He leaned down to kiss her cheek, and Deshawn did the same.

"Everyone at your church has been calling to check on you," he whispered to her. "Just rest and get better."

She nodded slightly. "Has anyone called Chloe?" she asked weakly.

Devon stiffened, and his eyes met with his twin's briefly. "I'll call her."

"You promise, Vonnie?"

"I promise."

Chloe dragged her body into her apartment, bone weary and tired. Today was the last day of the photo shoot for the new line of hair care products for women of color. Excitement was mixed with trepidation. Next week she would begin a twelve-city promotional tour on talk shows, and conduct interviews with radio personalities over the telephone, all to garner attention for the release date in two months.

At least the work kept her mind off Devon.

"No," she said aloud. "I'm not going to think of him."

She kicked off her soft Nine West ankle boots and hung her short sable mink in the closet of the foyer. It was late November and fall would soon disappear under the blanket of cold snow and the winter in December.

Chloe had every intention of closing up this apartment once again and returning to her home in Holtsville once she was finished with the promotional tour. She missed her house, the small town and the true friends she had made. She would just have to learn to live in the same town as Devon and not be with him.

They hadn't spoken since the morning he sneaked out and left her. Chloe figured he left, so he should call. Right?

Well it was obviously wrong, since he hadn't dialed her number once. Sighing, Chloe was on her way to the kitchen to make a cup of hot chocolate when she heard the answering machine beeping, alerting her to a message.

She changed course and headed back to her bedroom, where she pushed the PLAYBACK button.

"This is Chloe. Leave a message."

Beep.

"Chloe, this is your gorgeous friend. Call me ASAP."

Beep.

"Chloe . . . Chloe, this is Devon. Uhm, Nana Lil's in the hospital. She had a stroke. She asked for you to come back to Holtsville. I wouldn't ask you, but this seems really important to her. We're at the hospital, Memorial Regional . . . call me on my cell phone."

Beep.

The rest of the messages were incoherent to her because of the deafening beat of her heart. Nana Lil . . . in the hospital! She *had* to get to Holtsville!

Devon would admit it to no one, but he was afraid. All of his life his Nana had been a constant. What would he do without her now? He sighed and looked down at his watch as he sat on a small bench outside of the hospital. It was 8:55 P.M.

The smell of the hospital reminded him too much of death, and he had to get out of there. Visiting hours were over, but both he and Deshawn decided to stay there all night. Neither could bear the thought of leaving her at the hospital alone.

Sighing, he pulled his jacket closer around his body to shield himself from the cool November nights of South Carolina. Even as rain began to fall and the hour clicked to nine P.M., he remained outside, sheltered by the overhang of the building. He clutched his cell phone, foolishly worried he wouldn't hear it ring in his pocket.

Never had he felt so desolate and alone. Not since his parents' death. Devon dropped his head in his hands, shivering from the cold and the rain that fell around him. Chloe should have been here for him. Why hadn't she called yet? "Damn," he whispered as he thought of her. "I need you, Chloe."

Chloe sighed. The ride from the airport had cost her fifty dollars up front, but that wasn't her concern in the least. She was worried about the woman she had come to love and cherish as if she were her very own blood relative. *God, please don't take her now,* she begged silently.

"The hospital is just up on the right," she instructed the driver.

As the taxi neared the destination, Chloe leaned forward on her seat and looked out through the rain pelting the window. Her heart hammered in her chest when she saw the lone figure sitting on the bench, his head down in his hands.

He looked so desolate and alone.

"Driver! Pull up by that man!"

Devon felt near tears but he hadn't allowed himself to cry since his parents' deaths, all those years ago. So he breathed deeply and composed himself. If only Chloe were here, she could . . .

"Devon!"

He looked up and blinked as if he were dreaming. Was it his imagination, or was Chloe standing in the pouring rain next to a taxi? It had to be real because it was too bizarre not to be.

His heart hammered in his chest hard. She was here, just like she walked out of his imagination. He stood and she accepted her suitcase from the driver before walking under the shelter to stand before him.

Damn, he thought. *She's beautiful.*

They both became nervous.

"I got the first flight down as soon as I could. How is she?"

The concern in her eyes and her voice was evident. It was obvious that she loved his grandmother very much, even if she didn't love him. "She's resting comfortably with a lot of precautions to keep her from causing the aneurysm to rupture again or rebleed, which would cause another stroke."

Chloe looked into the depths of Devon's eyes and saw the pain and fear that he was trying to hide. Wordlessly, she wrapped her arms around his waist, holding him tightly to her. He stiffened before raising his own arms to return the embrace.

Chloe closed her eyes, riding the wave of pleasure, enjoying the feel of him, remembering the good times they had once shared. She enjoyed the comfort they gave one another, but wished it were under far better circumstances.

"You're soaking wet. You better take my truck and drive home. I'll call if there are any changes."

"Devon, I'm staying here with you," she said firmly.

She didn't know it, but inside he nearly burst with relief. He needed her. He hadn't known how to ask her to stay. His heart swelled with love for her. "Let's go inside. You can use one of the bathrooms to change."

He carried her suitcase as they made their way inside. Deshawn was sitting in the waiting room with the television on, although he didn't appear to care what was on.

Deshawn stood immediately to wrap Chloe into a tight embrace. "I knew you would come," he whispered into her ear.

She nodded and hugged him back. Slowly they released each other. "There's no other place that I'd rather be than right here with both of you. I just pray that Nana Lil . . ."

The rest of her words broke off with an anguished cry as hot tears streaked down her cheeks. Devon moved quickly to pull her into a tight embrace. "We're all praying."

Chloe slowly opened the door, peering into the darkened room before she entered. She had to bite back her gasp of surprise at the person lying in the bed. *That's Nana Lil?*

Lil looked as if she'd aged another twenty years, and with her eyes closed she looked— No! Chloe refused to even think of death. This beautiful, spirited woman was going to recover. She was too strong to do anything else.

Taking a deep breath to strengthen herself, Chloe stepped closer to the bed. She reached for her hand, lightly rubbing the wrinkled skin with her own hand. "I need you, Nana Lil, don't leave me. My mother's gone. My grandparents are dead. I don't have a father. You took me right in and loved me like one of your own. Please, it's like you're all that I have in terms of a parent. Please be strong."

A lone tear fell and softly landed on their united hands. Slowly, Nana Lil's eyes fluttered open. "Chloe?" she asked weakly, her grasp becoming a little firmer as she recognized her.

"No, don't speak. You have to be very quiet and stay calm."

"Don't . . . cry, Chloe. I'm not afraid of death." She breathed deeply, letting her eyes close. "I miss my own parents, and Tessa. Now I'll get to see them again. That's a blessing."

That only made her cry harder. "You're not going to die Nana Lil—"

"And I'll get to meet your mama. I'll make sure to tell her what a beautiful daughter she raised."

Her words began to slur. "Take care of my boys for me, Chloe," she whispered weakly before falling back under the effects of the sedation.

Chloe continued to hold her hand tightly as she sank to the seat near the bed. She cried so hard that she began to hiccup and her chest began to radiate with pain. Yes, Nana Lil was an angel, but surely it wasn't time for her to return to heaven?

Twenty-seven

Nana Lil's eyes opened slowly and she frowned at the recognizable stench of a hospital. Her time was near, and she knew it. She would have much preferred to be at home to pass on to the other side, but there was nothing she could do about that now.

She sighed, allowing her mind to drift to precious moments in her life. Clearly she remembered the sweetness of her first lover, the pride of her graduation from high school, the resilience of struggling in the civil rights movement of the Deep South, the joy and beauty of her simple wedding, the strength it took to bear her only child, the dedication of raising a son she was proud of. She could almost feel the pure pleasure of sitting at his wedding to Reena, and the happiness on the day of the birth of the twins. The soul-searing pain of the death of her son and his wife, whom she loved as a daughter, still affected her deeply. But she was left with many wonderful years spent raising her boys.

Her life played like a movie before her eyes. Moments of laughter or crying as she reviewed what she considered to be a long and fruitful life. She had done everything she was set on this earth to do. She had no complaints.

Her time had come.

She breathed deeply, wincing at the sudden sharp stiffness of her neck. Slowly the monitor showed her blood pressure decline and her heart rate increase. The alarm sounded at the nursing station that her vitals were nearing a danger zone.

But even before they reached her and attempted to revive her, Lil smiled in death and felt her spirit lift to the heavens.

Would life ever be the same without her? Already it seemed the sun was not as bright and the flowers had lost their fragrance. Everything was dull and lifeless. Everything was different, and it would never be quite the same again.

Chloe reached across the seat of the truck to take Devon's hand in hers as he drove home. She saw the grief and misery on his face. Would his pain ever go away? Would hers? She worried because, unlike Deshawn, he had not yet cried, not even when the doctor first came and told them that she suffered another rupture of the aneurysm before they could repair it, leading to the last fatal stroke.

She glanced over at him. It wasn't healthy to hold emotions in like that, was it? "Devon," Chloe began, not quite sure what to say.

Chloe just fell silent. She felt useless. She didn't even know what to tell him to make his grief lessen. But she was in pain as well. She had hoped never to feel the death of another person so close to her. Would they ever be able to get through it all?

Devon was numb. His body felt outside of itself. He moved through the motions like a robot. This had to be one of the worst days of his life. Nana Lil was gone.

No more wisdom and love, hugs and reprimands. All of it, her bluntness, her humor, her kindness . . . it was all gone.

Chloe reached for his hand, and he felt comfort but was still distanced from everything. He felt like he was watching his own life play before his eyes, trying desperately to push the STOP or PAUSE button to make this horrible scene disappear. But that was impossible.

He pulled the truck into Chloe's yard, and she gasped in surprise. "Oh my God."

Chloe got out of the truck, her mouth ajar in wonder. Who knew her front yard could look so beautiful? It was truly breathtaking. On both sides of the paved driveway were elegant lampposts surrounded by a climbing vine of clematis of the deepest purple blooms. Golden black-eyed Susans and pink coneflowers adorned the middle, and lush pachysandra evergreen ground cover surrounded the base.

The walkways, patio and driveway were complete and lined with square flower planters that perfectly matched the shutters of the house and were filled with beacon silver ground cover. Its striking white leaves had green margins that glowed. In between the boxes were ground lights that lit the walkway and helped the foliage gleam.

Corner gardens were on both sides of the house, made up of pink hydrangea, icy blue dwarf lilies, golden daylilies and lewisias in shades of salmon, apricot and plum.

It was all so beautiful and perfect with many more years of growth and blossoming to come and make it even better. If only winter wasn't so near, causing the blooms to fade. Chloe's eyes filled with tears and her heart swelled at the beauty of the landscape, but mostly because of the thoughtfulness and hard work that had gone into creating it.

Love built this garden, and she knew that.

Devon's footsteps crunched against the gravel and she turned to face him, a questioning look in her eyes. "It's all so glorious, Devon. Who did all of this?"

He held her suitcase easily in one hand as he looked down at her. Pain flickered in the depths before the obsidian pools became dull again. He nodded, "Nana Lil and I worked on it together. She wanted it to look nice for when . . . you came back."

Devon cleared his throat, moving to walk past Chloe to climb the porch steps. "You're probably tired and want to get settled in."

"Devon," Chloe said softly. "She was right. I was coming back. I just wish you would believe that, especially at a time like this when we need each other. I don't want to go through this without you by my side."

He paused on the last step, his foot almost suspended in air. "Chloe, don't do this . . . not now."

"You're right," she said, pain knifing her stomach. "I'm sorry."

She doubted the time would ever come for them to be together. There always seemed to be an obstacle in their path to happiness. Frankly she didn't know if she had the will or the strength to fight for it anymore, especially after the way he hurt her when he left New York almost three months ago. But not once during that time did her love fade for him. She couldn't stop caring for him, even when she tried.

There was nothing more she wanted in the world than to be in his arms and hear him say—

No! This wasn't healthy. No matter how much she dreamed for something, that wouldn't make it so. She couldn't make Devon love her.

Chloe took a deep breath to steady her nerves, but as she looked at the stiffness of his back as he entered the house, she saw the beauty of the garden and thought of the returning of one of God's angels to heaven. All of it overwhelmed her. *I refuse to cry,* she thought, wrapping her arms around herself and closing her eyes against a wave of pain.

When she opened them again, Devon was stepping back out onto the porch. She looked up at him, praying the desperation she felt was not in the depths of her eyes. But he could read the depths surely. *"Please Devon don't leave me alone to deal with this"* would be seen.

"I sat the suitcase in the foyer," he said, moving down the steps with controlled movements. "I'm going to head on home. Deshawn and I have to start making calls."

Chloe nodded, keeping her arms around herself. "If there's anything I can do, just call."

Like letting me love you, Devon.

"I'll let you know when the arrangements for the wake and funeral are made. There'll be a sitting up at the house once the town learns about . . . about, uh . . . it."

She could tell how difficult it was for him to even say that his precious grandmother had passed on. "Devon—"

"I'll talk to you later, Chloe."

She bit her lip, turning to watch him as he climbed into the truck and backed out of the yard. Would they ever be on the same wavelength in this game called love?

No mother, no grandparents, a deadbeat father, a best friend a thousand miles away, Nana Lil gone over to the other side, and no Devon. She felt hollow inside.

Chloe climbed the steps into the house, closing the front doors behind her. A wave of pleasure filled her at the familiar scent and sight of her home. This was where she was meant to be. Well, here *and* in Devon's arms.

She looked back out the window to the garden he had planted for her. He flew to New York after she told him and the world that she missed him. He broke his friendship with Alicia for her. Never would she forget the look in his eyes at the hospital when he first saw her standing next to the taxi.

It had been the look of—

Chloe's heart raced as she clearly remembered his eyes that night. Frantically she looked through her purse for the keys to her Navigator. She *had* to tell Devon that she loved him. She could not explain why, but something deep inside of her said to tell him.

With victory, she found her keys and raced out the door
to find her man.

Devon drove slowly, his thoughts filled with all the day's
events. His Nana was gone. When he went inside the house
tonight, she wouldn't be there. The house would never be the
same again. His life would never be the same again.

Chloe had come. When he needed her the most she had
been there, appearing suddenly as if she were his own guard-
ian angel. And she suffered to help him through this horrible
grieving he would have to deal with. What did he do?

Distance himself, afraid he would tell her just how much
he loved her, pull her into his arms and not let her go . . .
ever.

When he first started work on the garden at her house it
was a way for him to express the deep love he had for her.
Nana Lil had said, after she joined him in the planting, that
Chloe would love it when she returned. She had always been
so sure that Chloe was coming back home, when he had nothing but doubts.

And now here she was, as beautiful as ever and back in
Holtsville, but for how long? If only he could force her to
stay and never leave. If only he could force her to love him
the way he loved her, deeply and passionately with no re-
morse.

He thought of the look in her eyes when she came to the
hospital, stood before him and pulled him into a tight, comforting embrace. It had immediately warmed and soothed him.
A look of—

Devon slammed on the brakes, his mouth ajar as he made
a very sweet and indulging discovery. But was he wrong? He
had to know.

There was only one way. He had to tell Chloe he loved
her. Lord knows why, but he suddenly had the courage he
lacked all these months to do just that.

The tires squealed against the pavement as he did a wicked U-turn and headed back to his woman.

It was déjà vu. Just like their very first meeting. As they both raced down the road in opposite directions, their vehicles almost collided, both having to brake with a loud deafening squeal of tires. Almost as if by miracle, they stopped directly across from each other. They both jumped out of their cars and came to stand in front of one another.

They both swore they could hear the electricity crackle between them, just like their first meeting in this very same road, but there also was the sweet refrains of love this time. Clearly the emotion showed in each of their depths as Devon pulled her into his arms, and kissed her with enough passion to spread love across the world.

"Chloe . . . I . . ."

"Devon, baby I . . ."

They both spoke in unison, after they slowly broke the kiss, the words blended together in perfect harmony as they looked deeply into each other's eyes. "I love you."

"Now you know, I can get real used to this. I did more good up here in heaven to get them two together than I did down there with them."

Nana Lil smiled down on them from the heavens above. "Don't you worry, babies, your Nana will be with you always," she said softly.

She had found her own happiness on the other side as she reunited with family members and friends long since passed. Never had she known such joy as when she was again in the arms of her beloved mother. She felt whole as she then embraced her own son and daughter-in-law. But there was one person she had yet to greet and that was her next mission . . . meeting Adell Bolton.

* * *

Devon caressed the side of her beautiful face where they stood embraced in the middle of the road. "Chloe, I never knew when you came into my life that you were the woman who would make me whole, who would fill so many needs that I didn't even know I had. I've been a fool, afraid of my own feelings and still believing the worst of you. I love you from the very depths of my soul and I do not, no I will not live my life without you any longer. Say you'll grow old with me as my wife."

Chloe's knees buckled. She was so overwhelmed that this strong, brooding man loved her just as much as she loved him. Did anyone deserve such happiness? And now he wanted to share his life with her. "I have loved you since before I was willing to admit that I did. I don't want to ever go through what I've gone through these past three months. I have missed you until I ached. I'm sorry for whatever part I played in keeping us apart. We were meant to be. I love you so very much, Devon. I would be very honored to grow old with you, in Holtsville."

"Nana Lil would be so happy, I just . . . wish she was here."

His saddened voice hurt her as she wrapped him into a tight embrace. Soon she felt the dampness of his tears soak her neck. Gently she kissed his cheek. "She's here. You may not see her, but you can feel her in the wind blowing across your cheek, or the sun warming your body, or in the very air you breathe to survive. She's all around us. Nana Lil would never leave any of us all alone."

Epilogue

(Six Months Later)

"Now doesn't your baby make the most beautiful bride, Adell?"

Nana Lil came to stand next to her as they stood looking down at Chloe and Devon's wedding. Tessa, Odis, Adell, Daniel, Reena and Nana Lil all peered through the break in the clouds to the joyful gathering below.

Adell smiled. "This is the most beautiful I've ever seen my baby. It must be the love for your handsome grandson. And just look how pretty Anika is. She's like my other daughter."

"Yeah, it seems Deshawn has noticed that too."

They all laughed as they watched Deshawn attempt to attract Anika's attention, to no avail. "Seems I might need to be stirring the pot again. Lord know my boys can't seem to handle love by themselves."

Nana Lil hugged Adell tightly. "I wondered if those two would ever get it right, but here they are."

"I just wish I could be there with her like a mother should," she said softly, her voice filled with sadness.

Tessa came over to pull her daughter's hand into her own. "She knows you're always watching over her. Don't you worry, that's one wonderful grandchild you raised for me."

They all held hands and smiled down from the heavens at the union of their children. The vows were exchanged and the women all sighed as Devon kissed Chloe with such loving tenderness that they all felt warmed by it. It was a match made in the heavens.

Coming in September from
Arabesque Books . . .

TRUE LOVE by Brenda Jackson
1-58314-144-8 $5.99US/$7.99CAN
When Shayla Kirkland lands her dream job with one of Chicago's top firms, Chenault Electronics, she's in the perfect position to destroy the company for ruining her mother's career. But she never expects that CEO Nicholas Chenault will spark a passion that will challenge her resolve—and make her surrender to the most irresistible desire . . .

ENDLESS LOVE by Carmen Green
1-58314-135-9 $5.99US/$7.99CAN
Terra O'Shaughssey always did everything as carefully as she could—including managing an apartment building. But when handsome lawyer Michael Crawford becomes her newest tenant, Terra finds his party ways endangering her peace of mind . . . and her carefully shielded heart.

STOLEN MOMENTS by Dianne Mayhew
1-58314-119-7 $5.99US/$7.99CAN
Although widowed Sionna Michaels dreads confronting the man she holds responsible for her husband's death, the instant she sees David Young, her heart is set afire and she's certain of his innocence. There's only one obstacle in the couple's way—the truth about what really happened.

LOVE UNDERCOVER by S. Tamara Sneed
1-58314-142-1 $5.99US/$7.99CAN
When executive Jessica Larson meets FBI anti-terrorist agent Carey Riley in a remote mountain inn, she gives in to her most sensuous desires for the first time in her life. But when a dangerous enemy begins to watch their every move, the two must face down their doubts and fears about getting close . . . if they are to gain a love beyond all they've ever imagined.

Please Use the Coupon on the Next Page to Order

Fall In Love With
Arabesque Books

__**TRUE LOVE by Brenda Jackson**
    1-58314-144-8 $5.99US/$7.99CAN

__**ENDLESS LOVE by Carmen Green**
    1-58314-135-9 $5.99US/$7.99CAN

__**STOLEN MOMENTS by Dianne Mayhew**
    1-58314-119-7 $5.99US/$7.99CAN

__**LOVE UNDERCOVER by S. Tamara Sneed**
    1-58314-142-1 $5.99US/$7.99CAN

Call toll free **1-888-345-BOOK** to order by phone or use this coupon to order by mail. *ALL BOOKS AVAILABLE SEPTEMBER 1, 2000.*

Name_____
Address _____
City_____ State _____ Zip _____
Please send me the books I have checked above.
I am enclosing $_____
Plus postage and handling* $_____
Sales tax (in NY, TN, and DC) $_____
Total amount enclosed $_____
*Add $2.50 for the first book and $.50 for each additional book.
Send check or money order (no cash or CODs) to: **Arabesque Books, Dept. C.O., 850 Third Avenue, 16th Floor, New York, NY 10022**
Prices and numbers subject to change without notice.
All orders subject to availability.
Visit our website at **www.arabesquebooks.com**

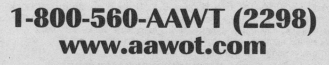

More Arabesque Romances by
Monica Jackson